SKIN

Books by C. E. Poverman

Novels

Susan
Solomon's Daughter
My Father in Dreams

Short Story Collections

The Black Velvet Girl
Skin

SKIN

STORIES BY
C. E. POVERMAN

Ontario Review Press/Princeton

Most of these stories have previously appeared,
often in a slightly altered form, in the following publications:
"Cutter" and "The Man Who Died" in *Ontario Review*;
"Africa" and "Desert Light" in *The Santa Monica Review*;
"Beautiful" in *Ploughshares*; "Intervention" in *Witness*;
"Children's Law" and "Father's Weekend" in *Epoch*;
"On the Ocean" in *The Sonora Review*;
"Skin" (under the title "Nam") in *The Canard Anthology*
"Beautiful" was reprinted in *The Pushcart Prize, XII*

Jacket photos by Linda Fry

Library of Congress Cataloging-in-Publication Data

Poverman, C. E., 1944–
Skin: stories / by C. E. Poverman
Contents: Cutter—Africa—Beautiful—Intervention—
Children's law—Desert light—Father's weekend—On the ocean—
The man who died—Skin—We all share the sun and moon
I. Title
PS3566.082S55   1992   813'.54—dc20   92-9249
ISBN 0-86538-076-7 (hardcover : acid free)

Typesetting by Backes Graphic Productions
Printed by Princeton University Press

ONTARIO REVIEW PRESS
Distributed by George Braziller, Inc.
60 Madison Ave., New York, NY 10010

for
Dana & Marisa

CONTENTS

Cutter

A T THE SAME MOMENT Jorge recognized the voice, the caller
started his story. It usually went like this: he had just
completed a rape, he was still in the victim's house or apartment, and he had dialed Helpline because he wanted to get
caught—he'd read a story in the paper about a crisis line tracing
a rapist's call. Hadn't they started a trace?

In fact, Jorge had done just that. He'd stood behind his desk,
and waving to Roberta, he pointed at the phone number beneath
the clock—police trace—and she called it in. Once started, it
could take anywhere from ten minutes to half an hour. When
they had the number, the police would call back. Many of their
traces had ended with a cop picking up the by-now silent phone,
telling the agency they were taking someone to the emergency
room, or that the paramedics were administering CPR—or
whatever it might be.

The caller was silent, then said, "Jorge, got it going yet?"
Jorge hated having to play along with this guy. He had the
feeling the caller thought of him as someone he had captured, a
kind of prisoner or hostage. Keeping his voice calm, he said, "Is
this Buddy?"

"Yeah, sure, you know it is."

"Buddy, if you really want to be caught, why don't you give

me your phone number and I'll be glad to send the police? Or, just turn yourself in. If you've hurt someone, that will keep you from hurting again. If you need help, we'll see you get help." Jorge picked up a plexiglass cube filled with viscous goo. He tipped it slowly.

"Can't you trace my number, man? Hey, I know you can do it when the chips are really down. When someone's bleeding or nodding off. What's the problem?"

"That's what I want to know, what's the problem? We're a suicide and crisis intervention agency; we help people who need help. Why are you wasting our time with games?"

"Games?"

"What do you want, Buddy?"

"I want you to find me." He said, "I was sure no one can." Something about that last statement wasn't right. The tenses. Jorge noted the phrase on his pad. He looked over at Roberta, who sat with her hand on the phone. They were the only ones in the office now. They looked at the clock. Three or four minutes since the start of the call. Jorge said, "You've just raped someone?"

"She's right here."

"Can you put her on?" You never knew. Maybe he'd be dumb enough to do it. Maybe the request would convolute into a challenge Buddy couldn't resist, and she'd blurt her address. Wishful thinking?

There was something muffled. A hand perhaps muting the mouthpiece. Buddy's voice came back on. "She won't talk."

"Why not?"

"She says she's scared."

Jorge decided to kick things up a notch and push it. "Well, then, after you leave, can you tell her to report the rape?"

There was a long pause and Buddy said, "She can't do that. She's too scared. She knows I'll come back."

Jorge said, "You're a nice guy. Who are you?"

Buddy didn't answer. In a standoff, they drifted into small talk. Jorge slowly tipped the plexiglass cube, checked the clock. Over ten minutes now. Across the room, Roberta waited for the police call-back.

"What's her name? Your victim?" Jorge pushed. You never knew what a caller would give you.

Buddy said, "I don't know. I didn't ask her. I do what I want, I always know no one could touch me." There it was again. Something funny in that sentence. Always know. Past tense. Present tense. "How come someone like me can get away with this, mi hijo? Hey, almost fifteen minutes for you guys. If I was bleeding, if I was full of pills and nodding off here, wouldn't you be able to connect?"

"Are you bleeding? Are you full of pills?"

"I'm waiting here for you, mi hijo. Why can't you find me?"

Trying to control his feelings of helplessness and anger, Jorge said, "Well, it's not my fault, Buddy, you and I are doing pretty well tonight but the police are so slow. Is that my fault?"

Buddy laughed. "No, mi hijo, you've done okay. I've got to go now. Give some of your other callers a chance."

"Buddy..."

The phone went dead. Jorge dropped the receiver on the desk, flung the plexiglass cube into the wastebasket. He looked at Roberta and shook his head.

Roberta said, "Good try. I thought you'd get him. The cops have been so slow lately." She glanced at the clock. "You kept him on fourteen minutes tonight. Last time, it was, what?"

"Eleven minutes."

"He's got something going with you, Jorge. I had three hang-ups earlier. It must have been Buddy looking for you to answer. And he's staying on longer each time. Next time he's going to stay on too long, they'll connect on the trace, we'll get him."

Jorge shook his head. Christ, who was he? What did he want? Jorge checked his notes, went to the files and pulled his other cards. *Buddy. Duane.* Tonight's call was consistent with his other rape stories. He'd been phoning on and off for almost a month; sometimes he said he was at his own home and was worried about a gay co-worker who kept calling. For this story, he used the name Duane, but Jorge knew it was the same caller and on his reports wrote in the names *Buddy/Duane* on each card.

Of course, there was no way to confirm whether these stories were fact or fiction, and Jorge rarely read the newspapers with the idea of confirming anything a caller might have said or done—suicides, crimes, family violence, obituaries. His first couple of years with the agency he had tried that, but it tended to make him a little crazy, and he'd stopped. Still he hadn't come across any articles about victims reporting or describing a rapist who hung around and made phone calls to a crisis hotline challenging them to catch him. Yet rape victims didn't always report rapes. And tonight, Buddy had said the woman wouldn't talk or give her name because she was afraid he'd come back— reason enough to remain silent.

Jorge looked over his notes. There was that odd thing about the tenses. The mix of past and present. And then, too, tonight, Buddy had called him *mi hijo*, my son. That was new. Jorge was the bilingual speaker for the agency, but he still didn't know what to make of this. It could be part of the ruse. Either the guy was very clever or very crazy or both.

And what did the caller really want? Jorge wasn't sure, but Roberta was right. Buddy's calls had been getting longer; one of these times Jorge was going to keep him talking until they could run a trace. That's what the caller wanted, wasn't it? To be caught?

Jorge looked around the office—the white fluorescent lights, the desks with their phones and glowing computer screens. There was Mondragon's old desk in the corner. Phil Mondragon. The weird thing, the hard thing for Jorge was that as he talked to the caller, he kept seeing Mondragon's face. His curly black hair, white skin, his dark brown eyes. He heard Phil in the caller's nervous energy, the taunting contempt. In fact, the very first time he'd heard Buddy's voice—before he'd told his rape story or gone into his history as Duane, Jorge had said, "Phil?" And the caller hadn't replied for a long moment.

Mondragon, Jorge knew, was capable of pulling something like this off. He was familiar with the agency and social services system. And if anyone had the voices, it was Mondragon. In his time at the agency, he had come to be referred to as *The Voice*. And when he'd been in one of his many personas as a counselor, he was great. Quiet, tender, yet firm and immovable with a codependent woman on her third go-around. Tough with a drunken, bullying ex-con looking to be convinced to get back on his medication, yet fighting it. In quiet times between calls, he'd do voices and characters: James Mason; Montgomery Clift; Muhammad Ali; Roseanne Barr; a perfect Betty Davis; an insidious Richard the Third courting Lady Anne, which he'd played in Drama School; a reprise of his raging Ned Weeks, from community theater's *The Normal Heart*.

But Phil had lost it. First, he'd quit the agency—they'd given him a party on what was to be his last shift and the end of his old life—to take a small part in a movie in L.A. The movie's financing had collapsed and after kicking around L.A. for ten months, he decided to come back and regroup. He'd returned to his girl's house in the middle of a sweltering afternoon, and just before ringing the doorbell, he'd heard sounds of love-making and done an about-face. He'd picked up his old job at Helpline, but had been unable to keep a sarcasm and taunting contempt out of his voice. Part of it, Jorge thought, was that Mondragon was so good and facile with voices and in seducing people into believing he sympathized with their situations, that he had come to feel an enormous contempt for himself and, subsequently, the callers.

One night Mondragon shook Jorge and made a believer out of him. Jorge had taken a convoluted phone call from a first-time caller who had identified herself only as Miranda H. Four marriages, fourth one breaking up. Husbands always untrustworthy and unfaithful. Molested by her father. A drinking problem. Two suicide attempts. Well, they weren't really attempts, but she'd mixed alcohol and sleeping pills and come to in the ER with her stomach being pumped both times. She was drinking now. He could hear ice cubes clinking in her glass and her speech starting to slur. She refused every attempted referral Jorge made for counseling. What, she said, was the use? She'd tried them all. He'd been unable to get her to give him her number and was thinking of starting a trace when she'd made an elegiac statement about life being a one-way journey down a lilac-scented path to death and hung up.

Jorge put his line on hold and went to the bathroom. As he'd returned, Mondragon, reading the paper at his desk, glanced up at Jorge. "Yo, brother, you looking whipped. Qué pasa, amigo-dude?"

Jorge mentioned the long call, Miranda H. Mondragon nodded sympathetically. Hey, did she keep talking about a big yellow dog—Biff?—with weak hindquarters, five hundred dollars on surgery for its prolapsed rectum? Jorge said, "That's the one. Have you talked with her before? She said she was a first-time caller."

Mondragon shrugged, "Nope, never talked to her," and then, picking up his paper, Mondragon slurred in her voice, "No matter what anyone says or does, I know life is just a pointless, lilac-scented slouch toward endless death. I'll probably see all four of my husbands there. If there's nothing you can say or do to change that fact, I don't see what we have to talk about."

The exact words of Miranda H. Jorge stared at Mondragon's raised newspaper. Biff with the prolapsed rectum. Mondragon, he realized, had placed the call from one of the back offices. They had often tested each other with little telephone games. But nothing like this. This was something else, a quantum leap, a tour de force. Mondragon had whipped him. Jorge hadn't had a clue.

But Mondragon had gone too far, even for Mondragon. After giving him repeated warnings, Jean, their supervisor, ran a check, calling and playing the part of a woman who wanted to leave her husband but was afraid she'd hurt his feelings so badly he'd kill himself and didn't know what to do. Mondragon had given her nothing but sarcasm, suggested she can the bum, be better off without him, and get a vibrator with six speeds. Not to mention that their standard opening, *Helpline,* had been a stuttering Porky Pig. HhhhhhELP LIllIINE.

Jean came out of the back offices and said, "That's all, Phil. I'll take over your phone as of right now—you can pick up two weeks' severance pay this Friday. I suggest you see a counselor yourself. You know the agencies, but take this." She handed him a note with several referrals. "Get help."

Now that he was fired, he suddenly seemed sorry and desperate, "Hey, I knew you were the caller, Jean . . . that's why I played it the way I did. I knew it was you."

She shook her head. "You didn't have a clue who it was when you answered the phone stuttering like Porky Pig. If I had been a caller and had heard that..."

Jorge watched Mondragon. With a tired, silly shrug, palms turned up, and a cartoon character's roll of his eyes, Mondragon smiled—a perfect little shit-eating grin—and stuttered in a Speedy Gonzalez accent, "Ttttthhhat's aallll, folks. Ttttthhhat's aallll, Phil." As he passed, he glared at Jorge, yet his eyes were blind with a moist fury; he kicked over a chair and slammed the door. Jorge was amazed by the outburst.

Hey, Jorge thought, as he fished the plexiglass cube out of the wastebasket and placed it back on the desk, Mondragon was definitely capable of pulling off the Buddy ruse. He checked over his scramble of notes, took out a card, but put his phone on hold. Christ, this place had really been bugging him lately. Was it just his mood, or had the agency come to overshadow almost every aspect of his life? There'd been the bad timing of the other night; *that* had been the agency, too.

He looked at a poster scotch-taped to the door. Across the top, it said: Miguel Angelo Rivera. Below, a fine-lined drawing, a length of tapered calf in a fishnet stocking, an impossibly high stiletto heel coming down on a smoking cigarette butt. At the bottom: Hotel Santa Cruz. Club Easy, June 28, 9 and 12 p.m. Which had been last week. Miguel, he just now realized, had been on his mind since that night, when Jorge had to rush off from the Club without a word. He'd felt uneasy since.

Miguel. Ten years ago, when Jorge was a young social worker running a group for disturbed children at Las Familias, Miguel had just been taken from his parents. His stepfather had been molesting him and his sister for years. Finally, a teacher who'd been observing the boy—his withdrawn and depressed behavior, his bruises—called Child Protective Services.

At eleven, Miguel Angelo was a beautiful boy, slim, with golden skin, blue-green eyes which tipped up at the corners, high cheekbones, full lips, and glossy, straight black hair which fell to his shoulders. In the group, he remained silent and withdrawn. Then, without warning or apparent provocation, he would weep, howl, pull his hair, tremble, and scratch his cheeks. Jorge would talk to him softly, and sometimes Miguel would let Jorge hold his hand, hug and console him.

In time, Jorge had taken Miguel to the movies and bowling and brought him home to his parents' for dinner several nights a week. Jorge wanted Miguel to be with adults, a mother and father, who could be trusted. He wanted Miguel to be with a Hispanic family. Jorge had not always been Hispanic or Chicano. For a long time, he'd seen himself as the world saw him: a spic, a beaner, a greaser. He'd been beaten and humiliated by his grade-school teachers when he'd lapse into Spanish from English. As a teenager, he'd been furious, reckless. He still had a tattoo from those high-school days, a stemmed rose entwined with a dagger dripping blood and rose petals on his chest. In the shower, an Anglo linebacker had placed his finger on Jorge's chest. "What's this, verga, it takes a tough man to make a tender chicken, some shit like that?" And they'd fought. One night, without provocation, his car had been pulled over by a cop. As he'd stepped out, the white cop had brought his gun down on his head and split his scalp open. Wherever he turned, there was trouble. It had been a Hispanic woman, a chicana, a social worker, who taught him who he was and why he was angry and how to value and accept himself. He understood Miguel. Jorge had retained a special attachment to him.

After a couple of years of hearings, pretrial motions, and delays, Miguel, as a thirteen-year-old, had testified against his stepfather in trial, and it had been his testimony and that of his sister which sent him to prison. Afterward, Miguel seemed to regress, and Jorge understood that Miguel, though relieved, felt that he had betrayed his stepfather. At times, Jorge even thought that Miguel yearned for the man, despite what he'd done.

By now, he was turning from a boy into an adolescent, *beautiful* being the only word to describe him. Whenever Jorge ran into him, he could see an enormous torment within Miguel's face. His voice had dropped to barely a whisper. He'd gone to the community college, studied art one semester, and then, painfully cut off from everyone, he'd disappeared.

For a while, there had been no word of him and then Jorge

heard that Miguel Angelo Rivera was down in Douglas on the Arizona-Sonora border, and that he did a stage show in a gay bar there called Serafino's; he dressed and sang as a woman and word was that he was beautiful and that he was knocking them dead. Jorge had no idea what to think, and last week, after more than two years, Miguel had come back to town, and Jorge had gone down to the Club Easy to see for himself what had happened to Miguel.

Club Easy was on the first floor of the old and dilapidated Hotel Santa Cruz. Inside, Jorge eased into a thick darkness. He sensed, then slowly made out a large crowd sitting with faces turned up to a raised stage where someone—Linda Ronstadt?—sang "Love Me Tender."

Jorge didn't know what he'd been expecting, but in the white lights, there was a beautiful, slender woman: long legs in sheer black stockings, high black heels, a black leather mini skirt, a short-sleeved white silk blouse. Then, the face, the high cheekbones, the blue-green eyes accented by bluish eye shadow, and the lips, the incredible, beautiful full lips, in glossy red lipstick. Though somewhere in him Jorge knew this must be Miguel, before he could check himself, he felt a leap of desire. Then, confusion and self-reproach. People stood around him all the way to the bar, and in the blacked-out room, with everyone motionless, each person's face turned up to Miguel Angelo Rivera lip-synching "Love Me Tender," it was as if everyone were dreaming this same dream.

Slowly, he started working his way forward through the crowd. Even as he got closer, Jorge could see that Miguel Angelo had none of the giveaway signs of the drag queen—large hands or prominent jaw. From time to time, he would stop and look from Miguel Angelo to the faces of the audience. Here, a row of women, silent, watched him. There, a couple, and beyond them, two men, arms around each other's waists. They looked silently into him, as if searching for a line of current where male met female.

Jorge had almost reached the stage when Miguel, peering out into the dark, spotted him. For a moment, he leaned forward and sang to him, and then, never breaking his persona, he pointed a polished nail toward the bar, and Jorge nodded, yes, he'd meet him there.

But before Miguel had been able to finish the show, Jorge's beeper had gone off—he was the Spanish speaker on call that night—and he'd gone out to take a two-hour long suicide call. He'd never made it back. He had no idea what Miguel had thought, his rushing out of there like that. After more than two years of being gone, had he taken it as a rejection of his appearing in drag? Uncertain how to reach Miguel Angelo, he'd called the next afternoon and left a message for him at the Club Easy—Miguel, sorry, called away on an emergency, I'll be back in touch. You were great. Jorge.

And he'd been meaning to see Miguel. But each day, something had come up. This, he realized as he looked at the poster—the fishnet stocking, the stilleto heel—was what had really been making him so edgy all week. Not Buddy or Duane or anything else that was going on at Helpline. Not really.

He circled back to his desk and reread his notes: rape call. Under caller, he wrote *Buddy*, and within moments, he felt himself being drawn back into obsessing about Buddy. At a recent staff meeting, each counselor had submitted a list of possible callers who might be Buddy—callers who had been overly threatening and contentious. By the time they'd finished, there were at least fifteen names. Several counselors, including Jorge, had submitted Dawn's name. Dawn was a very troubling possibility. Besides Mondragon, Jorge thought Dawn was the most likely caller. At times, he thought, she was the only real possibility.

Dawn had been molested by her grandfather, father, and uncles from the time she was two, and had also been used in satanic rituals. At fourteen, stressed by intense nightmares and flashbacks, Dawn had blossomed multiple personalities. She referred to them as the kids, and she had named them for Jorge, the way a mother would introduce children to a visitor, with affection, consternation, tenderness, exasperation, and, in her case, fear; there were the twins, Jody and Jan, they were ten and very sweet; there was the sluttish, angry teenager, Arlene, who had gotten in so much trouble cutting high school, getting arrested for drunken driving, and shoplifting; there was Jimmy Joe, a thuggish 19-year-old hood who took girls for rides in the desert, slapped them around, raped them. Jimmy Joe was rough and unpredictable. Dawn named eleven kids.

Jorge had only heard about Jimmy Joe from Dawn, but never actually heard his voice come out of her; could Jimmy Joe be the rapist? Dawn would call and say, I had flashbacks all afternoon and some of the kids came out. She'd say she couldn't stand it anymore, talk about killing herself. After several calls, it occurred to Jorge that if Dawn had multiple personalities, then who was Dawn? She said, "Dawn is someone I put together from watching the kids on the *Brady Bunch*, looking at posters of Farrah Fawcett—I have posters of her all over my room—and talking to shrinks. Dawn is the one who tries to take care of the kids."

Dawn's name had come up on almost half the staff's list of possible identities for Buddy—Dawn's Jimmy Joe as Buddy and Duane. As no one knew how to handle it, a wait-and-see attitude was adopted. When the meeting broke up, Jean cautioned everyone. No matter what each counselor thought, the caller—Buddy/Duane—couldn't be dismissed; this was the hard part. There was a very good chance that the caller was exactly who he said he was—a rapist—and that the calls were authentic. She acknowledged this held the agency hostage to the caller, but they'd just have to do the best they could until they got a break. Oddly to Jorge, Mondragon's name had not surfaced, and Jorge kept his suspicions to himself for the time being.

Jorge finished logging the night's calls and straightened his desk. Resolutely, he placed the plexiglass cube in a drawer. He walked to the window to check the parking lot for Jill, his replacement, who took the midnight to eight shift. Now it was ten of twelve. Jorge began to pace. He really wanted to get out of here and away from all this. Tonight, he was going to make it down to Club Easy and try to reconnect with Miguel. He felt a strange disquiet.

* * *

The show had just finished and people at the dark bar were talking about Miguel—how incredible, imagine legs like that on a man, they're better than mine; the amazing color of his eyes, the way he moved, his lips. Listening to the comments, Jorge worked his beer in circles. Someone in a white T-shirt and faded blue jeans slipped onto the stool beside him, and it was a moment before he realized it was Miguel with his long hair pulled tightly back into a pony tail. Except for nail polish, all traces of the make-up, lipstick and eye shadow, were gone, and no one recognized or noticed him.

Jokingly, Jorge said, "Hey, querido. Or," he added, "should I say, querida?"

Miguel smiled. Jorge said, "You were fantastic." He meant it. "Hey, sorry about last week, the way I just disappeared, but I got a call right before the end of the show." He tugged the beeper on his belt, Miguel looked down. "I'm the Spanish speaker for the agency, so you know, I had to run out to a phone. A two-hour suicide call." He shook his head. "Anyway, you got my note?"

"What note?"

"I was afraid of that. I left a note with the bartender. You know, I wanted to get back to see you sooner, but I've been jammed." As he said it, he looked at Miguel's red fingernails on the bar and wondered if he'd really been that busy.

Unable to pick up any kind of ease or rhythm, they spoke haltingly. Finally, Jorge thought to ask him about the border. Serafino's, where it had started. In a quiet voice, Miguel told how he'd gone there to get out of town; he'd started as a busboy. Anything was fine, he just wanted to make a break. After a few weeks, bored, he'd been playing with the mike late one afternoon, the place nearly empty—a few people at the bar, the waitresses setting up. He'd been pretending to sing to the jukebox. The waitresses laughed and encouraged him. Someone played Linda Ronstadt's "Ohh Baby Baby." He'd closed his eyes, forgotten everyone, drifted off, just flowed into the music. Halfway through the song, he'd looked out. Everyone had gravitated toward the tables and stood motionless, watching him. Within a few days, there was lipstick from a waitress, eye shadow, then the skirt, the heels, and stockings. Each just seemed to be there, inevitable, and he had not resisted.

Miguel's voice was barely audible, and now that he was off stage, his brilliance had receded into a distance, and Jorge almost felt a barrier in its place. Whose barrier, he wasn't sure. Maybe Miguel's. Maybe his, Jorge's. Miguel slid his fingertips up and down the neck of the bottle, drew circles in the moisture of the bar, his long red nails coming to rest near Jorge's hand, then moving away. The silence lengthened, and then Jorge, uncertain where to go next, asked Miguel if he could sing, if he'd ever tried—and Miguel said softly, "Oh, no, that doesn't matter. I have no voice. I can't even carry a tune." He'd shrugged as if nothing could be more self-evident, or beside the point, and Jorge, feeling stupid, nodded, of course it didn't.

Again the silence grew longer, and again Jorge felt that distance. Then, Miguel stood and, looking into the back bar mirror, remained beside his stool. "Gotta go. You can reach me here. See you later." It sounded more like a question and Jorge said, "Of course. I'll come back. We'll get together. Sorry again about the other night." Did Miguel believe him, that he hadn't been able to stick around, that he'd really had to take a suicide call? Jorge could only hope so. As Miguel reached the end of the bar, Jorge saw him as he might be in twenty years, a slight, shy man on the verge of middle age, and he couldn't help but wonder what it would be like to grow old as a drag queen. They nodded at each other and waved.

Jorge turned over and fought back the covers. He lay motionless, took several deep breaths, but the voices followed him like sonar. Buddy. Dawn. Mondragon. Mondragon as Miranda H. He heard Dawn saying in a small voice, "The kids came out today."

He reached over in the dark, turned on his radio, and searched for something without words, jazz. He settled back, followed the swift flight of a guitar, began to drift. Faraway, someone appeared out of a circle of light. He drifted. He heard someone crying and felt an ache of tenderness. He turned on his side and walked into a hot, dry wind of voices. The kids? The kids came out. Somewhere on a fault line in the night, he slow-danced feverishly with a beautiful woman in a white T-shirt and tight jeans.

June was gone and a week of July. Day after day, the desert sky was cloudless. Just after noon the sun drifted to a stop and, becalmed, hung overhead; the streets and alleys went from three- to two-dimensional in the white light, and everything dried up in the sun. Towering over the city, the mountains too, dried brown, looked as if they had been air-brushed onto a silvery blue distance. In the second week in July, an arsonist torched the mountain woods, and in high westerly winds the woods burned out of control. They burned out of control for days. Evenings, people came home from work to find deer and javelinas, foxes and snakes, coyotes and flocks of birds, drinking from their backyard swimming pools in the foothills. Nights, the dense blackness of the mountains blazed with thousands of beautiful, liquidly shimmering fires, as if the stars had come down out of the sky, and each star was burning on the mountain. A fine ash sifted over the city.

The fire triggered something in people, and day and night Helpline was flooded with callers. The chronics called and obsessed through old problems. They forgot or refused to take their medication and, hallucinatory, ranted into the phone. The incidence of domestic violence doubled and tripled, and Helpline sent women and children to battered women's shelters and told women how and where to get restraining orders. There were serious suicide attempts and Helpline dispatched the police. One night Buddy called with another rape victim at his feet and taunted Jorge to find him and stayed on seventeen minutes, but he couldn't be traced and Jorge called and berated a bored dispatcher at the police department who said she'd file a report.

Another night, Duane called about the gay co-worker who was phoning him at home, and Jorge pretended he didn't know it was Buddy's other voice, tried to trace him, and failed. Part of him said, as he hung up the phone, don't I know this guy? He became motionless in his swivel chair as a voice within jolted him: yes, you do, it's Miguel Angelo. Though Jorge couldn't say how or why, he was suddenly sure. Then he felt the thick, feverish dream of the other night envelop him, slow-dancing with a beautiful woman in a white T-shirt and tight jeans. That, too, was Miguel Angelo. What, was he starting to lose it completely? He felt his certainty give way.

Mondragon? If it was Mondragon, hey, maybe he didn't want to recognize it. Jorge liked Mondragon. He really didn't want to think Mondragon could be doing something like this. And doing it to him. And if he identified Mondragon, well, what then? What was he supposed to do? Follow through on the trace, send the cops, have Mondragon charged by the agency? Jorge didn't know, but if things kept up, maybe it was coming to that.

A few minutes later someone with a soft, husky voice called in and wanted to know if the people on TV, you know, the ones in the cop shows, bled real blood when they were shot or stabbed, and Jorge, after a long pause—genuine schizo caller, outpatient who needed a shot of Haldol, or just a bored summer-school student?—said, yes, they bled real blood, always real blood, the caller asked, who cleans it up, Jorge said he didn't know, but he'd check it out, before he could say more, he heard the dial tone. He pulled a card to him. Caller. Jorge wrote, unknown . . . he hesitated. Male? Female? Something in that voice. An alarm went off in him, loud and clear, and he went to the files, pulled out the great steel drawers, dropped to his knees, and began to dig in the S's.

He found the file under: Samantha/Sam. There were at least forty cards held together with a heavy clip, cards in a dozen different staff members' handwriting. Caller: Sam, Amber . . . Jean had crossed out each name and written in *Samantha* or *Absolutely Samantha*. Christ, how had he—how had they, the staff, and particularly Jean and himself—overlooked Samantha/Sam as Buddy/Duane? It had been almost a year since her last call, but still, what an oversight! That soft, husky voice.

Jorge leafed the cards. Many were in his handwriting. God, he had forgotten. She had started out calling as Samantha—hey, call me Sam, okay? A runaway teenager with a guy named Nicky just out of a correctional institution, they were trying to make it to Hawaii.... He flipped through the cards: Amber. Tiffany. All girls on the run with good/bad boyfriends. Jean had figured out they were the same caller. Then, amazingly, there was Howard, whose wife had taken their three kids and left him; he was going crazy. And Dell, with his soft Southern accent. So polite. Yes, sir, no, ma'am. Dell usually called at two in the morning while waiting for his girl to come home. She was out with another man, yes, sir. Again, both Jean and Jorge had finally grown suspicious, figured out Howard and Dell were the same caller, and then Jean also figured it out—that soft, husky voice—was Samantha. Even after the staff had been warned, Samantha went on hooking counselors for months. Howard. Dell. Amber. Perhaps her pièce de résistance had been Amorita. Amorita was a seven-year-old girl who was home alone. Her daddy was dying of cancer in the hospital. Her mommy worked. Staff workers read to her night after night. *The Velveteen Rabbit, The Cat in the Hat, The Black Stallion.* It had been months before Jean identified her as Samantha.

Jorge stood with the file. How had every single person in the agency overlooked this? Okay, the caller had been quiescent for a year, but still someone should have thought of Samantha. These callers were like weird strains of aerobically borne viruses or molds triggered out of dormancy by who knew what, electro-magnetic activity, X-rays from deep space, who knew? He wrote Jean a note: Buddy/Duane, our rape caller? He clipped it to Samantha's file and put it in Jean's box. Then, as he sat back down at his desk, his sense of certainty went out of him. What if Sam and Amber and Howard and Amorita were Buddy? They still had to catch him.

One night Jorge received a succession of calls which pushed him over the edge. The first, toward the last hour of his shift, had been from an unknown woman. The voice was so soft he could barely hear it, and he had thought of Samantha and Mondragon's Miranda H. He went ahead with the usual questions to ground the caller and bring her out. What's going on tonight? What'd you do today? Gradually, he got the woman to speak up, though he could still barely make her out. It was like this when they'd been crying, or when they were paralyzed by depression.

She said she hadn't gone out today, she'd been too depressed. She didn't have many friends. She stayed by herself. She had no close relationships, she lived alone. Within a few minutes, Jorge suddenly knew that she was going to turn out to be a cutter. Cutters, he had noticed, seemed to have similar histories: they were almost always young women who had been sexually abused; they had extremely low self-esteem and suffered numbing depression, like this caller. Softly and gently, Jorge asked questions into her paralyzed silence. No, she had not called the agency before. She didn't feel like giving a first name. Okay, that was fine.

Convinced she was a cutter, Jorge decided to head for it and started to set her up. She sounded very depressed. Was she in counseling? Sort of—she went to a group. What group? AMAC. Had he heard of it? Yes, Adults Molested As Children. And was it helping? Not really. Was she feeling suicidal tonight? Yes. Did she have a method at her disposal? Yes. What was that? Razor. The word hung. Razor. They were there. He listened into the phone. The silence grew longer. He had been doing it all for her, but now he waited. She had to make the next move. He watched the second hand go around on the clock.

The minute hand jumped twice before she said softly, "I have this strange urge to cut myself." Jorge nodded. He'd seen the arms of cutters, the thin tracings and maps left by razor blades. For some it was a kind of foreplay to wrist slashing. For others, cutting was release enough, an end in itself. Jorge said, "Have you cut yourself before?"

"No. I'm fighting it," she said in a near whisper, "but I'm feeling very alone."

"I understand," Jorge said. He knew that often it was just the sound of a human voice that could make a difference, and so he stayed on, searching for questions to ask her, trying to get her to talk. Finally, after a long silent impasse, he said, "If you think you're going to cut yourself, will you call us back before you do anything?"

"I'll try," she said in a halting voice, "Will you be there?"

He'd glanced at the clock. He was going off soon. "Not much longer, but there is always someone here."

"But *you* won't be there?"

"Not tonight."

The caller was silent. After a moment, Jorge heard her start to cry. As she had been unwilling to give her name, he could only make a kind of undefined sound into the phone. She hung up. Stunned, Jorge listened to the dial tone, then let out an exhausted sigh. There was something about the way she'd said *you*—*you* won't—which made him think of Mondragon's saying, "All we're doing is acting. We're pretending we're here for people, but we're not. It's a con job." Now Mondragon seemed right. Jorge knew he was exhausted. He put his phone on hold, went into a small back office, and turning off the lights, he stretched out on the floor and lay in the dark.

When he returned, blinking into the glare of the office lights, the moment he released the hold button, the phone rang. Picking up, he recognized Buddy. Or was it Samantha? He waved at Marilyn and pointed at the trace number. They'd gotten no more than two minutes into the call, when something in him snapped at the sound of the taunting voice; he'd been keeping it from himself, but there was no longer any doubt, and he stood suddenly at his desk. "Goddamnit, Mondragon, why the fuck are you doing this to me? Chinga tu madre! Hijo de puta!" He banged down the receiver. Marilyn and Roberta looked at him, then each other. He slammed out of the room and down the long dark hall of the office building, punching the walls. It was the first time ever in his career as a counselor at Helpline—four years—that anyone had pulled him out of his counselor's persona. Worse, somewhere in him, he was still just a furious seventeen-year-old pachuca with a rose and dagger on his chest.

Shaking his head, he walked the length of the hall several times, then took off early, and went for a long drive, finally coming to a stop facing the Hotel Santa Cruz. He left the engine running and stared at the hotel. Inside, in the Club Easy, Miguel Angelo wore a tight mini skirt and black silk stockings and lip-synched to Linda Ronstadt, Whitney Houston, and Janet Jackson in a circle of white lights. He saw Miguel's glossy red lips. His blue-green eyes. He saw Miguel's red fingernails drawing circles on the bar, his fingertips moving up and down slowly on the neck of the bottle, felt a wave of uneasiness roll through his stomach. He stared at the hotel. Something inside told him this was what was making him so edgy, not Buddy—hell, the agency had never really gotten to him before. He was divorced and between girlfriends, but turning queer? He liked women. He knew he liked women, not men dressed as women. He was sure of that. He revved the engine, slammed it into drive, and drove.

The next afternoon, Jorge had little trouble finding Mondragon's bungalow at the end of a narrow dirt road, and standing outside his garden gate, hand on the latch, he hesitated. The front of the house was surrounded by a six-foot high fence made of salvaged wood and corrugated iron, but which created, nonetheless, a pleasingly ordered pattern. Jorge peered through a crack and spotted Mondragon standing in the garden; he was partially hidden by roof-high sunflowers. He wore nothing but a black belt tied around his waist and a jockstrap, and sweating, he moved in a slowly undulating wave: tai chi. Jorge worked the latch, called out, and stepped inside. A neatly manicured dirt path curved toward the front door, and waist-high mounds of dirt were covered with flowers—marigolds, zinnias, verbena, and lantana—all giving off a pungent odor in the midday sun.

Without stopping his movement, Mondragon rotated toward Jorge and went into a slight crouch, his hands raised. Only a gringo like this could be doing tai chi or whatever it was gringos did in the desert sun in July. Mondragon's curly black hair had grown out, he was unshaven, and there was something crazed and contemptuous in his brown eyes which made Jorge uneasy.

Mondragon said softly, "Qué pasa, amigo-dude?"

"I'm okay. How've you been, Phil?"

"Just how you see."

Jorge wasn't sure how he saw. Mondragon stopped moving

and stood motionless among the towering sunflowers, sweat dripping from his chin and streaming down his chest. Damp with sweat and dry-mouthed, Jorge decided small talk wouldn't work. He said, "Phil, I know what you think of the agency—Jean, the way she fired you, all of it. And I know you had some trouble leading up to it. L.A. Your girl. I understand. A lot of the time I feel like you do about the agency. You were right about some things—the easy seduction, the way we're all maybe playing a part we can't deliver on, the way it's a kind of act." Jorge surprised himself and tried to shut up.

Mondragon stood still. Without turning to look, he let a hand inch away until it found a sunflower stalk.

Jorge went on. "And so, yeah, calling us, putting on an act, challenging us, I understand, Phil. It's the perfect reply. But listen, man, whatever you think of the agency, please stop calling us now. Buddy, Miranda H . . . " He trailed off. "Are you calling us?"

Phil curled his fingers gently around the thick green stalk. He said very simply, "Why would I call you?" Jorge watched him closely and thought Mondragon was masterful in his ingenuousness.

"I don't know. But if you are calling, please stop." Mondragon smiled, a gentle, pitying, slightly contemptuous smile. "Phil, if and when the agency does catch you, they'll press charges." Phil shook his head. "But the real danger here is someone's going to get lost in the shuffle and die in the confusion this thing is making."

Mondragon remained smiling at him. Jorge turned and walked back down the path. As he reached the gate, Mondragon called him. "Amigo-dude?"

"What?"

"Would you like a glass of water?"

Jorge hesitated. Brilliant. The sly guile, the contempt. Mondragon. Jorge shook his head no. Mondragon was unreadable, and now he realized that no matter what Mondragon had said, he wouldn't have believed him. As he closed the gate, he looked back once more. Mondragon, in his black belt and jockstrap, and holding the sunflower stalk, was smiling and looking up at the sun.

Several days later there was an emotional staff meeting. Jorge's explosive hang-up on Buddy was raised, and Jorge shook his head in disbelief that Roberta and Marilyn would rat him off. Unbelievable. Though Jean said no one was more sympathetic than she, the agency could not afford to deal with callers that way. And it still hadn't been established that Buddy was a hoax. Incidentally, that kind of uncontrolled response was just the payoff someone like Buddy was working for. Someone said to Jorge, "You're holding back anger. Talk about it." After a long silence, Jorge said, "Fuck you. How's that?"

In that deteriorating atmosphere, Jean went over possible callers. She thanked Jorge for the suggestion about Samantha/ Sam/Howard/Dell and said that she thought Samantha had to be number one on their list of candidates. When the name was mentioned, everyone murmured. Christ almighty, how had everyone forgotten about Samantha? Well, she hadn't called in over a year... yeah, but, still. Never mind. They would start checking her out, but as of now, it remained tough because as far as anyone knew, she had never had a social worker, never taken any referrals. She would be tough. Again, Dawn's name was brought up. Jean had recently spoken with Dawn and thought she was in a difficult, suicidal phase. The kids were coming out all the time now. Arlene. Jimmy Joe. Dawn was very afraid of Jimmy Joe, who was a dangerous and unstable personality. Jimmy Joe *was* a rapist.

Now Jorge thought of mentioning Mondragon, but just couldn't bring himself to do it. His old authority problems? Wasn't he keeping something from himself so he wouldn't have to dime Phil? Christ, he knew it was Mondragon. So what? Be like these gringa counselors, rat him off? Better to let Mondragon keep calling. Catch him or not, whatever. Another voice, cold and out of nowhere, said, or am I going crazy and can't tell what's what because I'm turning queer? And that one made his stomach roll over. The meeting broke up with nothing

resolved. Jorge stood and walked out quickly, pushing past staff
members.

Jorge made sure the catch on the window was in place and
leaned on the windowsill. Covering the late afternoon sun, an
ashen wall rose in the west. Dust. A while later, the wind bent
the palms and eucalypti, the sky went black, and when Jorge
leaned on the sill again, a fine layer of dust coated his hands.
Then it was hot and still, and slowly the stars came out. Jorge
took a call and after a few moments recognized the voice of the
woman, the cutter. She seemed very far away and because Jorge
was tired and could barely make her out, he momentarily
imagined her buried somewhere in that wall of dust. She was
very depressed. She had a razor. Had she used it? She didn't
answer. Maybe this would be a good time to tell me your first
name? After a long silence, she hung up. Jorge noted the time,
took a deep breath, and went to the coke machine.
    When he returned, there was a hang-up, and then Jorge took
a call and recognized Buddy's voice. He snapped his fingers at
Marilyn, who started the trace. Buddy didn't mention Jorge's
explosion of the other night. Nor did he begin in his usual
taunting way by asking if Jorge had started the trace. Instead,
talking almost gently to Jorge, mi hijo, he seemed to be going in
and out of a past and a meandering present, and suddenly,
Jorge knew that this guy wasn't Samantha or Mondragon, this
guy must be for real. He talked about how hard it had been in
prison, mi hijo, how much he had missed his children, how he
had never meant to hurt them, that no one was supposed to get
hurt, but he couldn't help himself, wasn't it that way, too, with
the way the government had put Indians on the reservation, mi
hijo? Jorge listened. Did he know this guy from somewhere? Or
was he going crazy himself? And what about Cortez? Jorge lost
him completely with Cortez. I'll tell you about Cortez. Much of
the rambling Jorge couldn't follow, but almost afraid to breathe,
he just kept murmuring, yes, yes, yes, I see, I understand, all of
the time thinking of Mondragon's saying how it was all just an
act, Jorge understood nothing. He watched the minute hand
going around, twelve minutes, fifteen minutes, eighteen min-

utes, Marilyn's phone rang, she wrote quickly, she held her hand overhead in a fist, a number and address, she called 911, sent the cops. Jorge went on listening. After a few minutes, Buddy said talking so much was making him thirsty, he was going to get a drink, he'd be right back, he had more to tell Jorge.

Buddy put the phone down and then it was silent, and Jorge paced behind his desk, listening into the receiver. The phone remained silent for a long time. Ten, fifteen minutes. Then, someone, breathless, picked up the phone, and Jorge's heart started to pound. "This is Sergeant Vega here...who is this? Who is this?"

"Helpline. Jorge of Helpline. I'm still on. We started the trace and sent you." Jorge explained quickly about Buddy, the rapist, the calls. "Who's down there?"

"Just the woman. The guy, whoever he is, he's gone. There's blood everywhere. We're taking the woman to the ER."

"Which ER?"

"Kino."

Jorge hung up, circled the office, took a hug from Marilyn, and then said, "Can you cover for me? I've got to go." In his car, he sat numb and then started driving. He drove south. In the hot stillness, undulating white clouds choked the silvery street-lights, and Jorge, stopped at a red light, could see they were huge winged grasshoppers swarming in from the desert. He watched a cloud shaping and reshaping itself. In his four years at Helpline, he realized he'd never seen a caller's face. This latest victim knew something. Jorge didn't know exactly what he wanted. He couldn't stop seeing Mondragon's face. He realized the summer, the heat, the weeks of taking calls from Buddy and Duane and Dawn and dozens of others, maybe he'd lost it more than a little. He drove south.

In the emergency room, people waited—mothers and fathers with crying children, a weeping woman, a man who lay on his side groaning. A huge, fat white woman was brought in by cops who had arrested her in a bar brawl; they couldn't take her to jail until she sobered up. Restrained, she cursed and abused everyone, momentarily broke away from the cops, filled the corridor with threats.

At the end of the hall, there was an alcove, and Jorge saw more cops and a woman's back. One cop stood by the woman and another was talking to the nurse a few steps away. Jorge could see they were about to take her inside, and that she was covered with blood. She turned as Jorge approached, and Jorge saw Miguel Angelo in his skirt and black stockings.

Miguel looked at Jorge and said in the small, not quite comprehending voice of the small boy he remembered, "Where've you been?"

Jorge looked at Miguel's face and then he saw the many faces moving beneath the make-up, the tormented boy, the boy who had sent his stepfather to prison; he saw the nondescript, middle-aged man he'd momentarily seen in the Club Easy, whom he now recognized as Buddy, the stepfather who had held his son hostage night after night; and, as Miguel held out his hand—the beautiful painted long nails, the bloody tracks of the razor up and down his arms—Jorge recognized his unknown female, his cutter, the woman Miguel had become.

Miguel said, "I'm alone. Where've you been?"

Jorge stretched out his hand into Miguel's vast, uncrossable distance. "I'm here, mi hijo. I've always been here." Jorge took Miguel's slim hand which was thick with blood. From down the hall, they could hear the fat woman cursing and the cops trying to restrain her.

Africa

E VERYTHING SEEMS A LITTLE BETTER. We are here now, Gracie and I, together with Zoeller and Madame Bardi, Madame's old house falling into disrepair above us on the hillside. Even though I see them daily, I'm not really sure what goes on between Zoeller and Madame Bardi, but that's okay. It is the small things which seem to be helping me. Chess with Zoeller under the tree. Strolls with Grace through the medieval part of the town. But when I think about the slides, I feel a queasy dread insinuate itself out of the white sunlight and rise through my stomach. I'm here because the director sent me.

I'm one of the curators for a museum in Los Angeles and I was supposed to curate a photography show to be called *The Faces of Love*. Right from the start, I had been skeptical. I said to Jim, the director, "Look, it sounds too much like *The Family of Man*. It's broad, it's infinite, it's the deep blue sea, it's too romantic, and in this age of disbelief, irony, satire, contempt, you name it ..."

Jim said, "You're absolutely right. And those are the very reasons we should do it now. You're the perfect curator for this. You're thirty-seven, neither young or old, but you've got experience, you're right in the middle of your life...." He was the director. It was his idea. We went ahead with it.

Several years before, I had curated a photography show called *Things We Live By*. I was just married then. I told my assistant: "Listen, Betsy, no bathrooms, no bums, no seagulls, no car parts...." Betsy started laughing. "No puddles, no bark, no roots, no peeling paint...." I was sure of myself.

The Faces of Love. This time I said to my assistant, "Listen, this new show. Jim's show. We're going to get an avalanche of work. Right from the top, I can say, no lovers looking out windows, no men and women with glasses of wine dreaming into cigarette smoke, absolutely no lovers sharing sodas, ice cream, whatever, you know what I'm talking about here, no lovers in parks, on branches... no mothers holding babies up to windows, no lovers lonely on beaches—I don't have to spell it out, the horizon, infinity, that stuff...." I glanced out the window and trailed off. The first time I'd seen Grace, I lost my breath. Her beauty. And a sense of recognition. Certainty. We'd been married six years, and for the last three years we'd been trying to have children. Lately, we'd embarked on a series of tests, my tests, her tests, sperm, ovulation, and the results had been ambiguous. I'd been trying to imagine life without children, Grace and I, our life. Sometimes I thought it would be all right. At times, I studied Grace and wondered if she was disappointed in us. I couldn't tell from her expression. Betsy turned to leave. "Forget what I said. Let's just look at everything."

We sent out press releases announcing the show, and the slides came in. I looked at everything. I'd see an image and get that hit in my chest, certainty, a while later, I'd look again and the same images were clichéd or sentimental or self-indulgent; how could I have missed it? For the most part, I had always just known—I'd look, I'd know. But now I didn't seem to know. I noticed my sentences started trailing off and things—rooms, furniture—looked smaller, as though they were shrinking. Grace, too, beautiful Grace, when she was curled up in an easy chair with a book, was far away. Everything was receding. Myself, too, I'd look at my hand, and it was way down there at the end of my arm. Jim, busy with his fund raising, new building, and grant writing, would pass me and ask, "How's the show looking, Nick?" And I'd nod. In the street, in movie lines, I stared at

people—men and women—wondering what brought them together, held them together, sustained them. I'd stare and go
back to the slides and look some more. It was as though I were
shouting down into myself and getting no echo back.

One morning, Jim called me into his office. He was miles
away behind his big oak desk. He spoke quietly. He wanted me
to take a leave of absence. He had something specific in mind.
There was a small town in the south of France, where an old,
little known French photographer, Charles Raymond, had a
body of work. Jim wanted me to catalog everything—letters,
prints, diaries, negatives, everything—and ship it to the museum. It would take a while. Maybe two or three months. There
was a small foundation in the same town—painters and sculptors usually stayed there—but he knew the woman who owned
the place and he thought she would put me up.

When he finished, I closed the door. "Jim, I know what you're
doing. Just give me a couple of more days and I'll pull the
show . . ." I trailed off.

"I gave Grace the letter of inquiry a few weeks ago and
I know she's already sent it on. I really do need this done."
He nodded. "It's a beautiful spot. A small town up in the Mari-
time Alps, maybe 20 miles above the Riviera. . . ." The phone
rang.

The show opened just before we left for France. Jim had
curated it himself. Maybe, seeing the show hung, I'd know
something, but the moment I walked into the opening, my heart
started pounding, and I felt a fine sweat mist my skin as if I'd
walked into a cloud. I hung on to Grace and then plunged
toward the door. "I have to get out of here. Take your time, I'll
be in the car."

A few days later we left for France.

We have been here since. Three weeks. As I finished packing,
I placed a box of duplicate slides from the show in my duffle.
Though I was off the hook, maybe I'd look them over. I hesitated. I took them out. Then I put them back in. After several
days of flying and trains and buses, a taxi had driven us from
the town square to Madame's and left us in a long narrow drive;

Grace and I stood disoriented and looked up at a stone Pro-
vençal house, shutters drawn against the August heat. At the
sound of the taxi, a second-floor shutter cracked open and an
old woman looked out, then down at us. "Who are you? What
do you want here?" she asked in a hoarse whisper. I explained
we were the Americans who had come to catalogue Charles
Raymond's work; I mentioned Jim, the Museum Director. She
rapped the shutter with her cane and called out, "Zoeller . . .
Zoeller!" in a louder whisper and closed the shutter.

I said, "Do you think that was Madame Bardi? She didn't act
like she knew who we were. Maybe there's been some mistake."

Grace shrugged. "If there's been a mistake, we'll go down to
the Riviera and have fun until our money gives out."

The house remained closed and silent. I looked around. The
hillside, once a vineyard, was gently terraced, the stones of its
retaining walls crumbling, and I could see a couple of small out-
buildings, paths meandering between them. The terraces sloped
down to a valley thick and green with pines and misted with
humidity. In the distance, a silvery-purple shimmer, I made out
the Mediterranean on the horizon.

When I glanced back, I saw someone coming up a path, and
when he was close, I could see he was maybe a head taller than
I and about my age. He had long hair which fell across his eyes,
regular features, an unreadable face. He wore jeans and a
Grateful Dead T-shirt, and because he was thin, he seemed even
taller.

He held out his hand. "Zoeller." Just then I heard a door slam
behind us, and the old woman came out a side door. "Ah," said
Zoeller, "Madame Bardi makes her entrance. The real countess," a mixture of admiration and contempt in his voice. Jim had
used that exact phrase, too, told me that she'd been born in
Budapest, had been an expatriate after the Communists had
come in, and had led a fascinating life. He'd added the singular
fact, "She's over ninety." We watched her pick her way over the
uneven ground. Though she used a cane, she had a beautiful
upright posture. And though she was frail, and her face webbed
with wrinkles, she had a kind of luminosity; perhaps it was her

eyes, which were a beautiful blue, deep and radiant. I couldn't stop looking at her.

Zoeller glanced at me and shook his head, "Another admirer." He walked to meet her, offered his arm, but she ignored him. When she reached us, she caught her breath, and then offered her hand to me so that I felt confused, almost as though I should kiss her hand. I took her hand gently and half bowed. I'd never done such a thing before.

Zoeller looked at Madame, at Grace, and hair falling over his eyes, he kissed her hand, "Grace, is it?" He looked up and smiled. "Enchanting to have such beauty installed in our digs, isn't it so, Madame?"

Madame Bardi placed her knobby cane on his shoulder, then smiled, and said softly and affectionately, "He is so insolent." She placed the tip of her cane over his heart and pressed lightly as if to run him through. "Zoeller, help them with their bags and get them settled in the studio." She nodded at us. "Later, we will take a drive." We exchanged a few pleasantries about our trip, what a beautiful spot here.... Just before I turned to go, I looked back and saw Madame Bardi staring at Grace.

In the studio, Zoeller dropped a duffle, turned on the fan, and gave us a quick demonstration of how the stove and shower worked. Then he stopped and looked us over. "So ... we are the only ones here at this decrepit old place and maybe I go any day now."

"It's generous of Madame Bardi to let us stay here," Grace offered.

He waved his hand. "It is just her way of having company and still believing she is the great woman. Painters come and paint her. Everyone kisses her ass. She lives on the dreams." He waved his hand. "Okay, Zoeller goes now. I'm over there." He pointed to a whitewashed studio across our terrace. "Los Angeles, huh? Hollywood. The American West. Maybe I visit you someday soon." He grinned, waved his hand, "Hey, don't be scared, I don't come so far, huh? I just knock, maybe half after four, that is when Madame Bardi bestirs her old bones, we take a ride, have a look around." And he turned, gave a mock half bow, swept his hair out of his eyes, and left. Later, as I nodded into a sweaty, afternoon nap, airports and trains, I heard a volcanic burst of drumming, a refrain, "A Night in Tunisia" in the white sunlight.

Zoeller called, "Hey, you Americans ... not making love, uh?" and knocked lightly on the screen door. "Okay, maybe so. Then Zoeller will give you a minute to finish your business. One minute, no more, no less, it's plenty of time." There was a silence. Zoeller called out, "Ten ... fifteen ... " Grace laughed, "Come in."

"Nah, come in, go out, this fatigues me, you come on, we go now, go with Madame in the car, have a look around." We followed him up the terraced hillside to the garage. "Okay, wait here." I looked in and saw a motorcycle in the shadows. After a few minutes, he returned, walking slowly with Madame on his arm, who barely came to his shoulder.

The four of us squeezed into a small, nondescript car, Zoeller's chin almost touching the steering wheel. He turned the key, the motor cranked, but wouldn't catch. Zoeller cursed in German, "Russian car!" got out and opened the hood. He tinkered. "Try it." I tried it. In the ensuing silence, I noticed a long descending whistle, the sound a kid makes imitating a falling bomb. Over and over.

I said to Madame Bardi, "What's that whistling?"

In her sweet hoarse whisper, she said, "Ah, that is Madame LeClerc's parrot, Jacques." She pointed toward a thick green hedge in front of us. "Zoeller has taught the parrot to make that sound. He does it all day long now. It is driving me crazy. That is why Zoeller did it." Facing forward, she said resolutely, "Someday, I will kill that bird."

"Try now!"

I turned the key, and the car started. Zoeller slammed the hood, wiped his hands, and got in. She touched the tip of her cane to his nails. "Grease. Machines. I know you through and through. A true German."

Zoeller looked back at me in the mirror. "I fix her crummy Russian car and this is what she must say to me."

We went bumping up the long drive, through the hedge to the street, deserted in the afternoon stillness. We drove around the town square, shaded by massive old sycamores, drove into the old quarter of the city, up past the memorial to the slain resistance fighters, looked out over the valleys and hillsides going down to the Mediterranean. We drove on. Zoeller pointed out the good markets, the Matisse Chapel, the road down to St. Paul; we passed men drinking red wine and smoking cigarettes and playing bolles as though they were on a poster, Visit France. After a while, we went back to Madame Bardi's where we were served dinner at a table under one of the olive trees and then the trip caught up with me and I suddenly felt exhausted and excused myself.

Lying in the dark after a shower, the smell of heat and dust beyond the screens, I said to Grace, "What do you think of Madame Bardi?"

"She's charming. And fascinating with all of her stories." Grace was thoughtful. "But she doesn't like women much."

"Why do you say that?"

"She just doesn't want other women around. It's something maybe women can feel or understand better than men."

I couldn't see it, but I didn't say anything. "And Zoeller?"

"Zoeller?" She laughed softly. "Zoeller," she repeated, and before she could say more, she was asleep.

In the morning, we again piled into the little Russian car and drove over to Charles Raymond's, where Madame Bardi introduced us; we had coffee and some of my rusty, college French even came back. I could see from Monsieur Raymond's fervency that I was the envoy from the magical kingdom across the water that every artist believes will some day arrive and validate his work. His fervency and the real reason I was here embarrassed me. He led us through his house and out-building: boxes of negatives, correspondences, prints, portfolios. A mountain of work, a lifetime. I tried to show some interest. As Zoeller peered into a darkened room piled high with boxes, he patted me on the shoulder and said, "Fack, man, I can see this will be fun for you, yah ... all this junk go to archive somewhere. Unbelievable." I was here because I couldn't successfully curate a show. I decided then and there I wouldn't try to assess Raymond's work. I'd catalogue, pack and ship it. I wouldn't think beyond that.

So every morning, glad that I had someplace to go, I rode a rusty bicycle over to Monsieur Raymond's and culled and catalogued until his wife served us a light lunch; we would talk in my rusty French, work another hour or two, and then, the town somnolent in the heat, I'd ride back to Madame Bardi's, where I'd arrive drenched with sweat, and take a cool shower. Then, dread sucking at me just beneath the sunlight, I would wrap myself up in crosswords. Reading. Chess and small talk with Zoeller under the tree.

From little things Zoeller and Madame Bardi said, I gathered that Zoeller had come here five years ago with a group of designers and sculptors from Berlin. Their project was to build a small house without any plans or leader—just spontaneously create it out of the forces which evolved between them. They had managed a foundation, which I discovered down in the valley, but then they had started to quarrel and drink, kept drinking, and finally gone their ways. Zoeller had stayed on, coming and going.

In my wanderings on the hillside, I had come upon a blinding flash of light. When I'd stepped onto a terrace, grass and weeds run riot, I saw a structure made of burnished stainless steel, a rhomboid, the joints flexible, now a wing, now a breaking wave, the whole thing, maybe one story high, coming to some indecipherable point of balance on a column. The structure turned silently, this way, that, extending, flattening, responding to the wind which, smelling of heat and pine, rose up the valley. Closer, I saw the name on the column, Zoeller. The whole thing was beautifully machined and welded and alive. The next time I saw him, I said, "Zoeller, I saw your sculpture down there. It's fantastic, the way it balances, the way..."

Zoeller waved his hands in circles around his head, "Yah, yah, the wind, the machine, the vector, the force, is all fack fack fack...." A while later, I heard volcanic drumming from his studio, the bray and cry of ferocious horns, and thought I recognized the African samba rhythms of Art Blakey. I didn't say anything more to him about his piece.

So we played chess in the hot afternoons, the falling bomb whistle of Jacques descending endlessly from beyond the hedge like a record stuck in a fever. Zoeller ran errands, did chores, appeared and disappeared in and out of Madame Bardi's cluttered house. Once he came back with a heavy green oxygen tank. "For Madame," he said as I helped him wrestle it up a narrow staircase to her bedroom. "She is old old womans." The four of us took excursions into town or drove into the country in early evening. Sometimes, late in the afternoon, I would see Madame Bardi and Zoeller walking together down the rows of olive trees, the sunlight slanting silver-green through the branches, Madame leaning on Zoeller's arm, the two talking softly in German. I didn't know what to make of it. Grace said, "Maybe it's just what it appears to be." Though speculations about them wove in and out of our daily conversations, I just didn't know what to think.

Things went along and were fine at Madame Bardi's until one evening. We'd had dinner and were sitting under the olive tree when Zoeller, who had drunk a lot of wine, pushed back in his chair. "So, Madame Bardi... the moment has arrived. Will you tell us, please, why is it you are always staring at Grace? Just now, again, I catch you. You stare at her. She is very beautiful, isn't she? And her skin is so smooth, like a child's." Madame Bardi looked away. "What do you see when you stare like this?" The candlelight lapped the underside of the olive branches like water. Zoeller had mentioned to me that Madame had been considered one of the great beauties of Europe. "And at ninety-one, it is inconceivable to me how Madame could still be so vain." Now Zoeller laughed. Madame Bardi didn't reply. There was a long silence. I said that it was late and I was going to bed. As Grace and I felt our way down the dark terraces to our studio, I could hear them, Zoeller's German, laconic, bluff, and Madame Bardi's voice, sharp-toned but almost inaudible. Once I heard her rap the table with her cane, and Zoeller's laughter rising as she rapped louder. But that wasn't the end of it.

In the morning, when Zoeller came up the terraces to breakfast, he was wearing pink frosted lipstick and as he reached for the coffee pot, I saw his matching nail polish. Each lens of his sunglasses had a small lipstick heart. Madame said, "Wipe that maquillage off your lips, Zoeller."

He sat down with his coffee. "Is not quite the right shade for Madame Bardi?"

"Go on." She waved her cane toward him.

He smiled. "But I think it is quite becoming." He held up the silver coffee pot, studied his reflection. "What do you think of the color, Grace?"

"Perhaps a little young for you, Zoeller. Maybe a darker shade."

Zoeller studied himself. "Hmm, what you say maybe has some truth ... no, no, I think it is just right."

"Go on, Zoeller," she said in a hoarse whisper, "wipe it off or take breakfast by yourself."

Zoeller said, "That is extremely antisocial, Madame. And consider the feelings of our guests." He placed a napkin in his lap, took a slice of melon, and ate. Madame stood. "Excuse me." With her beautiful, upright carriage, picking her way with her cane, Madame walked back to the house. I looked over at Zoeller. Was he mocking the beautiful young woman Madame had been? Or perhaps saw when she looked at Grace? Zoeller said, "Ah, this papaya...." When he had finished, he sat back in his chair, and licking the juice from his frosted pink lips, he stared through his lipstick hearts with a faint smile.

There seemed to be something restless let loose in the air and Grace and I were talking about catching the bus down to Nice for a swim when Zoeller rapped on the door. "Hey, you two Americans...." The lipstick and polish were gone. He wore jeans and a T-shirt. "How about we get away from this decrepit place—take the car to Nice for bathing, see the world."

"We were just talking about that. Let's go." I turned to get our things together.

Zoeller caught my sleeve. "Wait. No. I tell you how. You two walk to the cafe in town ... after a while, I come in the car and pick you up."

"Why don't we just go from here?"

Zoeller said, "Ah, then Madame will see us leave together and she will become jealous. She does not like to be left out of anything. Even the thing she is not so interested in, like bathing in the sea ... and she will accuse me of seeing the womens if she knows I go. Better this way. Believe me. I know Madame Bardi like no one else."

We waited in the cafe, and after a while Zoeller, hunched up in the little Russian car, came driving by and we wound down from the mountains to the sea, where we spent the afternoon on the crowded beach. We would swim and lie in the sun and sit up to our waists and chests in the water. I watched the children dashing in and out of the water. Occasionally, one would catch my eye or splash me and laugh. Throughout the afternoon, Zoeller, staring off at the horizon, seemed to be somewhere else. Once I asked him, "What was that with the lipstick? Madame Bardi?"

Zoeller just waved his hand. "Is all fack fack fack."

Grace and I swam far out until the beach and the promenade and the hotels seemed distant and, treading water, Grace wrapped her legs around my waist, and we drifted. We glowed a silver-green and far below was the mystery of sunlight slanting and disappearing down into a blue-green depth.

Late in the day, as we stood to go, Zoeller said to me, "You smell it out there?"

"Smell what?" I sniffed.

"Fack, man, Africa." When he said Africa, I felt something go off in me, as though he'd struck a gong which sent out multicolored soundwaves. I sniffed the air. He couldn't really smell Africa. He had to be kidding.

I said, "Does Nice have a zoo?"

Zoeller looked affronted. "What? Is everything the joke? I tell you, all day I smell it on the wind: the desert, the camel, Negroes, Arabs.... I go to Africa soon. I feel it. Something is coming. I know." He turned and we walked back toward the promenade, our steps making the rocks clatter.

* * *

We were sweating and playing chess, and Zoeller was, as always, beating me. He said quietly, "Uh oh, Madame Bardi comes now. I haven't seen her since we go to Nice yesterday. Just keep playing. I handle this."

Madame walked slowly up to the table and caught her breath. I said hello and she gave me a formal smile. Zoeller stared at the board. She studied the game, then said something in German. Zoeller replied laconically. She said something else. They talked. Then Zoeller looked up at Madame Bardi and spoke rapidly, and as he did, her blue eyes flashed, she raised her cane over her head, and trembled. She spat several words at him. Zoeller stared up at her contemptuously. She trembled, lowered her cane, and walked away. Zoeller watched her, then said quietly, "Your move."

I stared at the board. Finally, I said, "What happened?"

Zoeller said, "Oh, she asks me about yesterday. Where we go, what we do. I tell her. She asks why I sneak away. I tell her she doesn't like to bath so we go ourself to Nice. I talk talk talk. I tell her there is no womans. Okay. She says, go, now, take the car, do this and that, then take me here.... You know, she is a real countess," he said with contempt and admiration. "She gives orders. So I listen listen listen and then I get tired of it and say, 'Shut up, you wrinkled old woman, no one orders Zoeller, not even you.'"

"But why were you so insulting?" I moved a pawn to put pressure on his knight.

"Watch it. Keep your mind on the game. I take you with my other bishop and then it is not so much fun for me. Why? Because I am not a servant. She *is* wrinkled. She *is* old." From out of nowhere, he moved me into a knight fork—my bishop or rook. I started looking for a way out. "Everyone kiss her ass. She is the great woman, but I say to her, 'What have you done yourself? You were born a countess, just an accident. Your husband was premier for a short time, then the Communists throw him out. Did you make your money yourself? And what is a countess now? Tell me. You're so full of pride, but it is all ridiculous. You live in the dream.' I am the only one who dares tell her the truth and don't kiss her boney old ass—and that is why she keeps me here." With a sound of disgust, he polished me off in several moves, stood, and strode up several terraces. I heard the motorcycle start and, spitting gravel, rocket up the drive and fade toward town.

I was retracing our last few moves, when Grace, breathless, came down the path. "Come quick! It's Zoeller. He's cracked up the motorcycle. He's hurt."

I found Zoeller lying in the road, the motorcycle on its side a long way back. His clothes were shredded and he lay on his back, teeth gritted, eyes far away. I kneeled over him.

"Ah, so it's you. Fack, man, I think I hit a hole, fly over the bars. I fly fly fly. I travel long way in the air. I see and think about everything. Quite beautiful, really." He gritted his teeth. "I am maybe okay. Can you take me to the doctor?"

I was backing the Russian car out of the garage when Madame Bardi threw open the shutter. "Now where are you driving in my car?"

There wasn't time to go into it. "Grace will be coming in a minute and explain everything."

As I lifted Zoeller into the car, I was surprised at how light he was. He seemed to have the hollow, tensile bones of a bird. The rough road had skinned him at every point of impact— knees, shoulders, elbows, everything in between, and his cuts and scrapes were flecked with grit. As I drove, Zoeller slumped in the seat, and, oozing blood, sometimes moaned, sometimes mumbled to himself in German, once a faint smile appearing. "Quite nice, too, when you lift me up...I feel very light." He said, "There is a doctor, young, very lovely...." He directed me, here, there, through the narrow back streets of the old quarter, and finally, I helped him out of the car and up a long, narrow stairway. A secretary appeared, disappeared, and then a slim, beautiful woman, all business, came out and directed me to help Zoeller into her examining room. A while later, covered with bandages, he walked out gingerly, his arm in a cast and sling. "My wrist. Is cracked. Three weeks, maybe."

The doctor handed me a prescription, instructed me rapidly in French.

I was easing him into bed in his studio when Madame Bardi appeared at the door. Opening the screen door, she thanked me, and shuffled slowly toward Zoeller. The late afternoon light was slanting in through the screen, and even before she said, "Please leave us now," I felt something intimate take them in. Madame Bardi moved toward Zoeller, her eyes filled with anxious tenderness. And Zoeller lying quietly on his back, staring up at the ceiling, lay calm, waiting. As she reached his bed and began to lean over him, I stepped outside and closed the door. I took a short walk, and then I found Grace doing the Trib crossword in the studio. "Grace, I just saw it. They love each other—Zoeller and Madame Bardi...."

Grace said, "I know."

"I mean, they really love each other."

And Grace just nodded again. Though we slept and dreamed side by side night after night, I wondered at the difference between what she knew and I knew for sure. Then I said, "I think I knew. I had to. I saw. I knew but didn't believe it. Maybe that's not knowing." Grace wrote something in the crossword.

As I was drifting toward sleep, I was still seeing them: the afternoon sun slanting in the screened window, Zoeller, forearm in cast and sling, staring up at the ceiling, waiting, and Madame Bardi, her eyes filled with tenderness, coming to his side; I'd been seeing it for hours. I got up, dug out the box of slides, and heart starting to pound, I pulled off the lid. I sat at the table and held a slide to the light. I knew. This one was good. This showed me something I hadn't seen. And this. And this. But not this. Or this. I made two piles. When I'd gone through forty or fifty, I sat under the trees and smoked and then came back in. I picked up the first slide and looked. I looked a long time. Then I put the slide down. I felt the rise of queasiness. I went through several more. I couldn't tell anything. I pushed them back into one pile. Once I'd had a sense of knowing about myself and now it was gone. From the other room, I heard Grace sigh as she voyaged through sleep. I saw the Mediterranean stretching to the horizon in the sun: beyond, Africa. After a while, I lay down on the cot in the living room and closed my eyes and saw the children as they had been yesterday, running in and out of the sea, gleaming with water; I felt Grace's legs slip around my waist as we floated. When I looked back toward shore, I saw a caravan of lions and camels and men hooded in robes coming out of the sea just outside the studio.

Everyone seemed a little different after the accident. Arm in sling, Zoeller sat in a chair, sometimes reading, sometimes making sketches, or gazing out across the valley. He watched the play of wind in the trees, the small movement of branches, and said little. Something had been taken out of him, perhaps what Madame called his insolence. When he walked, he moved stiffly and seemed faraway. Grace, too, seemed inward, silent, almost as though she were sleepwalking. I was working with packers, getting ready to have the archive shipped. I was glad to be finishing, but I was also worried. It had kept me busy and I didn't know what next.

In the midst of this somnolence, Madame Bardi's oldest daughter arrived from Spain. Zoeller said, "She come for her inheritance. Three years ago, she get a few things, and then Madame throw her out. She wants the house and property." She, herself, was old and white-haired—sixty-five. She disappeared into the house. After several days, she exited hastily in a taxi with a silver service, several paintings, and Madame Bardi shouting down from the second-floor window, "Not yet, I am not ready yet. Go back to Spain."

Several days later, I returned to find Grace packing and cleaning out the kitchen. It had the look of a final cleanup. Confused, I stopped in the doorway.

"Madame Bardi has thrown us out. We have to leave now. This afternoon. Within the hour." I waited. "You know how I've been helping Zoeller change his dressings and massaging his neck and shoulders." I nodded. "Madame Bardi came in today, saw us, and has decided we're having a torrid love affair. She said, 'You can't deny it. You have the unmistakable bloom of love in your cheek. I know it. I see it.'" Grace touched her cheek.

"I'll go talk to her."

Grace shook her head. "Don't try. She won't hear it. Zoeller tried to reason with her. She's thrown him out, too."

"All three of us?" Grace nodded. "You mean, we just pack and leave. Zoeller, too?"

"I guess so. She's gone into her house and locked the doors."

I went over to see Zoeller. He was packing slowly with his one good arm. "When she get this way, there is nothing to do. I tell her she is wrong. I tell her she must apologize. She never apologize."

I went up and knocked on her door a long time, but she wouldn't answer. After a while, a taxi came and we went to town and took a hotel room where we stayed for several nights while I finished up at Raymond's. By then Zoeller had made connections with friends in Nice. He got hold of a painter who was just leaving for America; we sublet his place in the old quarter. Zoeller found a small flat not too far away. We took the bus to Nice late that afternoon, and when I woke up the next morning, we were no longer in the pines. We were three blocks from the sea, and the streets were so narrow and lightless, I had to stick my head out the window and look straight up to to tell if the sky was blue.

At first Nice was a good change, and Grace and I spent hours looking in the markets and museums, but whether it was the time of year—mid-October—or we had brought some of the misunderstanding from Madame Bardi's, everything receded into the distance. Grace remained inward and often, when I asked her if she wanted to go somewhere with me, she'd shake her head and say she was tired, you go. I'd check at Zoeller's, and he'd be out. Neither of us had phones. I'd come back and find Grace asleep. I discovered a Hitchcock festival and went to the movies afternoons. The original English had been dubbed into French, my French wasn't that great, and I understood just about half of everything said.

I took to walking alone. I walked everywhere, but usually ended up on the Promenade Anglais. I loved the long slow curving sweep, with the rush of traffic, the miles of hotels and flats on one side, the rocky beach—now barren of tourists—on the other. The bare-breasted women and gleaming brown children were gone until next summer. I'd walk for miles looking out at the horizon and occasionally stopping to sniff the air. I'd think of the slides and going back to the museum and feel that lurch of queasiness rise in me. So much walking made me thin and hollow-cheeked. I'd pass lonely Algerians in their baggy clothes, faces masked against their life in France, perhaps daydreaming of the Casbah; I'd pass punked-out kids smoking and gazing out to sea; smatterings of tourists making the best of being here in the wrong season; the unemployed. After a while, I journeyed the three blocks from my street directly to the sea where I'd crunch across the rocky beach and stare out. There, soles lapped by the chilling water, I realized that day and night I'd been thinking about Africa for weeks. I went back, found Grace waking from a nap, and started talking about Africa, that it was what we needed, where our lives went next. I said, "It's just over there," and pointed out the window. "We may never get another chance." She didn't say anything, and then, abruptly, I had nothing more to say. I suggested we get some air, maybe see if we could catch Zoeller at home.

As we turned into Zoeller's narrow street, we spotted the Russian car blocking his doorway. Hair in six-inch spikes, one of the local punks, who had hung around the cafe all summer, lounged against the car. Ça va? Ça va. Grace said, "Maybe they're having a reconciliation. Let's come back later." Just then, Madame Bardi stepped into the narrow street. She looked at Grace. Her beautiful blue eyes flashed, she said something in Hungarian, the punk opened her door, and they drove away.

We climbed the dark stairway. The door was open and there was Zoeller standing by the window. The cast was off and he stood stretching and flexing his arm. I could see places where his skin was still raw. He turned. "Ah, Nick. And la belle Grace.... " He hugged us.

"We just saw Madame Bardi leave. What's happened?"

His voice took on its bluff, laconic tone. "Ah, she says it is time for us to go to Budapest. Fall. Winter come soon. Every

year I drive drive drive her. She has a black-and-white apartment—all black, all white, nothing more. Is freezing there.
Nothing to do. I tell her she must apologize."

"For what?"

"Because I am Zoeller and she must."

"And?"

"She never apologize to anyone. So I tell her go to her black-
and-white apartment by herself." He shrugged. He stretched
out his mended arm. "I am going to Africa."

I nodded. "That's what we've decided, too." I glanced at
Grace.

"Good. We go together. Maybe I become zebra, dik-dik,
lion." He gazed out the window a moment. Then he made us
tea, took out a large map of Africa, and we started planning. We
would go here first. Later here. Then cross back to Cairo. We
would get jobs. Zoeller knew people in Cairo. Just the shape of
Africa made me happy; sometimes it looked like a face or
profile, sometimes it looked like a beautiful, many-colored animal curled up in a half sleep. Zoeller and I went on making lists
and plans while Grace cradled her teacup and seemed far away.

As we turned out of a narrow street, a car hit its brakes, and
Grace froze and pressed both of her hands, fingers spread,
against her stomach. I walked several steps. I stopped. The
spread of her fingers. Something I had seen. A woman in the
street. Belly. Holding something. I turned and looked at Grace
in the fading light. "You're pregnant? Grace?" She nodded.
"Why didn't you say something?"

"After the time it's taken us, it seemed a fragile thing and I
wanted to be sure first."

"How sure are you?"

"Maybe nine weeks sure." I nodded and put my arms around
her. We turned and walked on through the narrow streets. We
weren't far from the sea, and as we walked, I sniffed the air and
held her hand.

In early spring, Jim, the director, stopped me in the hallway
of the museum and told me that he'd heard from a friend that

Madame Bardi had died. She had just gotten tired of it all and turned off her oxygen. I imagined the heavy green tank. The valve. Just turning it off. The sunlight slanting through the rows of olive trees, Madame and Zoeller leaning against each other and murmuring softly in German.

A couple of months later, we got a long letter from Zoeller. He was in Somalia. He had been everywhere. Aden. Yemen. Egypt. He described everything in a kind of beautiful, broken English. Somalians. Berbers. Blacks. He had just come from Dar es Salaam, Tanzania: "I never saw such green befor! everything wet and green, hot and coulered birds, a waste of nature, I feel like becoming a plant, too. So many charming animals here, monkeys, dik-dik, gazelles, camels, I go right up and talk, I can't help it, I must laugh."

The envelope had a fat stamp with a gauzy, green acacia, acacias receding into a khaki veldt; that night, I trekked beneath those trees, and jungle, too, surrounded by glowing birds and animals. When I woke, Grace was lying quietly on her back, and even before she placed my hand on her domed stomach, I could see her skin quivering, and then felt the baby beating her belly inside like a drum.

Beautiful

L AST NIGHT LAURA CALLED and asked if I could stand in for her
at Bloomingdale's. Lancôme was doing a promotion, and
Laura was supposed to work at the cosmetics counter making
up from three to eight.

I always do my own make-up, but one ad I did for BMW,
they wanted a make-up artist. That's where I met Laura. The
BMW shoot. Laura's a make-up artist.

In the BMW ad, I'm on a big black BMW, we're coming right
into the camera, head on. I'm looking haughty and cool; there
was an incredible response to that ad. Sales. Guys called BMW
wanting to know who I was, where they could meet me. Men
live in a dream world half the time: where they could meet
me. . . .

After we shot the ad, I was knocked out. Everyone's always
surprised, oh, you're exhausted, all they did was shoot some
pictures, but you're not just sitting there, you're projecting
something. It takes pure energy. It's intangible, something you
learn to do, to project energy, a look.

So I sat there glassy-eyed, and the photographer pulled out a
mirror and we did some lines and then the guy who owns the
BMW dealership pointed to the bike, yes? and we got on, why
not? We're going along; over his shoulder I'm watching the

speedometer, the tach, and this clock. The clock has a second hand that is still and jumps a couple of seconds and is still again. I was watching that. All of a sudden he laid it into a corner, I grabbed him hard around the waist, and he laughed and shouted back, "You're beautiful, but you're no different."

"What's your big problem?" I shouted. He just laughed. I couldn't wait to get away from him. Men have to make a run at you.

Anyway, Laura did my make-up for that BMW ad. Laura herself is nice, nothing much to look at, but she does understand make-up. She works for one of the theaters and a TV studio. I like her, but when she asked if I could stand in, I hesitated. It's only ten dollars an hour. And then, you never know what you're going to run into on something like that. I mean, it's probably women who are unhappy with themselves or have decided to change or maybe they just want a miracle. I figure whatever it is, I'm not going to be able to make them real happy. If their problems were fixable, would a few more cosmetics help?

But I sensed something in Laura's voice—an appeal. Maybe something between her and her old man. She told me about him. Sometimes he knocks her around. Long sleeves once on a hot day to cover the black-and-blue marks. I figured he gave her a black eye or something and that's why she couldn't go out. I heard it in her voice. Pain. The creep! She got married when she was nineteen and they've been married ten years and he's an up-and-comer in real estate and has her talked into one of these deals where he sees other women and tells her about it and she pretends she doesn't mind, very enlightened, right? though it's half killing her. I'd never put up with that crap. And any man hits me—and ever touches my face—I'll kill him. But Laura puts up with it. One time he asked her to leave town for a week so he could have some slut in and she did, she left, dumb! she pays half the rent on that place. When she called to say she was coming back, he asked her to stay away another two days. And when she finally let herself into the apartment, the bed was unmade, there were wine glasses and cigarette butts all over the night tables, the place still stank from the bitch's perfume.

I met the guy once, Laura's husband, and he is a little short nothing, a pure nothing. I wanted to smack him for what he was doing to Laura. I hate little men anyway. I can't look at a man who isn't at least taller than I am. At least. When I asked Laura why she put up with him, she just got this quiet faraway look in her eye, really sad, I felt so sorry for her, she seemed helpless, she must have a terrible self-image. So I figured Laura had a black eye and I said, okay, I'd do the Lancôme promotion.

So here I am at home, getting ready, doing my make-up. Sometimes when I'm in front of the mirror, I feel like I've been here forever, making up, but you can't be lazy. Every time you step out, you're advertising yourself, whether it's for a job, a go-see, whatever. Everything has to be right. Hair, make-up, stockings, every detail.

I stand naked in front of the mirror, curlers in my hair, and then I start. Lately, before I put my curlers in, I check my hair for gray or white hairs. That may sound odd, I'm only twenty-four, but my grandmother, my mother's mother, went gray early—in her twenties—and I look a lot like her. So I check for gray, first. I'm not sure what I'll do about it, but...

Then I put the curlers in, step back and look at myself. The goddamned pill puts the weight on me, my breasts and just above the curve of my hips, and the camera always adds another ten to fifteen pounds. Between the camera and the pill, I sometimes wonder if I stand a chance. I hate the pill, the diaphragm is a mess and a turn-off and you never really know, either. I don't trust it. I tried the IUD for a while, but that gave me hellish cramps and an awful flow. And I don't think they're safe, IUDs. I've heard horror stories of perforated uterus walls. And a friend of mine got pregnant with one of the damned things. The IUD just disappeared in her. They couldn't find it. And she's pregnant. She decided to have the kid and when the kid is born, he has the IUD in his hand.

So I'm on the pill. I hate the pill but the diaphragm...

One afternoon, Richie and I are suddenly in the mood and then, you know, I had to pull away and go get the thing and get it fixed up with the orthogoo and when I got back, I said, "Here, you put it in."

He was turned off, but tried to hide it. "What for?"

And I said, "To know me better, I want you to know everything about me."

He still looked uncomfortable. I said, "Don't you want to?"

He looked at the diaphragm and said, "Well, I'm not really sure how it fits, or what to feel for, or when it will be in place."

"That's okay, that's the point, for me to teach you about me." I put the diaphragm down and got a piece of paper and drew him a diagram of female anatomy, simple, really. The uterus, the cervix, the vagina, and I started explaining how the lip of the diaphragm hooked onto...

I glanced over. He was sitting there staring at the pad, looking a little squeamish and kind of puzzled.

"What's that look on your face?"

"What look?"

He stared at the diagram. I pointed. "What do you make of it?"

He took the pencil and in the middle of the uterus, he drew a question mark and smiled a little and said, "It looks like circles within circles."

"This is a joke to you, isn't it?"

"I just want you to leave me a little bit of mystery. You know, the Grand Inquisitor says, mystery, magic..."

"Don't give me that! I finished USC, I know The Brothers K, too."

He's a big Princeton grad trying to turn all of his English lit into pop culture, he's trying to make it as a screenwriter, in the meantime he's doing PR for one of the studios. He did get something going last year, but it got put into turn-around after a few months. That's how we met. He was lining up some models for promotion work.

"A little mystery isn't so much to ask...."

He stared at the sketch. I snatched it from him.

"Don't have your mystery on me. There's no goddamned mystery when I end up on a table with my legs spread and a vacuum sucking at my uterus."

I've never really seen anyone turn pale, though I've heard the expression, but he turned pale.

"Kim..."

"I'm the one, not you. Women are always being prodded, poked, having fingers stuck in us, whatever. You don't want to put the diaphragm in, but you don't mind sticking your cock into me, do you?" I grabbed the diaphragm. "Here, maybe you guys ought to have this thing stuck up your asses once in a while to know what it's like."

I got up and walked out leaving him with the diaphragm in his hand. I felt bad right away and went back and tried to kiss him and apologize, but he pushed me away. For a second I thought he was going to hit me—though he never has—and I said, "Don't hit my face, Richie!" He just looked at me with disgust, got dressed and walked out. We didn't talk to each other for a couple of days. I really don't know why I got so angry with him—and suddenly. Old patterns, I guess. Anyway, we got over it. And I don't use the diaphragm now. I'm not even sure I can blame him for not wanting to stick his hands into all that mess.

I'm still making up when Richie comes out of the bedroom. Except for my pantyhose, I'm naked.

"Got an ad, Sausage?"

Sausage. The squeezed way the pantyhose makes me look.

"Sausage, yourself. No, the Lancôme promotion. I told you last night. Don't you listen to me?"

"Right. Forgot."

"Do you think I'm getting fat?"

"No."

"Here?" I squeeze some around my hip.

"Nope."

"Five pounds."

"Nope, it's lady-like."

"Come here."

"I'm here."

"Closer. Stand next to me. Look at yourself in the mirror beside me. Aren't you a pretty man?"

He looks embarrassed. I look at him in the mirror with me.

"See us. Look at you. You're pretty. Look, Richie."

"You look."

"I am looking. You look, too."

"If you want to look at me, why look in the mirror?" He tries to turn me toward him. "Why not look right at me? Here I am."

"It's different, that's all. Different perspectives. I've told you that before. Lenses, mirrors."

"But..."

"Oh, Richie, don't be a bore. Look at us. Together. I can't see us together without a mirror, that's all." I turn him back toward the mirror. But he doesn't look. I look. He can't. It embarrasses him for some reason. But I can look. I look at us. We are so different. They tell me I am beautiful, one of the prettiest women in L.A. They tell me I could make it in New York and maybe I'll go, I've been thinking about that. But beautiful or not, if I liked women, I wouldn't be the kind I'd go for. I'm just so pale. My skin is absolutely white and hardly ever tans. I have small precise features. Small features like mine are very photogenic. But I don't think I'd go for them. I look at Richie next to me. He's tall and slim and has incredibly soft skin, almost like a girl's. It's not fair for a man to have such soft skin. His skin is softer than mine, almost hairless, and a beautiful fawn color. He has long dark lashes and large eyes, also dark and soft, like a pretty colt or deer, and his face is full of colors, highlights, blushes, light and shadow. If Richie were a girl, he'd be the kind I'd like.

"Richie, you are pretty. Are you going to the studio?"

"In a while. They said I could work at home this morning, but to be there for a meeting at three. I'll be working late tonight...." He trails off, points to the molding. "Pawprints."

Richie didn't care about the molding until he repainted the bungalow.

"I didn't do that."

"I sure don't use blue eye shadow."

"Well, don't complain, you like the finished product."

"If you spent as much time reading as you did making up, you'd be..."

"I'd be some gimpy librarian."

He shrugs, turns, "I've got to change." He heads into the bedroom.

He kids me about make-up. He's got a little streak of the old Puritan ethic about cosmetics, but it kind of fascinates him, and a lot of times I'll look back in the mirror and catch him looking up from the paper and just staring at me. He'll smile shyly. I've tried to show him what I'm doing, each step, how it works, but he can't really let himself get into it. But once, when he got stoned, I told him I was going to make him up; he was just listening to the Moody Blues and hardly paying any attention, so I sat down and started, he didn't resist, he had a big faraway smile and was mumbling stony shit about the moon and stars, he is so sweet when he's stoned, and I just started putting the make-up on him, not really sure what I was looking for or where I wanted to go with it, but just putting on some basic contouring and seeing where it would lead, letting it take me where it would, and all of a sudden I knew just what I wanted, light, shadow, contouring, I saw this incredibly beautiful woman in him, I didn't want to scare him or threaten him, men are in a dream world half the time, anyway, so I started talking about a philosophy teacher I'd had and this thing he'd said about looking for yourself in the other sex and Richie was nodding and then I said, and looking for the other sex in yourself, I kind of reworded it a little, and Richie said, "Did you sleep with him?"

I think I would have been furious if I hadn't been stoned, but Richie and I can talk to each other stoned, we get more accepting, and so I laughed and said, "No, no, I didn't sleep with him...."

"Because," he said with a smile, "it would be alright, I'm just curious."

Not that I hadn't thought of it, sleeping with the philosophy teacher, he was very good-looking and had a real passion for philosophy—he made it seem like real life—but no, I decided to drop it and just kissed Richie and kept putting the blue eye shadow on him and he kept listening to the Moody Blues and when it was done, I stood back, I was really stunned, he was enormously beautiful, but still himself, completely a man, he played lacrosse at Princeton and has quarter-moon scars on one knee, inside and out, where he had cartilage removed, completely a man, but enormously beautiful, maybe he was the woman I would be with his fawn skin and beautiful large eyes, and I kissed him really gently and said, "God, you're beautiful, look at yourself," and he smiled from faraway; he was off into those Moody Blues and said, "I don't want to see," and I touched him a little gently to stir him and remind him he was a man and then brought over a mirror and put my arm around him and held up the mirror and said, "Look," and he looked a really long time with a trace of that faraway stoned smile and said, "Who is it, Kim?"

And I said, "It's you, and it's absolutely alright, it's you."

And he kept looking in the mirror, the Moody Blues turned up, saying, "Who is it, Kim?"

And I kept saying, "It's you, do you *see?*"

And he said, "Yes, I see, but *who* is it?"

And I said, "Never mind. Whoever. Don't ask those boring intellectual questions. That stuff's all a defense, anyway. It doesn't matter who it is. Don't worry. Whoever it is, it's beautiful."

I'm thinking about that as I'm finishing my eyes. When I look up, I see him standing behind me staring into the palette. "It's a regular rainbow in there." He's dressed and ready to go. "Here. Mind if I put this cigarette out. It's all ash. You always do this."

I shrug. "Put it out. Richie," I turn, "I don't want to scare these women. I mean, look too good."

He shrugs. "Then you've got a problem. Tell you what, I'll go with you and when they start to look a little scared, I'll tell them you snore and drool on the pillow and leave pawprints on the molding; that should help them. Okay? I've gotta go."

"Kiss me. Here." I point to my cheek. He kisses me. "I'll see you tonight."

"Yeah."

"Watch out for all those beautiful women, Richie. Women dig men like you. I shouldn't tell you that."

Then I kiss him, smear my mouth, and wipe his mouth with a tissue. He goes out and I'm alone. Suddenly, I look at myself in the mirror and I feel exhausted, absolutely exhausted, like something heavy is weighing down on me and I can hardly move, can hardly even breathe. I go in and lie down on the bed. I look over at the Chinese fern on the night table. Needs water. At the clock. I'm going to have to get moving, I'm already running a little late, but I don't know if I can move. If only it would let me go a little. One afternoon, I put on some make-up, high-light, foundation. . . . The mirror seemed so bright, I looked at my face, no eye shadow, no mouth, just a smooth, even flesh tone, I looked at the colors, it just felt like too much, and I went in and washed my face. Richie acts like it's all me, a big joke, but it's not me, or just me, something in his vanity, he's got to share some of the responsibility. I lie here exhausted another few minutes and then I get up, water the fern, and start taking the curlers out of my hair.

By the time I get to the cosmetics counter there are already a couple of women waiting and I don't really have much time to think about it, I just set up—Mrs. Adams, the woman in charge, helps me. I take one of the women, who isn't too bad, sit her on a stool, give her a smile, ask her about herself, try to get her used to the idea that I—a stranger—am going to be touching her in a few moments. She's kind of average-looking, a few basic cosmetics might help her some, maybe they'll help her feel a little better about herself, more confident. I start making her up, explaining what I'm doing, asking her who she is, why she came today. She doesn't say much. Some women stop to watch, talk nervously, laugh, move on. When I finish, the woman looks at herself, shrugs, and starts to leave. Mrs. Adams calls her back and gives her a loaf of French bread and a blue canvas bag which says, LANCÔME, Paris. They're part of the promotion.

The woman takes her blue bag and bread, and she disappears. I start on the next woman, then the next, and after a while I glance up and realize I've been working a couple of hours. The next woman is tense, but I get her to relax. Her face is actually starting to glow, she's talking about her job and her kids when she notices a group of women standing back and watching, studying her and making comments. She tenses up, says, stop, I say, never mind them, relax, you look fine, but I can't get her to relax and so I help her wipe the make-up off, she gathers her things and just about runs out of there. I kind of know how she felt, but you've got to be able to ignore stuff like that.

I take a break, drink some coffee, head for the ladies' room to straighten up. It's about five-thirty and I'm starting to feel hungry. I look at myself in the mirror. Whoever invented the fluorescent light didn't have skin in mind. What's wrong with some of these women anyway? They're so closed off to style, fashion. So afraid to try; is it immoral to be pretty, to try to make yourself beautiful? Is jewelry immoral? They act like it's the Russian Revolution or something. I've been half-expecting some of these dummies from the women's movement to come galloping up and issue a proclamation, let's scrub our faces with Ivory soap and wear blue jeans and feel self-righteous forever. I'm as independent—more!—than a lot of those whiners, and what a bunch of dogs. It's fashion, play. You accentuate what's good, what's strong—if you have a good feature, you display it. I read in the paper the other day how a woman met Cary Grant and said, "But you don't look like Cary Grant." And he smiled and said, "My dear, no one does." Cary Grant's not even his real name. Archibald Leach is Cary Grant, and Cary Grant knows that no one looks like Cary Grant. Not even Cary Grant.

When I get back to the counter, there's a black girl waiting, about sixteen, and I sit her down, she looks up at me, drops her eyes, we talk for a minute, and I start. She's real cute, has nice features, but I can tell she doesn't think she can be pretty, not really pretty, because she's black, so I start telling her what I'm doing and how nice it is to have such pretty skin, it allows her to use bright colors, wonderful colors, oranges, reds, lavender hues, I tell her she's really pretty, and she says, do you think so, do you really think so? and I know what she's really saying, she's surprised, I don't think anyone had ever told her she was pretty or could be; I tell her so, I hold up the mirror and say, you're beautiful, you're a real knockout, now remember what I told you about using bronze powder to set the whole thing, you're a real knockout, dynamite, and I am not lying. She leaves smiling.

The women keep coming, they're so vulnerable, they just come in and give themselves to me, they're asking for help, and it makes me care, feel responsible for them. I'm really hungry by now and my feet are tired, I've been standing up all this time, but someone brings me some coffee and I keep on working.

I'm just about ready to call it a night—I light a cigarette, take a sip of coffee, cold now. When I look up, I notice a girl standing off to one side. I look over at her, but she's kind of half turned away and doesn't seem interested. I start cleaning up. When I glance over again, she's a little closer, but she still doesn't approach, and finally I ask, "Did you have an appointment?" She looks at me apologetically and nods, yes. I half feel like telling her that I'm finished, my feet are killing me, it's not exactly a secret that high heels were not made for standing, not five hours, but I look at her, there's something sad about her, sad and timid and apologetic; it's in her posture, her eyes, her clothes, which do nothing to help, and so I say, "Well, come on," and pat the stool.

She says, "That's okay, if you're finished . . . "

I feel both sympathetic and annoyed, I almost feel like saying, look, do you or don't you want to do this?

But she comes over uncertainly and says, "It's just that you seem tired. . . . "

I hesitate and say, "It's not supposed to show, but I am. Sit down, anyway." I take her purse and set it behind the counter, "It'll be safe there." I smile at her. "Come on, sit down."

She sits and we try to make small talk while I look her over. She has large gray-green eyes—beautiful—long dark lashes, a nice nose, high, pronounced cheekbones, okay hair, a little on the mousy side, but that could be fixed, a pretty full mouth. She is almost beautiful, but there is something off, besides the fact that she is doing absolutely nothing to show off her beautiful eyes, show those cheekbones, the mouth. In another moment, I see it, of course, her chin, she has a receded chin, and so this beautiful face is not beautiful, but almost beautiful and gives the appearance and feeling of weakness. She looks at me hopefully, and I say, "What's your name?"

"Maureen."

When I tell her mine, she seems grateful. Just for that. I decide the best thing would be to build her confidence a little and so I tell her she has beautiful eyes, lovely cheekbones. She looks at me doubtfully, and I can see she's timid and so I ask her about herself and she starts talking while I apply highlight. The first time I touch her—just her cheek—she jumps, looks embarrassed. "I'm sorry."

"It's okay. I'm just going to rub this on, start beneath the eyes—it's highlight—then I'll put on this foundation. Okay?"

"Please go ahead. I'm sorry."

I ask her what she does and start putting the highlight on— it's really whiteface, pure and beautiful, and sometimes I think it would be nice to go around in just white face, so cool and calm, I'm thinking about what I'm going to do with her chin, she settles down, I go along, I'm listening to her, there's a sadness in her voice, an *if* to everything she says, I finish with the highlight and start the foundation, then the contour, explaining to her what I'm doing and how it works, she tells me she finished college a few years ago and was unsure of what to do next, so after working as a barmaid, working in a boutique, then as a landscape gardener, and a housepainter, she still didn't know what she wanted, so she began as a legal secretary, which is what she's doing now . . . just coming from there as a matter of fact.

I'm working on her eyes.

. . . but which is still not what she wants to do—legal secretary. She thinks she'd like to go back to school.

I nod. "Don't move. I don't want to poke you in the eye."

She stares straight ahead, but keeps talking. Her voice is a little stronger now, but there's that *if*. She loves her boyfriend, but she's not sure he's right or loves her right. She hesitates. She doesn't even know what she means by that, *right*. She'd like to change herself or make a change in her life, but somehow . . . she says she can remember a time when she used to be confident, really confident, sure of herself, but something happened, she's not sure what, or when it happened, or if anything at all even really happened, and now she's not sure. . . .

She hesitates. "Do you think men like make-up?"

"Mine acts like he doesn't. He jokes. Maybe it gets him a little nervous, but I think it turns him on. The playfulness, the invention . . . "

She nods uncertainly. "I've never done anything like what

you're doing. Some eyeliner and lipstick, but nothing like this.
I'm wondering what he'll say when I come home."

She looks doubtful. I start on her chin and say softly, "Light if
you want to bring something out, dark if you want to make less
of it."

She nods. We don't mention the chin, but I know she understands what I'm telling her and why. When I'm finished, I step
back. "Look." I turn her head toward the mirror. "Look." She
looks. She smiles. She raises her hand toward her chin, but
checks herself. "How do you feel?"

"Better."

"You should. You look wonderful. Beautiful."

She smiles at me. "Do you really think so?"

"I promise."

"Do you think...he'll like it? Oh, that's stupid of me, you
don't even know him."

"He'd be crazy not to. Don't you let him talk you out of it."

"I like the way I look. I really do." We smile at each other. She
says, still not mentioning the chin, "Do you know I'd been
thinking of plastic surgery. It just nags at me."

I shake my head. "You look great." We talk another moment.
I check with her to make sure she understands, to be aware of
lighting, since lighting has a big effect on make-up and what
works in one lighting situation might not work at all in another.
I tell her to practice with the make-up, then give her the blue bag
and French bread, remember to give her back her purse, she
laughs, delighted, thanks me, starts to leave, turns back uncertainly. "Light if you want to bring something out..."

"...and dark if you want to make less of it."

We smile, she waves the French bread, walks away. I watch
her go. I almost feel like asking her to go for coffee. There's
something about the way they give themselves to you which
makes you feel responsible, care. And she's really nice. I kind of
believe in something in her—I'm feeling a little lonely now for
some reason; I take a step toward her, but then stop. I'm tired.

I start cleaning up and when I'm done Mrs. Adams asks me
for my social security number, thanks me, and gives me a
couple of loaves of French bread and a blue bag, LANCÔME,
Paris.

* * *

In the parking lot, the white lines remind me of a children's game I used to play—the board—but I can't remember which one. I throw the bag and French bread on the seat, slide in, remember Richie won't be home until late. I'm stiff all over.

In McDonald's, the food suddenly sickens me, I throw the whole mess into the garbage, grab my purse. The ladies' room. I lock the door, take out a jar of Vaseline and some tissue, and wipe my make-up off. Streaks on the white porcelain, blues, flesh tones, magenta...I wash my face, throw everything in my purse. Back in the car, I remember half a pint of bourbon Richie left under the seat. I dig it out, take a sip, light a cigarette, another swallow of bourbon, this one relaxes me. I don't want to come back to an empty house so I put on an old Van Morrison tape, dig out the bourbon for one more swallow, and decide to take a drive out into the desert.

The moon is almost full and I'm driving fast—past a sign for Palm Springs—suddenly I turn off the Van Morrison, another swallow of bourbon, the desert is almost perfect and white and endless like the ocean, I miss the change of seasons, real changes, leaves turning, snow, only part I really miss about the East, things startle in and out of the headlights, the flash of a deer haunch, gleam of a coyote's eyes, quick prance off the shoulder, Maureen, her timidity, the way she jumped when I touched her cheek to apply the highlight, what would her boyfriend think, said she'd been sure of herself, once. What did he say when she walked in the door? Probably said, what the hell happened to you? Wipe that gunk off.

I wonder if she did. Probably did. Maybe I would have, too. No. Sixteen and I'd had mono and spent months home from school, Mother sent me to modelling school. Eight years later, big fight over it, she said I wanted to go, but I know she sent me. Big fight. Says she remembers. Thought I had a bad self-image, that it would be good for me. I didn't have any bad self-image, but I went anyway, just to get out of the house, away from her. But she still insists....

She's the one with the bad self-image. Projecting. Spent half her life doing dumb things, never made a decision for herself, married young, kids young, worked in an office, never exercises, reads, smokes like a fiend, no interests...

After Richie and I had been living together a few weeks, she called: "Are you there alone."

"Yes."

"Good, now I can talk to you."

"You don't have to whisper."

"I'm not whispering. Are you living with him—the one who answers the phone?"

"Yes. Richie's his name."

"Kim..."

"Don't. Please."

"Who pays the rent?"

"He does."

"Well, that much is right. He should at least pay for the privilege."

"What do you think, I'm selling something?"

"I don't go for this living together. Your father would be very upset. I'm going to keep this from him."

I don't answer. I'm here and she's there. One reason I went to school on the coast. I'll just stay. What scares her. She uses the phone like a musical instrument—pauses, inflections, wants me to feel guilty. She talks. Talk on.

"...if you live with him, if you give a man what he wants, how will you ever get him to marry you?"

Her bully-barter system. My brother a marshmallow, sister a ball-buster.

"Let's not talk about it, Mother."

"You think your mother doesn't understand?"

Maybe once she had some pride, dignity. Pictures of her taken during the war. Slim, face wasn't puffy, fire in her eyes. That picture of her taken outside of the Nugget. Eyes shining, she had her skirt hiked up above her knees, laughing. They'd gotten all the girls up on top of the bar, she'd won the contest for beautiful legs. Dynamite legs—for all the good it did her, never seen her eyes like that.

Twenty years in the same office, she takes the goddamned job so seriously, she comes up for office manager, she runs the goddamned office anyway, they give it to a young guy, turn around and ask her to train him, maybe that finally wised her up to something, I really did feel sorry for her. After that, whatever last little illusions she had, even she couldn't keep it up. Just let her white hair come in, had one of those mousy, middle-aged dye jobs, blondie, got this vacant look on her face....

Now Dad and she selling Amway, detergent, fertilizer. Amway conventions, positive selling attitudes. Last time home, come down to breakfast, Dad listening to an Amway cassette, like brainwashing or religion, she even wants me to do it, cram your Amway.

I keep driving and then remember some clothes in the trunk. Pull off the road, drive into the desert a little, dead silent, I cast a pale shadow on the desert floor, strip off the dress, change into a pair of jeans, one of Richie's T-shirts—Richie's smell as I pull it over my head—Adidas, sit down on the car, silent slow out here, just the metal creaking as it cools off, my innards still churning with engine speed, road speed, nerves. My shadow, the car shadow, pale, ground the color of chalk. If I wish hard enough, frost or even a light dusting of snow. Raise my arm and wave. There, my shadow. I touch my chin. Modelling director said I had a perfect face—shape, proportion. Almost heart-shaped. A valentine.

Maybe Maureen came in and her man loved her face, loved all of that light and shadow and color. Maybe he didn't. Wipe it off. But maybe she told him to get stuffed. Men live in such a dream world. I should have gotten Maureen's phone number, given her mine. Or we could have had coffee, gotten to be friends.

I hear something. Listen. Into the distance. Rising and falling. Here. There. Over there. Back here. Swooping rise and fall. Coyotes. Chilling and beautiful and pure, it raises goose bumps on my arms. I listen for minutes at a time, almost holding my breath, finally step down off the car, crunch around in the desert, bourbon from under the seat.

I should start back but don't feel like it. I listen to the coyotes, here, there, watch my pale shadow in the moonlight. The moon looks like it's far under water and if I jumped up and let go of the earth, I could swim down, stretch out my hand, touch it, Dad and I in a duck blind, moon still shining, but getting light, sound of the ducks flying over, beautiful and chilling and pure, giving me goose bumps, choked feeling, Dad standing, slight rocking of the boat, the sweep of his shotgun, graceful motion, four years in the Airborne, all over Europe, killing, the shotgun, muzzle flash in the smoky-dilute light, muffled splash, moon shining in the water. Then, cleaning them, their beautiful feathers, so many colors, sticking to the backs of my hands and arms, and a mountain of decoys by the furnace, handmade, beautiful, round, startled Egyptian eyes, decoys a silent reply to her bullying, his disappearing into the basement after supper and staying there half the night, wanted to be a veterinarian, but after he got home, started working and never stopped, a waste, but he stood up to her hurting me....

I look up at the moon, maybe I'm a little drunk. A little. I drop the bottle on the seat, spot the French bread, rip off a chunk, thick in my mouth, I get back in the car, drive back to the road and start driving, this time a little slower, feeling the light on my skin, the glass display cases, mirrors, glittery underwater light, like an aquarium....

She was surprised as hell when the woman who ran the agency told her how smart I was, seventeen and she was taking me to a competition in New York, scared, the Hotel Pierre, designers, photographers, knees shaking, I went out on that runway, they loved me, were dazzled....

Oh, then she was proud, saw dollar signs, thought maybe I'd make it in New York, but I sensed what it really was, USC she screamed, could it be any farther? how about Tokyo? can't you go to UMass? And I knew I wasn't really tall enough, five-ten, six feet on those runways, they want you to overpower, not quite five-seven, I could do print work, magazines, it's not real enough, anyway.

I see the lights of L.A. as I come over the mountains. My stomach tightens. USC. Math and philosophy, and good grades, too, people always surprised, professors, what'd they expect, cut my hair short, working nights as a cocktail waitress, sick of that, phone numbers on matchbooks pushed into my hands, then part-time as a sales rep for a big modelling agency:

I AM INTERESTED IN THE FOLLOWING CAREER PROGRAMS:
Acting_____, Modelling_____, Personal Development_____
MY INTEREST LEVEL IS:
High_____, Moderate_____, Just Curious_____

Mothers hopeful with daughters, like mine, crazy sleeping people walking through these doors dreaming, and you want to give it to them, they need it, they sit in the waiting room, look at all of those unreal portraits, lips eyes hair shining, all lights and make-up, they sleep-walk into the interviews, tacky guys good-looking in obvious ways, guys who do a little modelling, extras, male go-go dancers, they want to get into the movies, TV, they look at your tits, ask you out, that forty-five-year-old guy who hardly said anything the whole time and then at the end said, I have money, will you marry me?

As I hit the freeway, I feel the fatigue, my arms, my legs. I fumble out another tape and put it on.

By then my hair was growing out, and everyone in the office said I should go to New York, that I had it, and Sonia gave me some stretching exercises, heard of a girl who stretched an inch-and-a-half. I start hanging from a chinning bar, morning and evening. One night, I'm hanging from the bar thinking of my spine getting stretched out and suddenly I burst out laughing, can't stop, next day I'm at work, suddenly I walk out of my cubicle, I'm laughing again, and waving Hegel—I've got class afterward—I'm walking up and down past the cubicles, Joyce and Betty and Sonia, all made up and sensational, Joyce had great legs and had once done a commercial for Hanes, Betty sang jingles for granola and floor wax, Betty had taken voice lessons for years, Sonia had been the lips in a Revlon commercial, they came out of their cubicles, they were kind of laughing, I was losing it, I pointed to Joyce's legs, finally could say, between Joyce's legs, my tits, Betty's voice, Dee's ass, we've almost got a whole broad here. I couldn't stop laughing, sud-

denly grabbed my books, said, I'm sorry, I can't do this anymore, and walked out of there. It was another year before I
thought of modelling again and that was because I was desperate for money. So you get back to it. Somehow it's always there,
the face, and you turn away, and when you turn back around,
it's there again, the face.

The bungalow is dark. Inside, quiet. I peer into the bedroom,
Richie's sound asleep. I close the door so I won't wake him,
undress, take a shower, rub oil into my skin. I sit down naked
on the sofa, smoke a cigarette.

Richie stirs as I get into bed. It's warm and the sheet is kicked
back. He says my name in his sleep. I kiss him gently, his breath
deepens. I listen to his breathing. I kind of want to make love,
but I don't want to wake him, and I'm just too tired to start.
Sometimes it's hard to start, the toughest part, even. I drift into
sleep, wake, close in here, I get up and open a window, settle
down, drift back to sleep, colors, eyes, the women keep coming
and giving themselves to me, help me, they're so vulnerable,
their eyes are bright, glittery, pained in the underwater light, it's
like an aquarium, mirrors, glass, bright light, their eyes keep
disappearing underwater, colors all over my hands, my arms,
clinging to my lips, metallic greens, beautiful feathers, getting in
my throat, the startled Egyptian eyes, black, the beautiful band
of white so startling, I am gluing feathers on their eyelids, light
to bring something out, shadow to lessen, feathers in my nose.

I wake, gasp for breath.

I reach over and touch Richie's shoulder. The hall light falls
into the room. I look at him. Pretty fawn colors, white hip,
bathing suit, no sun. Where he has kicked back the sheet, the
crescent scars on his knee, faint shadows. I touch one. Too
smooth for skin. I kiss him gently and he stirs and goes on
sleeping. I lie there beside him, listening to his breathing.

A few days later, I'm coming out of the photographer's
studio. We've been shooting the fall catalogue for hours, I'm
wired, I'm in nylons, high heels, full make-up for bright
lights...there's a crowd and up ahead people are getting off a

bus, the bus pulls away and I see someone familiar, it's Maureen, she must work around here, I start walking quickly, pushing through the crowd, the light changes, more people come up around me, I break into a quick walk, almost a trot. I stumble in my heels, this time we'll have coffee, we'll talk, I want to know, did she keep the look or not, what did he say, and if he didn't like it, did she tell him where to go, maybe that night was a turning point for her, a beginning, she disappears ahead into the crowd, I break into a trot, a couple of steps, wobbling in the heels, debate, then shout after her, Maureen! Maureen! I finally get up to where I can reach out, I touch her on the shoulder, Maureen, I smile, she turns, looks startled, no make-up, none at all, a lot older, not at all like Maureen, her eyes startled from far away, sad, too. From the back, though, for a second, there was something familiar. I apologize and watch her walk into the crowd. I glance around nervously—for some reason, things like this have always embarrassed me, but I look around quickly, people, they're all just walking along and I don't really think any of them noticed.

Intervention

THE PHONE'S RING CAUGHT HIM as he turned off the shower.
"Kramer," she said, "you sound breathless. Am I getting
you at a bad time?"

"I won't say it's bad, but I'm standing naked in a puddle of
water. If I get electrocuted, I hope this was important."

She laughed, disgusted. "You and Frank are just the same."
Kramer decided not to make his case and went for a towel.
When he returned, Karen asked, "Have you spoken with Frank
lately?"

"It's been maybe a couple of months. Why?"

"You know he moved back in with me six weeks ago."

"He didn't tell me."

"No idea what's going on?" Karen sounded suspicious. "Can
I count on you not to tell him I phoned? I'll explain, but before I
say another word, promise me. Kramer?"

"I guess so. . . . Sure. What's happening?"

Kramer waited. He had the feeling she was going to ask him
to come out there. Early last spring, Frank had called and after a
rambling oblique conversation, asked Kramer if he could fly in
for a few days, things had gotten weird. Frank couldn't explain
on the phone; he no longer trusted phones. Kramer canceled his
appointments and took the morning flight, Phoenix to L.A.,

where he'd spent four days listening to Frank. In a combination of monologues, laconic asides, jokes, and earnest conversation, Frank made a kind of ongoing confession to Kramer about his various girlfriends, one night stands, problems with Karen, sleazy clients. Having failed his bar exam the first time, Frank had become a private investigator until he could save enough money to take the bar again. Now lawyers owed him money; he also kept talking about a lot of money he had just lost. When Kramer asked him how much, all Frank said was, "A lot." Frank wouldn't say exactly how he'd lost the money, but kept dropping hints, and finally Kramer got the idea it involved something the cops wouldn't be too thrilled to hear about; Frank said there was an investigation in progress, but he didn't think it could lead to him. "I had no real part in it, Kramer. I left money with a few players. I started with ten grand. They ran my share up—way up. I thought I'd get out, but my guys got nailed before I found the door. I was getting ready to live on the scratch while I studied full time for the bar." In the end, Frank said to Kramer, "Loose lips sink ships." That had been last March.

Now Karen went on. "He's started again. And it's not just booze. He's doing a lot of coke. In a way, this call has nothing to do with our marriage or what went on last spring. I know, Steve, you and I haven't always had the best relationship. And that you take Frank's side..."

"I don't..."

"Kramer, you don't have to bullshit me now. I know. I even understand. He fools everyone, even his best friends. He only lets them see what he wants." Kramer wrapped the towel around his waist. He could never put his finger on what it was about Karen, but he could feel it now in his irritation. "Frank has a way of leaving things out. All of the macho stories, the strokes he gets for being so funny. He doesn't tell you how scared he is. And Frank can be very convincing.... It's part him, part the alcoholic personality." Since Karen had started going to Al-Anon, she made these kinds of assertions with authority.

"I'm making this call for Frank's sake and Frank's alone." Her voice was high, strained. "He's totally out of control. It's been going on for weeks. He's out half the night. He says he sleeps in his office, comes home shaky and paranoid. His business is going to hell. Something's got to be done."

Kramer carefully dried his shoulder, wiped the phone and pressed the receiver between his shoulder and ear.

Karen said, "I know how this must sound ... you're thinking I'm hysterical or it's just another quarrel. But if you could see him, Kramer.... I know he respects you because you stopped drinking ten years ago. But to tell you how distorted his thinking can get, there are times he says that anyone who can stop drinking overnight—and on his own—must be cold and can't be trusted.

"Frank doesn't trust. Or know how to trust. It's, 'Trust and you get fucked.' He's always been secretive. And being an investigator has just played on that. His world now is dealing with people who are trying to con him and going them one better. But the important thing here, Kramer, is you did call his bluff four years ago, somehow got through to him, and took him to AA. And he thought enough of you to go."

"Have you tried getting him to AA?"

"Of course. I'm the last person he'd go with. Anyway, it's way past AA, Kramer."

"He won't see a shrink?"

"No...."

Kramer dried his legs and glanced at the clock. He had a meeting in half an hour, and he was already running late. "Do you know what's set him off?"

"Could be a million things. You've worked with him, you know his life. Lawyers run him hard, he's out all day and night. He does their legwork and makes their cases; they make the money, take forever to pay, and rarely thank him. Lawyers and the Public Defender's office owe him twenty grand. Meanwhile, he can't pay his bills. He's angry. We have problems. As you know. The bar exam hangs over his head. And I sense there's something big he hasn't told me. I mean beside all the other little things he never tells me."

Again Kramer thought of the lost money. He sat down on a kitchen chair. "Okay, Karen, Frank is over the line and won't go to AA or see a shrink. What do you want to do?"

"I really believe the only thing left to do is call an intervention." Kramer was silent. "Do you know what I'm talking about?" She paused, went on. "I have to say, when I first heard about it, I didn't like the idea. But I've now come around to thinking it's our only chance—his only chance."

Karen described how she'd been talking to a psychotherapist who specialized in interventions. She'd been reading her books and articles. "We would meet in her office. Myself, people who are important to Frank. And each of us would confront him. With love. And honesty. But tell him. 'Frank, you're doing these things. This is how it looks. Cut it out and we're with you, we'll support you. But if you don't stop and get help, here's what we're going to do.'"

"What can you do?"

"I can say, 'Frank, get help and I'll be there, I'll love you and help you. Keep drinking and doing shit and I'm gone.'" Kramer was silent. "What, Kramer?"

"I don't know. Pretty cold."

"Look, Kramer, if you love him and care about him, this hard choice has to be made." Kramer looked at the clock. He had to get off the phone. "He's a con man, Kramer. One of the best. He's conned all his friends, he's conned himself. I'm the only one he can't con and that's why I'm the one he stays with. Kramer?"

"I just have a lot of questions. Look, Karen, I've got a meeting in twenty minutes."

"You don't have time for this?"

"I didn't say that. I said I have a meeting and I'm going to be late. I'll call you back."

"No. Whatever you do, don't call me back." Her voice was urgent. "Give me a time and I'll call you."

They agreed on a time—3 p.m.—and Kramer hung up and rushed to dress for his meeting.

But Kramer couldn't keep his mind on the discussion. He kept thinking about Frank, last spring. After he'd left L.A., he'd heard nothing from him for weeks. Kramer called the house, but

always got the answering machine. Same at the office. He let it
ride. In early June, Frank surfaced. "Sorry I haven't called,
Kramer, and I'm in a rush now, but wanna tell you what's been
happening." Five days after Kramer's visit, he'd referred all of
his cases and checked himself into a detox place; he'd been there
for the last six weeks; he felt great and had come to a lot of
realizations. Just being away from Karen made him see she was
a good part of his problem. He'd decided not to move back in
with her. He'd started seeing one of the alcohol counselors. He
thought he was in love with Sidra. Maybe they'd go to Austra-
lia. "Hey, I know how it sounds, but... "

When he'd finished, Kramer said, "Why do it all in one fell
swoop, Frank? You went, you detoxed, that's great. Why not
just slow it down with Sidra?"

Frank said, "Hey, I'm jammed, I've got to meet a witness,
we'll talk," and hung up. A week later, Frank called again. He'd
gotten his own place, Sidra and he were better than ever, he had
a dozen new cases, was doing great, and though Karen was
begging him, he was determined not to move back in with her.
And yeah, he was broke, but he'd registered for the next bar
exam. Two months had gone by, and now Karen had called
telling him Frank had moved back in and was stoned. Kramer
didn't know what to believe.

At three on the dot, Karen called back. She started right in.
"You had questions about the intervention."

"Right. I do. Let me think. You know, one big question I have
is how do you get Frank to an intervention if he won't even go
to AA?"

"Leave that to me."

"Okay, I'll leave that to you. And let's say you can get his
friends together and we confront him. What then? I once saw
Frank serve a subpoena to a cop right there in the station, the
cop threw it on the floor, Frank picked it up and jammed it in
the cop's pants. I mean, he's not going to take it lying down."

"Kramer, I know what he can be. Look, no one gets the whole
story from Frank. Everyone gets a piece of the story. The idea
here is that by bringing everyone together, we can get all of the

stories in the same room. The point is to put a dent in his denial."

Kramer looked out into the yard. Karen seemed to have answers for everything.

"You know, Karen...If Frank is drunk..."

"He is drunk! Why *if*? Drunk and stoned!"

"I still don't like interfering in a friend's life. When he bottoms out, and when he wants, he'll get help."

"I've just gone through that with you!" She stopped. Sounding miserable, taut, she said, "I don't mean to raise my voice, but it is so hard to make people see.... Look, you'd pull a child from in front of an oncoming car. You did take him to AA."

"I asked him if he wanted to go. He said yes. There wasn't all this conniving and secrecy...."

"Well, it's too bad it's come to this, but it has."

"I'm afraid it will knock him to his knees."

"Can't I make you understand he is on his knees?! There's nothing else left to do. And the intervention is supposed to knock him to his knees."

"I thought you said he was already on his knees...." Kramer said. "Is it supposed to knock him flat?"

"Kramer...please don't, Kramer. Look, it's a disease."

Kramer said with impatience, "Okay, Karen, say we have the intervention. Then what?"

"I have a thirty-day inpatient program lined up for him, detox and intensive counseling. It's in another state where he can't get drugs or see friends. Before he can work the intervention into his denial system, we take him straight from the therapist's office to the airport. The detox people are waiting on the other end."

"And if he won't go?"

"I know he'll go," she said quietly. "If his friends show up, he'll go. I've scheduled the intervention for a week from this Sunday. I'm asking you, Sean Connelly, Jules Levine, his sister, I'll be there..." She listed several people. "Are you coming, Kramer?"

Kramer hesitated. "I'll tell you, Karen, I don't know. I'll have to think about it."

"Christ! What's there to think about! God, why won't people believe me! What do I have to do, write it in blood! I'm talking about saving Frank's life! There's not much time and I need to know from people if I'm going to be able to make this happen. You're supposed to be his friends! Are you too busy?" She quieted, said with resignation, "Look, I'll send you some of the therapist's articles on interventions. Her name is Germaine Blumenthal—the therapist—and she's very well known. I'll call you back in a few days. Kramer, I'm hoarse, I've been on the phone for days calling people; I realize I sound stressed out. I've been dealing with Frank for weeks. I know you don't really like me. . . ."

"Karen . . ."

"It's okay. This is for Frank. I do know what I'm doing. I'll say one last thing. We're all part of his system—you, me, his close friends. Like it or not, we have helped create him. He may even be acting out our unconscious desires."

Kramer suppressed a sound of contempt. He knew this was Al-Anon talk. He said, "He may be a beast, but he's our beast?"

Karen went on without replying, "We've laughed at his jokes and bullshit, given him strokes for being a wise guy. . . . I'll admit it, I've loved him for going over the line. We all have. And that's why I'm saying, we're all responsible now." She lapsed into silence. In a tired voice, she said, "Okay, think about it. However you decide, promise me you won't warn him of this out of some misguided sense of loyalty."

"I already promised you."

"I know. Right. I believe you. It's just that I'm so used to dealing with Frank. . . . "

"Call me in a few days. Bye, Karen." He didn't wait. He hung up.

Kramer could come to no conclusions. He thought of Sean Connelly in Chicago. Karen had mentioned him for the intervention. And Sean had known Frank since they'd been altarboys. Kramer called him. Had Karen phoned? Oh, yeah, two-hours worth last night. "I'll tell you, I don't know what to think, Kramer. I talked to Karen about a month ago—that was just after Frank had moved back in. She kept talking about Sidra. Karen visited Frank when he went to that detox place last spring. Came the day Sidra gave a lecture. Karen thought she was on a big power trip. According to Karen, Sidra gets up there and gives this well-rehearsed speech, 'Let me tell you how it is, I've been to hell and back.' Afterward, Frank's sitting out by the pool, and Sidra comes walking out in a string bikini and sits down next to him. Karen says she must have had a lot of contempt for Frank to go after him when he was so fragile. She says to me, 'Christ, there are a lot of desperate 38-year-old women out there hunting for men.' She told me she was going to sue the detox place."

Sean was quiet. "Karen said, 'To Frank, she's a complete fantasy. No dirty socks in the hall, nothing. It's one thing losing out to a real woman—flesh and blood. That's bad enough. But it's humiliating when it's a fantasy, the big tit in the sky.' "

The receiver whined with static. Sean said, "Is that my phone—or yours?"

"Must be mine. I drop it every other day." They fell silent. Kramer said, "I don't know what's going on—why he went back to Karen, if he's drinking, if she's lying, what. And detox places are expensive. Where's the money supposed to come from this time?"

"She wants each of us to put up a thousand bucks."

"She forgot to mention that little detail. Christ. Are you going, Sean?"

"I don't know. I'll give you a call when I decide."

Kramer was on his second cup of coffee when the phone rang. "Good morning, is this Steven L. Kramer?" The official tone of voice made Kramer feel a stab of nervousness.

"Yes, it is."

"This is James Lucky of the Phoenix Police Department. Do you own a blue 1983 Blazer, AZ license plate number: PGN 121?"

"Yes, I do."

"We have a report it's been stolen and been involved in a jewelry store robbery and a hit-and-run, pedestrian fatality."

Confused, heart starting to pound, Kramer walked the phone to
the window and looked out. The car was sitting in the driveway. Frank started to laugh. "Gotcha, didn't I, Kramer?" Relieved, Kramer laughed. "What's been happenin', dude-san?"

"Work. June and the baby. What about you?"

"I'm in my office. My client's going to trial in two hours.
Tyrone Davis. What it is, Slick, two niggers living in a rooming
house. My man, Tyrone, is a sweet guy, keeps to himself; he's a
composer and keyboard player. Jamal Kelly lives downstairs.
He keeps threatening Tyrone, pushing him around. Kelly steals
Davis's keyboards, but Davis can't prove it—I just turned them
up in pawn. Anyway, Tyrone, he scared, he get hisself some
heat. Finally, Jamal, he get fucked up behind hubbas, forces his
way into Tyrone's room, this happens, that, Tyrone shoots him
with a .357 magnum. Good shot, too. Right in the forehead.
Levine's arguing self-defense. Kelly really was a bad nigger—a
long record of assaults—so my job's been easy."

"I thought you and Jules Levine had fallen out over money."

"Well, yes and no. But everything's cool again. For now. You
know, Levine be cool when he need me. I'll tell you when I've
got more time. Hey, when did we last talk? A while, right? Have
we spoken since I moved back in with Karen?"

"No, I don't think so."

"The thing with Sidra got to be too much. Nice woman,
but... Fact is, fucked up as we are, I love Karen. She said if it
was over with Sidra, then come back and let's put it behind us.
But what's happening, Kramer, is she keeps looking for evidence that I'm with Sidra—and not just Sidra, but other women.
I can tell, she's been going through my things. She's looking for
letters, phone numbers, anything. I don't know what Karen
thinks she'll find. But if she thought it through, she'd realize that
whatever it is wouldn't be at home anyway."

"I don't know, Frank."

"Karen says, 'Forgive and forget.' But why haven't I learned
by now, Karen never forgives and forgets anything? Kramer, I
think she's up to something, maybe calling people and telling
them I'm doing this and that—drinking, whatever. She's trying
to discredit me with my friends." Kramer was silent. "Hey, I've

gotta get outta here and meet an attorney...you know, Slick, she can dig all she wants, but I'm really not doing anything. Has she called you in the last couple of weeks?"

Kramer looked out the window at the Blazer. "Why would she call me?"

"I don't know. I've just got this feeling she's up to something. Let me know if she calls you, okay, man?" Kramer didn't answer and therefore told himself he wasn't really lying. "Later, Slick, Tyrone, we gonna walk him.... Hey, you know something, Jules and I have done some numbers, but this time it really was self-defense."

June held out the phone as Kramer came in the door. "Kramer! Christ, I've been trying to reach you for three days. Where've you been?"

"Living. Talking to my wife. Playing with my kid. You could have made it easier on yourself if you'd left me a number where I could leave a message. Maybe a secret password. You know, 'This is Don Carlo. The ship has docked.'"

"Has Frank called you since we spoke?"

"As a matter of fact, he has."

"Kramer..."

"I didn't say anything."

"Kramer?"

"I said I didn't. It's just a coincidence he called. He doesn't know, but he has instincts something's happening."

"I really pray you didn't say anything, Kramer. He'll con you. He'll sound absolutely normal and in control. If you warned Frank, we'll never get him to the intervention."

"I haven't told him. And if you question me one more time about this, I'm hanging up."

"Alright. Sorry. I believe you. I do. I'm just stressed out. You got the Blumenthal articles I sent you?"

"Yep."

"And you've had time to read them."

"Sí."

"Well, Kramer, I need to know. Are you in or out? Remember, this isn't a matter of our marriage. This is Frank's life."

"A couple of more questions, Karen, if you don't mind." He heard a sigh of exasperation. He waited.

"Go ahead."

"Last time you mentioned a detox place."

"Right."

"Those places cost a fortune. Where's the money coming from?"

"I've borrowed some. And I thought each of Frank's friends could put in something ... "

"How much?"

"Money's not the issue here! And it will all be paid back."

"We run Frank thousands more into debt for this without his say-so?"

"Under the circumstances, of course it wouldn't be with his say-so. It. Will. Be. Paid. Back."

"He's already in debt."

"He's also got money owed to him."

Kramer knew she had no idea of the money lost last spring. "Okay, it will be paid back. How much do you want from his friends?"

"A thousand dollars each."

"Great, Karen. Actually, I knew that. Why didn't you tell me before?"

"Kramer, I've been on the phone for days to half a dozen people. You're something. If you don't want to do it because of the money, just say so. Has *that* been your big hang-up?"

"No, not at all. But it is something you left out."

"What a friend even to be thinking of money at a time like this."

"Karen ... " Kramer held himself back. They were silent. Finally, Karen said, "Yes or no, Kramer? I have to know. There are only four more days."

Kramer didn't know what to believe. He decided he couldn't know anything for sure without going. "Yes. And for your sake, Frank better be drunk."

"Drunk is the least of it. You'll see. And thank you, Kramer." He heard a softening in her voice. "There's a map, all the information is in the envelope. Everything. You can just go up and wait in Blumenthal's office. It's scheduled for Sunday at one p.m. I'm telling Frank that we're going for lunch and that I'm stopping to pick up a friend from work there. One last thing...you read in her article how each participant reads a letter: what they care about in him, what he's been doing, and what they'll do if the person doesn't stop abusing?"

"I read it."

"Well, you could give that some careful thought. I'll see you Sunday."

Kramer hung up. He called Sean. Sean said he'd gotten as far as plane reservations, but canceled. He couldn't really explain.

Kramer climbed the carpeted stairs to the second floor, saw *Blumenthal* on the half-open door, and walked in. There was a waiting room and, beyond, a consultation room with a circle of chairs. Kramer saw Barry Mannis standing by the window. Mannis had worked part time for Frank as an investigator. Frank and Barry had had an explosive turbulent working relationship. They'd fought over everything. Money, hours, details large and small. They'd also won some big cases together. They nodded and shook hands. "You fly in for this?"

"Last night. Karen summoned me. What's Frank up to?"

"He's drinking. And fucked-up behind a lot of blow." Kramer waited. "Scheming and hustling. He's everything he's always been but more. Who knows anything about Frank for sure."

"But I mean, can he live his life? Should we be doing this?"

Barry shrugged. "Tough one to call."

"You guys still working together?"

"Oh, yeah, but there are so many hassles. Always money."

Kramer nodded. They circled the waiting room, froze as a door opened and closed downstairs. Jules Levine, in slacks and sports jacket, walked in alone. He paused to catch his breath and take command of the room; everyone shook hands. Frank had been his investigator on a dozen big cases, looked up to him at the same time he resented him—rich kid. In another moment, Catherine came up the stairs. Frank's younger sister. She was in her early thirties. She thanked each of them for coming and walked into the consultation room. Kramer looked at the clock.

It was almost one. A door at the back of the consultation room opened, and a woman, obviously Germaine Blumenthal, mid-thirties, looked out at each of them and disappeared. Kramer's impression was fair-looking, helped along by an expensive veneer, uptight, and in persona for the duration.

Downstairs, they heard the door open and close, a woman's voice interweaving with heavy, syncopated steps. Karen stepped into the waiting room: curly blond hair, a jogger's thinness peaked by stress, good features. Flushed, winded, Frank stepped in behind her. Kramer hadn't seen him since late last winter—six months. His face was now full, his handsomeness being swallowed by weight. He stopped and glanced at each of them. He peered into the consulting room. "That you, Catherine?" He paused, said offhandedly to the room, "This it? You all bringing me in?"

Kramer stepped over to him. When he took his hand, it was cold and limp. Frank looked past Kramer. "Hey, you hadn't heard from Karen lately, right, dude-san?"

"It was a hard one, Frank."

Frank said offhandedly, "Life is like a dick, Kramer, when it's hard you get fucked; when it's soft, you can't beat it."

Barry put his arm around Frank. Frank said, "What, my big buddy, you think I owe you money, right? There's the guy who owes me, Slick. Tell you what, Barry, you collect it directly from Jules; you won't have to protect your investment, and I'll go take a walk."

Karen held Frank's arm and said, "They all love you and care about you, Frank; we all do. They're just here to help."

"I know it, honey," Frank said in a fey aside. He rolled his eyes straight up, sucked his lips in one of his ten fag variations. "We'll all just get in touch with our feelings, go through it together, right?" Without thinking, Kramer had backed up a step or two. He'd seen Frank explode at people under less trying circumstances.

Frank asked, "Excuse me, did I say hello to you, yet, Jules?"

"Sure, Frank." Jules smiled indulgently.

"No, I didn't. Good afternoon, Jules." When Jules didn't say any more, Frank said, "Guess he's not talking to me."

Germaine Blumenthal came to the door with Catherine. Frank said, "You girls want me to amble on in, that it?"

As yet, Kramer couldn't tell what Frank was going to do.

Karen said, "Come on, Frank."

"I thought we were meeting someone for lunch. I'm starved."

Karen said quietly, "It's over, Frank, and you know it. Please come. We love you. We care about you. You don't have to keep it up any longer. Just let it go. Trust us. It will be alright."

Frank said, "Karen tell a little fibby about lunchtime. Anyone want to go for lunch?"

Barry said, "After."

"Kramer?"

"After."

"Jules?"

"I'll take everyone to lunch after."

"That'll be a first."

Jules put his hand gently on Frank's shoulder, said quietly, "I've been there, Frank, it'll be okay."

Frank remained motionless. Karen said, "Come in, Frank, and we'll have a life. Go out into the street now and stay there, don't come home, that's it."

"Oh," Frank said. "That's a good one, honey. Guess I better play along, what'd ya think, Kramer? Kramer leave Junie and the baby and came all the way out here to do this. I better be good." Karen went ahead. As they walked in, Frank looked Germaine over and, leaning back, said softly to Kramer, "Hm, there's some styrene, dude." In spite of himself, Kramer laughed. Karen gave him a hard look. Frank said, "Uh oh, you're in honey pooh's doggy house now, Stevie."

Catherine tried to hug Frank, but he kept his arms at his side. He surveyed the circle of chairs. "Oh my, pick just any place?" Again in one of his fag voices. He sat. Karen sat beside him. In another moment, Germaine Blumenthal had closed the outer and inner doors, and everyone was seated. She introduced herself and made a short statement laying out the ground rules of the intervention. Everything was to be said in a caring way. There was to be no vindictiveness. She told Frank that all of these people were here because they were concerned for him.

Still in his leather jacket, Frank sat pale and motionless. His face was unreadable. Germaine said, "Do you know why we're here today, Frank?"

Frank said, "You talk, I'll listen."

Germaine said, "Fine. I hope you will. I'd like to start by getting people's impressions of what they see happening to you."

She paused and looked around the circle. No one said anything. Then Karen made a determined statement about why she'd called the intervention with a long account of Frank's behavior. Frank didn't say a word, which seemed incredible to Kramer: to have Karen go on like this and not to hear the echo of Frank's mocking wisecracks and mimicry. When she was finished, Catherine gave her account, variations on Karen's themes. Jules went on to say that Frank was a special friend to him; as an investigator Frank could do amazing things with people and situations. And he'd say now in front of everyone, Frank had made many of his cases. But though Jules recognized there was a lot of stress in what Frank did—the people, the hours, the deadlines—he still thought Frank went too far—fights over money, unpredictable and inappropriate behavior. Specific incidents were brought up. Barry echoed Jules in his statement. When it was Kramer's turn, he said that he thought Frank could be difficult at times, he'd never liked his three a.m. phone calls, the little money games, but that he'd always had the greatest of respect for his ingenuity and talents; they'd had a lot of good times together. Frank listened to each with almost no expression.

When Kramer checked his watch, he was surprised to see that an hour had gone by. Now Frank's cynical and desensitized language was being taken to task by Catherine and Karen and Barry. Niggers, spics, beaners, gooks. Pussy. Styrene. You name it. Frank was educated and well-read. He was also very feeling and generous. And as he'd gone on talking like that, they assumed it was Frank's trying to protect himself from the people he was dealing with. But now it just seemed that Frank had become brutalized. Kramer thought they were misreading Frank's peculiar sense of satire and provocation, but said nothing.

Then Germaine Blumenthal asked them to read their letters. What each cared for about Frank. And what each would do if Frank didn't stop abusing and change his behavior. In one way or another, each praised Frank for his humor, energy, and resourcefulness. Each said, change, and we'll be there. But keep on as you are, and we're through with you: don't call, we'll hang up; don't come home, we'll change the locks. When it came to Kramer, though he felt the group's disapproval, he couldn't bring himself to give Frank an ultimatum. When Kramer looked up, Frank was sitting motionless, but tears were streaming down his cheeks. In all of their years of friendship, Kramer had never seen him like this. It was as if Frank, with his endless motion, his unpredictability and temper, had lived his life to avoid this moment. Kramer looked at the floor.

Now the question of the detox center was raised. Karen described the location and program. What about it? Would Frank consider going, thirty days, inpatient? Frank wiped his cheeks and said quietly, "Where's the money coming from?"

Karen said, "The money's not a question, it will be covered."

"Hey, you know, I've got a business. Twenty-four cases open now and I'm supposed to meet a defendant at four."

Karen said, "Frank, it's been thought out. We'll take care of everything. We'll contact lawyers, refer your cases, Barry can keep things going until you get back. I'll pay your bills, take care of the paper work." Karen had her hand on Frank's arm. She watched his face.

Frank took a breath and wiped his cheek. He said, "You're saying give you the keys to my office?"

Karen said, "I'll take care of things."

Frank said to the group, "I don't trust Karen to have the keys to my business."

Karen said, "Frank, I know there have been terrible things between us, but we're letting them go. You can trust me. I won't go into your files; I'll pay your bills, Barry and I will collect your messages, that will be it. I know how hard it is for you to trust, I understand. We understand. But it's okay now. It's time for us to move on."

Frank was silent. He looked slowly around the circle of faces.

When Frank looked at him, Kramer didn't know what his face showed. After a long time, Frank reached into his pocket and pulled out a large ring of keys. He looked at Karen. She returned his gaze. He gave her the keys. Everyone shifted, relaxed.

Several more minutes were spent discussing details. A flight was leaving in three hours; Karen would call the people at the detox center, have them waiting at the other end. That left time for Frank to go to his office with Barry and Jules and pull things together. Frank said, "Hey, do I go naked?" Karen said his bag was already packed and in the trunk. Frank said laconically, "Honey pooh has thought of everything."

Within another moment, Karen stood, thanked each of them for coming, and crossed to Germaine. They hugged each other. Frank, without much inspiration, sucked his lips and rolled his eyes, "Sisterhood, ya know." Kramer saw her write a check for two hundred and fifty dollars. Frank said, "Not a bad hustle for two hours work, doctor. Let's talk some time. Hey, I'm starved, do I get to eat now?"

As Jules and Frank went out, Karen grabbed Barry's arm, "Once he hits the street, he may try to slip away. Whatever you do, don't let him out of your sight—not even to go to the bathroom. It's not over until we've actually put him on the plane. Have him at the Continental counter at four-thirty." Barry nodded and took off down the stairs after Frank and Jules whose voices were already fading in the street.

Kramer was almost surprised, perhaps even a little disappointed, to see Frank walking toward Continental at four-thirty with Barry and Jules on either side of him. Barry shook his head. Knowing that Jules and Barry were staying on him, Frank, of course, had been leading them all over. Frank said, "Kramer, I've got to talk with you a minute." He walked out into the crowd. Kramer ran after him.

Outside, Frank said, "Relax, Stevie, I'm not going to bolt, much as Karen has set you up to think I will." He stopped in front of a bar. "And I'm not going to sneak a drink. I'm going to have one out in the open. And yeah I had some blow at the office." They sat down at the bar and Frank ordered a double vodka martini, Kramer a tonic. Then Frank turned to Kramer and said, "I won't say whether this was right or wrong, but thanks for coming today. That's twice in the last six months and I won't forget my friends. Here's my side. I've been drinking and doing shit. I won't deny it. But I'm also exhausted and overworked. You try investigating eleven murders gone to trial in the last eight months while you keep the rest of your cases going, don't get paid—you remember the scratch I lost last winter...?" Kramer nodded. "You know what it is, out all hours of the day and night. Karen has always been suspicious of that. Is what it is, dude-san. I could tell you some stories about Karen pooh, but love and trust are the order of the day here.... Hey, if you guys want to bail me out for a while, I welcome this chance to rest. More than anything that's what I need. Rest."

From the moment Frank began to speak, Kramer had the overwhelming feeling that there was really nothing wrong with him. He worked hard. He drank and did some coke. So did a lot of people.

"I'll tell you, I'm flat broke. Not even pocket money." Frank took out his wallet and put two fifties on the bar. "Jules gave me a couple of portraits of Ulysses S. Grant for my trip to the gulag. What are you going to give me, Kramer?"

Kramer said, "Nothing. I've already come all this way for you." After some cajoling, Kramer gave Frank a twenty and then, after more kidding, Kramer, shaking his head, gave Frank one more twenty.

At the gate, everyone hugged Frank. Frank's face was expressionless. Karen led him off to one side, her arm around him, and they stood by the window talking softly, faces together, and then Karen gave Frank a tender kiss, Kramer could hear her, I'll be here for you, Frank, and Kramer could see that Frank was again crying. With a stewardess on one side and Karen on the other, dwarfed by his shoulders, they walked him down the tunnel and onto the plane. A few minutes later, Karen came back alone. She remained apart from Barry and Jules and Kramer as the plane was pulled away from the building. Catherine, too, stood by herself. No one left. They watched the plane work its way into the ground traffic.

Barry said, "He took me aside and, I swear, he almost had me convinced he was okay and that it was just everyone else sticking it to him."

Kramer nodded. He saw it clearly. That's what had been going on in the bar. As an afterthought, Kramer said to Jules, "You gave him a hundred bucks. . . . "

"Who?"

"You. Frank showed me the two fifties."

The Continental jet wheeled into position on the runway and started to wind up its engines.

Jules dug out his wallet. "Jesus. I had my wallet on the table for a couple of minutes in the restaurant. He must have taken the money."

The plane went down the runway and lifted into the low fog.

Kramer said, "He showed me the fifties, shamed me into giving him forty bucks. And I felt bad for not giving him more."

They looked at each other and broke out laughing. Overhead, lights blinking, the plane banked into the twilight. As they turned and started to drift through the airport, Kramer, despite an uneasiness, had the feeling the intervention had been the right thing.

For the next ten days, Frank called to talk with Kramer from the gulag, which was in Minneapolis. He thanked Kramer for trying to help him and said that more than anything, what he really had needed was sleep and a sensible diet. He said that it was a very special and loving thing that Karen had done—the intervention—and that he would always be thankful to her. When he got home, they'd have a life.

Then a letter arrived, Frank's handwriting, three sheets of yellow legal paper. Frank started right in. Karen had broken her word. She had taken the keys, gone into his office, and rifled everything. Every file, the rolodex, all of his drawers and closets. She had found letters, names, phone numbers, what she'd always feared. She'd already burned a lot of his papers. She'd canceled his credit cards. She'd called women all over town, cursing and threatening them. She had called him ten times last night, threatening to kill him, kill herself. "The thing is, Kramer, except for Sidra's letters—and she knew about

Sidra—they were just some old girlfriends, things that were over years ago. Some even went back before we were married. She just found what she had to find. Almost any woman's name was confirmation. She's totally out of control. So far she's threatened several defendants, an assistant prosecutor, four attorneys, all women." Frank went on to say, "A lot of bad things had happened—I won't deny them, but I had sincerely apologized to her, I took her at her word that day—remember, Kramer, love, trust, we're putting it all behind us? Well, I have no one to blame but myself: trust and you get fucked." As an afterthought, he added, almost hopefully, that maybe Karen had tried to keep her word, but just couldn't help herself. Kramer talked about it with June. June handed back the letter and said, "After ten years, didn't he know what she was going to do?"

Three days after he'd finished detox and reached L.A., Frank called Kramer to tell him he'd come back to find all of Karen's things gone. She had moved from their duplex in Venice and taken a place over in Manhattan Beach. Two hours ago, she'd had him served with a restraining order and divorce papers.

On a spring day six months after the intervention, Kramer had reason to be in L.A. Frank met him at the airport, and after serving a subpoena in Inglewood, they drove on to Santa Monica Beach. There was a strong wind, a big shore break, and everything seemed to be shining. They got out of the car, walking slowly. As they reached the sand, Kramer said, "So how're you doing, Frank?"

Frank nodded, "Not bad. I'm staying clean. I'm up and down. Got a lot of cases, I'm busier than ever; clients were really understanding about my trip to the gulag." After a moment, he said, "Hey, you know, the fact is, it's hard for me without Karen." He looked at Kramer. "I know what you're thinking. How can he say that after all the shit, but it was ten years, and," he shrugged, "you know, whatever it is, it's your life...." Kramer nodded. The wind gusted, picked up sand, lashed it around their ankles. They walked toward the water, pants and jackets whipping, hair standing up. Frank said, "It's over between us, I know it. The divorce is going through. And she suckered me, man, but I still love Karen, maybe more than ever."

"You think Karen suckered you?"

Frank nodded. "Oh, hey, listen, Slick, no doubt about it, I don't think, I know. Karen suckered me. She suckered all of us. I know what you're going to start thinking, that whatever I say is going to be part of my denial and the rest of it." Frank stopped and turned to Kramer. "I'll flat-ass say it, Kramer. I was using, man. I was drunk, I was high, I was over the line. And that was getting to be a little problem." Frank turned and faced the water. "But what Karen did with that opportunity..." Frank shook his head. "Look, when I walked into that office, I didn't have a clue. I make my living by reading people, defendants, witnesses, figuring out when they're lying, when they're telling the truth, what they're up to. I never saw it coming.

"She's doing this to save my life, right? That's what she tells me, you, Barry, Jules. Everyone buys it. You buy. I buy. She gets a thousand out of each of you, puts me another five grand in debt, tells me it's going to be love and trust from now on. I'm knocked off balance. I still have big reservations, I'm not dumb, but I go along. I give her the keys to my office: everything will be okay, honey."

Kramer thought that Frank was obsessing, but just decided to let him get it out of his system. "That's what she wanted, Slick. She wanted that key. That's what it was about. Or that's what I thought. Once she had that key—well, I wrote you about it. She thought I was fucking every woman in the Rolodex."

Frank turned suddenly. "Kramer...I don't know if I'm getting through to you. I thought she left because of what she *thought* she found in my office. When I got back, I drove over to Manhattan Beach to see where she was living. There were a few cars in front of her duplex. I get the license plates and run them through the DMV, get some names, social security numbers, routine stuff. I started making calls to banks, following checks, this and that."

They watched the skaters and bike riders drifting down the bike path toward Ocean Park and Venice in the distance. "When I put it all together, what it tells me, Slick, is that Karen had this lover, Brad Moreno, back before I got into it with Sidra. And that's its own thing. But the real point here, my man, is when I pull up these accounts, I see that she's made a check out to Moreno for four hundred dollars—half his rent. The check says it: rent. It's dated May 1. That's two weeks before she sent me to the gulag. She never had any intention of living with me again when she put me on that plane. So you can call this my denial or whatever, but there it is. Deny that check and its date."

They walked on in silence. Frank grabbed Kramer's arm. They stopped. "Kramer, don't feel bad about it. I know you were trying to help me." Stunned, Kramer could only nod. "Hey, I've done some numbers, but step back and look at this; it's a real masterpiece. Karen took several of my closest friends and associates, five completely different people, and put on a little circus. She conned them all. She conned me. Her timing was impeccable." He looked back toward the surf exploding in the sunlight. "She screwed me completely. It was beautifully done. It was elegant. Whatever else you might think of Karen, you've got to admire the girl for this." And looking out to sea, Frank smiled, a tender, wistful smile, filled with love and fury.

Children's Law

SALLY'S KID IS HOME SICK IN BED and so we are overhearing *I Dream of Jeannie* reruns from the next room because Sally is being permissive and letting the kid watch daytime TV for a while. I am more than a little disappointed Sally is back from Texas—Sally, the kid, and all of her books, floor to ceiling, already arranged in alphabetical order by author. Tony, her husband, is not back from Texas. He will remain in Texas. Don't get me wrong. I am not disappointed that Sally is back from Texas because I do not like Sally. I do like Sally, though she can be a little difficult. But no, that's not it. I am disappointed Sally is back from Texas because I needed her there and me here, which is this East Coast college town, wherein resides the Great Gray U. My needing Sally in Texas is not merely spurious, though I am certainly not against the spurious as such. I had a real need to have Sally Bernstein Murphy distant.

So much so that the morning she left, I was already composing letters to her. Fairway by fairway. Her plane could not have been farther than Ohio. *Dear Sally*...Not playing, caddying. I'd been working for the city, kind of a PR job, smoothing things over between the city administration and the minorities, but my man hadn't gotten reelected, so there I was. After fifteen holes, it started hailing, big carooming balls of ice and bolts of blue-white lightning, my god, one guy seriously wanted to play on, *Dear Sally*/Hailing here....

Sally and I are not lovers, though we tried to be. It—the chemistry—just wasn't there; I believe in chemistry. And then, there was too much sympathetic identification, which was perhaps the draw, but somehow it vaporized on contact, neutralized us. Our fathers. Lying there in bed, my bed, only vaguely attracted to each other, we talked about our fathers for the first and last time. We were both the children of famous fathers, both in *Who's Who* by the time they were thirty. Both of us had done time at the Great Gray U, both of us had in some unmentioned way been expected to do great things, but never had. Mutual recognition unconsummated in bed. Too much sympathy for sex. Chemistry, sympathy, and a spark of antagonism, the big three which fuel love's carburetor.

Anyway, both of us had it, the humid spiritual hypochondria, the famous father disease, which is: whatever you do, child of famous father, a voice inside says, it doesn't matter, not *really*, the life lived by your father is more real than any life you can possibly live. Now the children of famous fathers are often not as stupid as it is necessary for them to pretend to be, they know it is an illusion, but knowing is not as real as feeling, and knowing and feeling often won't make friends. All of which is to say, I knew I needed Sally in Texas.

Before Texas, though Sally had grown fat and thin, thin and fat, married and had the kid, it seemed that her life could most purely be charted by academic degrees. Ph.D. in English back when students and faculty drank sherry and talked with English accents and women wore black leotards and behaved like women in Jules Feiffer cartoons: I dance my homage to spring, flowers strewn here and there. Sally had even married a Ph.D. in English, their marriage like a match-up of Airedales with A.K.C. papers. Tony Murphy and Sally Bernstein, married by her father in the garden behind the family house in Mamaroneck. Her father, among other things, was a justice of the peace. I can't remember if I ever told Sally that my father was an honorary deputy sheriff and carried a heavy brass star pinned to his inside jacket pocket.

In the wedding album, Sally smiles the same blind smile in every picture. She told me she couldn't see anything—her mother insisted she looked better without her glasses—and so half the time she had to be led around by Tony, her mother, or anyone else available. It is night and the bridal party looks startled and aqueous as if photographed from a bathosphere in the Mariana Trench. Incidentally, I couldn't see anything *that* imposing about her father.

Just as she had been finishing up her Ph.D., along came Vietnam, the Resistance, May Day, the Bobby Seale trial. Sally had been some kind of marshall on May Day. I remember a spent tear-gas canister wrapped in a plastic baggie and displayed on her mantle. All of the lush rhetoric of the New Left fanned by the mistral of Women's Lib decided Sally on going back to get a law degree. The people! Community action! Law for the people. Metamorphosis, Ph.D. to LL.B. She passed the bar exam about the time Tony, the other Ph.D., had not gotten tenure at the Great Gray U. But Texas welcomed a Great U boy with open arms. That had been six or eight months ago. So off they'd gone to Texas, the marriage strained, but maybe a change...

I had been counting on Sally's letters from Texas to show me the way, to cast some Georgia O'Keeffe light into the Dostoyevskian gloom. I wanted her letters to be magnificent, Sally to be my Scheherazade of the Far West, voice from the Sun Belt, the New West, tapping out a ghost dance of instructive riddles. I would reply, *Dear Ariadne*...

What a rude shock when I look up from the raisin and coconut granola in the food co-op, and there she is in the date granola bin. The kid is whining he doesn't *like* date granola, and Sally is saying, sotto voce, you haven't ever had date granola. Just that morning, I'd written her a letter, a little masterpiece, had it right in my chest pocket. I stare at Sally with this sinking feeling. She hasn't seen me. I turn, start for the cash register. I will mail it anyway, please forward.

Sally reaches into her pack, pulls out her own plastic bag, good girl, let's hear it for recycling and saving the earth, and starts bagging the date granola, all the while reasoning with the kid who won't be reasoned with. Date granola it is, kid. Again, I start for the checkout. I'll just go on writing her, pretending she's in Texas, maybe she'll go on writing, pretend she's in Texas, too.

I hesitate, walk over, and say hello. She greets me in her almost inaudible voice. "Oh. Hello. Jack." That's what she says. "Oh. Hello. Jack." Touching her glasses nervously. Sally does go inaudible. Soft. Softer. Not softest, but inaudible, the voice falling away with a shrug so one must swan-dive toward her in slow motion as she finishes a word or phrase. "Oh. Hel. Lo. Jack."

The kid looks up at me and likes me a lot less than date granola. He tugs hard at Sally's hand. "Mom." The kid and I have never been able to hit it off. Scheherazade of the Sun Belt, back, and with the kid.

While the kid practically dislocates her arm, she tells me to come by. Scrawls an address. Stumbles once as the kid yanks her away. "But in a week, Jack." I watch the kid drag her toward the organic bubble gum. I pull out the letter.

"Sally."

But she doesn't hear. I stuff the letter back in my pocket.

Dear Sally . . .

So I come by and visit her one day a week later, and here I am visiting her again. Let me say one thing. Sally did in fact write me for six or eight months. She really did. And she started telling me something. Some pointillism of the spirit in metamorphosis. What it is, or was, I can't say because the Texas epistles were never finished. Maybe I'll dig out those Texas letters for another look.

Meanwhile, here she is living in this communal household— big, old rambling house. The whole country to choose and she comes back here. And this household. So solemn. Everyone does his chores and there's a house meeting once a week around a scrubbed and oiled oak table, everyone talks everything through, gripes, problems, it's all so civilized, self-conscious and humorless—full disclosure on feelings, being a single parent, yak yak yak, while the no-nonsense jars stare down from the wooden shelves and proclaim, Oats, Granola, etc. I know there are halfway houses for ex-junkies, ex-alkies, ex-cons. They have names like Reality House or Westward Look. I don't know what the people do here, but I do already know that they are all ex-somethings and this is *One Step Back, One Step Sideways House*. Bad name, it will never play. Everyone has at least one kid—sum total, lots of kids. These are the people who use words like *parenting* with such solemnity. Perhaps the best of the household is the kids' proudly exhibited artwork, crayon drawings, poster paintings, and general incandescent mushings spreading from cabinet to wall like some beautiful aerobic mold. I admire the artwork, feeling both baffled and moved by its familiarity and strangeness.

In the next room, sudden canned laughter. Jeannie. Makes me uneasy. Reminds me of my draft card matted in my wallet back then. Mid-sixties. I say, "You're letting the kid watch daytime TV."

She shrugs in her easy chair. Movements of the eyes behind the thick tortoise-shell glasses. I decide to drop it about the kid and daytime TV.

Before we can say anything else, the kid pads in and stands there in his Bugs Bunny pajamas like Benito Mussolini, fists on hips, Il Duce. He looks hard at me. He wanders over to Sally where he kind of sags toward her breast-heart-ventral self. She puts her arms around his head and shoulders. Enfolds him. In a soft voice, "What is it, Pumpkin?" She smoothes the hair off his forehead. He kind of whimpers, whispers, glances back once toward me. "You know Jack . . . get back in bed and I'll bring you some ginger ale and we'll check your temperature."

The kid rubs his eyes hard as he walks past me. I'm really not sure I've ever been able to like this kid, though I sense it's not his fault, not my fault, no one's fault. I've never been able to reach out to him. No chemistry with Mom, bad chemistry with Kid. First, I can only think of him as kid or refer to him as the kid though full well I know his name is Scott. Sally is always giving him the sotto voce, the voice of the understanding, patient mother. Christ, he is so full of need!

Sally in a series of stories written in an inaudible phase surprised me by calling him the kid, too. In these stories, a woman, Faye, unhappy for unspecified reasons, lives in a university environment, also unspecified, but with a certain too familiar grayness; she complains and argues with her husband over nebulous small concerns, also unspecified. This woman, Faye, who cannot eat or else eats compulsively at other times, and who has a way of getting fat and then starved-thin, much like Sally, usually takes the kid and after walking a long distance, either hitches or takes a bus somewhere. Then she walks some more. The kid walks beside her until he gets tired and finally begs to be carried. Though he is too old—and too heavy—to carry, Faye usually takes him up on her back, all the time answering his precocious, ironic questions. Often these stories end with her getting to some alien place where she puts the kid to sleep on a sofa, comforts him, then feels blank and ends up staring out a window which the pre—or false—dawn is turning gray. In one story, I remember she ends up sitting with the kid in an all-night donut shop. She is surrounded by giant photo reproductions of donuts on the walls. I mean, they are the wallpaper. For lack of anything more kind, I told her I thought the image of the donuts was startling.

The kid is back in the bedroom, the TV gets louder, and suddenly this progressive little kid, offspring of two Ph.D.s and an LL.B., who could read before he went to school, and who is sensitive and perceptive enough for Sally to carry on her much-vaunted adult relationship, this kid starts flicking the TV tuner so fast the thing sounds like a machine gun, and Sally calls out, "Pumpkin, wouldn't you like to color now? Remember our agreement. *I Dream of Jeannie* and then, TV off. Pumpkin?" No reply. "Scott?"

Sally smiles at me. Or her lips part, rise, fall. The muscles of her jaw seem to have thickened almost as if they've been exercised. The tuner stops at something murky and melodramatic. Shots and screams. Sally stands.

"Excuse me." Soft, very soft. She starts for the bedroom. What's she so afraid of—all of these guarded movements, this soft voice—all of this suggesting and diplomacy and treating the kid like an adult?

Sally once told me she was a genius. Something she had

overheard a psychologist tell her mother: "...but just treat her as though she's an ordinary child and she'll be alright."

I don't know if she'd been alright. I don't even know if there had been any psychologist or any such conversation. In a way, it sounds invented, invented and believed in. But maybe Sally figures the way around the unhappy childhood problem is to propagate no further childhoods. Still, why can't she just tell the kid to kill the tube now or she'll knock his fucking block off.

Sally disappears into the bedroom, no sound from Sally, but Pumpkin says no several times, each time louder. The TV goes off, there is a scream, Sally returns with crayons and a coloring book, time to develop some manual dexterity, Sally is so quiet and self-possessed I think she is going to scream, go ahead I want to say, scream, let it out, you and the kid can both scream, come on! I'll scream, too. Let's break everything in the house. Start with the dishes. But no, another concerned parent for discreet TV viewing comes out of the bedroom, heads off to the kitchen for ginger ale, must keep up the fluids, no TV, plenty of crayons....

The kid comes to the door, crayons clenched tightly, he glowers at me. I shrug. "See, it's frustration. You want something—TV, gratification—and you can't have it. I understand." The kid glares at me. I shrug again. "It won't do any good. I don't make the policies here." Il Duce glares at me in his Bugs Bunny pajamas, turns smartly on his heel, and storms back into the bedroom.

Sally seems to be hunting around for something, she's on her hands and knees, she's standing on chairs, has her nose in cabinets.

"What?"

"Oh, the coloring book's too confining for him, he wants to do something big—a mural."

Shelf paper. Guernica coming up. She sits on the edge of the bed, gets him arranged, finally kisses him, she's walking back toward me.

"Mom?"

"What is it, Pumpkin?"

"What should I draw?"

She sighs. They debate this for some time, and finally it is Pumpkin himself who suggests he might draw something about Texas. Sally sits down and gives me the frozen smile, the wedding smile, as if to say, you understand, you know how it is, and in a way, I guess I do, he's just a kid, he must be having a tough time, Texas and back, the separation and impending divorce, I understand, sure, but Sally looks so drained by all of this, isn't there some other way; her shoulders sag, her skin is actually gray, her hair hangs limp and falls forward like a cowl, covering most of her face. She doesn't bother to push it back.

We sit for a few minutes, and I keep involuntarily reading the titles of her books. C.S. Lewis and all that hot air. Finally, I make an effort and tear my eyes away. Outside, through the trees, I can see Red Rock, a raw outcropping left after the glacier sliced through here. The yard is overgrown with weeds, a rusty clothesline with plastic rope angles toward a peeling fence, an orange cat picking his way through the weeds stops, listens and raises his head, listens, and continues on. I sigh.

"Sally, what happens now?"

"I don't know," she says softly.

I'm thinking: *Dear Sally*/Why didn't you stay in Texas where *I needed you to be...*

"You could do a lot of things with the Ph.D. And the law degree."

"Not really."

God, dare I ask her why not really. Four years for the Ph.D., another writing a thesis, three more for the LL.B., not really? She's done more time than a convict.

She shakes her head. Her voice is soft, tense, her face pinched. The hair hangs forward and she says, "Please...I don't know, I don't know."

I hear overtones of the peculiar accent which once cost her a legal aid job. A friend of hers had been at the meeting after the interview and reported the question of her accent had come up. What was that accent? No one talks like that in Mamaroneck. Would the clients understand the accent? Poor? Mostly black? It was decided that they would not. This accent can come and go mysteriously.

"I don't know." She sounds adamant.

I want to reach over and put my arm around her and say, "Alright, Sally, alright," but everything is misinterpreted. Beyond that, there is Pumpkin, and he might really misinterpret. It's just that she is sitting over there, she looks cold, freezing, actually, her hand rests on her stomach, and she seems to be in real physical pain. And the way her hand rests on her stomach—tenderly, tentatively, as though her fingertips have ears and are listening to something growing, spreading inside.

"You remember, I tried working for that law firm...." She trails off.

"There must be others."

Before she can answer, the kid calls out, "MOM."

"What is it?"

"Come look."

"In a minute, sweetheart."

"Now."

She gets up slowly, and staring bleakly ahead, she walks into the bedroom. A couple of half-hearted exclamations, a big kiss, and she's back.

I say, "Well, how are you going to get along?"

"Unemployment."

I'm not sure what it means, but lately I have heard a small voice in me saying, "It's not that you can't find work, it's that you are unemployable." I almost blurt it out, "Sally, you and I, we are unemployable." But I don't. I start a short letter.

Dear Sally,

Look around you—up, down, to the sides. Reach out your hand. Take something, anything. It's being offered. This is your time, blacks, women, Indians, you could have anything your heart desires. Anything. Sally, don't be afraid, don't question, it's your due, your historical moment being served up on a platter, you're all like Columbus returning to Spain, treasure ships filled with guilt and reproach, you can have anything. Take something. Everything you can get. You can't go on refusing forever.

But I can't hit Sally with this avalanche. Unmailed letter. We don't say anything. From the next room, the table groans once. The kid's pressing hard. She says in a tentative voice, "Jack, do I look somehow different to you?"

This is very unlike Sally. She is not vain and has a kind of common-sense approach tempered with some scruples from women's consciousness raising groups about looks.

"Different from before you went to Texas?"

"Yes, I guess so. Just somehow different."

She has her fat phases, thin phases, pinched, soft and inaudible phases, she waxes and wanes haggish and beautiful, but now she looks just awful. Beyond phases. Is that somehow different?

"Well, do you feel different?"

Her glasses catch the dull light from the window, glint.

"I don't know."

"What do you mean, you don't know? Do you or don't you feel different?"

She's holding her hands tightly in her lap. "My body feels far away. You look far away, too."

Then the hand resting tentatively on the stomach, the fingertips listening.

"I'm not far away. I'm here. Right here. Maybe you have what the kid has."

"I took my temperature; it's normal."

I decide to lie. Definitely. Someone has to draw the line somewhere. "You look a little tired, that's all. But not different." I peer out of the corner of my eye. What's the kid up to? The kid is bent over his table, ass in the air, face almost touching the paper, consummating his drawing. Sally looks inconsolable. "Sally, you're worried about the kid, aren't you?"

"Not really. Tony and I both agreed Scott is better with me now. He'll visit Tony during vacations."

"That's it?"

"Not exactly. I've agreed to give him up at adolescence." She drifts off. "It's good for a boy to be near his father at that time in his life though it will be awful for me."

"Sally, you're talking as though your life's over. You'll meet someone else. Maybe have another kid or two. Come on. You're only thirty-four."

"Another kid . . ." she says softly. Thinks of something, shakes her head. "I'll stick to our agreement when the time comes. I have a couple of friends who wanted to be with one parent or the other at some point in their lives, but they couldn't be. You know, it still poisons their lives. I won't stand in his way, no matter how lonely I'll be."

She stares into the overgrown yard. A hint of deepening emotion in her voice. "Maybe it's the divorce, but lately I've been thinking a lot about how the law applies to children. A professor referred to it several times in lectures. Children's law. We have all these assumptions and do all these things to children and they have no say whatsoever in what happens to them . . . do you know they're the only group in our society that has no rights or representation?"

Sally looks a little wild-eyed behind her glasses. I think of all these children going out and hiring attorneys. The kid. Pumpkin. Pumpkin could hire a lawyer whenever Sally makes him turn off the TV and color.

Sally is saying something about our philosophical assumptions regarding children, we're pre-Declaration of Independence, worse, medieval. . . .

Philosophical assumptions. It's going to be another ten years in school somewhere, five years of philosophy laying the groundwork for five years of specialized law.

"Sally, that's a great idea, go ahead and practice children's law." Anything to get her out of that chair.

"I should probably go back to school to check out some fine points."

"No, Sally, no more school. Just do it. You're ready."

Her eyes vague over. Layers of nervous silence enshroud us, the air goes stale in the room. I think I want to get out of here now. Come back another day when we're both feeling better. Yes, I cross and uncross my feet. Yes.

"Mom!"

Sally winces. "Yes, Pumpkin."

"Come look, it's finished. Everybody! Come look."

Everybody. Me, too? I glance over at Sally. Sally nods. We troop in. The kid sits back from the drawing. Surveys it. The drawing is huge. Maybe five feet across. Mostly yellow with red undercurrents pulsing through it. As a matter of fact, except for one corner about the size of a palm, which is pale blue, the whole piece of paper is yellow. Sally smiles uneasily.

"No people?"

"Not this time, Mom."

The longer I stare at this drawing, the more uneasy I feel. The picture, whatever it is, seems to be pulsing with a kind of direct, unmitigated force. Sally must be feeling it, too. She has a funny gesture of working her sleeve down into her palm with her fingertips when she is not delighted about things, and she is doing so now. The kid looks up at her.

"Don't you know what it is, Mom?"

"No."

"Guess!"

Sally's voice. Very soft. "I don't think I can guess. Let's see what else you can do? How about some people and animals this time. You always were a terrific people and animal drawer." Sally reaches to turn the picture over. The kid presses it flat with both palms.

"Guess!"

I stare at this huge pulsing yellow thing with its red undercurrents. I kind of wish it would go away. Sally looks a little light-headed and out of focus.

"I can't guess. I think I'm going in the other room now, Pumpkin."

"The sun! Remember, it was going to be about Texas! The sun."

Sally, an intake of breath, working the sleeve into her palm.

"Yes, Scott."

"Can we put it up?"

Sally doesn't answer. Finally she says weakly, "Maybe tomorrow. Let's see what else you can do."

The kid looks at her oddly, hesitates, glances at the dark TV, and starts a new drawing with several stabbing motions.

Wondering what Sally is going to do, I leave her staring into the overgrown yard.

What Sally does is: Sally takes a lover. Klaus. That's the way Sally would think of it. I have taken a lover. The early Sixties, Jules Feiffer lady, kicking off her Guatemalan sandals. Ta Dum. I have taken a lover. Flower petals. Ta Dum. No, Sally has no real Ta Dums in her now. Small ta dum. Klaus is the geometry teacher and soccer coach at one of the local high schools. Long before he turned up on Sally's doorstep, I noticed him jogging through the neighborhood in the snow, teeth clenched, blue eyes narrowed into the distance. Fingertip push-ups on the frozen ground in the park. Gasps of exasperation as he sidestepped people laden with grocery bags, walking dogs, and so on. Serious training going on here, out of my way, blighters!

We meet not long after Klaus' BMW comes to be more or less permanently and constantly in a state of disassembly beneath Sally's window. Klaus leaving, myself coming in. Klaus, reddish-blond hair, beard carefully trimmed, shoulders self-consciously squared. Klaus, with thick-soled boots. High heels built up in layers. An edge, I must have an edge on other men! A streak of engine grease below one eye. As we meet, Sally lightly touches Klaus' sleeve, one of those secret reassuring gestures. I don't think Klaus is much reassured. He looks me up and down, sniffs the air, offers his hand: Hand. Here it is. My hand. Against my better judgement, I give him my hand. Klaus does exactly what I expect. He tries to crush my hand.

His clothes, his hair, his beard emanate the explosive smell of gasoline. He sniffs at me again. Is he going to drop to all fours, sniff my cuffs, piss on my leg? Chemistry. We hate each other on sight. I believe in chemistry. Chemistry, sympathetic identification, a spark of antagonism—the big three.

There's not much point in my wondering what Sally sees in this little martinet. I can see she's got the chemistry and a real blaze of antagonism. I don't say anything to her, but deep inside, I sense there is something about her attraction to Klaus which embarrasses her.

But not for me, Sally, I want to say. I do wonder a little. Does he wear his boots to bed, those soles thick as burned pork chops? Does he make her wear a spiked collar, walk her around on a choke chain? Maybe as a kind of foreplay, he should tie her up and burn her books, page by page, A—C, C through...

I start another letter.

Dear Sally,

We're like animals in a movie about Africa. Here we all are in our camouflage roaming the veldt of love, you, me, Klaus, the kid, Tony in Texas. Sometime, sometime, we must all come out, sunset, sunrise, and drink at that dangerous water hole, tenderness, drink long and deep, ears cocked, flanks exposed. Sally, punishment is not necessary for love, is it? You can be who you are. Just reach out and take a little, you are all so bleak in this miserable, single-parent house....

I abandon this effort and decide to dig out the Texas letters. The handwriting has a reduced, carefully formed look, almost as if written with a sewing needle dipped in black ink, not a drop spilled. I read the letters over several times, close my eyes, and float into the hot white light of Texas. Heat rising in waves. Shimmering. Suddenly, the pulsing yellow field, the kid looking up at us, Sally and me, it's the sun! and Sally making that gesture with her fingertips and sleeves.

"Day and night," writes Sally, "everywhere, the sound of air conditioners. Incredible as it may seem, I am freezing here."

I thumb another letter. Read:

...wrecked the car, Tony was absolutely furious. I can't blame him. I still don't know what happened. One moment, I'm driving along, next thing, I'm hanging upside down from my seat belt, every single window is shattered, the sunlight is shimmering through the splintered glass. Of all things, my only thought looking at all that shattered glass is how absolutely beautiful. Like being under a mountain stream. Somewhere far away, I smell gas. It is lovely. I feel peaceful. Almost happy. I'm completely unhurt. A cop kneels down beside the car and tells me not to worry, he'll have me out in a minute. I don't want him to have me out in a minute. I'd like him to go away and leave me alone. I feel peaceful. Almost as though I'm falling asleep. But instead of telling him to go away, I smile, upside down, and say, thank you very much.

I start looking for the letter about Sally's interview with the lady lawyer. As far as I know, this was her last attempt to find a law job. I find the letter and scan it.

Sally writes she can barely keep her mind on anything. She stumbles into furniture. Walls. Doors. She trips. As she is getting dressed, she notices bruises—black-and-blue marks. She finds her way to a huge office building. Inside, it is freezing. Why doesn't she ever remember to bring sweaters? She has goose pimples. Aren't these people freezing? Why do they keep it so cold indoors? She gets off the elevator, walks to a window. Fingertips on the bronzed glass. Cold. Sunlight pouring down on the city, beyond the skyline, the plains. She finds her way to the suite. Is shown into a beautiful office, thick rugs, mahogany desk, beautiful furniture, beautiful paintings, it is all so beautiful, do people really work here? A woman comes out from behind the desk. Middle-aged, dark-haired. She is wearing rings. Bracelets which jingle softly. A massive necklace. Sally can see a picture on her desk, but she can't see who is in the picture. It is angled away.

I stop skimming and read:

> . . . she stares at me, takes my hand, holds it, and looks me in the eye a long time. Finally, she smiles and says in a soft voice, "Ah, you're a witch, too." Then she sat me down and we talked a long time. I can't remember what we talked about. I remember the sun moving. All the time I kept wondering if she had really said that, the sun moved on the wall behind her. I could see it moving. Onto her desk. I kept wanting to ask her, but my tongue felt so far away. Oily and small and dark. Like an olive pit. I must

have said things to her, but all I remember is the sun coming slowly across the rug and wondering if I would leave before it touched my feet. She was close to me, all of her jewelry shining and ringing softly. Her voice was soft, too. I couldn't keep my mind on anything. I almost asked her if she would mind terribly if I lay down on the sofa for a few minutes. But I didn't. The sun kept inching toward me across the rug. Back at home I realized we had never said a word about law. Not that I could remember. I don't think she ever even considered me for the job. In a way, I found it hard to believe any of this had actually taken place. I kept walking into furniture, knocking things over. I found myself in front of the mirror. I took off all my clothes. I was covered with black-and-blue marks. When? Where? I kept hearing her voice. It was so soft. Ah, you're a witch, too. I looked in the mirror and thought, am I turning into one of those women?

One of those women? I stare at the thin handwriting.

Sally goes on having her love affair with Klaus. I never say anything to Sally, though sometimes I feel her waiting.

It's been a couple of weeks since I've last seen her. She seems completely preoccupied. Suddenly, she is up out of her chair. After several moments, I begin to understand.

" ...I can not, I will not go back to these old, possessive monogamous relationships. If it means being alone, then I'll be alone." She cuts the air with the side of her hand. "Over. Done. I will not let the dictates of my body run my life. I simply will not."

Sally whirls. Suddenly she is glaring at me and defending Klaus. I have not said a word about Klaus, now or ever, but she is defending him to me. Did I know that there was a lot more to Klaus than I saw or wanted to give him credit for? That Klaus was sensitive? Artistic?

I groan and watch Sally rant around, glasses flashing, hair flying. I stare up at the ornamental door molding. I start a short letter. After a moment, start over, addressing it to myself:

Dear Jack,

Everyone in this house has the disease. I don't know what the disease is, but everyone here used to be married to someone else or used to do something else and wants to do something else or simply refuses to do what he/she can do. Everyone writes for the counter-culture paper—Klaus, film criticism, Sally, fillers on anti-nuke stuff—everyone wants to be an artist, potter, poet, everyone understands children and carries on these very intense adult relationships with these kids—maybe they'd just like to be left as kids. No one can make up his mind about anything, everyone pauses weightily to speak and finally mines his/her sentences with alternate this and viable that. Everyone refuses—perversely, arbitrarily, refuses—the verb is intransitive here because refusal seems to be the pure liquid oxygen of assertion for its own sake, will as pure will....

Sally stops, grabs her stomach, sinks into her chair, drops her head, takes several deep breaths. She's pale. "Sally?" She doesn't move. She holds her stomach. "Sally..." I'm out of my chair. "What is it?" She doubles up a little more. "I have a friend who's a doctor. I'm going to call him."

"No, Jack."

"He lives near here, he's a good guy. He won't mind coming over." I start dialing.

"Jack, put the phone down. I don't need a doctor. I know what it is." She hesitates. "I had an abortion a few days ago. The last one I'll ever have." I stop dialing. "Please put the phone down, Jack."

I put the phone down. Stand beside her chair. Awkwardly, I put my hand on her shoulder. "I'm sorry, Sally."

She reaches up and squeezes my hand lightly. Doesn't say anything. Drops her hand.

"What do you mean, the last one you'll ever have?"

"It was enough. Enough. I had it done."

"It?" Sally stares at the floor. "It? Done? You mean, you

had ... no, no. You're too young. Your tubes ... tied?"

Sally hesitates. Softly. "Not tied. Burned."

"Burned?"

"That's what they do. Burn them." Sally touches her abdomen. "They make a small incision here and here. Really, it's very simple, then they ... "

"Stop! I don't want to hear it!" Suddenly, I grab a handful of books and wave them. "Sally, you are not turning into one of those women. You were not. Are not! Fat, thin, loud, soft, all of your dodging and feinting, you're not a witch. That woman, the lawyer in Texas ... " She looks up startled. "No, I'm not clairvoyant, you wrote me about her, you yourself, how she said you're a witch, too, that's why you won't do anything. If you just sit here, maybe it won't happen."

"Oh, nonsense," she says, both stricken and uncertain.

"Not only won't do anything, but run out and get your tubes ... That woman in Texas, for all you know, it was some Lesie mind-fuck...."

"You should hear yourself, whenever men don't understand something about women, they shout *lesbian*."

"Okay, she sure was right, you're a witch. Beat me around the ears with a rolled-up *Ms.* magazine."

"Please, Jack."

I sink back in the chair. "I'm sorry, Sally. Look, you and I are unemployable. I may work at things, but I am unemployable. I needed you to be my Scheherazade of the Sun Belt, voice of the New West. I needed a message. A clue. I was depending on you. We're both Martians; I was figuring if you could make it out of whatever we're in ... "

"Anyone could?"

"No, Sally, I needed you to stick it out. I needed your letters. I was looking for a clue."

"That's right, women who go away and change have always fascinated you. Your medium to yourself. How obtuse of me to forget, what was the name of that woman who left you and went to Hong Kong, you used to read me sections of her letters, you started to believe you were really in love with her only after she'd written and said she could look off and see mainland China—Red China—lying low in the distance. You loved that *low in the distance.* She had you there. What was her name, anyway?"

"I forget."

"You do remember the *low in the distance?*"

"Stop it, Sally."

"I'm sorry. What is it, Jack?"

"I don't know." We sit in silence. I notice the way her hand rests on her stomach and look away. "Sally, how could you do that...?"

Sally looks at me almost sympathetically. "I think men tend to get more emotional about these things than women. We're always being stuck on examining tables and poked and peered into. Gloves. Fingers. Jack, you're just not a woman."

"No kidding."

"You can't understand."

"Anything but that, Sally. Beat me soundly around the ears with a rolled-up *Ms.* magazine. Anything. Please."

"Look, I had to keep myself from letting it happen again. Pregnancies aren't really just accidents. Part of me always wants pregnancy—always. My body. This time I just couldn't let it have its way."

"Right now, Sally, you, talking to me, are you the one that wants pregnancy always?"

"The me talking to you now? I don't know, Jack."

"Or are you the one who has to prevent the other?"

"I don't know." Her voice fading. "I don't know."

I have an urge to see the kid. I get up blindly and walk into his room. Shadowy. The kid sleeping. Toys underfoot. I look down, listen to his breathing. Sally beside me. We look down at the kid sleeping. I reach out and touch his hair. He stirs in his sleep. Moans something. For a moment, I think maybe I might want to hold this kid, make friends with him.

Outside, I squint in the light. I turn and put my arms around Sally. She presses her face against my chest. I hold her. I want to say something, but I don't know what. I just hold her a moment more and leave without a word.

* * *

Winter comes. *One Step Back, One Step Sideways* house is always drafty, all of the children get colds, give them to each other, the parents. Someone's always sniffing or coughing or bringing someone a foul-tasting herb from the food co-op, drink it, it'll be good for you.

It is a long hard winter and perhaps I'm not as good a friend to Sally as I might be—or wish to be, but I don't see her for weeks at a time. Part of it is the kid. There seems to be such a tug-of-war with the kid. And something familiar about him, which I can't seem to get over.

Then it is spring. Suddenly. It's rained the night before, one of those cold, incomprehensible rains that make the flowers come up anyway. Everything smells fresh, the sky is filled with puffy, white cumulous clouds, dirigibles, faces, wonderful things aloft. When the sun is out, it's warm, though with a chill in the air. I decide to see Sally.

As I approach the house, I hear sudden laughter. Wild. Delighted. I look toward the overgrown yard. Nothing. The laughter seems to be outside here with me, in the grass, the trees, the air. I glance about uncertainly. Some of the trees have started to leaf, a tender green, the color breath would be if it were green. Another burst of laughter. I glance along the side of the house. The porch. Nothing. On one side of the house, a window is open. I walk toward the window.

I can see the children. They are lined up on the sofa, sitting in chairs, they are wearing party hats, and they are looking up, eyes wide, expectant. Scott is there in his Bugs Bunny T-shirt, Bugs with a rogue's grin and a chomped-off carrot; the kid's eyes are bright, his mouth is half open. He is delighted. There is a birthday cake on the table, candles unlit, the cake with a large red eight on it, a color red I recall loving when I was a kid. Real red. The adults stand back and to one side, pasty-faced, circles under their eyes; it's been a long winter, and they too watch whatever it is, though with only traces of faint amusement and pleasure. I don't see Sally among them. I come closer to the window. The children's eyes jump, all at the same moment, like sparks. A flash of red silk, an empty hand offered, suddenly a rabbit in the hand. I can't believe my eyes. I burst out laughing. The children laugh, they bounce in their seats, their hands come to their mouths, they gasp, laugh, jump up, point at something. "It's in the other hand, the other! Show us the sleeve, the sleeve!" First one, then the other empty sleeve is offered in the window. From out here, I peer up the sleeves. Nothing. Wonderful.

Inside, the frontier kitchen—the large glass jars, OATS... I stand in the kitchen doorway, glance in the living room, which is crammed with children. The magician stands by the old upright piano in his black tuxedo. A couple of the people in the house wave at me. I glance around. Sally? I walk through the kitchen to her room. Empty. Not in the kid's room, either. I walk back to the living room, shrug, lip out, "Where's Sally?"

Someone waves, points vaguely toward the ceiling. I back uncertainly through the kitchen, spot a dark doorway I hadn't noticed before. The magician has started another trick. I can hardly tear myself away. I step into the doorway. A back staircase. So narrow my shoulders almost brush the walls. Several times I lose my balance on warped steps, and once my foot comes down on a toy.

At the top, I duck my head for the low ceiling. The house has settled deeply to one side. "Sally."

A sudden burst of laughter wafts up the dark staircase. I step back toward the first doorway, look in. Sally sits on the edge of a narrow cot which is pushed against the wall. Chill white light from one low window. She has worked both her sleeves down into her palms, she seems to be hugging herself. "Sally?"

Silver glints from the part in her black hair as she glances up. I step toward her, the floor is so warped I almost lose my balance. Reach up suddenly, afraid I am going to hit my head on the low sloped ceiling. "What are you doing here by yourself?"

She stares at the floor. "Sally?" She hugs herself harder. "Come on, let's go down." I glance around the room. "It's chilly up here."

A sudden burst of laughter beneath our feet—high, crazy, delighted. Sally seems to be shrinking in the laughter, huddled in an icy wind. "Let's go downstairs."

Another burst of laughter beneath the floor wafts up the stairs, the children shout something in unison, I can't quite make it out.

"Come on, Sally, we'll go down and watch the magic."

Sally tries to look up, manages to shake her head. "I hate magic." I can hardly hear her as the children stamp their feet. "I have always hated magic." Her eyes are dark and flickering with fright.

"Sally . . ." I don't really know what to say to her. I cross over. "Sally, it's not so bad." She is hugging herself. I gently reach down and pry one of her arms free from her side. She resists, but not hard. I take her hand. It's cold. I warm it between my hands. Her hair falls forward so her face is hidden.

I pull her up gently from the bed and lead her to the door. She follows a step at a time, her hair hanging over both sides of her face. Down the narrow stairs. In the kitchen, the laughter and shouting is louder. I glance toward the kitchen; the magician is pulling coins from the children's noses and ears. The children gape, burst out laughing. I gape. Sally is staring at the floor, hair hanging forward, face averted. I squeeze her hand. Cold. I lead her outside.

In the yard, we pass the window. I glance up and watch the magician's back, his hands moving, objects floating in and out of his hands, appearing and disappearing in the air. We walk around the side of the house, the children's laughter fades, I put my arm around Sally as she stumbles, no idea where we are going, past the front of the house, down the walk. The sun goes behind a cloud, chill, then dapples the walk again, another burst of laughter, applause, something shouted in unison, I can't make it out.

I push Sally's hair back out of her eyes, off her face, she keeps her eyes on the walk. There is a park near here, Red Rock Park, a softball diamond and some swings. We wander in that direction, my arm around Sally, half supporting her as she stumbles from time to time.

We come to the park, wander toward the softball diamond, just vague dirt paths. Somewhere between the mound, which is a puddle, and second base, we come to a stop and seem to kneel, sink, lie down, myself on my back, Sally with her head on my chest, the way lovers and friends all over the world have always gone to sleep. I cradle her head gently against my chest, lie back, back, close my eyes.

Overhead, Red Rock seems to spin against the clouds, the clouds aimless and gentle. Faces. Dirigibles. My eyes close under the warmth of the sun, the ground with winter still going to sleep, chilly against my back. I feel Sally's hair warm under my fingers; my eyelids thicken, Red Rock above us, I doze, recall in the last century a hermit who lived somewhere up there in a cave. He started building a boat. Occasionally, someone would straggle up from town and ask him how he was going to get the boat down, but he never answered. Maybe it's still up there. I don't know. Anyway, from the top of Red Rock you have a nice view of the ocean, it's a thin line and shines blue-silver like a razor blade on the horizon. Now high-school kids pull their cars precariously close to the edge, park, and the braver ones scale the cliffs and spray-paint their graduating class, declarations of love, and obscenities on the rock face.

I feel Sally start to relax, perhaps doze. I smooth her hair, say softly, "Everything's alright, Sally," though I don't know what everything is, or if it's alright, but in some way, it is, it's not a lie, even with the vague terrible knowing that the stars are shining right now behind the blue sky. Sally's breath deepens slightly, she says something I can't make out. I feel her breathe on my fingertips, we doze, drift. I suddenly feel her jerk, stiffen. I open my eyes. Blinded. So bright. Sense someone standing close, I hear Sally's voice, very soft, almost inaudible. "What is it, Pumpkin?"

My eyes focus. Hands on his hips, he looks down at us. The Bugs Bunny T-shirt. An ice cream stain. She raises her head from my chest. "Pumpkin?"

Above us, the trees, laced with their tender green capillaries, seem to be spinning. My eyes ache in the bright sunlight. I pull myself up slowly, grass and chill mud stains on my knees and elbows. I pull Sally up. We kneel; the kid, between us, is our height. The kid is staring at us, his eyes hot and blurry with hurt and reproach. She touches the kid's hair and starts to talk softly. I want to say something, I am no longer angry. I really don't know why I have been so angry with this kid, but I don't know what to say. I feel as though I am standing both inside and outside, looking at him, looking at us.

Sally goes on talking, but he just stares at me. I see the vast ballpark, Red Rock spinning above us, the trees spinning against the clouds. It is all in motion and beautiful, familiar.

Suddenly I hear myself say the kid's name, softly, and feel a kind of sadness and longing. I put my hand on his small shoulders, and he stiffens, but doesn't pull back. I don't know what to say, but I feel an ache in my throat. I stand. He looks up at me. There is a question on his face. I smile, take his hand. He doesn't exactly take my hand, hold it back, but he doesn't refuse, either. After a moment, Sally stands and, together, we turn and walk slowly across the diamond.

Desert Light

G RACE REACHED THE AMTRAK STATION a few minutes late and
parked in a red zone. Most of the passengers had already
drifted away, and Grace walked quickly, looking for her younger
sister. She had reached the far end of the platform when Jackie
came out of the ladies' room and sat down on a bright red
suitcase. Grace waved. "Jackie!" Jackie looked up and before she
saw Grace, she smiled. Grace would later remember Jackie's
face in that moment—the late-morning, desert light of June, the
brilliant blue eyes with their struck gaze, almost as if they were
a natural element, water or sky, her blond good looks. She
walked toward Jackie, and they kissed.

Grace patted the suitcase. "Is this all?"

"Well, it's only going to be two months, right?" She smiled.
"It's summer. Shorts, a couple of dresses..."

Changing off carrying the suitcase, they walked toward the
car. As Jackie slid it into the back seat, two men turned to look
at her beautiful legs. In the car, she fanned herself. "You said it
would be hot."

Grace pointed up at the bank: the temperature against the
blue sky and glare. 103. She looked over at Jackie. "It's the
desert."

"Don't worry about me, it was hot at home."

Grace pulled into traffic. "What were you doing?"

"Oh, I was working part-time for a caterer. Taking a couple of courses toward finishing school. And I was seeing Tom. He's so nice...." Her voice trailed away in a lack of interest. "Did you ever meet Tom?"

"I'm not sure. Blond. Kind of pleasant. Law school. That the one?"

Jackie nodded. "He felt bad when I left, but I just needed to go...I don't think he understood, really." Her eyes went vague. "He was starting to talk about getting married. But it wasn't that. I just had to go." Jackie wiped the sweat from her hairline.

"We can take a swim later."

Jackie said in a far-off voice, "That'll be nice. Just a shower would be nice. It seemed like a long train ride. The desert was endless once we left L.A. I kept watching it in the moonlight. Beautiful, like water, but so white and endless. I was glad to see the mountains rise up this morning before we reached Tucson."

As they drove, Grace interrupted to point out restaurants, main streets, neighborhoods. She looked over in the middle of a sentence to see Jackie staring at her. "Grace. You look so beautiful."

"Well, thank you."

"No, I really mean it. Your hair's shiny and thick, your skin has a glow." She shook her head. "You always were the beautiful one."

"Oh, you got your share. Lisa. Annie. All of us."

"I remember the way you looked the night you were the Winter Queen senior year and went out in that white formal. Chet Davis came for you wearing a tuxedo."

Grace laughed. "High school. Chet Davis." She shook her head. Jackie must have been eleven. "You remember that?"

Jackie nodded. "Whatever happened to Chet?"

"Last I'd heard, he'd been sent to a detox place. I haven't seen him in years."

Jackie said, "You love Michael, don't you? You have a good marriage." Grace nodded. "Maybe things work out for people. I got the idea you went through some hard times before you met Michael." She shook her head and smiled. "But what am I saying? That's really none of my business." The smile remained, and Grace recalled that it was winning until it became a response to everything.

She turned out of traffic onto a quieter street lined with eucalyptus and mesquite, many of the houses a blend of Spanish mission style—red Mexican tiles, white stucco. In another minute, they swung into a drive. "This it?"

"This is it."

Inside, Jackie stopped in the front hall, then walked slowly into the living room. She looked at the tile floor. The house was cool, and there was a feeling of order and quiet balance. She looked at Grace's framed photographs, drew a book from the shelves. "Oh, Frank Lloyd Wright. I've heard of him." She walked to a sliding glass door; outside, a closed courtyard green with plants in large Mexican pots—red blooming hibiscus, Florida oleander, broad leafed philodendron. The plants had just been watered, and Jackie's face lit with the soft green and watery reflection from puddles. "Beautiful," she said softly.

"Here, I'll show you your bedroom."

A few minutes later, when Grace returned with a towel, Jackie was already in the shower. As she put the towel on the chair, she noticed a worn black Bible creasing the bedspread. Grace picked it up, held it, and then put it back in its crease.

After she'd said goodnight to Jackie, Grace closed their bedroom door and started sorting clothes; stretched on the bed, Michael thumbed a magazine. She turned from the closet and said in a lowered voice, "Michael, I think I'm a little worried about leaving Jackie alone in the house." Michael looked up at her. "I don't know what it is. There's something, young, vulnerable—I'm not sure what word to use—about her."

"How old is she now? Twenty-four?"

"Twenty-five."

"Well, come on, Gracie."

"Maybe I'm just used to thinking of her as a little sister. Except for a few visits home, I really haven't seen her in years. I left when she was eleven."

"Well, she's not eleven. And lots of women live alone. You were living alone when we met." He smiled at her. "Can you remember back that far? Three whole years."

"I remember. We didn't sleep the first four weeks." They smiled at the recollection. Grace said, "But this is different. For one thing, I was older, twenty-nine."

Michael smiled. "Grace ... "

"Okay, it's not age, it's just that I've always known something."

"You've always said that and I've always asked you what and you can never explain it. Just that you've always known something."

She nodded. "Some awareness."

"Right, you know something no one else in your family knows. Oh, and you were the love child of the family," he said in a playful voice.

"That, too."

"What were the other sisters? Accidents?"

"I know that by the time my mother got around to having Jackie and Lisa, she was tired. Exhausted. And maybe I've imagined this, but I have the idea she wasn't there for them the way she'd been for Annie and me."

Michael sighed. "Well ... "

"Oh, it'll be alright, Michael. I don't know what I'm reacting to. Probably just that I'm used to thinking of her as my eleven-year-old sister. She said she wanted to get away for a while. She'll house-sit for us, she'll get a summer job here, she'll be fine."

Grace went on sorting things in her closet. From beyond the window screen, the soft smell of the garden and cooling desert beyond—creosote, dust—drifted out of the dark.

Grace spent the next few days organizing the house. She went through personal papers and locked them in a filing cabinet; she kept adding to a list of people that Jackie might call. She introduced her to neighbors and made a watering schedule for the plants and yard. Jackie circled ads for summer jobs and made a few calls, but nothing definite panned out. By mid-afternoon the temperature would be over a hundred, the sky a silvery blue glare, and they would lose their momentum and go down to the University pool for a swim. Later, they'd run a few more errands. Just before leaving, Michael helped Jackie buy a used ten-speed bike. And then, perhaps in deference to the uneasiness Grace had voiced, he added several extra locks to side windows which were hidden by oleander. On the fourth morning after Jackie arrived, Grace and Michael left for San Francisco.

A few days passed and Grace called Jackie. Was she comfortable? Did she feel safe? She was fine. The house was so peaceful, it was just what she needed. Some day she'd live in a house like this. She was a little lonely, but a person had to have faith. She'd found a job in a hotel restaurant downtown and was busy. It was very hot—a couple of days it had been 114—but she was keeping everything watered; the courtyard was so beautiful, she just loved to come home and look out at the plants. It was a little world back there, like the green heart of the house.

Grace gathered from small things Jackie said in the next few weeks that something was happening with a man. After the phone calls, her sister's voice would come back to her like a muffled echo: his family is really nice; they like me and think I'm a good influence on Ruben; when he wants, Ruben can be one of the kindest, gentlest people in the world. Don't worry about me, Grace, everything's fine here. Grace didn't know what she heard in Jackie's voice. Something.

One night, just as she was falling asleep, the half statements and hesitations came clear, and Grace knew that the man, whoever he was, Ruben, was living in the house and that things were not alright. She sat up in bed and looked at the clock. Michael stirred. She went downstairs, closed the door, and called her sister. After a long time, Jackie answered. Grace tried a few awkward exchanges of small talk which didn't go with the late call, hesitated and then said, "Jackie, I've been thinking about some of the things you've been saying. I want the simple truth. This man you've mentioned, Ruben, is he living there with you in the house?"

There'd been a pause, and then Jackie said in a voice which rose and went hoarse, "No...no, why do you say that? He visits me, but he's not living here."

"Is he there now? Can you talk?"

Jackie said, "Uh huh. No. Not here."

And then Grace knew that he was there, that she couldn't talk, and from the tone of her voice, that she was afraid of something. "Okay, Jackie, I don't really know what's happened, I don't expect you to be an angel, but I did ask you not to have people staying there." Jackie didn't say anything. "Whoever he is, I want him out of our house. I can tell from your voice that something's wrong. Call me first thing in the morning when you're alone so we can talk. Do you understand?"

"Yes, okay. I will. I'm really sorry. It's hard to explain. Grace? Please don't be angry. I didn't really intend it to be this way. Somehow it just happened. I don't know. I just want..."

"Let's save it for tomorrow when you can talk freely. Okay? Call me."

"I will, Grace. I really will."

When Jackie didn't phone, Grace called her back, but there was no answer. She tried for several days and then she called the hotel restaurant. There, they said she had taken a short sick leave. Finally, Grace thought to call her mother in California. Yes, Jackie had been home for a couple of days, but then yesterday, a man had come to pick her up. Ruben. He was very nice—big, soft-spoken. Didn't say much. Nicely dressed. So neat. Clean. Looked a little like Jackie except that he had black hair. And with the bluest eyes. Something about the quiet evenness of her mother's voice infuriated Grace. Soft-spoken. Nicely dressed. Whatever was happening had been missed completely. Where'd they gone? Why, he'd come all the way up to get Jackie and driven her back to Tucson. They left a couple of hours ago. He'd gone to church with her just before starting out. Sunday service. Everyone thought he had such nice manners....

When Grace reached Jackie, she was back in the house. Grace said, "Jackie, I've been trying to get hold of you for days. You said you'd call me."

"I meant to. I just felt so bad about the whole thing. I needed to get away and think."

"You went home."

"Well..."

"You told me you left home so you could be alone and think. Then you went back home to think. Where can you think?"

"Grace! What is this?"

"I'm sorry. Look, all I asked you to do was call me. You said you would. You didn't. I've been worried."

"It didn't make me feel any better knowing you felt suspicious, asking if someone was here with me."

"I wasn't suspicious, I'd been listening to the things you were saying about this man and realized..."

"You know, Grace, some things you just don't understand." Jackie's voice rose, distraught and defiant. Just because it was her house didn't mean she had to pass judgement on the way she was living, after all, she was doing her a favor house-sitting, and you know, you lived with Jeff back when you were a twenty-year-old hippie, you did what you wanted—not in someone else's house, Jackie—and Mom cried that whole first year, now that you have some money and are married, everything's suddenly different for you, Ruben may not be an architect like Michael, people aren't calling him to come to San Francisco to work on design projects or whatever it is, okay, but he's still a good person, Ruben is trying hard, I know he can be better, I see the good in him, it's just that no one's ever really believed in him.... It went on. Grace was amazed. "Jackie, will you listen to me for one moment. Please."

"Go ahead."

"I can't come back right now. If you are comfortable staying in the house, I'd like you to stay. I really would. But I want this guy, whoever he is, whatever his shining virtues, out of my house! Do you understand?"

"Yes, but I just want to say..."

"Is he out of my house, Jackie?"

"Sort of. I mean, most of his things are."

"I want all of his things out. I've offered to pay your way home if that's what you want. I care about you. We've been on the phone an hour. What do I have to say or do? I am asking you to get this person out of my house. Please. I'll talk to you later." Grace hung up.

She debated talking to Michael about Jackie, but her pride made her hesitant; this was her sister, a situation of her making. And Michael could be unpredictable. She saw him, what? taking the next flight home. She called a neighbor and asked if there'd been a man with her sister, and after a lengthening pause Grace said, "It's okay, you can tell me." Norma described Ruben, big, neat, he was there all the time, added that two squad cars had been to the house late one night; no one knew what it was about. She added, "Beside the fact that I personally don't trust men who wear cologne, there's something about this guy that makes me very nervous."

Grace thought it over. She could call the sheriff to have him evicted, ask a lawyer for advice.... What was going on? Police in the middle of the night. File a restraining order? Days went by. She could fly back there. The thing was to get her sister safely extricated from the situation. What was the situation? She thought about it constantly, but no approach seemed right, and she realized in a couple of weeks they'd be going home.

When they returned in mid-August, Grace looked down at her sister's red suitcase in the front hall. There was the postcard she'd sent: their expected date of arrival—today. She walked into the living room. Something different, the light. Outside, in the courtyard, the plants were brown and shrivelled in their pots, the grass was dead. She turned as Jackie walked quickly out of the bedroom.

Jackie held up her hands, "Grace...wait, Grace, I know, I'll pay for it, just let me try to explain...." Something about her stopped Grace from speaking. A puffiness around her eyes, which were red, perhaps from crying, and tiny, almost lost.

"Jackie," Grace said softly.

Michael put down a suitcase behind her. He looked into the

courtyard. He looked at Grace and Jackie. He walked slowly through the house, returned.

Jackie said without hesitating, "Michael, there's no one I respect more than you."

Michael started to say something. His voice went hoarse, there was a leap of anger in his eyes. He broke off, turned and went out, Grace following. "I'm not going to ask you or her about this now, but please make sure she's gone by the time I get back." He got in the car and drove away.

Inside, Jackie sat at the kitchen table, her shoulders silently heaving. Grace put her hand on Jackie's back. Jackie let out a long strangled sob. "The look on Michael's face...I don't blame him." She felt Jackie's body trembling as she cried. Standing behind her, Grace stroked her hair. She could see the silted hasty strokes of a mop on the tiles at her feet. When she turned, something in the bookshelf caught her eye. She walked over and pulled out a design book, which split in two at the binding. Grace held the two halves. Jackie said, "Whatever I say, I just know that I can't... Grace, he's never been to college. He just kept looking at the books, so many books...." In the closed slats of the blind, dust drifted, secret, between thin blades of white sunlight. Grace opened the sliding glass door into the wall of baking heat. She stood Jackie's bike up. It's frame was sprung and twisted. Jackie shook her head. "Oh, please, it's like you're looking for things...can I tell the truth without always being judged?"

Grace said softly, "Is that the way you think it's been for you?"

"Gracie...I don't know...I came home a little late from the restaurant...the place was so busy...Ruben wouldn't listen. He was just so jealous. He went crazy; he smashed the bike with his weights. God, I know what you have to be thinking." Grace noticed the weight bench under the porch. The weights were gone. There were several deep gashes in a post supporting the porch. "Afterward, we read the Bible together; he felt so bad he was just about in tears."

"That made it alright?" Grace said in spite of herself.

"Inside, he's good. He really is."

At the distance between them, Grace felt an exhaustion overtake her. She eased the bike back down, looked up at the wilting Chinaberry; she extended a hose across the courtyard, watched the water gush over the roots. Inside, she said quietly, "So hard to do, Jackie?"

"I knew I'd never be able to explain."

Grace looked at her sister's face hidden in her hands. "No, go ahead, explain," Grace said quietly. "Is it judging you to say I don't understand?" Jackie shook her head. Grace looked at her sister's profile, her hair hanging. "Would you like to get away from this now?" Jackie nodded. She only seemed to be half listening. Grace said, "I'll talk to Michael and he'll calm down, but it would be better if you were gone before he gets back."

Jackie nodded. Grace picked up the phone and dialed an airline. As she asked for a schedule of flights, Jackie said, "Grace, Grace, hang up. Please." She looked down at the table. "I can't take the ticket."

"Why not?"

"I just can't." Jackie looked at Grace out of the corner of her eye. Her face was swollen from crying. She blurted, "I married him three days ago. He's coming by in a few minutes to get me."

Grace just stared at Jackie. She hung up the phone. Jackie began to sob again.

"Is that what you want? To be married to him?"

"I don't know, his family was so kind to me, they said I was good for him, I just felt under so much pressure...."

"Marriages can be annulled."

"Can it be?" Jackie asked hopefully.

"I'll call a lawyer. Why don't you just go lie down."

A horn sounded outside. Jackie stood. "I've got to go. That's him. I married him," she said as though that explained why she had to go.

"You don't have to do anything you don't want to! If he loved you, would he have pressured you like this?"

Grace looked out the front window, saw a dented Ford Fairlane burning oil at the curb. Someone in the driver's seat. When he spotted Grace in the window, he looked away. Jackie picked up her red suitcase and Bible in the front hall and wiping her face with her fingertips, she opened the door. "Please forgive me. I'll pay you back. I'm really sorry."

When she was halfway down the walk, Grace said, "Where are you going?"

"We've got a little place. His mother gave us the first month's rent."

Grace stepped outside. "I'll call the police if you're afraid of him. You're my sister. You don't have to do this. Come back inside, Jackie."

She shook her head. "I can't."

"Jackie, if there wasn't something dishonest, wouldn't he get out of the car and introduce himself, your new husband? Wouldn't you want to introduce him? Jackie?"

Jackie opened her mouth. She smiled a pained smile. "Grace, there's so much that's impossible to make anyone understand."

"I guess so. That's all you've said to me. What is it that no one can understand?"

Shaking her head and blinking quickly, Jackie walked out to the car. Ruben leaned over and opened the door. Jackie slid her suitcase onto the seat, got in. Without ever once looking Grace's way, Ruben stepped on the gas and turned the corner, the tires squealing. In the silence, Grace listened to the hot desert wind going through the eucalyptus overhead.

For the next few days, Grace cleaned the house. She pushed the living room and kitchen furniture onto the patio and scrubbed the tile floor. She vacuumed the rugs, washed the bathrooms, stripped the beds, and washed all of the sheets and towels. She scrubbed the counters and stove, ran the dishes through the dishwasher, and cleaned out the refrigerator. She made a list of things which were broken or needed replacing. Dishes. TV. Added small things which were missing.

She found herself talking about Jackie, the house, this man, Ruben, on and off for days, a broken monologue which she couldn't quite bring to an end. Michael listened, asked questions, listened, said as he finished lunch, "Grace, I feel sorry for Jackie, and when I get over my anger, I'll feel sorrier for her, but I don't want her in here again."

Grace nodded, "I understand. The thing is I know she's going to wake up in two weeks, get this thing annulled, and go home. One day she'll look back on this in disbelief."

Michael said, "Is it just some weird sex thing?"

Grace shook her head. "I don't know what it is."

"Because if it's that, why didn't she just lock herself in a room with him for a week and do whatever? Why'd she have to marry him?"

"Jackie always has that Bible with her and I remember now Mom said she had joined a Baptist church back home. I once heard Jackie say of a friend who'd gotten divorced, When you marry, you marry for life. That's the one thing that really scares me about this."

"Why couldn't she at least keep the plants watered?"

Grace shook her head, "I don't know, she's my sister, but I just don't know. I don't even know where she's gone to live."

Jackie appeared at the front door several weeks later. When Grace answered, Jackie smiled. "Hi, Gracie...I know you probably don't want to see me. I won't stay long." She wiped the sweat from her hairline.

"You walked?"

"Only from the bus stop."

"It's blazing out there. Come in and have some juice."

"No, that's okay. Well, water would be nice."

Jackie stayed in the front hall. Grace said, "Sit down."

"I can only stay a minute." Jackie reached into her jeans and pulled out several bills. One at a time, she untangled each from the pocket and placed them, crumpled, on the table. A ten. A twenty. A five. Several ones. "Thirty-seven dollars. I'll have more soon. I know it must be much more...just tell me.... How much do you think it will come to?"

Grace brought her a glass of ice water. "I don't know."

Jackie walked to the sink and fished out the ice. "I think ice is bad for you in heat." She drank the water. "Oh, you've been to the nursery. You've got new plants." Her face softened. "They look so good. Just tell me, how much were the plants?" Grace didn't say anything. "It's okay, Grace, I'm going to pay it all back. And Michael's books, too, of course."

"Jackie, let's not do this today. Some of the books are expensive and I know you don't have much money right now. Actually, I'm on my way out, let me give you a ride."

"I can hop the bus. I'm used to it."

"Come on. It's hot out there."

Grace drove Jackie back toward the downtown to a cluster of mission-style studios built in the Forties, off-white, dusty. From the curb, Grace could see a cracked pool green with algae. Ungroomed Mexican fan palms. A man in a red tank top sat in an iron porch chair and watched a couple of kids playing in the dirt. As they'd driven, Jackie asked Grace if she'd come in for a minute, but when she saw Ruben's Ford parked in front, she said, "Oh, he was supposed to be looking for a job...." She got out without saying anymore.

"Jackie." Jackie leaned back into the car. "Give me your phone number."

"We don't have a phone."

"You're still working at the restaurant downtown?" Jackie nodded. "I won't ask you why it's like this. But any time you need my help, call me. Please."

"I'm okay."

Grace said, "I love you."

Jackie's eyes went watery with tears, and she turned quickly from the window and walked toward the studio court.

Shortly after that Grace started getting phone calls from Jackie at all hours, phone calls from work, from pay phones. Sometimes she'd be crying; she'd start to explain something, break off, hang up. Sometimes she'd say I've got to leave him, but if Grace said something in support of Jackie, she would say, "Grace, why is it always this way? I call to talk and you end up criticizing my life, criticizing Ruben when you don't even know him...."

Grace would fall silent. "You've never brought him by and given me a chance to know him. He's never introduced himself."

"That's because I know—and he knows—you don't want to meet him. You won't give him a chance. Don't even pretend, Grace."

"A minute ago you were telling me how you couldn't stand it

and had to leave and now you're saying I'm criticizing you. You're the one who called me."

"I thought I could."

"You can. Where are you, Jackie?" There was a silence. "Do you want me to come pick you up? Let me come pick you up and we'll talk."

"Grace, I'll call you back. I'm really sorry." Jackie hung up.

After these phone calls, Grace would feel speechless and crazy. Gradually, she became aware that Jackie was getting her to play a part, and that as she did so, she felt less than herself, as though a ghost were marching her like a sleepwalker. From this, she had a small sense of how it must have been all the time for Jackie, driven, marched. She tried to become more cautious, more neutral in her responses. She was almost silent during the phone calls, just saying, yes, uh huh, right, right.

It came to the climax Grace had imagined it must several weeks later. It started with Jackie coming to the house, as always, on foot. She had circles under her eyes and a bruise on her cheek, and there was a hardness Grace hadn't seen in her before. She sat at the table and said, "Grace, you offered me a plane ticket a while ago. Can I take you up on the offer?" In a cautious way, Grace said, yes, of course. Jackie worked her fingers together. "I want to go back home."

"Do you want me to call for you?"

"Would you? The next flight."

As Grace dialed, Jackie said, "We were riding in the car yesterday. All of a sudden he slapped me." She held her hand to her cheek. "I couldn't believe it. I asked him why. He said he saw me looking at some guy crossing the street. I said, I wasn't looking at any guy. He slapped me again for lying. I said what am I supposed to do, close my eyes. I really wasn't looking at anyone, Grace. He kept slapping me, right there at the traffic light. People were watching."

Grace kept writing down flight times. She said, "There's something in a little over an hour."

Jackie nodded. "Please, Grace. I'll pay you back." Grace dictated her credit card number, hung up. "We argued on and off all night. This morning he held a knife to my throat. My neighbor looked in the window, saw us, and called the police. They took him in. He said he'd never let me go. He'd find me wherever I went. That was the last thing he said as he got in the car." Jackie gazed out the window, twisting her fingers. She stood. "Should we get going?" Grace nodded and put her arm around Jackie as they walked to the car.

They were silent in traffic, and in the silence, Grace feared she was losing her connection with Jackie, but she didn't dare talk. As they approached the airport, the long shapes of jets passed over the car. Jackie watched airplanes taking off in the distance. She leaned into the curve of the windshield, and peering up into the sky, watched the jets. She sat back. She stared straight ahead. She said, "Grace, I've got to go back." Grace kept driving. Jackie said, "Grace. Did you hear me? I've got to go back."

"We're almost there."

Jackie shook her head. "Please, turn around."

"Jackie."

"Stop, Grace! If you're worried about the ticket, I'll pay you back."

"I'm not worried about the ticket. I'm worried about you! Jackie... Jackie.... Please. Will you just let me drive you as far as the airport and then see how it looks to you?"

Jackie shook her head. She put her hand on the door handle, opened the door. "Jesus, Jackie, I'm driving!" Grace veered across two lanes and up onto the shoulder, and as they came to a stop, Jackie threw the door wide and jumped out onto the shoulder, her blue eyes tiny and almost white in the sun. A jet went over low, wheels and flaps down, its shadow rippling over them, engines screaming.

Grace yelled, "You don't have to stay married to him for life! Let's go see a minister together! Anyone you like!" Jackie stepped in front of the car. Grace yelled, "People make mistakes! It's okay!" She watched the oncoming traffic, then bolted. She reached the island, ran to the other side. Grace slammed the door and pulled back into traffic, found a break in the median divider and made a U-turn. She came up behind Jackie, pulled off. Jackie was walking quickly. Grace opened the window. "Get in, Jackie!" A car swerved around her, horn blaring. Jackie kept walking. "I won't take you to the airport. Just get in!"

Jackie stopped and got in. They drove back to the city in silence. As Grace dropped her at her place, she said, "Don't call me, Jackie." Jackie looked at her, sidelong, her face swollen. Grace turned the rearview mirror toward her. "Look at yourself! Look!" Jackie looked at Grace as though she were pleading. She opened her mouth. Grace said, "Don't say anything. Don't cry. Don't do anything. Just get out."

Several blocks away, Grace pulled over, closed her eyes, and placed her forehead against the steering wheel. Then she straightened the rearview mirror and drove home.

Though Grace made herself stay away, an awareness of Jackie was always with her like some small, misshapen thing which she had swallowed, a stone or pit, and which she couldn't digest. Sometimes she'd go over the first days when she'd figured out Jackie was living with someone in the house and wonder if she could have handled things differently. Maybe she should have flown home or gotten the sheriff. Part of her was still waiting for Jackie to show up, early morning, middle of the night, and say, "Take me to the airport." This time they would make it. From time to time, Grace called information to see if they'd gotten a phone, but information never had a listing. She took to calling her mother and youngest sister, Lisa, for news. Her mother, who had a small voice, spoke almost inaudibly when speaking of Jackie. That she spoke about Ruben and Jackie matter-of-factly offended Grace, as though she had given up on getting Jackie back. When her mother told her Jackie was pregnant, Grace felt a wave of sickness go through her, felt Jackie move out of reach.

Grace drove over to Jackie's, walked up the stairs to the studio and knocked. There was no answer. She looked in the window: a broken box spring in a bedroom, a chair overturned. The morning sun slanted across the painted cement floor.

"You're the sister. . . . " Grace turned and saw a man looking at her through a dusty screened window. "You look a little like her. I seen you..." Cigarette smoke curled through the screen into the sunlight. "You didn't know they moved? I got the address somewhere. Hold on." The man coughed, said in a hushed voice, "The manager's pissed. They didn't pay their last month's rent—comes out of his salary. Here, come around the front, I'll give you the address." The man pushed open the screen door and handed her something scrawled on a brown bag.

When she knocked—it was the same kind of place—Ruben came to the door and looked at her through the screen. He didn't say anything. He pushed open the door, extended his hand, and said, "Hello. My name is Ruben." Grace looked at his hand and hesitated. She said, "I know your name." It was as everyone had said. He looked like Jackie. He excused himself and walked into the back bedroom.

A Sixties formica table, three chairs, the vinyl torn and patched with duct tape. Dishes in the sink. Jackie came out sweeping a lock of hair off her forehead with the back of her hand. She smiled. "Oh, Grace...what a surprise. Come on, sit down." As she went by, she turned off an iron on an ironing board.

Grace looked at her sister. Face. Middle. Maybe a little more weight. Not showing. Grace said, "I'm only here for a minute."

Ruben returned from the back bedroom. His shirt and jeans were pressed. In his self-conscious neatness, there was something of the mother's boy about him. Without looking at Grace, he said, "Nice to meet you," and went to the door. Grace didn't answer. "See you later, Jackie." He slipped out, and after a moment, given the way things had happened, Grace felt the full insult of his mannerliness.

Jackie said, "He's going to see about a job today."

"Doing what?"

"Landscaping. Gardening. He just wants to be outdoors. If he can be outdoors, he's okay."

"And if he can't?" Jackie blinked once, kept her eyes closed, opened them slowly. "Never mind." They sat down. Grace said,

"You doing okay?" Jackie nodded. "Mom told me you were pregnant."

"It's a little sooner than I'd imagined."

"How do you feel?"

"Oh, okay, not bad. If you like puking every morning." They looked at each other, then laughed.

Grace said, "Do you like puking every morning?"

"Oh, I love it. I think I'm through for today."

"Do you need anything?"

Jackie said, "We're fine. Ruben's going to get this job, I just know it. . . . I'm working at the restaurant. We'll be fine." Grace took two twenties out of her purse and slid them over to Jackie. "Oh, no, Grace . . . "

Grace said, "Just put them away." She nodded. "Please."

"Grace . . . well, thank you. That's so sweet of you."

They talked and then Grace could find nothing more to say and began to ache. She reached across the table and took her sister's hand and looked at her. Jackie said, "I'm okay, Gracie," and smiled. "Really."

Grace stood. She looked down at Jackie. She touched the bottom of the iron, quick—cool now, off—and left.

Jackie had her baby, and shortly after, Grace, too, had a first baby. Sometimes they'd meet in one of the parks with strollers and talk. Sometimes Ruben brought Jackie by. He always stayed in the car, usually slumped down listening to the radio. Whenever Jackie came in, Michael left the room. Once, after she was gone, Michael came out and answered Grace's look. "I'm not trying to make a point. I don't like to see her eyes—there's a lie in them."

Every few months, it seemed, they would move, each place much like the last, the wobbly kitchen table, the torn screen door, sometimes no hot water, usually a church close enough for Jackie to reach on foot. There would be long silences, and then there might be a single phone call from Ruben: was Jackie there? Or perhaps a short weeping call from Jackie, nothing more. The phone calls were like shadows cast by unseen figures. Several times, when Grace called her mother, Jackie was there or had just gone back. One time, she disappeared for two weeks, and afterward Grace found out she'd been in a battered women's shelter.

In an ongoing way Grace couldn't keep herself from asking what it was that could have made Jackie accept living like this: no money, no hope, cut off; most of her friends, on a first meeting of Ruben, had long ago withdrawn. At times it seemed to Grace that Jackie had silently harbored a terrible virus, and almost overnight, in the right conditions, it had multiplied. No matter how Grace looked at it, how much she talked with Lisa or Annie or her mother, she couldn't understand. None of them could.

Each time Jackie left Ruben, Grace, in spite of herself, would feel a small hope. Maybe this time she would leave him for good. Each time, Jackie went back. Without intending it, Grace let the intervals grow longer between seeing Jackie. They got together briefly on their kids' birthdays—by now each of them had a second child—gave each other presents for Christmas. Because Jackie never had a phone, Grace, when she had an important call from their parents, might drive over to wherever Jackie was living or working. Sometimes they met for a walk in the park. Sometimes months would go by without them contacting each other.

That's how it had been when their sister Lisa came for a visit one October, and after a weekend of Lisa coming and going, Grace drove her over to Jackie's Baptist church. Lisa wasn't a Baptist, but she went to church, and this was her way of being close with Jackie. The sky was still too blue, the streets glaring. Motor running, Grace parked in front of the red brick church, and fanning themselves, they waited. Then, down the street, Grace saw someone elongating through the silvery heat mirage. Lisa pointed, and as Jackie approached, Grace felt a tender pain and refusal mingle in her.

Jackie smiled her quick smile. She hugged Lisa. She leaned in the car. "Gracie, how've you been? Always so beautiful."

They kissed. With no make-up, skin chapped from washing in cold water, Grace realized Jackie had the look of hard poverty. Her eyes seemed smaller, her cheekbones higher, her gaze feral. Grace looked for something familiar in her sister's face.

Jackie said, "Gracie, will you come in with us?" She added playfully, "Never know when it will come to you." She tugged her sleeve. "Come on, Gracie."

At that moment she didn't want to refuse Jackie. She turned off the motor and followed Lisa and Jackie into the church where they sat quietly in a back pew, and Grace felt herself engulfed in the airless hush. She listened to the young minister, took a deep breath and let it out slowly. Behind him, she noticed a painting which filled the entire space behind the altar, floor to ceiling. It was painfully clumsy, the depiction of a forest primeval beneath a blue sky, touching in its literal-minded representation. A silvery blue river came from out of a distance, wound through the trees, got bigger, and as Grace studied the perspective, she realized it was to give the illusion that the river flowed behind the altar.

After the service, Grace wandered to the front of the church. She climbed the two low steps and stood behind the minister's lectern. Beneath where the river widened, she looked down into a large, old-fashioned bathtub. Jackie stood beside her. Grace couldn't think of anything to say. Finally, she said, "Have you been baptized here?"

Jackie nodded. "Three times."

"Three?"

"You can be baptized as often as you want. I've gotten Ruben to come and he's been baptized, too."

Grace glanced from the silvery blue river to the tub. "How do they do it?"

"Oh, they dress you in a robe.... They ask you if you open yourself to receive the Lord Jesus Christ." She laughed a little awkwardly. "You step in, kneel. You take a deep breath. And they put you under, immerse you completely."

Grace was silent.

Jackie smiled and started to say something, but her lips trembled back into a smile again. Grace stared down into the deep porcelain bathtub. She noticed her sister's chapped hand hanging at her side. She touched Jackie's hand, turned and left the altar.

Long after she had driven Lisa to the airport and everyone was sleeping, Grace was still walking through the house. She'd lie down, close her eyes, get up, walk to the windows. Sitting in the dark, she dozed into a summer day several years back. Midday. Driving down a deserted street silvered with mirage, she passed a woman bending over to pick up a child at the bus stop. She'd felt something, a deep atavistic tug, slowed, and reversed. She rolled down the window. As the woman looked up, it seemed, in the two-dimensional desert light, as though a layer of skin had thickened over her face and obliterated her features before she shaded her eyes with her hand and said, "That you, Gracie?" Grace helped Jackie and her two kids into the car. She drove them to their turnoff where they got out and walked the rest of the way home.

Father's Weekend

Y ESTERDAY MORNING, SATURDAY, I was bringing them presents. Now I follow the dark country road back home. Again I feel the pressure of his hands, sudden and firm like some delicate move from aikido. The flat of his palms against my shoulders, once. Perhaps an hour ago. I feel it again and again as I drive and absently fidget the radio dial. Still nothing but static.

Yesterday: this road is beautiful in early morning sunlight. New England. Somewhere between the interstate and the camp, the radio begins to fade. I fool with the tuner, but the stations disappear one by one, blocked by hills and valleys. In the silence, the winding country road becomes more immediate: a stream rushing on my right, dense woods overhanging, sun and shadow speckling the road.

I am on my way to see my sister's boys at overnight camp. My nephews. My sister was badly injured in an accident several years ago. Her husband deserted her at the time, there followed a divorce, he has since disappeared and never tried to contact them in any way. After much pain, trauma, and anger everyone seems more or less reconciled to these conditions, and now my father and mother are raising the boys.

I myself live and work in the Southwest—I'd never imagined

myself living in the desert, where there is no ocean, no sharply demarcated seasons, not like New England where I grew up. But that's where my job took me. Sometimes I wake up in my house and wonder where I am or how I got here. And lately, when someone asks how long I've been out West, I have to think before I say uneasily, five years, somehow wanting to add, but not really. But yes, really. Without seasons, it's often hard for me to distinguish one year from the next.

For several weeks during the summer, I return to New England. I visit my parents, who still live in the same house. There I feel lost, restless, uneasy, morose. I pace, sleep badly, drink too much. If I am still here when Father's Weekend comes, I go. My father has gone once, but it is too hard for him to follow the boys around in the July heat and humidity.

Besides, as he said, "You're more the age their father would be, they need a young man—it's better for them, for you, too, you and they are going to be around a while after I'm gone. Anyway, what do they want with an old guy like me?"

I try to tell him he's not old, but he just makes a noise and waves his hand at such a brazen, well-intentioned lie.

"I'm old, alright," he says, with more an intonation about the human condition than self-pity.

He is right—it's better for them to have a young man even though they don't usually see me the rest of the year. I go. At Father's Weekend, there are a few men my age—thirty—with young sons, but many are at least several years older and most are in their late thirties and early forties. A few look almost my father's age. I myself am unmarried.

I slow down as I come up behind a camper swaying along. A trout leaping by the screen door. In the side-view mirror, I can see an old man dreaming. He's wearing a Red Sox cap. I can't pass. I glance out at the stream below us, both banks dense with ferns, trees, the water an incandescent green, speckled with rocks beneath the surface. I would like to pull off, walk by the bank, wade in, feel the cold water, the sun hot on my back.

Forced to drive slowly, I feel the distance already travelled this morning at my back, the small towns between the interstate and this last stretch of winding road, New England factory towns, each with its beautiful green, Victorian gazebos, war memorial—honor roll, cannons and cannonballs. A man in a helmet, head high, jaw thrust forward, knee raised in midstride, walks into a pastoral eternity. He looks over his bayonet at a girl in curlers too young to be pushing her pram. She is coming out of the variety store with the remodelled facade. She squints and steps into the Edward Hopper light. At the end of the street, curving down toward the river, the dark bricks and broken windows of an abandoned factory. Above it all the spire of a Congregational Church so white it momentarily seems to be blue air against the sky.

The camper pokes along. I'm already a little late. I shift about. Notice a dead tree, branches stripped of bark and silvering, an open sweep of sky through the branches. I feel an ache in my chest, a longing. For what? I have no idea. The dead tree, bare branches. Winter. Snow. Luminous light, blue sky after snowfall.

I force my thoughts ahead to camp, to how I will greet the boys, which with the older, Richard, can be difficult. I have brought presents. All of the fathers bring presents. I glance across the seat. The bag opened and strewing the floor, for Timmy, a water pistol, balloons, a whiffle ball, a frisbee, some comic books, which my mother discouraged. "Oh, come on, Mom, a few comics . . . " All the wonderful things I myself loved as a boy. Also, some candy. My mother insisted, no candy—and filled a bag with plums and peaches, but I know Timmy won't eat plums or peaches, and have gotten him a little candy, and know against my mother's purist dictums, no comics, no candy, that Timmy will be delighted today and suffer no lasting psychic or cellular deformities.

Richard, the older boy, fourteen, doesn't read comics, but is devoted to science fiction, and so I have brought him a sci-fi novel, a new *Galaxy,* and a lead figure—a dragon—for a game he loves, Dungeons and Dragons.

I am still filled with a longing for snow as I spot the turnoff for the camp.

* * *

Cars parking on the ball field, drifting clouds of dust, fathers following their sons with baseball gloves, bats, volleyballs; frisbees drift bright against the sky, the deep greens and shadows of the woods. I begin to fight a deep lassitude. There are only males here, of course, and I hate being among only males. Determined, I get out of the car, but I feel leaden, dazed. Sunlight glares off windshields, bumpers.

I walk down to the office to register—the cool lake through the trees, the sunlight off aluminum canoes, triangles of white sails. I get directions to the boys' cabins, decide to find Richard first. The camp is permeated with fathers and sons drifting in and out of the woods and paths, counselors, boys playing four-square. The sound of bouncing balls, sudden shouts of excitement. Deeper voices of counselors, fathers, the sharp cries of the boys.

I find Richard's cabin. His counselor looks up from a clipboard and introduces himself. Richard is at archery. Without my asking, he seems intent on giving me a report—reassures me he understands Richard's situation, though his solicitousness and hushed, confidential voice make me uncomfortable. I'm being positioned for a sympathy neither I nor Richard want. I look over at Richard's bunk as we talk, his cubbyhole. Unpainted pine shelving, books arranged neatly in alphabetical order. A large dictionary. Socks. Underwear. Flashlight. Baseball glove. I decide it's much more important I actually be with Richard now, and so I cut short the counselor by thanking him at the first possible moment and leave for the archery field.

I walk along wondering how to give him the presents. Here you go. Or: here are a few things I thought you'd like. No, neither way is right. Maybe the casualness would be mistaken for indifference. It's just that I don't want him to feel obligated.

If I told my father about this difficulty, he would look at me incredulously: oh, look, just give him the presents, he'll be glad as hell and won't think twice about it.

The path through the woods is strewn with rocks and foot-polished roots. I think about the boys. Of the two, Richard was the harder hit by the accident and divorce. The accident was the end of his close relationship with his mother; subsequently, his father. Richard was young, but not so young that he doesn't remember the way they'd been. His safe place with them. When he was younger, and after his father had gone, Richard asked after him constantly. Now it is rare that he asks anything at all about either his father or his mother. He never hears from his father. Neither birthdays, Christmas, nor any other times. Not a word.

At fourteen, he rarely makes a comfortable move. He often stumbles, doesn't ever quite know what to do with his hands—large, shapely hands—and though he is very bright and well-read, and has a huge vocabulary filled with obscure words from sci-fi, science, technology, and mythologies of all kinds, he blurts as though inarticulate, stepping only with great reluctance into the minefield of language. I sensed his loneliness last year and this year's counselor has again confirmed it; he has used such phrases as coming along, and doing a lot better, but still something of a recluse—the boys don't know quite what to make of him, all of his reading—they're just not completely comfortable, though he is not the kind of outcast who is bullied, he has too much innate dignity. He's more held at arm's length, you know. Not spontaneously included. They don't realize he's had to deal with some things most of them haven't yet had to imagine. He seems to do everything a little differently.

Yes, I think, even his real father doesn't come to visit him on Father's Weekend, just his uncle. I walk through the woods, still contemplating how to greet him. It's a delicate business, greeting a boy in front of his peers and particularly after an absence. I almost remember; part of me still feels like a boy to the extent that occasionally when I give my age, or see a picture of myself, some man, it feels like that couldn't possibly be me. Still, when I puzzle over greeting Richard, that time has grown just a little too far away. What would he want? How did I greet him last year, my arm about him, comradely?

As I walk, I remember my father's visiting me at camp. A different camp, the early Fifties. A sense of embarrassment and deep pleasure when someone yelled, hey, your father's here, he's looking for you. What was my embarrassment? He was a little older than most of the fathers, already gray, though I was thankful he wasn't shiny bald like some, and he never involved himself in the daily sports. An indifference to displaying athletic ability, so important to a boy? Was it that, or his aloofness? Or perhaps, more, a sense that his presence might jeopardize the person I'd become to others all summer. Make me less? I don't know. And I can't remember how he'd greeted me. A hug didn't feel right, though he often hugged me; I particularly remember the scrape of his white whiskers, alarmingly sharp and delightful after he'd brought someone's boat back; they'd been caught in a gale—the thrill of the word *gale*. November, dark, loud whining gusts, broken branches and matted wet leaves in the streets. After several days, he'd appeared late at night and hugged me. He'd never been afraid to hug me. But hugging me at camp? Possibly his hand on my shoulder....

As I walk, I glance into the bag, fumble around, draw out the lead figure, a dragon with a coiling serpentine tail, pterodactyl-like wings. Snarling mouth. I'd asked uncertainly about the lead figures for Dungeons and Dragons in the hobby shop, and the owner, chain-smoking and heavily tattooed had shown me a display case full of them and explained how Dungeons and Dragons was a very heavy game. "I got doctors and lawyers coming in here, they love it as much as the kids. You know, when they're playing they're not worrying about bills, problems, the wife and kids. Very creative." He'd reached up, touched a model hanging overhead, stated both sagely and enigmatically, "They get out of it what they put into it."

Dungeons and Dragons calls itself an adult fantasy role-playing war game which builds on the medieval world of Tolkien's *Lord of the Rings* trilogy, classical mythology, and anything else the referee, or Dungeon Master as he is called, might want to use—Burrough's Martian adventures, Howard's Conan Saga, or any other science fiction or fantasy—all of which Richard reads exhaustively, both because it fascinates him and to fuel his inspiration for being a more formidable Dungeon Master.

Being involved in a game with so much groping in dark and treacherous pits, I can understand how this dragon I am holding in my hand can be a wonderful ally, for the attributes of dragons are that they can see equally well in daylight or darkness. They have excellent sight, smell, and hearing, and because of these keen senses, all dragons are able to detect hidden or invisible creatures. . . .

In the distance, I can see a clearing, beautiful bright targets through the trees—concentric whites, reds, yellows, blues—and hear the whiz and thud of arrows. Now I feel foolish lugging these presents all the way down here.

Richard is at the other end of the firing line, back to me. In front of him, arrows sprinkle the target, some in the yellow and blue, more in the ground before and behind. He takes an arrow from the stand, looks around, glances among the fathers watching from the shade. He turns my way. Does he spot me? I wave. He nods, starts to turn and realizes he is walking toward me with bow and arrow half-drawn. I wave for him to shoot. He hesitates, turns back, stumbles slightly; carefully, he resumes his stance with exaggerated care—legs spread, bow arm outstretched, elbow high—he draws back the arrow; the arrow flies erratically, lands in the dirt almost at his feet. He raises his hand to his head in dismay. Someone laughs. He puts down his bow and walks toward me. Bright blue eyes.

"How are you doing, Richard?"

He makes a funny embarrassed sound. "Humm, not so good." He crosses his arms in front of him.

"What's not so good?"

"Well, that last shot for one thing."

"Oh, that was nothing. Look at all the arrows in the target."

"Humm."

As we're talking, he keeps turning from side to side and nervously keeping an eye on the other campers, sneaking glances at what their impression of this exchange might be. I become self-conscious; am I alright, or am I embarrassing him, wearing something that's taboo among fourteen-year-olds this summer? T-shirt, jeans, running shoes, like everyone else. Perhaps my hair's too long for his comfort.

He squints at me. Looks at the ground. Nothing more to say right now. "I have some things for you."

"Oh."

"Don't you want to see them?"

"Humm, I suppose so."

This is not indifference, I remind myself, but confusion, uneasiness at how to show emotions. I hand him the bag. He pulls out a water pistol. "No, that's for Tim."

"About his speed." A paperback. "Oh, Ursula LeGuin!" His face falls. *"A Wizard of Earth Sea.* I read this one."

"Dad said you wrote for it."

He sighs. "No, it was the other one. *The Tombs of Atuan."* He can't hide his disappointment.

"Richard, I'm sorry."

He shrugs. "This is a good *Galaxy.* I've been waiting for it. There's an article about lasers." I nod. "I want to check the rules and see if lasers can be used in D and D."

"D and D? Oh. Dungeons and ... "

"Dragons." He looks skeptically. How slow can this uncle of his be? He reaches in, pulls out the lead dragon, weighs it in his hand. He turns it over, studies it, balances the dragon. Says softly, "Nice."

"It can see in the dark."

"Infravision, 60 feet." He cups the dragon in his palm, carefully places it in the bag. "Thanks, Uncle Jack."

He starts rubbing one eye hard.

"Richard, what's wrong with your eye?"

"Nothing."

"Stop rubbing your eye, it's turning red."

"Hum. Uncle Jack?"

"What?"

"I've been chosen as assistant stage manager for the camp show."

"Good. Is that good?"

"It's kind of fun and you get to put up all the props and lights and stuff and you don't have to go out on the stage and be in those silly skits."

"Well, good."

A counselor blows a whistle. Richard thrusts the book back at me. "Uncle Jack?"

"Yes."

"I have to go pick up my arrows now."

"Go ahead."

He takes a step and turns. "Will you swim with me later?"

"Of course."

He trots out and begins picking up arrows. He shoots several more rounds, each time scoring about the same. When the activity is over, we take the path back to the bunk where I suddenly remember Tim. It's already late morning; I explain as apologetically as possible to Richard. "I'll be right back."

He picks up the *Galaxy* and thumbs it, carefully places the dragon on the shelf above his bed.

"Where will you be?" He shrugs. "Do you want to come with me?"

"I can't. We're supposed to stay around here."

I wave, start across the camp. A voice behind me. "Jack!"

I turn. Someone walking quickly up the path, head down.

"Tom."

We shake hands.

"Which way are you going?"

"I'm going to see Tim over in Pioneer Village."

"I'll walk with you. I'm going that way myself."

Tom is six or eight years older than I. He'd been a dean when I'd been a freshman and had been sent to him for discipline over some harmless disturbance. I've seen Tom on and off since, saw him up here last summer, but I have no idea if he recalls my having been sent to him freshman year. Dean's office: Tom in a three-piece suit behind his desk, my either avoiding his eyes or else staring at him with contempt, a posture struck against whatever usurped authority he represented to me, and finally his standing behind his desk and warning me that such incidents would only work against me in the future, a letter in my file, etc. I'd been intractable and contemptuous in every silent-sullen adolescent way possible, and he'd stepped out from behind his desk and said, "That's all," in a voice that telegraphed resignation to my unpenitent attitude. As I'd reached the door, he'd said, "Just one moment." I'd turned. "I don't expect to see you here again or the tone of things will be very different." I didn't answer. "Understood?"

"Yes."

He leaned forward and peered. He took a step toward me. "Are those things sideburns?"

I didn't answer. I looked out the window past him. He shook his head and with a combination of humor and derision, commanded, "Get out, Jack, and don't let me see you in here again."

We follow the path side by side. I know Tom has a couple of boys here. He's aware of the accident, the boys and their situation so there's nothing to explain. We talk easily about this and that, my work, the West, staying in shape; I mention that he looks much lighter than last year.

He is pleased. He explains he'd decided to lose some weight for his twentieth high school reunion. His diet: no sugar, butter, or desserts. More than I want to hear. And jogging four miles a day. He beams. "I've lost twenty pounds. I weigh exactly what I weighed when I was eighteen."

And except for a mustache he grew in the late sixties, he looks almost the same as when I'd first encountered him as a freshman dean.

We're getting to Pioneer Village. Ten-year-olds playing in a circle of bunks. Tether ball, volleyball, four-square. Tom points into a group of boys. "That one's mine."

Tom calls his son, and the boy leaves his game, runs over, and throws himself into Tom's arms, Tom closes his eyes and softens his voice as he says the name of his son, hugs him. Tom introduces me. Makes a point of introducing me as Mister and before the boy goes back to his game he tells him say goodbye to Mister...

I spot Tim, wave, he runs toward me. He is too young to remember the accident. He moves freely, unencumbered, charmed, curly-headed, loved by everyone, courted, his presence always hotly contested, who will get to sit next to him on the canoe trip. He dashes at my waist, throws his arms around me, presses his cheek to my stomach, hugs me hard as he can. "Uncle Jack!" His arms don't reach around my waist. He lifts his feet off the ground, hangs, wraps his legs around the back of my calves, works them up behind my knees, he wants to wrap himself around my body, shinny up me like a tree. He smells of sweat, hair, strong camp laundry soap, palm sweat from much-handled balls.

When I hand him his presents, he takes the bag, digs in. Water pistol, ball, frisbee, forbidden comics! candy! each one delights him more than the next, he jumps up, dances, everything's wonderful. He calls a friend. "Look what my Uncle Jack brought me!" He dashes off to fill the water pistol, squirts it here, there, can't resist a few shots at friends, enemies, even a counselor, now a friend can use it, five shots, hey, that's more than five, give it back! a brief struggle, Tim! share it, is that me sounding like a grown-up, Tim! I laugh. Tim! Listen to me for a second.

Richard is on his bunk reading *Galaxy* when I get back.

"Is it good? The article about lasers?"

"It's so-so. I knew most of the information. I want to check and see if they can be used in D and D." He contemplates the springs of the upper bunk. "They're supposed to be medieval weapons. But maybe . . . "

"How do you find out if you can?"

"Maybe I'll write Gary Gygax. He invented the game, sort of. He and some friends. Maybe I'll just do it, anyway."

That's what I want to tell him. You want lasers in your dungeon, just do it.

He pulls out a notebook and begins printing in slanted block letters. He presses hard, using a dark pencil, his hand smudging the soft pencil and clouding the page as he writes. He thumbs the book, prints something on another page. Adds a detail to a drawing. I can see the foreshortening of comic book art combined with his own carefully detailed style. Creatures writhe. Glower. Squirm in death agonies. Fangs. Forked tongues. Blazing eyes. Hydras, harpies, lizard men, lysanthropes, elaborately armored knights, halflings, dwarves, elves, animated skeletons, giant spiders, dragons, unicorns, bearded wizards in marvelous conical hats covered with quarter moons and stars, long witchy fingers beaming spells. On one page, I glimpse an elaborate, multileveled labyrinth of dungeons inhabited by creatures. He writes intensely and when finished, stares out the window, eyes far away, then carefully fits the notebook in its place among past issues of *Galaxy,* sci-fi paperbacks, and books on Dungeons and Dragons.

"What was that you wrote?"

"An idea for my dungeon."

"Do you have people who play here?"

"A few. We have a club, sort of." Outside, a bugle call. He stands up. "Hey, Uncle Jack, that's a free swim. You said we'd swim."

"We will. Come on."

He goes out and comes back with his suit—sun-stiffened from the line. He hesitates. Changing. Past years, his changing, sometime long back, my changing. The intense strained silence of boys doubling away from each other, hiding groins, the embarrassment of buttock and penis. The source of his fiddling in his shelves, looking for a towel, straightening clothes; I conveniently offer to find the john, which is a separate cabin.

In the bathroom, Tom has just unbuttoned his shirt. He nods and smiles. "A swim. Just in the nick of time. It's turning into a real scorcher." I agree and peel off my shirt, start unlacing my shoes, draping my clothes over one of the sinks. Suddenly, nothing to say, we undress in silence, both of us momentarily shy, hard to believe; when we think of something to say, our voices strain, does he or doesn't he remember that incident freshman year, almost fifteen years ago, is that it? this shyness, some authority adhering to him, three-piece suit of early Sixties deanship, two adult men hiding their groins from each other, so odd to me after years of team sports, locker rooms. At last, maybe all of two minutes, safely in our suits, clothes under our arms, we walk quietly out of the washroom, somewhat relieved, a diminishing tension left behind us in there. When I get to the bunk, Richard is ready.

As we walk down to the lake, I debate asking Tom if he recalls that freshman incident. Richard says, "Tim thinks he's so cute."

"What do you mean?"

"Everyone says he's so cute."

We're coming down to the lake. A long line, fathers and sons, files past the swim counselor who gives each pair a number attached to an elastic loop. I slip the loop on my wrist. Richard makes his noise several more times. Hum humph!

"Don't worry about it, Richard."

"What?'

"Tim."

"Hum."

"How's your swimming this year?" He shrugs. I pat him on the shoulder. "Come show me. You improve every year."

We walk onto the crowded float. Fathers and sons everywhere. On the beach, on the floats, fathers who dive right in and swim easily, fathers who ease themselves down the ladder, shrinking with every step. Some of the fathers have remained slim and still have boyish, athletic bodies—narrow waists, good muscles; some have rolls of fat, are misshapen, pale white. On the main float, a tall slide. Everyone loves the water-slippery aluminum track and lines up by the ladder, on up the steel rungs, one behind the other. Richard and I take a quick cooling plunge, get in line for the slide. I look around slowly as we go up the rungs. Each father is buddied up with his son and with many there is some physical feature, often prominent—a nose, the tip of the eyes, shape of the lips, slope of the shoulder, set of the ears, which identifies the son with his father. If there is no physical feature—rare—then there is some intangible, a way of turning the head, the posture. Something tender and vulnerable about it—this fragile but definitive identification—which suddenly touches me, these fathers, gentle, swimming with their sons in this July heat, gleaming with water, each son so aware of and aching toward his father. I, who have not the immediate comfort of my own son, who no longer have the bodily comfort taken by a boy in the mere physical presence of his father, height and deep voice and gravity, suddenly feel lonely in the sunlight, the racket of boys and fathers laughing and calling each other's names—watch this! Dad! Watch!—a beautiful, fragile chorus in the stillness of the lake.

Richard's turn on the slide, he's just above me stepping from the top rung onto the slide. Still gripping the steel handrails, he takes the weight onto his arms, swings his legs forward, pushes off, pinches his nose, closes his eyes. Blond hair dark with water, he accelerates down the slide, back gleaming, aluminum glinting beneath him, I yell, open your eyes, it's only water.

When I see his head clear, I repeat his movements, knees drawn up, the warm-cold aluminum; at the bottom, sudden lurch, almost weightless, midair. Dozens of voices, cacophony, watery entry, translucent darkness, silence, momentary body fright from long ago, the darkness, rise toward light, silence, burst of air and voices.

Lying on my side, head propped on one elbow, I watch Tom and his sons weave through the clusters of campers eating off paper plates. They sit beside us—myself with Tim and Richard—and we eat potato chips and burgers, drink cups of bright pink fruit punch. I lean back and watch the smoke from the grills curling up through the top branches of the trees—birches, oaks, pines. It disappears into the stillness and silvery blue humidity above the trees. The boys gulp their food and dash back for seconds, finally asking to be excused to run through the sunlight and shadows. Tom and I lie in the broken shade of our tree, hair almost dry, and watch the boys and fathers. I prop myself up a little more. "Tom?"

He glances over. His thinning hair is more noticeable since the swim. "Do you remember my being sent to you freshman year? My freshman year?"

He smiles. "Of course." Suddenly we grin. "I remember it well." He picks at some grass, shakes his head. "You were one of the more angry freshmen. Though I can't recall what it was about, can you—the incident?"

"No, I can't."

"It stood out in my mind because for freshmen at the time—remember those days, the beginning of Vietnam and much of the student activism—Berkeley Free Speech was about it, but most students coming in for discipline were already scared as hell, apologetic, I'd say a few words and that was the end. I knew I wouldn't see them again. But you weren't about to kiss the dean's ass. I decided to handle you very gently."

"I didn't realize I had required any special handling."

He smiles. "You needed a lot of special handling. Gentle handling. I wondered if you were going to make it. I passed the word on down the line. As I recall, there were a couple of other marginal scrapes which we watched but didn't do anything about. I thought if anyone said one word to you, you would blow up."

"Thank you, Tom."

He smiles. "Apparently you did make it."

"Did I?" I ask half-seriously.

"Sure. How do you like living in the West?"

"I like it, but for some reason, just this morning, I suddenly realized I'd been missing the New England winters. I don't know why. I left the East with no regrets. I was relieved. It's a different sky here, closer, you don't realize how close until you're going West, somewhere, maybe an hour past Chicago and just before the Mississippi, you can feel the sky start to open up, and in the West, the sky is open and endless. And in the desert, blue, day after day. Absolutely blue.…" I trail off. I glance around. "It's so green here. Another world. So much water. They say the desert is running out of water. Will run out of water.…" I falter not knowing where I'm going with that. Tom looks at me. I force a laugh. "The West is fine. I just never thought I'd miss the winters. Maybe it's not even winters I miss. I don't know."

We're silent. We glance about the grove. Groups of fathers and sons.

"You know, Tom, I'm worried about my sister's kid—Richard. I don't have any kids. Maybe I don't understand. I think he's a good kid. Seems to be. But he's so wound up and isolated in himself." I explain his preoccupation with sci-fi, Dungeons and Dragons, recalling the fierce tableau in his notebook. "I don't know, maybe it's got a purpose. A safety valve for his feelings."

"Jack, some of this is being fourteen."

"I know."

"But some of it is the accident, the divorce, the disappearance of his father. I know your parents are doing a good job with him, but they are much older."

"I know that, too. But he's so lonely and I don't seem able to do anything for him."

Tom nods. "He'll be alright, though. He's smart. I do see what you're talking about, the isolated quality in him."

"A friend of mine has a theory that you just get dealt good kids or bad kids. Like cards. And it doesn't matter too much what you do—within limits—the good kids grow up good, the bad kids grow up bad. Is that too romantic?"

"Maybe there's some truth in it. But most kids are good and turn out pretty well. And whatever, Richard will be alright." He smiles. "Like all these kids will be. Sometimes they need a little gentle handling." He smiles at me. We watch the smoke curling up through the trees. Shift positions.

"What were you so angry about, anyway, freshman year, college?"

I recall the sense of anger, but nothing more specific. "I don't know, Tom. Maybe just scared of something."

We become thoughtful, and then spontaneously start getting up and brushing off. He picks several leaves and twigs off the back of my shirt. "You're still angry, do you know that?"

"Maybe. I don't know."

He pats me on the shoulder. We start scrunching through the leaves looking for the boys.

"Don't worry too much about Richard. He'll be alright. And whatever attitude or behavior he's showing you now—today— it's very important to him that you are here. He knows it and you know it. It's important to you, too. For now. And for later."

He looks at me significantly.

Later, I think, what does he mean by later? My father. Old. I return his look, and we nod together.

As the day goes on, I make rapid apologetic departures from Richard to see Tim, rapid apologetic departures from Tim to return to Richard, who I think needs me more; in the middle of the hot afternoon, we go on a long involved treasure hunt which takes us all over the camp. Then another swim, the cool plunge into the shadowy lake, and now it is late afternoon, almost dinnertime, something has been building up in me. I decide to tell Richard I need to take a short walk by myself. He gives me a look of interest, but doesn't seem to mind. I take a path which leads me off beside the lake. Stop. Look up. Above the tree tops, fragments of sky, now deep blue. I sit under a tree. Long shadows in the woods. Ferns. Heat. Ants in orderly procession. Birds hushed. Occasionally, a loud isolated voice reaches out here, distorted. The clang of a paddle against an aluminum hull floats across the lake. A nickname. Something like Rosie. A shortening of his last name, Rosen? Rosie. I'm pretty sure. A counselor. Blond hair, thinning in front, quiet blue eyes, deep set, a long face. Lean, muscular, sinewy. A quiet voice which made you feel calm because you sensed he'd be fair with you. I stare through the trees at the lake.

And it was something with me, then. Nine? Ten? Something inconsolable, a new fear composed of the long shadows in the woods, the night sky filled with stars, the deep part of the lake where the boulders made black shapes and the sunlight faded down into the blackness. Something terrible down there, in there, in that darkness. I suddenly didn't want to do any of the things I loved. Baseball, volleyball, swimming, what could they matter? Didn't they, everyone, know it was there? I'd heard some counselors discussing me, the word homesick, what was wrong? homesick, but I knew it wasn't homesick. It was a cellular terror of the woods and lake and stars. Almost a panic, I felt myself floating away, being taken away, people getting farther and farther, the vastness of the woods and stars drawing me away.

I was vaguely aware of Rosie's quiet presence, of his shepherding me aside once and studying my face. One morning soon after, he asked in his quiet voice, did I want to take a trip with him, a special trip?

We loaded a canoe and paddled through narrow passages from lake to lake, at times stopping to untangle lily pads and stems entwining the paddles, while bubbles rose and burst mysteriously beside the canoe. We paddled until finally late in the day, one last widening passage, the water getting choppier as we approached a larger lake, a lake I'd never seen, but heard of—the big lake. The sun slanted through billowing cumulus clouds, their underbellies smoky gray, tops flushing and coloring, and the clouds casting deep, purple-black shadows on the wind-whipped surface of the lake, great shafts of rapidly moving sunlight between.

Then, darkness, the air chilly, the black shape of the canoe pulled up on the sandy beach, the lake quiet, Rosie sitting across from me. Dinner. Scrubbing the pans with lake sand and cold water. The warmth of the fire on my face. Rosie sat feet toward the fire, loosely joined hands draped over his knees. On one foot, his sock had pulled down and I could see a deep red line. I hesitated, then asked.

He slipped off his moccasin, peeled down the sock. The scar was red and deep. It made a groove from the top of his sock down across his ankle and the top of his foot. The skin seemed to fold in on itself. As deep as a pencil.

Something in his voice conveyed an acceptance, a dignity, awful things could happen to a person, he could still have himself, care for himself, come back to his life.

Did I know anything about the war? Not the one going on now in Korea, but the last one? Bigger. Much bigger. No, just a little. Rosie pulled his sock back on, slipped on his moccasin. So many people died. The way he said it made me feel as if he'd seen a lot of them die. We were over Germany, B-17s. His voice so quiet. Shrapnel. Bursting everywhere. Planes falling out of the sky. Above us. Below us. Shrapnel shattered the bone. Someone used a tourniquet. Lost a lot of blood. Copilot made it home. Saved the foot.

Something about the way he said *over Germany*. It seemed so high. So black. Over. I didn't dare tell him that I'd seen a B-17 hanging from a string in a model shop and wanted it. Over Germany.

"How high?"

He started to say something. Changed his mind. "So high we wore oxygen masks and heavy jackets and boots lined with fleece—sheepskin."

I looked up. The sky filled with stars. Up there. In the dark. In oxygen masks and fleece-lined coats.

"There's no oxygen up there?"

"Not enough to breathe."

"And it's cold?"

"And cold."

"Even in summer?"

"Even in summer. There is no summer at 30,000 feet."

"Had you gone many times? Over Germany?"

"Fifty-three."

"Is that a lot?"

"Once is a lot."

"Where did you go from?"

"England."

"And you flew the plane?"

"I flew the plane. But there were other men. A navigator and bombardier and gunners and a copilot. A lot of men."

"And you dropped bombs?"

He nodded. "We dropped bombs."

I looked over at Rosie. His pale blue eyes were so sad and quiet and intense. So different than Buddy Burke who also talked about the war. Rosie. Buddy Burke. It was confusing.

Buddy had reddish-gold eyes and looked like that actor called Spencer Tracy who had been in the movie we'd seen earlier in the summer, *Northwest Passage;* it even seemed to me it was Buddy leading Roger's Rangers. Buddy was the rifle instructor and you never ever made the least little mistake on Buddy's rifle range. You did everything exactly the way he said or you would lose your shooting privileges and sometimes even be banished from the range for the entire summer, Buddy said that, *Banished,* we'd heard of someone two summers ago who had been banished, and besides banished, Buddy would be furious with you, no one wanted Buddy furious at him, everyone wanted to be best friends with Buddy. Anyway, Buddy said his rules were for your own good. He had broad shoulders and thick forearms glowing with reddish-gold hairs and freckles and a dark tattoo of a globe and a wonderful fierce eagle. Underneath, U.S.M.C. He'd been a marine! The tattoo seemed to be slightly out of focus and starting to drift and fade away into different directions in his skin, but it was still beautiful, just beautiful, and I spent hours and days figuring where mine would go and what it would be. But sitting here with Rosie, hearing him talk, seeing his sad eyes, I felt confused, I . . .

I gaze at my feet. The ants crawling. The silent ferns, the sunlight slanting through the trees. It has grown very still, and I stand and start back, still thinking about Buddy and Rosie, but unable to keep my mind on them as I hurry toward the dining hall, which sits beside the lake. After a few minutes, I make my way out of the woods.

The lake is glassy and still and boats lie motionless on their reflections. The docks and floats are dark with water from the last swim. I'm late. Fathers and sons crowd the wide porches; as I approach, the building roars with one indistinguishable voice. Which, as I climb the stairs, becomes single words, phrases, overlapping exchanges; you were terrific, today . . . no, you have to choke up more . . . don't worry about him, take the inside position, plant your feet, and keep it. . . . I make my way around the porch looking for Richard and Tim. Richard spots me and waves once, frantically, then looks down.

"Where were you so long?"

"I told you I was going for a walk." He scowls. "I'm sorry. I lost track of time." We don't have anything to say. He doesn't help me. "Are you hungry?" I try.

He shrugs. I peer around the porch, fathers' arms around sons, sons leaning against their fathers, they rub against each other, breathe each other's scents, inhale each other.

Richard and I regard each other. "Where's Tim?"

"He's a waiter for the dinner so he's already inside. He told me to make sure you sit at his table—ten."

"Are you sitting with me?"

He looks annoyed. "You know I can't. It's a fathers' table."

"I forgot. I'm sorry I was late."

"What were you doing?"

"I remembered some things I'd forgotten."

"What?"

"Some people from when I went to camp."

"I didn't know you'd gone."

"I did. Like you."

"This camp?"

"No, another. But similar, I think."

"Did Mom go, too?"

Mom? I'm a blank. Mom. My sister his mother mom Mom so rare for him to ask anything about her since the accident.

"Yes, to a girls' camp."

"Huump." He looks out at the lake and rubs his eye. Stands with a strained effort at looking relaxed. The other boys lean against their fathers, hang onto them. Suddenly the doors open and everyone presses forward—smell of wood, disinfectants, food, sweat—clambers to the tables, I shout to Richard, "We'll meet out here after dinner."

He yells. "What?"

"Out there! Meet me!" He looks confused. "Meet me!"

We're pulled in different directions by the crowd, the noise. I see him at the other end of the dining hall, he sits shyly at a table. I find my way to table ten, nod to some of the men who eye me curiously, a little young or awfully well-preserved to have a son here, not impossible of course, but also lacking, what? perhaps a certain paternal gravity; they study me. At the far end of the dining hall, a large sign with Old English lettering: I CAN I WILL. The dining hall quiets down, a nondenominational prayer, we sit with a great scraping of chairs. It is hot and noisy, everyone sweats, we bump elbows and shoulders and hold our arms in at our sides; to be amenable, we try to talk to each other, ask questions, but that requires shouting. I notice Tim staggering quickly toward our table with a huge aluminum tray; he heaves it onto the stand, the fathers smile at his effort, encourage him, he smiles, but I see he is serious about doing this well. First one platter, then another, he lifts them into the circle of fathers. He looks up at me after each serving, I play the buffoon and applaud his efforts, which delights him; he goes back to bring the rest of the food, returns. In a moment of relative silence, someone has just asked me which one is your boy and the rest of the table pauses and listens; I hesitate, anything but yet again this complicated story of sister's accident, divorce, disappearance of father and ensuing solicitousness. I look into the circle of faces, the fathers, most gray, some bald, all sweating, tired from a day of following their sons; my shirt is soaked with sweat, I can feel the drops rolling down my back. I take a deep breath, I'm about to reply, which one is my boy, when Tim says, "Me! I'm his boy. He's substituting. He's my substitute father. Richard's too." They turn to him. He tips his chin up slightly. He is a little undersize for his age, but the way he picks up his chest makes the fathers smile. Substitute. He must have gotten that word from school.

"I'm his uncle," I say. "His parents are divorced and so I come to visit." Now the shortcut comes easily, Tim grins, and I smile and suddenly feel very thankful to him, what a good kid. The fathers, too, nod, their intuitive confusion about me cleared up, a man pats me on the shoulder, lets his hand rest there, good, good for you, several nod, nice, good, very nice, *mensch.*...

Toward the end of dinner, a loud series of announcements, then the boys chant and sing, some words English, some sound Indian, yelling and thumping at critical junctures, stamping their feet until the dining hall shakes. I look over at Richard. He's looking out the window. The fathers drink cup after cup of hot coffee from dented aluminum pitchers, sweat, smile and endure this awful din, their sons. Finally, the dinner is finished, fathers drift out into the twilight, the flash of a match, click of a lighter, the glow of a pipe. I lean against the wooden rail and wait for Richard. Take a deep breath and sigh into the cooling air. Tim comes out, sees me, walks over and puts his arms around my waist, pressing his face against my stomach. He leans against me. I put my hand on his head, stroke his hair. "You're a great waiter."

"I know." I smile. "Are you coming to the camp show?"

"Of course."

"Good, I'm in two skits."

When I look up, Richard is leaning silently against the rail. He stares at the floor. Never anything to say. I suddenly feel annoyed. Don't just stand there waiting for me to produce something. Say something, try! In the next moment, guilty. "Richard." Softly. "Are you ready for the show?"

"Huh!"

"Is that yes?"

"Yes."

As easily as Tim had placed himself against me, he separates himself. "Hey, Uncle Jack, I've gotta get ready now."

"Okay, I'll be out there watching."

"I know." He runs off the porch. Stops in the dark. "Uncle Jack."

I turn. "What?"

Several squirts into my face. Maniacal laughter joined by my own, the crunch of his feet running on the gravel path in the twilight. I wipe my face, turn to Richard. Hands deep in his pockets, his strained ease. He shakes his head. "What a baby!"

"Richard..."

"Hey, Uncle Jack..." He pulls his hands out of his pockets. "What?"

"I've got to get ready, too. Help with the props."

"Good luck, it's going to be great."

Alone. A pipe glowing at the end of the porch. The gleam of the lake is rising into the long silence to meet the twilight. Across the lake, the trees have massed with night. I can smell the lake's coolness.

I see a flashlight bobbing through the trees. Buddy. The flashlight appears again, farther away. Disappears. Rosie on the other side of the fire. Deepset blue eyes. Over Germany. Buddy Burke was so different. We'd watch for his flashlight. Twenty hundred. Sharp. On the dot! That's what Buddy called it, twenty hundred, and everyone had to be in bed, lights out, bunk battle-ready, no feet on the floor, or you would lose your visit. The bunk with top inspection got an extra visit from Buddy and all day everyone would boast, Buddy Burke is coming to our cabin tonight. We'd post a watch and wait for his flashlight to start appearing and disappearing in and out of the trees until someone would yell he's coming! and we'd dash for our bunks— we'd know it was his because he'd be whistling. He was a great whistler. We'd watch the flashlight drift closer and hope he wouldn't stop off too long at the counselor's shack where there was a yellow bulb and the sound of a silly song which always went... *when your baby/sends you a let-ter/of Good-bye...*

Just the sound of his boot on the step outside was wonderful and exciting and maybe once we had Buddy to ourselves he'd never leave. He'd walk between the bunks, fist on hip, shining the flashlight looking for dust balls, inspecting our shelves, and we'd just hope when the light stopped that someone hadn't messed up and that the bunk really was battle-ready so we wouldn't lose our story. If you were very lucky, he'd sit on your bunk and would tell strange wonderful stories of places we'd never heard of—Guadalcanal, where I knew there must be a beautiful canal and perhaps bunks like these. There were palm trees and beaches and coral and jungles. Buddy told stories about patrols and fighter planes and naval bombardments and how one soldier from their side, Buddy called him a Jap, got caught in a booby trap one night, they heard the explosion in the dark, and in the first light of day they could see him, head blown off, body still facing downhill, knife in hand, he'd been crawling, sneaking! All of the blood had drained out of him and run down, that yellow Jap was pale white, boys, and one of our guys crawled out there and picked him up, he was light as a feather—it's blood that gives your body weight, so don't lose too much if you can help it as you go through life—and he danced out there with the headless Jap, his arms flopping around as the sun rose, and boys, it was a sight to see. In the dark bunk, we could see it. We loved being near Buddy who handled guns every day, could handle all the guns he wanted without ever having to ask permission, and who had killed, we knew, just knew, he had killed. When he had finished, we would beg for more. But he would say, that's all for now, boys, got to get your sleep.

Hushed voices in a broken chorus, we'd say, "Thank you, Buddy."

And he would say, "Goodnight, boys. God bless you."

And we'd listen to the slap of the screen door, run to the screened windows, watch his flashlight drift through the trees—and then talk feverishly about everything he'd told us, everything. It was wonderful. Buddy was fearless, wonderful.

But sitting in the firelight with Rosie, it seemed different. He'd been to the war, the same war, wasn't it? And it made Rosie's eyes so sad and he had that groove in his ankle and foot, so deep you could trace the tip of your finger in it. Rosie's war seemed different. Much sadder than Buddy's war. It was the same war, wasn't it?

I thought it over carefully and then asked, "Have you ever heard of a place called Guadalcanal?"

He nodded.

I was thoughtful. He watched me. I was looking at Rosie's arms for tattoos.

"Are you thinking about Buddy? Buddy Burke?"

I nodded. "It just seemed different than what you told me."

He looked at me across the fire. "You like Buddy, don't you?"

I hesitated. Was it still alright to like Buddy? "Yes."

"Good. I wouldn't want you to stop being friends with him because of anything we've talked about here."

I nodded, a little relieved. I could be friends with Buddy, too.

Then we slid down into our sleeping bags. It was clear and still and there were more stars than I'd ever seen. The Milky Way glowed like the numbers on my watch and I pressed the crystal against my eye, but it was like a river, a luminous face or profile, the whole sky sprinkled with single bright stars everywhere.

I stared up into the sky, my face chilly, my body warm in the sleeping bag, and then Rosie said something. So quietly, I wasn't sure I'd heard it. I gazed up at the stars. Maybe I only thought I heard him. I looked over. His profile between myself and the low fire. I whispered his name softly, "Rosie?" From his breathing, asleep. Try not to be afraid? Is that what he'd said? Had he said anything at all? The stars got blurry and closer, it was still alright to be friends with Buddy, Rosie was just beneath the stars, he wore an oxygen mask, there was no oxygen, freezing and losing blood, the Jap lost his head and all of his blood, light as a feather, Rosie wasn't afraid, just sad, staring with his deepset blue eyes as he floated in the cold blackness between the stars. Floating away. Try not to be afraid. Come back to earth.

When I look up, the silvery lake has all but disappeared and I am alone on the porch. I force myself to start for the ballfield.

The fathers are sprawled on a high grassy bank behind third base, the primary colors of their shirts flattened into one color in the twilight. Behind them, dark woods. A flatbed trailer has been pulled up outside the left-field line: the stage. Now, white light and activity. Boys running. In and out of the lights. Costumes. The fathers sit cross-legged, Indian style, sprawl propped on one elbow, lie on their backs, hands cradling their half-raised heads. They have blades of grass in their mouths, they stare up into the sky, they fiddle, doze, a medicinal smell of 6-12 hangs over them. Twilight deepening, air cooling, stars brightening one by one above the circle of open woods.

"Jack." Tom pats a place beside him.

I pick my way through a sprawl of arms and legs. "How are you holding up?"

He smiles. "Not too bad. The boys in this?"

"Tim. Richard is doing important things backstage."

"Here, you'll need this." He hands me a spray can of 6-12. We sigh and lean back against the grassy bank. I gaze up at the brightening stars. Once Tom lets out a single snore, jerks awake. We laugh softly.

The program begins. First, counselors wearing false handle-bar mustaches, a barber shop quartet. Very good. Then the skits. All are surprisingly funny. The places where the boys forget lines and simply stand dumbstruck until loudly prompted are received with tenderness and amusement. Many of the skits involve buckets of thrown water, shaving cream, pies in the face, tricks, a Punch and Judy roughness. But the skits which draw the loudest laughter are ones where the sons dress up as girls—grotesquely huge tits, flouncing silly walks, great padded asses, mincing falsetto voices. Though the men are married, love and honor their wives, have daughters, the sight of their sons dressed as girls sets off waves of laughter across the dark embankment, the laughter acknowledging some shared secret; tonight, nothing could be funnier or more grotesque than the characteristics of womanhood: breasts, long hair, pronounced hips, a high voice. Tom, who is a professor, who is well travelled and active in community affairs, laughs the same loud laugh. We laugh as one. It is a powerful conspiracy of love and mockery, this mimicry of women, which says: we are one way, the same; women are other.

Afterward, flashlights come on, drift, appear and disappear and reappear fainter, bobbing. I find my way into Tim's bunk where the boys are still excited and running around. The counselors manage to quiet them down, get them scrubbed and into their bunks. I kneel beside Tim's bunk. He's still got greasepaint along his hairline and traces of lipstick on his teeth and upper lips. "Did you see me?"

"Of course. You were terrific."

He sighs. The legs of the boy's father on the ladder, the sound of their voices above.

"I was a girl." He laughs. "With..." He starts to giggle. "Titties." He giggles uncontrollably saying the word over and over, "Titties." He pulls out a tennis ball from under the cover. Giggles. I place it carefully on the shelf.

"Tim?"

"What?"

"Do you have another one in there with you?"

He gives it to me. Giggles. Stares up at the mattress springs. Becomes thoughtful. "Richard thinks he's so great."

"Why do you say that?"

"Being a stage manager—assistant stage manager."

"He doesn't think any such thing. You had fun. He had fun."

"He does. He thinks he's great."

"Okay, Tim. Just remember, Richard's your brother."

"I don't care."

"Goodnight, Tim."

"Hey, Uncle Jack! You're sleeping in camp, aren't you?"

"I sure am."

"Good!"

He throws his arms around my neck and hugs me, and I kiss him goodnight.

Up at Richard's cabin, we sit on his bunk, myself leaning back against the wall, and we try to talk about the day; I ask him how he thought the show went—I realize I saw no traces of him, though I looked off to the sides of the stage frequently. He says it went well, though he frets over a couple of skits that had to go on without certain props because someone had misplaced them. I ask him if he likes his counselor, what activities he likes best, but on everything he is noncommittal, he answers with a shrug, an *okay*, an *I-don't-know*. I realize then that of course I saw no traces of him. And he as much told me earlier, being an assistant stage manager, he wouldn't have to be seen. Drowsy and starting to nod, I shake my head clear, make a last effort to talk to Richard, get up. "Well, you should be proud, the skits went well." He sits on the edge of his bunk playing with his fingers. I put my hand on his shoulder. "Goodnight, Richard." I shake his shoulder, playfully, encouragingly. He shrugs and taps his foot once.

I take the path to a large recreation hall set back in the woods. A porch. Footsteps and flashlights. Smells. Dry wood, tar, shingles. Pine resin. A makeshift father's dorm. Inside, cots. Heat. Dim light from bare bulbs on the rough pine planking. Dark knots. I debate taking a blanket and going to sleep under a tree, instead, wander around the old hall looking at framed yellowing group photographs of campers which go back to the turn of the century. They make me feel lonely. I know that several of the fathers had been campers here. They love return-ing. They rest their hands easily on each other's shoulders as they talk. Buddy and Rosie—if alive would most likely be in their early sixties now. I try to imagine how their faces would look. I can't. I sit on the porch awhile, footsteps thumping the stairs, creak and slap of screen door.

The hall hasn't cooled off much, but I wander into one of the rooms. An empty cot. In the light from the hall, half-lit men, covers kicked back, in shorts or pajamas. The curve of a shoul-der. Bunching of a pectoral muscle. Fan of hair on a pillow. They sleep on their stomachs and sides, they sleep on their backs, forearms thrown across eyes.

I lie down on a cot. Sweaty. Though exhausted, I'm tense. Lonely. Aware of the space under my mattress and the floor. I drift. The men toss and turn, springs popping under the mat-tresses; once I open my eyes. Glare of hall light. All of the men have moved, shifted; when I turn over, all have moved again, silent, like constellations; they snore, groan, whisper the names of women, wives, blurt words, phrases, sigh, gasp, momentarily gag, the rush of air in their nostrils and throats; they smack their lips, whimper, become absolutely still, frown; outside, sigh of pines, the rise of a hanging sheet, soothe of wind, Northwest Passage, when your sweetheart sends a letter of Goodbye, danced out there with that headless Jap light as a feather, floating between the stars, no oxygen, freezing, no summer at thirty thousand...

The racket of morning. Screen door slamming, porch thumping footsteps, cots empty. Whistling. Sunlight on blue and rust-white strips of mattress, swirl of sheet. I feel hungover with exhaustion, a sense of confusion and displacement. The sunlight is too bright and other, everything is removed and unreal and too real at the same time—the heat, the sudden shouts of the boys, the bouncing of balls, roar of dining hall, clatter of silver. I can hardly finish sentences, and once I am so overcome with drowsiness, I doze off watching a softball game. I have trouble keeping myself here and barely make it through the day.

Finally, after dinner, it is time to say goodbye. Outside of his cabin, Tim says, "Will you come back again for the second session in August?"

At this moment, the thought is overwhelming. "I don't know if I'll still be here—on the East Coast. You know I work in the West and I'm just visiting." He can't hide his disappointment. "But maybe I'll be here, Tim. And in the meantime, if there's anything you need, you'll write—you have those stamped and addressed postcards I gave you."

He nods. "Okay." I'm kneeling. He rushes into my arms and hugs me hard. I hug him, kiss him, tousle his hair. His ribs, his body, feel hard and feverish with health, like some high-strung animal. "Okay, Timmy, I'll see you later."

It feels wrong to turn and walk away, but there's nothing else to do. When will I see him later? Small lies. I start for Richard's cabin. Turn. Tim watching me. I wave. He waves. What's he thinking? Determined not to look back, I take the path wondering how I will say goodbye to Richard.

His cabin ahead through the trees. Squares of light, the screened windows, gauzy figures moving inside, and from the toilets, the splash of a shower, several adolescently deepening voices in the half-light, a high sudden laugh. On all sides of me, the woods are already dark, but overhead, the sky has a whitish-blue radiance, a mare's tail lingers, blending into the rising night. Walking quickly, head down, I almost bump into Richard.

In front of me. No towel or soap dish, he's not on his way to or from the washcabin. His feet are comically large in the grass and weeds. Red track shoes. Arms and legs long, chest thin. I'm startled. He wasn't here a moment ago.

"Richard, I'm just on my way to see you."

"Oh, hello, Uncle Jack. Figured." He looks around nervously, crosses his arms in front of him, cradles his elbows.

"Is everything okay?"

"Oh, yeah."

I'm not sure what to say. "Is there anything you want to tell me, Richard?" I realize with sudden annoyance that is what my father has always asked me and that it has always irritated me, precisely because it seems to put everything back on me. In reply, I have always said, no, to shun him, to teach him, to tell him that's not what I want from him. He has either never caught on or else never wanted to change. Maybe I was supposed to catch on and say, yes, there is something I want to tell you.

Now in reply to me, Richard shrugs.

"Or anything you want me to do for you? Or send you?"

He shakes his head, no.

"How about Ursula LeGuin? The right one this time, *The Tombs of Atuan*." I try to joke about it.

He shrugs. "No, that's okay."

"I'll send it."

He shrugs. He is still shifting nervously. Dry leaves crunch underfoot. Everything feels out of rhythm—our attempt at conversation, this shifting back and forth. His loneliness and isolation are overwhelming. He watches me nervously, and I realize his nervous gestures are like those of an athlete psyching up before a contest.

"I'll send it," I repeat, "*The Tombs of Atuan*."

I still don't know how to say goodbye, but I want him to feel loved. I hugged him last year. Though my father and I have had violent disagreements, at times not spoken, I still continue to hug him, kiss him goodbye. Old man's grind of stubble on my cheek. Richard crosses and recrosses his arms.

"Goodnight, Richard."

I step toward him. He places his palms against my shoulders and pushes me back. A light firm pressure.

We look at each other. He cradles each elbow with the other hand, lifts his arms like some awkward bird settling his wings, places hands in pockets, takes one out and holds his chin with his hand, still not right, he cradles his arms over his stomach.

I reach out and carefully and determinedly pat him—once, firmly, on the shoulder.

"Goodnight, Richard. It's been good to see you. Write if you need anything. I'll send the book."

"Goodnight."

In the few moments we've been standing here, it's gotten much darker so the voices seem further away, the lights to the cabin brighter, the space we've been standing in larger, emptier.

I turn and start down the path through the woods, a coolness now reaching out of the darkness. I stumble on roots. Several times I stop, confused, hesitant, feeling as though I've forgotten something, then go on.

I follow path after path through camp until I come to the large baseball field. Cool and smelling of dust and the departing day's heat. A few cars. I wander disoriented around the field and then find the car. It seems a long time ago since I was here. Things that happened last year feel more recent than yesterday morning. The car is completely veiled with a fine layer of dust and seems to have become shapeless, aged, anonymous. The keys. The door light, the familiar smell of a closed car which has gone through a day of heat and has cooled again—upholstery, leather—a tired, comforting smell. I step back from the car and piss facing the woods. The splash of urine is something I know.

Inside I sit, hands in my lap, and stare straight ahead through the windshield. My eyes are used to the dark and I can make out the woods—darker. I can't yet bring myself to turn on the lights. Richard a few moments ago. The space outside the cabin, the splashing shower, the voices, the continual stir of grass and crunch of leaves beneath our feet as we circled each other. The look on his face. Apprehension. Resolve. Fear. I have an urge to find Tom, ask him. He would know. He's a father. I pull on the lights—the long hood of the Caddy covered with dust, the woods. I drive slowly around the baseball field looking for Tom's car before I hear my father's voice suddenly, Go on, you make too much of things. It's more the tone in the *go on*, which makes me feel foolish, another way of seeing completely: the world is simpler, more physically there; this network of doubts and reasons is not possible in his *go on*. My father's world seems more self-evident, plausible, easier to live in.

The car, its lights, its workings, are a comfort, a distraction; I drive slowly, following the unpaved road back to the country road. Once or twice I try the radio. I feel the pressure of his hands, sudden and firm. The radio sends bursts of static.

The isolated stretch of country road reaches the first of the small towns. Out of the dark. One by one, I pass slowly through them, each with its center green unnaturally metallic under the mercury glow, the heavy elms shadowed motionless into the streetlamps; the Victorian gazebos and bandstands, the war memorials. Back into the darkness, another stretch.

Rosie's profile between myself and the fire. Try not to be afraid. Did Rosie say that as we were drifting off to sleep? Or did I think it? Plunge off the slide, darkness of lake, old cellular terror. For a moment, one moment of certainty, I think that is what I might have told Richard. Try not . . . His circling·in the grass. Maybe said, let's take a walk. Changed the opposition of our bodies. We would have walked side by side; that's what Rosie had done, hadn't he? Taken me out of the camp completely, probably with little or no forethought, but a sure instinct to do nothing more than be with me, beside me, show me care.

Now I remember writing to Rosie. How had I forgotten? And my mother saving his letters in a box, telling me how nice of him to write me. Maybe she still has those letters put away. When I get home, I'll ask her, look for them. I wonder vaguely if I could find Rosie, trace him. Would he remember me? Or that day passing from lake to lake? That night? And if he did and I found him and we talked, or even just saw him, would those images— the lake, the fire—afterward remain the same, intact, or would they, after a conversation with a sixty-year-old man, leave me, vanish. I'm sure, if he is alive, that his eyes still have that same quiet, that same sadness, his voice, that gentle kindness.

Ahead, I see signs for the interstate. In another few minutes, I'm merging into the onrushing traffic, a flood of cars and blinding headlights. I half-close the window against the buffeting wind, turn the radio up. News. More music. Ball scores. Yankees, Red Sox. West Coast, games getting underway. Sweet smell of mown grass from the median divider.

Though all of the windows are open, the family house is hot and stuffy, the downstairs lights off; I open the refrigerator, close it. Stand in the dark front hall. Upstairs, the sound of the TV. I climb the dark staircase slowly, come to the door of my parents' bedroom. Hesitate. Flicker of the TV light. I enter.

My father sits shirtless in boxer shorts, TV tuner on his chair arm; his wispy gray hair stands up in a cloud, his cheeks are sunken; he really seems to be gazing at some point beyond the TV. In the pale half-light, my mother dozes shapeless under a sheet.

I walk toward the TV screen, wave. My father punches the mute. How are the boys, when did I get back, was it as hot there as it's been here.... We talk. The boys are fine. Healthy, eating well, tan. I almost tell him about Richard, our saying goodbye. I decide not to. The boys are fine.

My mother rolls over, opens her eyes momentarily, doesn't see me, says something I don't understand in a hoarse voice, her breath deepens, she goes back to sleep.

My father and I talk for several more minutes. I watch the gray light flickering on his ankles. He tells me there's some leftover chicken in the refrigerator. As I leave, he punches the sound back on. Says it's wrapped in aluminum foil.

I take a long cool shower, and then before I dry I find myself wandering through the bedrooms. My sister's old bedroom. My old bedroom. Still beaded with water, towel around my waist, I catch sight of myself in the mirror. The other day, my mother gazed thoughtfully at me.

"Your body's changed."

"From when?"

"Oh, in the last few years."

"I've weighed the same since college."

She smiled vaguely. I'd asked her what she'd meant, but she ended up patting me on the cheek.

A few days later, she said, "With you living so far away and coming home only once a year, I might see you only four or five more times."

"Mom..."

Her eyes had given away little. I stare at my body in the mirror. I can't see it, what she meant. The TV from the next room. My father's brittle ankles in pale light. My mother shapeless under the sheet. In the desert, there are retirement communities. They are advertised on billboards and in the Sunday paper. Ads with too-bright color. A man and a woman smiling on a golf course. Living on savings and investments and interest, having lunch by the pool, watching the evening news. Though my father is older than many of these people, certainly the man in the ad, I can't imagine him that way—or living that way. He says he could never retire. He shrugs. And play golf for the rest of my life? I'd be bored. I look at myself in the mirror, turn and start drying water gathered in the hair at the nape of my neck.

I stretch out on the bed and for a moment think of the hot desert air. Walking in the desert. Stopping. Silence. Dry wind milking my body. A wick. Cactus mottle the desert floor, each cactus casting a hard-edge shadow. Cholla. Prickly pear. Ocotillo. I turn my head to the right. The left. Overhead, a hawk remains motionless and time inches to a stop in the hot air; perhaps because there are no real seasons, one has the illusion time hasn't passed, isn't passing. I stand motionless, body losing water. One day I will reach out, and like some fallen cactus perfectly preserved in the dry air, my past will crumble at a touch.

I try to read. After a while the TV goes silent, the house dark. I walk into my sister's old room. Back to Richard's room. I lie down. On one wall, Richard has taped up a mythical kingdom which he has drawn. Islands, gnarled trees with faces in them, mountain peaks, trolls, dragons. It is beautifully detailed, drawn, and painted. I turn off the light, but can't sleep. Sit up and wonder at the finiteness of my feet on the floor.

I pull on a pair of shorts and wander aimlessly through the house, picking things up, putting them down. Hot. Still. Outside, it's cooler. I sit on the front steps of the dark house and look at the mountain laurel and magnolia. The blossoms are gone now. In spring, my mother walks slowly through the yard passing her fingertips lightly over the flowers and saying softly, oh, the lilacs... And the tulips! The mountain laurel! She will cut a sprig of mountain laurel, the pink flower and circle of shiny green oval leaves, and float it in a crystal vase which she will place in the middle of the dining room table.

I gaze up at the elms towering into the dark. I look down at my body. I weigh just the same. I take a deep breath, let it out slowly, and stare up into the thick motionless leaves.

On the Ocean

S ANDY WAS GOING TO MARRY HER. Most of his friends were disappointed, though they had expected it.

The first time Gallagher met Renee, there seemed to be something familiar about her, though Gallagher couldn't say exactly what. He studied her—her gray eyes, her straight blond hair; she had a sensual pouty underlip, but something tight and sour around the mouth, something strained about the eyes that reneged on that promise of sensuality. She wore Wallabees and dressed in gray or black sweaters which hung from her narrow shoulders. Gallagher knew she'd had a tough time—her first husband had walked out, leaving her with the two kids. Gallagher couldn't get over the feeling there was something familiar about her.

They were to be married out at the summer house. It was an old Victorian house that Sandy and Gallagher had shared off and on since college. Three floors, with rough shingles, a deep screened porch, and a wide lawn shaded by tall oaks and maples; the lawn narrowed into scrub oaks and wildflowers—daisies and buttercups; became a footpath which lost view of the water for several steps and then opened onto rocks and a view of the Sound. On clear days you could see the white bluffs of Long Island low in the distance, and looking across the bay, you could see the family house—Sandy's. It, too, was right on the water. Sandy and Gallagher usually shared the summer house from June until Labor Day. After that, on weekends. The house had no insulation and by mid-October most of the logs stacked by the gravel drive had been burned and it would be too cold to stay any longer. Gallagher and Sandy would meet one last Saturday afternoon, sweep the house, wash out the ice-box, straighten up, have one final beer on the porch, look at the leaves changing, look out at the Sound, and leave with a sweet sense of remorse; the house would be closed up until next season.

Renee and Sandy were to be married on the lawn in mid-July, and Sandy said to Gallagher, there is no place in the world I'd rather be married.

Shortly before the wedding Gallagher ran into an old confidant of Sandy's. She was married and had a couple of kids, but she and Sandy had remained close. They had never been lovers, though she smiled and said to Gallagher, we came near a couple of times ... too bad, but it was never quite the right time ... mostly for Sandy.

They talked about the approaching wedding and after a few moments, she shrugged and said, Sandy doesn't have to marry that woman to prove anything to himself. Oh, I hate to see it, really I do. And those two kids of hers ...

Sandy likes the kids.

His younger brother's married and has two kids and Sandy's thirty-two already, that's all, and thinks he's getting old. It's so unnecessary for him to put himself through all of this. For what? He can just accept himself the way he is.

Gallagher wasn't sure how much Sandy might have confided in her; he decided not to venture talking about Sandy accepting himself the way he is.

Instead, Gallagher said, oh, it'll come out alright. She shook her head, I hope it will come out alright, but I have serious misgivings. This business with his father ... and Renee? What kind of a woman is Renee? I mean, I get the feeling she doesn't

even like being a woman. Christ, any woman who has to spend
the day in bed every time she gets her period can't like having a
woman's body very much.

Gallagher thought that was pretty unreasonable. Who the hell
knew about women's periods, anyway. They talked a few
minutes more and then Gallagher said he had an appointment—
he was a legal aid lawyer—and got away.

Gallagher did think it odd, though, Sandy and his father.
Sandy's father was recovering from a mild heart attack, but
Sandy was sure his father was dying. Gallagher tried talking
him out of that, but Sandy said, it's not me, it's the old
man...he thinks he's dying. I know he doesn't want to live.

Why do you keep saying that?

He's wasted his life...the booze...AA...being a salesman...he could have been someone, he had the brains, the
chance, but he didn't do it. Why didn't he do something? He
doesn't know. But he does know what he is. Now he goes
around the house and garage putting things in order for my
mother like he's going to be gone tomorrow. It's getting on her
nerves worse than the drinking ever did. He just wants to die,
Gallagher. I know it!

There was no talking Sandy out of this.

Considering what Sandy thought about salesmen, Gallagher
couldn't understand why Sandy would be taking over for him.
He'd already started going out on the road with his father,
meeting customers, attending sales conventions in Boston and
New York. Last week he'd gone and gotten a haircut so his
father could introduce him to old clients at one of the conventions. Walking across the lawn in a blue cord suit, white shirt
and tie the day before leaving, Sandy really did look like a
salesman.

Since college—easily ten years—Sandy's father had been after
him to take over. For ten years, Sandy had refused. He'd gone to
his father's college and been in his fraternity. His father had
been a basketball and baseball star, but Sandy hadn't gone out
for anything. After graduation, he'd been in the March on
Washington, gone into the Peace Corps, gotten out of the draft
with a bad knee, campaigned for McGovern, gone back to

school and gotten a teaching certificate, and since, he'd been teaching in a big inner-city high school. That's where he'd met Renee. She was a guidance counselor.

Sandy was popular with the students and faculty. When he'd walk into a basketball game, the students would see him and cheer. On Thursday nights he played bridge with Mrs. Leibowitz, a history teacher; Tom Bailey, a city councilman and justice of the peace; and Ethel George, a black math teacher who was turning into a spinster. She had been a freedom rider back in 1964 and been jailed for sitting at a white lunch counter. She told Sandy that she had only hoped the mob couldn't see how hard she was shaking when the sheriff led her out into the street to the van. The four of them had been playing bridge together for almost five years. Between hands, and afterward, they would talk local politics, the death of the inner city, how the neighborhoods might be restored.

Sandy himself lived in a run-down three-story house in a black and Puerto Rican neighborhood. The second floor was Sandy's. The first he rented out. He drove a series of beat-up old cars, driving one until it would finally break down completely; he would then start on another. It was the same with everything Sandy owned—house, car, fishing rod, clothes, furniture . . . everything always seemed on the verge of falling apart, breaking down. Sandy's friends thought it was kind of funny—part of Sandy's charm.

Gallagher once drove up just as Sandy was trying to carry in a table from the street. It was trash collection night.

Ah, Gallagher, just in time, grab the end of this.

You got that out of the trash, didn't you?

Touch of paint, new leg, it'll be great.

Come on, Sandy, leave it. Get yourself a decent table. I mean that's awful.

You know me, Gallagher. I could never buy anything new. Too much guilt.

Don't give me that. Come on, leave it. But in the end, laughing, Gallagher had helped Sandy carry the table up the stairs.

* * *

Before he had made up his mind about stepping in for his father, Sandy would say periodically to Gallagher, the old man is after me to take over for him again.

He's still after you?

Oh, two or three times a year; he never ever really gives up. I'm not sure, I think he starts on me just before he goes off the wagon. Sandy laughed. I'm not sure what the correlation is, but that's my present theory, anyway. He doesn't give up easily, I'll say that for him.

Why doesn't he ask your brother?

Tim tried once. I think he lasted two weeks before the old man drove him crazy. My father's just not that easy to get along with. Matter of fact, he's impossible. You know his sarcasm, his quiet sarcasm. Anyway, who the hell really wants to be a salesman?

How bad can it be? You'd be making twice what you're getting teaching high school. Aren't you tired of teaching high school?

Yeah, dead tired. And it's not twice. It's three times. I'd be making three times what I'm making if I took over for him. Don't think I'm not tempted at times. Sandy sighed. When I was about ten or twelve, my father took me on the road with him. We went to all of these different stores and my father's voice was so quiet—you know the double edge in my father's voice, the softer it gets, the sharper... You can never really tell where you stand with him.

Everywhere we went, the store owners and managers were really glad to see him. My father can make himself immensely likeable. His voice would get quieter and quieter as we'd go from place to place. Sometimes I could barely make him out. He'd have this distant look in his eyes. He wouldn't really sell to them. He'd just ask them about their wives and kids, they'd talk for a while, then they'd ask him what he thought they'd be needing, he'd look around, make a few suggestions and write up orders. Half an hour, he'd make three, four hundred dollars in commissions. I remember looking up and watching them shake hands. When we got back in the car, my father said, see how it's done? I didn't answer, but I knew I wouldn't do it. Oh, he's good, no doubt about it. He's a master. But he told me once he wanted to be a doctor. Sandy thought for a minute. I don't know what kind of doctor he'd have made.

Sandy had always been easy to like. He had lots of friends. A number of them couldn't stand each other, but they all liked Sandy. He had clear blue eyes and hair which was never cut right, but looked fine, anyway. He'd never done anything to get in shape, but he had a good build and an easy, athletic way of moving, and he always seemed comfortable in beat-up old clothes—flannel shirts, corduroys, army jackets. He liked to drink in rundown bars, play pinball and pool and watch the ball games.

When Sandy and Gallagher got a little loaded, they would hold up the bottle and Sandy would ask, do you find yourself needing a drink to mix socially? And both would answer in a chorus, YES!

Gallagher would then ask, do you have a tendency to drink when you're depressed? And both would answer in a chorus, YES!

They would keep this up, pouring each other shots. Occasionally, Sandy and Gallagher worried about drinking too much, but never to the point of quitting for more than three or four days. Once a year Sandy quit smoking from New Year's morning until Washington's Birthday.

All of Sandy's friends had the sense that whatever he was doing at the moment, it was the very best thing a person could be doing. They prized his friendship.

Now on nights in the summer house, Sandy often stood, looked into his drink, spread his arms, swayed, smiled, Jesus, what a night, is this a great night? Let's go fishing, you wanna go fishing, Gallagher?

Gallagher always wanted to go fishing. Sandy would ask Renee, did Renee want to go fishing, and Renee would shake her head, no, she didn't want to go fishing.

Sandy would wave his hand, it's beautiful out there. He'd wave beyond the screened porch, the dark lawn, the ocean. We're going to catch fish tonight, Renee. I can feel it. Everything is perfect. Incoming tide, half moon, bunkers in the bay. There's a fish out there for each of us; wouldn't you like to catch a fish, Renee?

Again, Renee shook her head, no, she wouldn't like to catch a fish.

But one of them has your name on it. Renee.

Then I'll leave mine swimming.

Gallagher, don't misunderstand, she's a good woman, but she's Midwestern, she's not like us, she doesn't understand what it's like to be out on the ocean at night. She doesn't have it in her blood.

Renee looked up. What is in your blood, Sandy, is alcohol.

Sandy laughed. Oh, there is nothing finer, nothing, than to be drunk and on the ocean at night. He laughed. Oh, yeah. Come on, Gallagher, let's go across the bay, get the old man's boat, and wet a line.

They would drive the road around the bay, coast into the driveway, ease the doors shut quietly, return from the barn with the gas tanks, rods, a rusty knife, and pliers. Eventually, stumbling around and laughing, they'd get everything, themselves included, into the boat, and pole silently away from the seawall. Often, they'd stay out until the horizon separated itself from the darkness and the sky turned a pale gray.

It was the way he enjoyed himself which made Sandy's friendship prized. Then, several years before meeting Renee, he seemed to change. Gallagher didn't know exactly what was happening. They'd gone on a canoe trip. Gallagher would say something or joke and Sandy didn't seem to hear, or else he'd make a tight smile, his eyes expressionless, and look away. Several times he started to say something, then changed his mind. Finally, Gallagher, starting to feel uncomfortable, asked if there was something wrong.

After a long time, Sandy nodded, yeah, there is something wrong.

Gallagher waited, but Sandy didn't say any more. They cut the trip short. On the ride home, they were silent, but when

Gallagher pulled up to the house, Sandy said, come in and have a drink.

Gallagher didn't want to, but the offer seemed to be some kind of apology.

Inside, Sandy took a shower and Gallagher poured himself a drink and fell on the sofa. He was leafing through a magazine when he heard a door close, footsteps, and then Gallagher was surprised to see someone he didn't know standing in the doorway; his face was open and expectant. He had a key in one hand.

He held up the key and said, uh, I thought Mr. Johnson was gonna be away a few more days. But then I saw the light on. So I thought he was home. I was supposed to keep the plants watered for him.

We came back early.

Didn'tcha catch no fish?

A couple.

The boy looked uncertainly around the room, said to Gallagher, well, I'm just gonna water the plants, anyway, and returned from the kitchen with a plastic pitcher.

Gallagher watched him. He moved awkwardly; whether it was his adolescence or his Dr. Scholl's sandals, he seemed on the verge of tripping or skidding. Gallagher couldn't make out the scene on his shirt, it was a silk body shirt, and it had a scene of some kind. Each plant he watered carefully, and each time he leaned forward, his blond straight hair fell in his gray eyes and caught at the corner of his mouth. Finally, after clomping back and forth from the kitchen several times, he held the hair out of his eyes with one hand against his cheek. Was it his color? The circles under his eyes? Gallagher thought he looked sick or unhealthy.

Gallagher looked up in time to see Sandy stop in the doorway. He was combing his wet hair. Saying something. Then he said quickly, Hi, Peter. Peter, this is Gallagher.

I thought you was gonna be away for two more days, Mr. Johnson.

We were, Peter, but we cut it short. Nice to see you're so

dependable. Sandy said toward Gallagher, one of my students. Gonna get myself a drink.

Gallagher finished his drink. In the kitchen, Sandy was smashing an ice tray against the counter.

Warm water does it.

Sandy didn't look up.

I'll see you later. I'm going to get some sleep.

Stick around, we'll grill some burgers.

No thanks, just want to sleep.

As Gallagher stepped into the street, he could hear Sandy smashing the ice tray against the counter.

Next time Gallagher saw Sandy, there was a pause and then Sandy said quickly, I'm really concerned about Peter—the kid who was watering the plants.

I remember.

I had the kid when he was in the tenth grade. He's flunked two or three times. His father's gone, his mother's always loaded. He just stays with different people in the neighborhood. A few days here, a few days there. Now he's getting into drugs.

He didn't look too good when I saw him. His color or something.

Sandy said distractedly, yeah, no one feeds him. I mean, real food. He just eats Big Macs and fries and cupcakes. I try to have him over at least twice a week to make sure he has a good dinner. Maybe the kid would be better off in the army.

I can't see that kid in the army.

Neither can I, but he's thinking of it. What else do you do when you've flunked tenth grade three times?

Gallagher hadn't seen Sandy for a while when they ran into each other at a big, noisy party. They tried to talk for a few minutes, then simultaneously waved at the music and noise, shrugged, and moved away. Then it was late, the party had thinned out, quieted down, and Gallagher was on a sofa, when someone dropped down beside him.

Gallagher . . .

Sandy, lost track of you there for a while.

Gallagher, he repeated. Gallagher looked up.

Sandy blurted, for Christ's sake, I'm queer.

Gallagher knew he had to say something, but instead, he was remembering years ago, college, they'd gone out in the old man's boat, a hot summer day, Gallagher had brought a friend. Changing into suits, Gallagher's friend kicked off his pants, Sandy looked away sharply and Gallagher had thought it odd.

Then Gallagher wondered if he was going to start seeing everything this way. Finally, he said, Take it easy, Sandy. Jung says we're all bisexual. . . .

I don't care what Jung says, I'm not bisexual, I'm queer.

Take it easy.

I've started seeing a shrink, but I can tell it's not going to help.

How do you know?

I just sit there and cry.

The thought of Sandy's paying some stranger to sit and cry didn't seem good to Gallagher. He wondered, vaguely, if Sandy had ever been attracted to him, but then that passed, and Gallagher felt certain they would go on being friends.

Sandy said, lately, I keep wondering what my father would say if he found out.

He won't find out. Parts of people's lives can be private.

It's not what he'd say so much, the words. It's the sound of his voice I keep thinking about.

Sandy made deprecatory remarks about seeing the shrink, but went on seeing him. After six months, he started going to church. Gallagher couldn't believe Sandy going to church, although he remembered one time they got drunk and started singing hymns, which wasn't going to church. Sandy tried to joke. The shrink says I'm in a dangerous phase. Said this was one of several distinct possibilities. Said he wasn't surprised when I told him I was going to church. Smart, isn't he? Well, I don't give a shit, I feel like going to church, I'm going to church. I know how it looks, but . . .

After a while, he stopped going and later, whenever he referred to it, there would be a sardonic edge in his voice, ah, yes, my Jesus phase, predictable, just like the shrink said. . . .

Sandy and Gallagher went on sharing the summer house. Things were pretty much as they'd always been. They fished, drank, the house was a mess, bathing suits drying on the porch; water-stained John MacDonalds on the mantel; last year's and this year's tide table by the telephone; ashtrays full; trash overflowing with beer cans; bait of questionable freshness in the vegetable bin and always distressing to Gallagher's girlfriends, who seemed to last no more than a month, sometimes a summer. The house was never locked and Gallagher or Sandy often returned to find friends waiting on the porch with a gin and tonic and a fishing rod.

At times Sandy seemed so preoccupied that Gallagher, finally, having asked him something three times, shouted, do I need speech lessons, or have you gone deaf?

Sandy would get moodier and moodier and then finally disappear for days on end and then return to the house and sleep. After that he was calm and more like his old self—open, friendly. But within a week or two, he was withdrawn, moody, and irritable. Then he would disappear again for several days. Toward the end of the summer, he brought two or three different women out and the women stayed the night. One of them was Renee. Meeting her for the first time, Gallagher thought there was something familiar about her. Sandy brought her out to the house several times and though Gallagher was friendly, she could only manage a curt, tight-lipped hello or nod.

After a few times, Gallagher asked, does Renee dislike me? She always seems kind of pissed.

Sandy shook his head, no, that's just the way she is. I know she likes you.

Renee had a self-conscious habit of staring straight ahead, sometimes pursing her lips and frowning. She never wanted to fish or have a drink or play tennis. She'd read a novel. Sometimes take a swim. Though she had two kids, she had no marks on her stomach or hips, no marks at all on her pale body. She never tanned. As she would walk across the lawn, Gallagher wondered what it was Sandy liked about her.

As the summer went on, she started bringing out her two boys. The younger wore glasses which were always smudged with fingerprints, the older always wore different colored socks and sulked a lot. The kids screamed while everyone tried to talk, blew out Sandy's match as he tried to light a cigarette until it wasn't fun anymore, climbed all over everyone, fought with each other. Sandy and Renee would make no attempt to control the kids and Gallagher often went for a walk in disgust. It got so Renee and the kids were there all the time. Sandy and Gallagher had always split the rent on the house and never said anything to the other about who showed up, but Gallagher now felt as though the house had been taken over. Why, of all the women in the world, did Sandy have to pick this skinny one with two kids?

Often Gallagher came out from town to find Sandy standing on the lawn and staring out at the ocean. He would be holding the younger boy in one arm, holding the older boy's hand, and Renee would be standing beside him leaning her head against his shoulder, her arm around Sandy's waist. All three holding on to Sandy—or Sandy holding on to all three, Gallagher wasn't sure. Though Gallagher supposed it was for the best if it made Sandy happy, the sight of them standing on the lawn like that staring out at the ocean made Gallagher hurt.

Sandy had been seeing Renee a year, two years, and then he debated moving in with her. He said to Gallagher, it's not a decision which just affects Renee and myself. It's the kids, too. They're already attached to me, and if it doesn't work out, well, I wouldn't want them to have to go through that again. They've already had one man disappear and the older boy remembers. It still bothers him.

Sandy debated several months. Then he rented out his second-floor apartment over in the black section, Renee gave up her place, and they moved into the first floor of a duplex. They split the rent; Renee wouldn't allow Sandy to pay for any of the children's shoes, food, and so on. She said, after all, they're my kids, not Sandy's, why should he have to pay for my kids?

Each time Gallagher saw Sandy, he seemed more relaxed, more comfortable. He even put on enough weight so there was just the possibility of a roll around his middle. Renee still frowned, but she laughed more. The noise and confusion of the children followed Sandy everywhere and Gallagher knew that if he wanted to talk to Sandy, he would have to talk through the screams of the children.

One night at the summer house, Renee and the kids asleep, Sandy stood up, tipped back his head, laughed, what a night, what a beautiful night, let's go fishing, Gallagher, you wanna go over and get the old man's boat and go fishing?

It was clear, no moon, the stars bright, the Milky Way glowing overhead. They lay back on the thwarts, stared up at the stars, drank. Gallagher got a hit and fought whatever it was up to the boat. In the flashlight beam, they could see the beautiful silver flash of the blue rocket beneath the surface before it dove, disappeared into the dark. The blue thrashed, took off more line, Gallagher had the blue back up to the boat and Sandy was ready with the gaff when the line broke and that was that. Slowly Gallagher felt the adrenalin level down. They laughed and guessed at the size and after a while Sandy sighed, what a life.

Not bad, huh?

Not bad, not bad ... not great, either. Not what I thought it would be. Then, somehow, Sandy started talking about the whole business—that was the way Gallagher had come to think of it—which was unusual for Sandy. He talked for a while and then said, I don't know what I'm going to do. I ignore it for as long as I can. Which seems to be about two or three weeks. By then I'm really moody and irritable. I can't stand it. I give in. Go out and pick someone up. Got the third floor attic fixed up into a little apartment. That's the only thing I use it for. I rarely see them again.

And Renee?

Oh, she knows. It freaks her.

Gallagher took a hit off his bottle. He could see Sandy darker, against the water, the glow of his cigarette.

But you're still going to live together?

Yeah, I've told her, parts of my life are going to have to be like black holes, you know ... nothing comes out. She can have them, too, if she needs them. People are entitled, Gallagher. If we get married, it will be the same. I know it freaks her. But she also knows I love her. Sandy took a long drink from the bottle and let out a deep sigh. We're separate people, Gallagher, we really are.

Sandy was silent. Then: Sometimes I can't help thinking about what my father would say if he found out.

Gallagher looked up and noticed the constellations had moved. It was late.

Forget what he'd say. Take a piece of your own insight to heart. You're separate people.

They talked about other things, got a few more hits.

It was late when Sandy cut the motor and they drifted in toward the seawall. Sandy raised the flashlight, something red, Sandy raised the flashlight higher, the massive chest matted with gray hair, pectorals going soft, belly hanging over the bright red golf pants. The white water reflections rippled across his body, blue eyes pale in the light, white hair whiter, he seemed to be rising out of the water.

Sandy was laughing at something. He stopped. He raised the light higher.

His father placed his palm over his eyes and squinted against the light. Sandy, for Christ's sake ... His voice so soft they could hardly make it out. A bottle beside him.

Sorry, Dad.

The tip of his cigarette reappeared as Sandy lowered the light. Crabs moving in the seaweed. His voice out of the dark. You two jerks get anything?

A few hits. Gallagher had one up to the boat, but the line broke.

Nice going, Gallagher. Striper?

Blue. Big one.

Nice going. You two jerks so lushed you going to leave my boat a mess like last year?

Sandy didn't answer.

After a long time, his voice, soft. Sandy...I'm talking to you.... Did you hear me?

Sandy didn't answer.

That winter, Sandy was involved in an incident at the high school. He'd broken up a fight between several blacks and Italians. All had been brought to the principal's office. Accusations and counter-accusations flew, things flared up, and someone sucker-punched Sandy and knocked him to the floor.

Sandy found himself holding a blood-drenched handkerchief in Mrs. Leibowitz's office. She locked the door. He stood motionless. Then ten years of something went out of him and he burst into tears. Mrs. Leibowitz put her arms around him, he sobbed, tried to pull away, I'm bleeding on your dress, but she held him tighter and he sobbed harder. Then she drove him to the emergency room, a doctor put eight stitches in his scalp, and she drove him home.

Not long after that, Sandy's father had the heart attack, again asked Sandy to take over for him, and this time, after vacillating, and even joking, the old man sure timed that right, Sandy accepted, and almost at the same time decided to marry Renee.

Renee said she thought marriage meant nothing, the ceremony, the institution, and for a long time she had said she would never marry again. But finally, if it was what Sandy wanted, she wanted it, too—if it would please Sandy. Sandy also thought marriage in this day and age was a little ridiculous—after all, they'd been living together for the last year. Each said separately the marriage, the ceremony, was for the other's parents—it would make them happy. If it didn't make any difference one way or the other, then what the hell, they might as well make their parents happy. And Sandy said to Gallagher, it's a good excuse for a party. Though I'm really worried about having booze at the wedding...the temptation might be too much for the old man...ever since he's had his heart attack, he's been going off the wagon. He quit smoking, but I don't know, it wouldn't be too much of a wedding party without booze, would it? I mean, we've got to have booze.

The wedding was set for mid-July. It would be a simple ceremony out on the lawn of the summer house. They'd have to hope for good weather because they weren't having a tent—if it rained, it rained; they would have to crowd into the house.

Renee would drop her married name, but not take Sandy's last name. She would revert to her maiden name, though the children would keep her first married name. Sandy hopefully offered her a diamond, but Renee thought a diamond was ridiculous, a simple gold wedding band would be enough, Sandy might just as well spend the money on something worthwhile—like getting the car fixed. Sandy wanted to give Renee a diamond, they fought briefly over it, but in the end, Renee flatly refused to accept a diamond.

Sandy started getting up early and going out on the road with his father. Late in the afternoon, he'd come walking across the lawn in a cord suit, tie down, collar open, sigh, stop and look at the ocean.

For years he'd been telling Gallagher he couldn't get along with the old man, they couldn't even agree on how to put the boat in the water every spring. But Sandy said it really wasn't that bad.

Not as bad as I'd thought it would be. We spend a lot of time driving and he reminisces. He talks about college, about baseball season his senior year at Dartmouth, about when Tim and I were kids, anything. He introduces me to the customers. Sandy shrugged. It's kind of boring, but it's a lot of scratch. Thirty-five to forty grand a year, good years, fifty. I just can't turn my back on that kind of bread anymore.

Sandy joked, of course, I have no illusions, there's never been a time when I wasn't in debt, cash reserve checking accounts have been my undoing. The more I have, the more I spend. How's the water?

Perfect. Nice tide, too. Almost high.

I'm heading up to the house and change into a suit.

Sandy turned, hesitated, I suppose it's only a matter of time before I join the country club and start voting Republican.

He walked up toward the house.

A week before the wedding, Renee's mother came in from the Midwest to lend a hand, look after the kids, help with the preparations, whatever. Renee sat both of the children on the kitchen table and gave them haircuts. Renee's married sister and several cousins, aunts, and uncles arrived from different parts of the country. Gallagher gladly gave up his room and moved to town even though they were in the middle of a heat wave.

Mrs. Johnson called the morning of the wedding to tell Sandy that his father had gone off the wagon last night, but she thought he would be alright by three—the hour set for the wedding. Could Sandy drive across the bay, give her a hand with a couple of things, and talk to his father for a few minutes?

He'd be right over.

Did she want him not to have booze at the wedding? If she thought it would be better, Sandy would cut the hard liquor, just serve champagne.

No, no, she wanted nothing of the kind, they would have liquor at the wedding, everyone would have a good time, and Sandy's father would and could control himself.

At two-thirty the guests started walking slowly across the lawn and gathering in the shade to talk and fan themselves. It was hot and still, the second week of the heat wave. Beyond the lawn, Sunday sailors drifted on their reflections, sails slack. Everyone started drinking and Sandy and Renee mingled with the guests.

Tom Bailey, the justice of the peace, arrived, sweat darkening the back of his linen suit. After a few minutes, he looked questioningly at Sandy. Sandy checked his watch, glanced around, didn't see his father, and said, wait a few minutes, Tom. What are you drinking?

It was after three when Mr. and Mrs. Johnson came walking

slowly up the long gravel drive. Mr. Johnson was flushed and moved slowly, heavily, against Mrs. Johnson, who seemed to support him—or else just held his hand tightly.

Mr. Johnson walked slowly across the lawn, seemed to gaze with disapproval. His eyes were bleary; large circles showed beneath his flushed skin. His clothes were dark with perspiration. He smiled at some of the guests, but his pale blue eyes didn't smile as he made his way.

Gallagher saw him coming. He reached the bar. This your domain, Gallagher?

Gallagher tried to smile.

Nice to see you doing something useful. How about a Seven-Up with plenty of ice.

Gallagher handed him the drink and he took a long swallow. You the last one to avoid this vale of tears, Gallagher?

After a moment, Gallagher understood he meant marriage.

I guess so.

Mr. Johnson took another drink.

Tell you the truth, Gallagher, I never took you to be that smart. Jesus, you must get a lot of ass.

The wedding guests had already been drinking and talking on the lawn for almost an hour and there was the easy but inappropriate feeling that the whole affair had turned into an afternoon cocktail party. Now Sandy's brother and several of his friends eased the guests toward the edge of the lawn. Suddenly it was quiet except for the hiss of feet through the grass. The guests followed Sandy and Renee, and as Renee walked, she turned once and said in a mocking, but pleased voice, excuse us, we're going to get married, we'll be back in a minute. Her gray eyes were bright.

The guests formed a loose semicircle around them; the neighbor children crouched on the rocks. Sandy and Renee placed an arm around each other, an arm around each of the children and drew them to their sides.

They had written the ceremony to be short and simple. It was over in a few minutes. They exchanged gold wedding bands, kissed each other, knelt and kissed the boys; the wedding guests surrounded them and started to kiss and hug Renee and shake Sandy's hand. The children ran off to play with the neighbor children, champagne was passed around and there were several toasts.

The party spread out on the lawn. Gallagher could see the guests were managing by themselves so abandoned the bar. He was thankful he wasn't there when he saw Mr. Johnson make himself a strong gin and tonic, a few minutes later, another. Gallagher looked over to see Sandy watching his father apprehensively.

Sandy watched a moment longer, his face tense, and then walked over to Gallagher. The hell with it, just the hell with it, this is my wedding and I'll do what I want, let's get drunk, come to the bar and have a drink with me.

They had a couple of drinks. They could see Mr. Johnson sitting in a wicker chair across the lawn. His blue eyes were pale against his flushed skin, he was talking to someone, but not looking at him. When he spoke, his lips barely parted, and the muscles around his mouth had slackened. He was drinking steadily.

Sandy turned and walked to the house.

Standing in the shade and watching the guests, Gallagher noticed someone who had to be Renee's brother. Like Renee, he had straight blond hair which hid most of his face, but Gallagher could see the upturned nose, the gray eyes, the pouty mouth. Then it hit Gallagher. He walked over.

Peter. So. You've been in the army?

Peter shook his drink and looked around. Yeah, I got out six months ago. It wasn't too bad. I've been traveling around, but I just got back.

Perhaps this was the boy Sandy felt himself to be, sullen and full of thwarted feeling. Perhaps nothing of the kind. Gallagher didn't know. He saw Peter had a wedding present.

Does Sandy know you're here?

I don't think so. I just got here. When I heard Sandy was getting married, I just wanted to come and give him my best wishes even though I wasn't invited. He was the only person who cared about me or even helped me.

Gallagher looked across the lawn at Mr. Johnson. What did he know? What could he put together? Maybe he would be too drunk to see the resemblance. That would be best. Renee was across the lawn, and that was good, too. Gallagher was sure if they stood near each other, people would see it. Even Sandy might see and, Gallagher thought, that would be the worst.

Now Gallagher suddenly felt Sandy's long-time fear, what would his father say? He glanced around. Saw Renee stopping to talk to guests, but making her way slowly toward them. Best to get Peter out of here quickly.

Well, look, Peter, Sandy's in the house, come say hello to him, it's cooler in the house. I'm going back to town so I'll give you a lift.

That's okay, I got a car. Peter looked up from his drink. He's not in the house, anyway. He's right here.

Sandy was stepping off the porch. Gallagher could see from the way that he walked that he was much drunker. Sandy looked over, saw Peter, took a deep breath, looked over toward his father, and then walked slowly and unsteadily toward them, stopped, swayed, said in a soft voice, ahh, hello, Peter... you came to my wedding.

I brought you something, that's all, I just heard yesterday, I didn't mean to crash your party.

Peter handed him the wedding present. Sandy's eyes looked pained, sad. His voice softened, ah, Peter, how nice of you, how nice.

Sandy looked at the present, lurched, Gallagher reached out and steadied him. Sandy smiled at Gallagher. He looked at the wedding present. He put his arm around Peter and said, this is so nice of you, Peter.

Gallagher felt Renee beside him. Sandy put both his arms around Peter and hugged him.

So nice of you.

Sandy's fingers tangled in Peter's hair at the back of his neck.

Across the lawn, Gallagher saw Mr. Johnson hoist himself out of his wicker chair and start walking slowly toward them, face flushed, eyes bloodshot, the ruins of his great athlete's body evident beneath his sweat-soaked shirt. He walked slowly and unsteadily, bumping into people.

Sandy swayed, his arms still around Peter, but he must have heard or felt someone behind him. He turned and looked at his father.

Mr. Johnson swayed. He looked at Sandy. He looked at Peter, then Renee. Some unbelieving look of recognition seemed to pass across his face for a moment. Then his eyes emptied.

Sandy leaned heavily against Peter, his arm still around him. He stared at his father.

His father said in a soft voice which Gallagher could barely make out, For Christ's sake, Sandy...sober up.

Renee lifted Sandy's arm from Peter, slipped his arm around her, placed her arm around his waist, and led him off to a quiet part of the lawn where they stood with their backs to the guests holding each other and looking out at the ocean.

The Man Who Died

SIX WEEKS AFTER what came to be referred to as the incident, Tom Fields—Doctor Fields—was arrested. He'd just returned home from a faculty meeting. He was charged by two plainclothes detectives who read him his Miranda rights. He couldn't believe it. He was handcuffed and walked out to the unmarked car in front of his house.

His first glimpse of the county jail was what seemed to be miles of razor wire gleaming silver on top of a chain-link fence. He was walked from the parking lot into the jail where, on opening the door, the smell of Pinesol hit him. Several doors were unlocked and relocked behind him as he was led inside. Papers were processed along the way. The handcuffs were removed. He was fingerprinted and photographed. Finally, he stood at a counter with a wire grating, and there he was directed to empty the contents of his pockets. The deputy placed his wallet, keys, change, and a penknife in a brown manila envelope. He was allowed to keep a quarter for the pay phone across the room where he called a friend—an attorney with a civil practice—who said he'd drop everything and get Tom a criminal lawyer.

When he hung up, a deputy took him by the biceps, led him down a corridor where a block door was unlocked, and Tom

Fields was placed in a cell. As the door closed, he was overwhelmed by the cloy of stale food, sweat, the racket of a radio and prisoners shouting. He walked to the far wall and looked through the bars and glass at the desert glaring white in the sun, then cautiously checked the other prisoners. He sat down on a metal stool bolted to the tile wall and placed his elbows on his knees.

Someone said, "Got a cigarette?"

Tom patted his pockets. "No, I don't smoke."

The prisoner said, "The fuck ya check for?"

Tom shrugged. He stared at the floor and started thinking about the girl but couldn't get her into focus.

His dinner sat still untouched on a tray, when the deputy came and led him back down the corridor. He again saw his lawyer waiting for him on the other side of the cell-block door. "Bail's paid. Let's get out of here." Tom walked toward him, offered his hand.

Outside, Tom took a deep breath. The mountains were throwing long deepening shadows across the desert. As they walked toward Levy's car, Michael said, "Did they try to get you to talk to them when they arrested you?"

Tom shook his head. "No."

"You didn't attempt to explain anything?"

"No, they just took me in."

Levy nodded. "And they Mirandized you—they read you your rights: 'You have the right to remain silent...'?" Tom nodded. "Okay. Good that you didn't talk." Levy stopped at a silver BMW. "This one." He looked back across the parking lot at the jail. "Not much fun in there."

Tom took another deep breath and got in the car. He knew Levy was about his age—forty—had seen his name in the paper for years. They'd once met at a party, but Fields doubted Levy would remember. Again, he tried to recall the girl. The detectives cited the incident as having taken place five weeks ago, which he didn't remember, but a close friend of his had been killed two months ago, and he knew that date. Jim had been killed riding his bike—he was training for a triathlon—and had been struck by a hit-and-run driver in Marin County. Tom had been away skiing and hadn't heard about the death until ten days after the funeral. By then, all he'd been able to do was make a few phone calls to Jim's parents and ex-wife. Shortly after the death, Fields became vaguely aware that his tongue thickened in his mouth when he tried to speak, and he felt off balance and forgetful. One afternoon, unaware, he ran a red light and came within a moment of being hit. According to the detective, he'd met the girl two days later. He checked over at Levy—curly blond hair, dark eyes, a boxer's face flushed red in the setting sun. As they drove, he wondered if Levy thought he was guilty of the charges.

Several days after his release on bail, Fields had impulsively driven back to Levy's office without an appointment. He'd been remembering his initial appearance. When his case had been called, Fields stood with Levy and walked to the front of the courtroom. When her name was read as the victim, Susanne Raine, Fields recalled telling her that she had a beautiful name. It was impossible to know if he had actually believed this, but there had been something...

Now Fields caught up with Levy in the corridor outside his office. Levy was walking out and Tom fell in beside him. "Michael, look, I've been thinking, maybe if I just gave the girl a call and talked to her, I could straighten things out..." Levy took his arm.

Outside the office, he turned to face Fields. "Tom, listen to me carefully. A twenty-year-old girl has charged you with kidnapping and sexual abuse. They're serious charges. I know from our conversations that you're confused—anyone would be under these circumstances—which is one reason you have a lawyer. And I can see you're an emotional guy, anyway." Levy paused. "I've got your statement, the police reports, her state-ment; we've got a pretty good idea what we're doing. Everything's under control."

Levy's New York accent, his lowered, confiding voice, com-forted Tom. Tom was an Easterner, too. Levy put his hand on Tom's shoulder. "Whatever you do, promise me that you will not try to contact Susanne Raine in any way and for any reason." Tom nodded. "Okay. Good. Look, you're exhausted. Just try to get some sleep and put this out of your mind as much as possible. I know it won't be easy, but try." Levy studied him, then patted him on the shoulder. "Got to run. We'll talk." Levy walked quickly across the bricked courtyard.

Tom took off his tie and jacket and slid into his car, baking hot in the February sun. He opened the windows and drove toward the exit. Since the detectives had come to his door three days ago, he hadn't really slept. He'd doze off and then jerk awake, sometimes to the clamor in the jail cell. He'd think about the girl. No matter how hard he tried, he couldn't remember exactly what had happened, though he was sure it was nothing. She'd come to the house. They talked. There'd been some hugging, some rolling on the sofa. She'd left when she'd wanted. They hadn't seen or contacted each other after that.

He hunted up the ticket, dug out his wallet, and paid the attendant, who raised the gate. Tom fumbled his sunglasses off the dash. Levy had reminded Tom—it was in her statement, but Fields had dismissed the conversation—that there had been further contact between himself and the alleged victim. Susanne Raine had called him three weeks later. As they talked, Tom had been able to recall fragments for Levy. She'd started by saying, "Do you know who this is? Do you remember my voice...or have you forgotten?" He stalled. "Of course, I remember you." "You do? Oh, good." She'd talked aimlessly, and then out of the blue, "Why did you touch my groin area that day I came to your house?" And he'd been so struck by its clinical sound, he hadn't known what to say. "No answer, huh?" She'd gone on. "Well, I guess you've been very busy." Several times she circled back to a beginning. "Well, how've you been?" Hoping to connect with her, he'd said, "Look..." She'd picked up on it. "Susanne. Susanne Raine, the girl from the mall. I knew you didn't remember my name, that's okay, you remember me, and I certainly remember you." Something about her voice and tone were making him nervous. She said, "You didn't remember my name. But now you've got it. Susanne. Hey, that's okay, Tom, I don't hold it against you, but one thing I'd really like to know is why you masturbated against me." He was silent. "You know, as in hump." He really had no idea what she was talking about. Finally, he said, "Susanne, I don't remember anything like that. You came to my house. We hugged. We liked each other. You hugged me. We were affectionate." Then, because he imagined she wanted to hear it, he said, "I thought we'd get together again, but I've been very busy. Maybe we can still do something." She said, "Oh, sure, maybe." Just before they'd gotten off, she went back to the clinical tone, "Tom, I just want to know why you masturbated when I came to your house? Can you give me an answer?" This confirmed to Tom that she was crazy. Excusing himself, he hung up. That had been three weeks ago.

Tom swung into the drive-thru at Wendy's. Levy said it was a good thing that he hadn't argued with her. And that he had admitted nothing because, Levy told him, the police had been taping the phone call. She said so in her statement. Levy had shown him her statement to the police. Her account said they'd met at Thunderbird Mall where she worked part-time at the information counter. Fields asked her for directions, and then they'd started talking. She told him she had the mall job, was a waitress three days a week, and was also a student at the university. He said he was a professor. They'd talked. He'd asked how much her job paid, and told her he thought he could help her find a better job at the university. He left his number and told her to call if she was interested. She said he genuinely seemed to care about her. That's why she called him.

A few days later, she went to meet him at ten in the morning. She was surprised when the address turned out to be his house—she'd thought they were meeting in a university office. Fields greeted her at the front door which opened directly into the living room. He was wearing jeans and a sports shirt. She thought he'd be dressed a little better. She'd dressed as though for a job interview. Skirt. Blouse.

As she'd walked into the living room, she heard him lock the front door behind her. He showed her around the house a bit. The living room, den, kitchen. They looked into a bedroom, but did not go in. He also showed her the garden. He offered her coffee, which she refused, and he remarked on her good figure and overall look of health. She sat on the sofa opposite the French doors which opened out into a backyard garden. He sat down at the other end of the sofa. They talked about everything but the job. He asked her personal questions about her life, her studies; he asked her what she did to keep so physically fit and she said she was a dancer, but that lately she'd been having lower back pain. He told her he'd had some pain in the same area, but had done exercises which helped him. He stood up to demonstrate a few, then suggested she try them. She was hesitant, but he seemed genuinely to care and so she got up and tried several—there were three or four.

When she sat back down, they were closer together. He put his arm around her, told her he thought she was incredibly beautiful, that she really held something for him and she must know that, and he began to hug her. She let him for a minute, mainly because she was surprised and confused and didn't know what to do next. He moved closer. Then somehow, in the way he moved his body, he got her to lie down beside him on the sofa, began to touch her breasts and groin area. She asked him to stop; he went on hugging and touching her. She decided not to struggle, but wait for the right moment to move. He seemed very excited. This went on for a while. Then she felt his excitement peak. It was then that she knew he'd ejaculated. She could feel it in his body. She pushed away, stood up. She walked to the front door, unlocked it, and then asked him if there had ever really been a job. He didn't answer and she left.

As a result of this incident, she said in her statement, she had been depressed, unable to sleep or concentrate. Her stomach had been upset and it had not been possible to have relations with her boyfriend.

Tom leaned out of his window. One more car before he'd reach the drive-thru window. He swallowed. He had no saliva. When he'd finished making his own statement and been shown a typed copy, his first reaction was: is this all that stands between me and her charges? There was so little to the incident. His account was very much like hers, though he knew he had never locked the front door. She was free to go at any time. It was she who had asked to see the house and had not seemed interested in talking about the job. It was true, he had shown her some exercises. When they sat back down on the sofa, they had hugged at the same time. She had kissed him. There had been some affectionate touching, though he couldn't say where. She pushed away once and then started hugging him again. When she pushed away again, she said that he reminded her of an elementary school teacher who had touched her improperly. She had then become very agitated. He tried to talk to her, but she stood up suddenly. She walked to the front door, asked him if there had ever been any job, and before he could answer, she left.

Tom pulled up to the window. The girl handed over the drink, and one of them fumbled the coins. He took a gulp of the iced tea, and then kneeling on the hot pavement, he gathered up his change.

Several days after his arrest, there was a brief article on the front page of the morning paper: "University Professor Arrested for Kidnapping and Sexual Abuse." He had scheduled two student conferences that day; he had a short faculty meeting and later a graduate seminar. He debated, and then decided it was crucial that he keep his appointments.

One of the students didn't show for his conference, but students did sometimes forget. The other, a graduate student, whom he considered a friend, appeared at the right time, but just to tell him she had a scheduling conflict and couldn't stay. She gave him a searching look, then left abruptly.

In the halls and in the office, the faculty seemed to avoid him. At the meeting, no one said anything about the article in the paper. No one said or intimated they were sure Tom must be innocent of the charges.

That afternoon, the students in his graduate seminar watched him out of a distance and curiosity. No matter what he said or did, he couldn't bring much back from them. He hung on as long as he could and then dismissed the class early. As he walked from the room, he had no idea how he would finish the semester.

In the following days, he greeted people, but several ignored him. He developed a preoccupied air when he was out, acknowledged almost no one, and avoided restaurants; he began to shop in grocery stores outside his neighborhood. There was something familiar about this isolation and banishment.

Alone, unable to concentrate on his work, he put his energy into training for a triathlon which was to take place in Hawaii late in May. At sunrise, he followed the bike path to the edge of town where the suburban streets released him, the desert took him in, and, his shadow elongating across cactus, palo verde, and mesquite, he peddled hard. Afternoons, he jogged or swam laps outdoors, the pool an enormous twilit room electric with white sunlight and the plunging arms and legs of strangers.

Even under the fluorescent lights of the courtroom, Susanne Raine's reddish-blond hair gave off a kind of heat. Tom couldn't keep himself from looking over at her. The preliminary hearing. She told her story. Questions were asked and answered. She seemed very sure of herself. He told his story. More questions were asked. They stuck to their stories. He wanted to stand up, cross the room, and ask her why she was doing this to him? At the end of the hearing, the case was bound over for trial, and Fields entered a plea of innocent. A trial date was set. As she left the room, she gave him an expressionless look, and Tom caught the sharp smell of his own nervous sweat. He turned to Levy. "Jesus Christ, Michael, what does she really want?"

Levy said, "She wants your ass. I'm going to have my investigator check her out—see if she has a psychiatric history—or if she has a habit of getting herself into these kinds of situations and bringing charges. We'll see what comes back."

He came awake sweating, took a deep breath, let it out. Her hair. The way she'd been that day in the mall. She was just ahead of him, sipping a coke. Sunlight slanting through a skylight high overhead. She walked, her toes out, a dancer's walk, physical health and power in her movements. He got out of bed, turning on lights as he went. In the living room, his bicycle leaned against the fireplace; the hardwood floor creaked with each step. He retraced her path: she looked around, said, "Beautiful house...you live here by yourself? You professors really have the life. Work a few hours a week. Live like this. Is this your study?" She tipped her head to read book titles. "These books and articles have your name on them.... What do you write about?" Unsure she'd accept it, he said, "Making people more comfortable when they're sick and scared." And she'd nodded and said, "That's nice. Noble. Kind. No, really," the flirtatious contempt in her voice exciting him.

Fields walked to the French doors. Outside, the softness of the desert night; he stood in the garden, the mesquite and olive trees behind him. Near the wall, the prickly pear had bloomed, yellow flowers glowing in the dark. He looked into the house at the sofa. He stared at the cushions. He was sure nothing had really happened, but she'd been so convincing at the hearing.

As the trial date slowly approached and the semester went on, the students and faculty remained distant. Fields realized that even if he was found innocent, his reputation was already so badly damaged he'd probably be unable to teach or work in the community again. Some of the time he believed this; some of the time he wasn't sure. He started looking for jobs elsewhere.

Levy was a little late. He came in quickly and took off his jacket, hung it on the back of his chair. He looked for a file and then stood reading behind his desk, stroking his chin. When he looked up at Fields, he said, "My investigator has been checking on Susanne Raine. I've just received the report." Fields waited. "So who is she? She's a twenty-year-old part-time student who has a 3.0 average at the university. She's changed her major three times; her latest is education with a minor in computer science; she'd been studying dance until recently. She has a boyfriend...." Levy took a breath, puffed one cheek. "I could go on, but the point, I think, is that she's a typical college student." He closed the file. "She has no history of bringing sexual assault charges, nothing psychiatric."

Levy paused. A fountain splashed softly in the courtyard. "We're scheduled to go to trial in three weeks. We've pleaded innocent. I know that it's extremely important to you to be found innocent." A secretary peered in, closed the door. Levy toyed with a letter opener. "Listen to me. We take this to trial. There are no witnesses. It's a swearing contest between you and the girl. The jury watches and listens. You invited Raine to your house to a job-related interview that never took place." Fields started to say something. Levy held up his hand. "From a jury's point of view, Tom. Your house, not your office. Maybe for a job that did not exist. Okay, we're in trial. You get up there. You wear a white shirt, blue suit, tie. The jury looks you over. You're forty-one years old, you're six-one, have a good job, a successful career. You're educated, sophisticated. You tell your story. You talked, you showed Ms. Raine a few exercises, there was some hugging, a little of this, a little of that, she left. Okay?

"Then Susanne Raine gets up there. The jury looks at this young, very pretty girl. The D.A. will have her dress the part—something modest. Maybe with some good directing she'll stumble through the emotional parts of her testimony. Maybe she'll cry. Who knows. They'll hear she works at a couple of part-time jobs, she's putting herself through school. She'll make a strong impression on a jury. They'll feel sorry for her. Then the D.A. will get you up there on the stand and ask you some questions which will make you look bad no matter how you answer." Levy swung in his chair, faced Fields. He leaned on his desk. "Tom, I personally believe you are guilty of nothing more than very bad judgement here. Really. They have a poor case. The kidnapping charges are a joke. But juries are completely unpredictable and you're exposing yourself to a lot of jail time. As your lawyer, I recommend that you plead no contest. You're taking an enormous risk bringing this to trial." Fields started to speak, but Levy put up his hand. "Tom, please. Don't give me an answer now, but think it over carefully. Will you do that?" Fields stared out the window. Levy said, "I've seen juries convict people for less."

A very small part of Fields was marginally aware he'd done exactly what Susanne Raine had accused him of, but hadn't there been the way she'd guided and held his wrist as he'd placed her coffee on the table, something about the way she'd brushed his shoulder as she sat down? And then, too, wasn't there her look of flirtation and hard contempt which said, try me; the way she'd moved against him when he did; yes, she'd pulled back, but only after she'd fit herself to him, moved against him; and hadn't she still been saying, try me? It was nothing like the charges. Kidnapping. Sexual assault. Nothing had really happened. That's what Tom remembered.

Fields requested and received permission to take a formal leave of absence from the university, put his house up for sale, and accepted a position back East in the same town where he had grown up. Ten days before he was scheduled to go to trial, he flew out to Hawaii for the triathlon. He knew he wasn't ready, but the thought of not entering seemed worse. Six hundred and forty-one had entered, four hundred and twelve finished, and Tom Fields finished one hundred and seventy-one—his best time.

The next morning, he rose and slowly walked across the hotel room to the balcony and looked over the palms at the ocean and sea mist thrown up by the distant surf. Hilo. He could still feel the rise and fall of his body in the swells as he'd come ashore, his skin crusted with salt as he pedaled his bicycle. What if the jury didn't believe him? Susanne Raine had been so sure of herself at the preliminary hearing. He sat stiffly on the bed and picked up the phone. Reaching Levy in his office, he asked him to change   his plea to no contest. Levy told him that although it hadn't been completely worked out, he thought that in return for Fields' changing his plea, Levy could have the kidnapping and sexual assault charges reduced to one charge of sexual assault—a misdemeanor.

As part of his change of plea, he answered a request from the Adult Probation Department to meet with one of their investigators and assist in the preparation of a presentence report. He waited on the fifth floor, cold in the overly air-conditioned room, staring through the tinted glass at the hard edges of the distant mountains. He hated refrigeration. It made his flesh feel as though it were just meat strung on bones. Northern winters were one of the reasons he had come to the desert.

A woman walked toward him and introduced herself. She

was tall and slim, almost as tall as he was. He followed her into her office. As she moved to her desk, she indicated he take a chair. Behind her, the blue sky, the mountains from a different angle. She explained that she was the investigator in charge of his presentence report and that she was going to ask him questions and take his social history, a phrase which momentarily preoccupied him. She had a file open on the blotter in front of her.

She clicked on a hand-sized tape recorder: Jean Davis, investigator; she stated his name, the time and date, the case number, the superior court judge in charge of the case, the victim's name, and then placed the tape recorder on the desk between them. Tom Fields noticed that she wore no wedding ring, thought that she had beautiful hands. He saw a framed photo of a boy, maybe eight or ten, who was grinning and holding up a trout, and felt a sudden rise of emotion. He looked away. Sure she was divorced, he couldn't keep himself from seeing her, the boy, himself—the three of them—together at some future time. He saw them by a stream. He looked at the floor. He knew that as an investigator her evaluation would influence what was done with him.

With several long, self-conscious pauses, he began by responding to her questions about his parents and childhood. As Tom Fields progressed, he became acutely aware that he was coming to something. He talked about his one younger brother, a lawyer, now married and with two children; an ambitious father who was a prosperous businessman; and then his mother, a career woman, a set designer. They'd lived in Connecticut; his parents commuted into New York and were so busy with their successful careers that he and his brother were mostly raised by a grandmother. He saw his parents holidays and weekends. He mentioned that he realized in his twenties that his father was an alcoholic who often verbally abused and demeaned him. Though he was the captain of his basketball and baseball teams at a New England prep school, his father never came to see him play.

He went on to talk about college; an early marriage; a job as a salesman which he had found pointless and demeaning; a stint in the army—he'd avoided Vietnam; another job as a salesman;

a growing sense of purposelessness; and the birth of his son. He gazed out the window, felt something begin to hollow in himself. The tape recorder clicked. The investigator turned over the cassette, clicked it on, and nodded, go ahead.

After a long uncertain pause, he explained that his parents were no longer living. His father had died in his sleep two years ago. It had been seventeen years since his mother had died of cancer. He felt the hollowing in him widen, deepen. He said that his mother's death was the turning point in his life. He stared at the cluster of microphone holes. "After seeing her humiliating death in what was supposed to be one of the best hospitals, I promised myself I'd change the nature of dying in this country." He went on now to talk about getting a Ph.D. in Public Health, going to England to study their hospice program on a National Science Foundation Grant.

When he had regained control of his voice, he started giving the investigator an even, measured account of his mother's death. His mother was still young—in her late forties. She'd had a mastectomy, followed by chemotherapy, lost her hair, but had kept up her spirits. She seemed to be recovering when an examination revealed the cancer had metastasized into her stomach and lungs. She went back into the hospital.

The cassette clicked to an end. The investigator checked her watch and stood. Fields looked out the window. The mountains had taken on definition and were casting long purple shadows in the distance. She asked him if he wanted coffee, he shook his head no, perhaps water. She returned with coffee for herself, placed a plastic cup of water in front of him. The air conditioning made him ache. She replaced the cassette, clicked it on. He resumed speaking in a shaky voice.

Realizing it was to be his last chance with his mother, he spent hours by her bed, talking to her, holding her hand, reassuring her, telling her that he loved her. Everything that happened in those days imprinted itself on him. He noticed that as long as he was touching his mother—a hand, an arm—that her pain was eased. The sound of his voice, too, calmed her. When doctors came into her room—they rarely came alone, but usually in twos and threes—they stood back, almost never touched her, averted their eyes, and left quickly. His mother and his family were never asked anything about what might be wanted.

What he remembered most clearly was that when the windows were darkening with oncoming night, his mother, knowing he would have to leave, grew restless, tossing and turning in the bed. And when visiting hours were over, and he let go of her hand, she would get a wild, abandoned look in her eyes, and start to moan with pain. The hospital administration refused his request to sleep in an adjoining room. As he walked toward the elevator, he could hear her begin to howl.

Mornings, as he stepped into the hall, he heard her begging for painkillers, and the nurse explaining patiently as if to a child that she would have to wait, just another forty minutes, that they couldn't deviate from their schedule. Some mornings he helped the nurse lift his mother and wondered at how light her body was becoming.

He went silent, noticed the sunlight had moved across the investigator's desk. He followed a series of images. Every night he walks away from the hospital and across the street to a parking lot which is piled with black snow. The air is cold, smells of soot. He goes home to his wife and young son where they live on the second floor of a duplex. He sees the rooms, sees his wife waiting at the kitchen table, his son playing on the floor, sees the furniture in the different rooms, the double bed in the shadows. There is silvery condensation on the windows from their breathing. One night he gets into his car to go home, but cannot turn the key; he feels the hospital at his back, his apartment waiting. He gets out of the car and walks to a nearby bar. The bar is warm and quiet, the lights low; he takes a stool and has a beer, another beer, a shot, then notices someone, a girl who works at a desk in the hospital. Recognizing him, she nods, they slide down several stools. Later, when they walk out together, it is sleeting, the trees and bare branches are encased with ice, the streets glazed. As they step off the curb, a car comes down the street in a sideslip, the driver motionless, and passes through a red light. Steadying each other, they walk toward her car, which is frozen in ice. They begin to chip at the lock with keys. From inside, distant lights are formless shapes through the iced glass. They turn to each other, kiss, and start pulling at each other's clothes.

After a long silence, Fields spoke. He said that his mother died six weeks after she'd returned to the hospital. She died sometime after evening visiting hours ended and before the next morning; he hadn't been there. He walked into her room to find the bed empty, an orderly tucking in fresh sheets. When Fields tried to find out if someone had been with her when she died, he could get no answers.

He gazed at the photo of the boy with the trout. He remained silent. He'd loved his wife, but couldn't go home to her. There had been dozens of brief sexual encounters, which he could barely remember, as if the women were met and embraced while sleepwalking, and after two years his wife had divorced him. He'd seen his son each summer. He was a junior in college now.

The investigator looked at her watch and clicked off the tape.

At the second interview a few weeks later, she was asking Fields about a newspaper article. There was a picture of him in a suit and tie. He was smiling. His cheeks were hollow. It went back twelve years and referred to the first major field study he'd undertaken after returning from his hospice research in England. The article was titled "The Man Who Died," and described how Fields had faked cancer. To do so, he'd lost twenty pounds, had a biopsy scar incised on his neck, and shaved his head to simulate hair loss from chemotherapy; he'd had ultraviolet burns on his abdomen to simulate radiation burns, and i.v. marks in his arm. Unshaven and unshowered, diagnosed as having terminal cancer, he'd been admitted to the surgical ward of a large city hospital. Only two of the most senior administrators knew what he was doing. Within forty-eight hours of being admitted, he'd developed real symptoms—pain, vomiting, nausea, and listlessness. Afraid that painkillers would dull his ability to observe, he'd remained in this state in the ward for two weeks. He'd told the investigator that there he had confirmed everything he had observed during his mother's dying six years before. In their daily visits, the doctors had avoided eye contact, stood at a distance from the patient, and spent less than five minutes per visit with him. He had gone on to write up his findings and recommendations; many had been put into practice. Several well-known thanatologists had worried about the long-term effects of such an experiment on his psyche, but Fields had said in the article and repeated now that he couldn't let things like that stop him. His supporters had praised the study as brilliant, though dangerous to his personal well-being. His detractors had called it a morbid stunt. The article had concluded with Fields being quoted as saying, "The dying teach us to live. They have finally dropped their masks and see life as it is."

Fields could see the investigator had underlined the phrase *dropped their masks*. She swivelled in her chair once. He stared at her beautiful hands. Fields waited. She seemed to debate, then turned the article over and went on.

At the end of the interview, she asked him about his plans, and he said he hoped to go on with his work. He hesitated, then asked how her report would be used. She closed the file and said that all of this information would go to the Superior Court Judge in charge of his case. "If you have questions, your lawyer is the person to talk to."

His house sold quickly. He took a job in the East at the end of the summer. His mother had left him a house on some land in the country and in August he moved in. He walked across the fields, remembering how when he was a boy the trail to the pond had seemed infinite and mysterious. In cleaning out the house, kneeling in the corner of a second-floor bedroom where he and his brother had slept, his head at the windowsill, he stopped. Something had happened in this room with his mother years ago. She'd spanked him for something his brother had done and nothing he'd said could convince her it wasn't him. She'd held him here. His head not quite reaching the window. The sudden terror of her taking hold of him. Here. He stood slowly with the dustpan carefully poised, looked out across the fields to the woods, his weight off balance where the floor had settled. Outside, it was raining beneath a white sky.

Levy was on the phone. "I just want to keep you up-to-date. You've gotten some great letters of support from various professional people around the country. And one man in particular wrote how you'd helped his father die peacefully—calmed him for days, refused any fee. But you also have damaging letters. One woman wrote that she knew of several women who had gotten involved with you, but were too ashamed to come forward afterward. Another wrote of being drawn in, but asking around she said she found out that you had a reputation for collecting young women. I'm quoting phrases from the letters. These aren't my words." Levy paused. "Your good letters should far outweigh anything negative—it's a first offense and the charge is down to a misdemeanor, but I want you to be informed."

In early November he returned to the desert for sentencing. As Tom stepped off the plane, he felt the blue sky open over him, the clear light of fall, and realized he'd been aching for this light without knowing it. The next morning, he met Levy at his office, and they went to court together. The maximum jail sentence for the misdemeanor could have been four months, but the Superior Court Judge said that considering the many good things Fields had done, a jail sentence seemed pointless. The judge gave him a year's probation, a fine of fifteen hundred dollars, and ordered him to undergo counseling.

The next morning his picture appeared in the newspaper. It showed him in a dark suit, with close-cropped hair and a marathoner's hollow cheeks. He was staring straight ahead with no expression. The caption was: *Thomas Fields awaits sentencing in Superior Court.* Later, when he went to his department to pick up a box of his books which had been left behind, he saw two faculty members leaning over the picture. Tom Fields heard one of them remark that it was the only time he'd ever seen Fields look completely at peace.

Skin

SOMETIMES—LIKE THIS AFTERNOON—when Vicki and I sit here in her apartment, I can feel her studying me and wondering how it could happen. She wants to ask, what was he like? Even if I wanted, I could never explain—how it happened, what he was like. Not for the shrink's reason—traumatic amnesia. I don't really believe in shrinks anyway—besides the fact that people like us don't go to shrinks. But not for the shrink's reason. No. It's that I never found out myself. Simple enough.

And what I did and who I was with him, well, sometimes I feel as though he invented me, made me up, took me to Nam with him. Vicki lights a cigarette, looks at me over the match, she is wondering, but why you? why were you the one? She blows out the match, exhales. Turns back to the tube. The *$25,000 Pyramid.* I notice my painted nail. Red. Chipped. My left index finger. I tried to paint my nails last week. Got that far. Stopped. I still can't face lipstick, nail polish, eye shadow, any of it.

I myself have asked the shrink, how did he know I was the one? And the shrink has said, it wasn't me, that most likely I triggered something in him that was there and waiting. In him. Lewis.

Then it comes back to me and goes around and around; I

can't tell if he invented me, made me up, or if I invented him; and if there was a we, or even became a we, then the we that we were, like another country or world you travel to—*we*, beyond him, beyond me, a third place, Nam—where exactly is that place on a map? How did I get there? Or how did he get me there, and how did I get back? Am I even back?

Nights when I finally do fall asleep, I fall asleep exhausted from unceasing imaginary conversations I can't remember and wake exhausted from unceasing imaginary conversations I can't remember. I am talking to Vicki; I am talking to my mother; my father; my sister, Donna; to my brother, Martin; we are having endless conversations; I am talking to the shrink; to Woo; to the detective; to Mary Beth who drove me to the airport; I am talking to everyone but Lewis. Lewis and I do not talk. Lewis and I listen. Lewis listens to me and I do not say anything. I listen to Lewis and he does not say anything. We listen to each other the way you listen to plants or stones.

We look at each other. I do not know what Lewis sees when he sees me. Saw me. What he saw. The shrink said it wasn't me. I triggered something. I don't believe him. I sit here with Vicki watching the *$25,000 Pyramid*. Vicki knows me. We've known each other from first grade. Vicki's just Vicki. I don't know what he saw.

Or what I saw when I looked at him. What I thought I saw. I don't know. Even before I met him, I noticed his skin. He had the tightest skin I've ever seen. . . .

We're sitting in these broken-down easy chairs. I come here to get out of my parents' house for a while. Even when they're out, the air is thick with unspoken things. Secrets. Anger. At Vicki's, it's better. Vicki never left home to go to college. I did, the first person in my family to go to college at all. My mother hysterical, of course: why can't you take some courses here at the community college. . . . Her baby leaving home. I left, went away, got on the dean's list, but then it all happened, and so here we are, Vicki and I, now it's all come to the same thing, and my mother's got her baby back home.

I glance over at Vicki. Traces of a black eye and swollen nose. She got drunk and smashed up the car ten days ago. A few days before, she'd been broken into, which was why she was getting drunk, I guess. Across the room, smudges of fingerprint powder on the windowsill, we're still coming across splinters of glass in corners, on cushions—they smashed the window. And if you look closely, you can make out fingerprints in the powder. Occasionally, the phone rings late at night. When Vicki answers, there's never anyone there. Vicki's sure it's the guys who broke in. She listens. They listen. She says, how's the stereo? They don't answer. Pretty good? Like the cameras? Vicki thinks they took the phone number, that they're the ones who call. They know when she's in, when she's out, they can come back whenever they want. When the phone rings, I feel sick to my stomach, so lately we disconnect it for an hour or two.

But phone or not, still I like to be here with Vicki. I know her. Vicki's prematurely gray at twenty-one. My grandmother went white at twenty-five and I've often wondered what I would do if that happened to me. Bleach it, I guess. One of Vicki's eyebrows is almost completely white, as if she were hit by lightning. She's a little stocky, wears her jeans slouchy-low on her hips; she's asexual tending toward mannish, but perhaps it's more body chemistry than anything else. She has maybe two or three irregular periods a year. Fucked-up hormones. Chemistry.

I remember our junior year in high school, Vicki believed Jim Morrison wasn't dead, that it wasn't Jim Morrison in his grave up there in Montparnasse, but someone else and that Jim Morrison had disappeared into the desert in Africa and was living a new life under another identity. She showed me an article which proved it. She was serious. I went away for a couple of weeks that summer and when I came back, not another word. Jim Morrison not-dead just disappeared back where he came from.

But that's all okay, because Vicki knows something. When Vicki was nine, she came to school with this look on her face, like she was seeing through things, like things were weightless and floating, or she was. Maybe it's because I know her, but I can still see traces of it, that look. She had just found out her father had a second family—a wife, kids, another house, everything, two hundred miles away. The mirror image of a life.

Which one was the other? And he had kept it a secret all those years until somehow her mother found out. Vicki had that look on her face. Like she was looking through things, seeing them, but not seeing them.

Vicki wants to be a professional photographer. The other day, she dug out some pictures she took of me in high school. When she got to the short-hair ones, the ones after New York and The Pierre, she said, "You never really believed that stuff your mother was always saying about men, but still, you were ambivalent about being beautiful. Don't you remember? You said you felt too visible. Anyway, you were beautiful even with your hair cropped." I looked at the pictures. My eyes stopped somewhere. I can see I believed something. Hot-shit little model.

After a bout with mono, my mother thought I was depressed, had a bad self-image, and sent me to modeling school, though she always says I nagged her to go, that it was my idea when I remember clearly that it was her idea—just another thing we fight about. Now since all of this, I'm sure she's feeling that she was always right, that now she's won. She hasn't said anything—she's too smart for that—but I can tell. Anyway, in modeling school, the director told me I had natural poise, she helped me with my walk, my sitting, taught me how to move a little better, showed me makeup. Told me I had a perfect face, heart-shaped with small features, and sent me to a big competition at The Pierre. New York. All of those big designers, fashion photographers, society people. Sixteen, almost seventeen, knees shaking, I went out on that runway and I knocked them out. They stood up and cheered. I do not know what they saw, but they loved me.

I looked at the pictures. Before I met Lewis, I had this cocky look on my face. I see it in Vicki's pictures. Just before Vicki's cameras were stolen, she took a few pictures of me. On a pier. Under trees. In the fog. Arty. I'd been back home three months. First time I'd been photographed since Lewis. Beside the twenty pounds lost and the circles, I looked dead—eyes open, but seeing nothing. In one I have my head cocked to one side and I seem to be listening.

We watch *The Edge of Night*. Vicki looks over at me and

wonders and finally I get up. She jiggles her legs, stops. I glance at yesterday's paper, read "Jogging slows President's heartbeat from 63 to 40."

She nods and smiles as I go to the door, open it, look up and down the hall. No one there. I step out. Reach back in. Wave and say in a phony Southern accent. Bye. It comes out, Baaaa-ah. That's the way they talk down there. Baaaa-ah. Ya'all come back now. I close the door behind me, my stomach tightens, I start down the hall.

On my way home, I continue my unceasing conversations with everyone. I think I will make it home easily this time, though I jump and turn at every sound. Still, I think I'm better. Two months ago I couldn't go out. Days would pass. Sometimes I went out with my father when he came home from work. We'd go to a shopping center or something. I walk along the streets and I talk with my mother, with Vicki, I talk with the shrink. I do not talk with Lewis. I listen. He listens.

I pass the community college set back on a hill with a large lawn. Like our high school. Brick and glass, a factory. My mother, well, what's wrong with it, it comes out of our taxes, where do you want to run off to? Sure, ten blocks from home, I could imagine myself living in my room, my mother screaming, what time did you come home last night? Who knows, I might have, too, but then I got a high 700 on my math boards, felt differently about myself and went away. My father stayed out of it, but I could tell he was silently pleased. He was in the 82nd Airborne during World War II, he wanted to be a vet, loves animals, but after the war, he started working, then kids, and he's never been able to stop. Merry-go-round. Thirty years in a manufacturing plant. He's smart and still has interests, he's always had interests, but my mother drags him down. Even though he'd never heard of the college, he was pleased. I could tell. A small girls' school, mid-Southern. Jeffersonian architecture, rolling hills. Beautiful. And I started making the dean's list. He was proud. My mother still must think I went away to spite her. That's the way she thinks.

. . . He listens. We look at each other. Even before I met him, I noticed his skin. Lewis. He had the tightest skin I've ever seen. I was aware of his skin before anything. Before his face. After his face. Even in all of that noise, smoke, confusion. He was a grunt. The grunts came over from the base. Grunts. Rednecks. College girls. Local guys. Armenian's. Armenian was nice. It wasn't a bad place to work. Just noisy.

Beside the juke box, there were pinball machines and video games in back, Star Wars, Raiders, Defenders, Astro Fighters. There were always hollow, mechanical explosions and glowing blips disintegrating and grunts machine-gunning into those video screens with rapt drunken expressions on their faces.

After work, if it wasn't too late, I'd go over to the pool, calm down. The pool was set deep between trees on a green rolling lawn. Glass on three sides. I'd swim slowly, turn over, float on my back, stare at the lights high above; if I was the only one in the pool, I could feel my heartbeat rocking my body. Feel the voices and Star Wars explosions draining out of me into the water. Lie back floating so long my nose and cheeks would dry to single beads of water, my face became an island. I'd think about things. Anything. Surprises, I wouldn't be afraid. The other night it suddenly came to me how I'd wanted to play field hockey in high school, but my mother wouldn't sign the permission slip, she was afraid I'd get my face messed up. Kim a cheerleader. Funny things like that. I reached up to touch my face, started to sink. Floating. I'd turn over on my back, swim quietly. Sometimes half a mile.

Afterward, I'd wrap my hair in a wet towel and feeling calm, peaceful, clean, I'd walk home, the night air soft on my skin. The first year, I lived in the dorm, and then I moved into this old Victorian house with Mary Beth. Moving out of the dorm. Another fight with Mother. Anyway, the house was worth it. Wide porch. Front lawn with beautiful old trees. Front door with oval glass beveled at the edges. Then a long wide staircase with a carved oak bannister. Beautiful. Mary Beth and I had the second floor. When we moved in, we spent a solid week painting at the end of summer. Mary Beth, Tommy, me. Pure heat. Paint. Gallons. Day and night. We painted it different colors, the rooms, and it was just great to use real colors instead of the old repressed off-whites, beiges. Every house I've ever lived in was off-white. A Sears living room. Off-white bedrooms, living room, beige den, lemon kitchen. When Mary Beth and I finished, that place was blazing with colors—magentas, fuchsias, plum, blue. I loved it. My bedroom, fuchsia. I loved it.

Sometimes I laugh when I think of Mary Beth. Southern, dark, black hair, dark brown eyes, about my size, very smart. Studying microbiology. Never knew what to expect with her. One night I came in from Armenian's, I was counting my tips on the kitchen table—clumps of damp dollar bills, bar money is always damp—when Mary Beth came to the door, kind of breathless, eyes bright. She waved to me. I looked behind her. Could see Tommy was out. Tommy is her long-time steady, almost always there, like the music always coming out of her room—Allman Brothers, Boz Scaggs—Tommy's an easy-to-take, laid-back Southern boy, long blond hair, brown eyes not quite even, likes to play cards, drink, get stoned, he plays fiddle in a country rock band. Anyway, I could see he wasn't there so I followed her into the bedroom.

Mary Beth closed the door, went to the closet, reached in, pulled out a box, and dumped all of this stuff on the bed. Lingerie. Lacy underwear, bikini panties. Bras with the tips cut out. She reached in, grabbed something.

"Here."

I laughed. "What, Mary Beth ... "

"Try one."

I shrugged.

"Oh, come on," she laughed.

I slipped on panties and a bra. My nipples sticking out. We looked at each other and giggled. I struck a pose. She looked at me expectantly.

"How do you feel?"

I shrugged.

"Close your eyes."

I closed my eyes.

"Now?"

I opened my eyes. Lingerie on the bed. Twisted up into tight snarls, knots, they reminded me of my father's trout flies. I just smiled. I couldn't get into it. We laughed.

Mary Beth has gone with Tommy forever and she couldn't imagine being without him. One day they'll get married, but in the meantime, she has this little thing. She told me about it one night when we were getting high in the kitchen. Every once in a while she gets this urge to sleep with a golf pro. I remembered laughing. A golf pro. She laughed. A golf pro. Guys on the tour. So when Tommy goes off with the band some weekends, she heads out somewhere to follow the PGA tour. At first I thought she was kidding, it sounded so unreal. And she said it with a twinkle in her eye. Made it seem like good fun, a joke. Said Tommy had no idea. It made me feel funny. She said it would stop when she and Tommy got married. I wonder. I don't think you can turn it on and off like that. I know she loves Tommy. A golf pro...

Mary Beth. Except for that, when I think of her, I have to laugh. But she was no fool. And when the time came, she was right there.

All of that was before Lewis.

I was doing pretty well, I loved where we lived, I was making the dean's list. It was elating to find out I was smart. My mother'd spent half her life screaming at me. Making me feel like an idiot, nothing. I loved studying math and chemistry, they were so orderly. And even the job wasn't too bad. But all the time I was working in Armenian's, on some level I was aware of Lewis. I must have known he was always there, though I don't think I'd actually noticed him, separate from other grunts. I was aware that there was a center to one of the grunt tables, and that it was someone, a presence, laughing, buying drinks. I always avoided guys like that in high school. Hey, I was a cheerleader, we'd ride on the team bus to away games—football. Vans to basketball games. I knew a lot of jocks in high school. White. Black. Guys posturing. The black dudes walking around, belts unbuckled, buckles hanging, you know, fight or fuck, I wasn't any little Alice in Wonderland, I knew how guys could be, but this wasn't that, this was different, knowing he was there. This was different.

I don't know exactly when, but once I became aware of his skin, I was always aware of him—his skin—in that room. He

was about six-three, and where most of the grunts had those
white marks around their collars and sleeves, he was perfectly
tanned. He didn't have that meaty look men have, that raw
grunt look. I'd catch glimpses of him as I'd pass, but I'd never
look his way. And though he'd never look my way, either, I
could sense him watching. After a while, I knew that not only
was he watching me, but that his horsing around, his laughing
and clowning, were for my benefit. Odd, because whatever he
thought he was doing, nothing could have turned me off more.
I hate that kind of stuff.

Still, I could sense him in all of that noise and smoke and Star
Wars explosions. Even with my back to him, I could say where
he was, what he was doing, if he had his back to me or away
from me. If he was looking at me. I never went near him. The
grunts were usually over on the far side of the room, those
weren't my tables, and everyone was glad to give them a wide
berth. Sometimes I had the sense that he was over there waiting,
almost daring me to cross the room, and I was over on my side
hoping he never would cross and wondering what I would do if
he did. It got so that coming to work would give me a nervous
fluttering stomach, opening the door would make me more
nervous still, and when I'd walk in, I'd get a jolt when I felt him
out there. I didn't know what it was, that jolt, and I didn't really
want to find out. It was enough I could feel him waiting for me.

I knew I didn't like him so it was strange to find myself
wondering about his skin, how skin could be so tight, what it
would be like to touch. Feel. The way you'd want to feel
anything that was taut and of itself like the suede toe of a shoe,
a snakeskin wallet, a silk kimono. But most of the time I put it
out of my mind. I had enough else to think about.

I'd study Woo's lectures before work, look over my calculus
problems, and by the time I'd get home, they'd be half solved.
Having them in my head was the beginning of a meditation
which would help me keep calm, separate me from the music,
the voices. Woo, my math professor, was Chinese, we got to be
friends, we would have coffee together, it got so I saw and
heard my math in the delicate accent of his lectures; when I'd be
working, I could still maintain a thread of that reasoned deli-

cacy like a mobile softly turning and flashing from invisible wires.

Once he looked at one of my math solutions, smiled, nodded and said, elegant, I think you might perhaps do anything you wish.

He made me feel wonderful. He was small. Maybe five-five, not as tall as I, delicate, wore thick glasses, goofy plain sports shirts. I saw him once with his wife and three little kids. He was so gentle with them. He wasn't like most men. Something magical. I imagined him with his tiny feet and hands moving like a gymnast or dancer, silently, gracefully. I had a little crush on him. Sweet man. And I could tell he admired me, cared for me.

A few days after he'd said that, do anything you wish, I saw an old Gray's *Anatomy* in a used book bin, and on an impulse, I bought it. Just a sudden impulse, maybe a doctor. Why not me? I started reading a page or two a day, secretly memorizing the diagrams.

I come to a shopping center. K Mart. Sears. My father loves Sears. He buys most of his tools there. Clothes. Even suits. Traffic is rushing across a wide intersection. I can see people moving in there. In and out of stores. Cars. The intersection. Exhaust. It didn't really bother me on the way to Vicki's, but now it seems bad, a long way back. I step down off the curb and start walking. It's cloudy and humid, the sky a flat white. I can feel the heat from the engines. I can't quite make out the faces behind the reflections on the windshields, but I can feel them in their cars. It's a long way to the other side. I keep walking. I can hardly feel my feet hitting the ground down there.

One time I almost walked right into him, he was coming out of the men's room and I was walking away from a table, we turned into each other, both of us stopping that far apart without touching. I stepped back. The first time I'd looked him directly in the face. His eyes were so gray against his tan they were almost pale white, the color of a cigarette ash, and his skin pulled so tight across his cheekbones it was highlit. I could

hardly breathe. Cropped blond hair, eyes blank, and then a look
of sudden recognition, he started to smile, couldn't breathe, my
thinking, beautiful, thinking, no, he opened his mouth to speak,
I sensed there was something we knew about each other, I said,
excuse me, blanked my eyes, and turned away quickly. I sensed
him smiling, maybe even laughing or mocking me, I could feel
him watching me through the crowd. I put my tray on the bar,
went through the kitchen to the back door, and lit a cigarette.

Armenian looked up from the oven. "What's the matter,
Kim?"

I waved my hand at him. "I'm okay."

He shrugged and smiled. Armenian is nice. He takes care of
us, the waitresses, doesn't let anyone mess with us, he feeds us,
sometimes lends us money, doesn't lech after us.

I smoked and looked at the trees and thought maybe I should
quit and work somewhere else. And maybe I should have, but I
liked Armenian, the job was decent money, and anyway why
should I have let myself be forced into quitting over some dumb
grunt. Even if I'd quit, he probably would have just gone
looking until he'd found me. It was a small town.

My heart stopped pounding, I stepped on my cigarette and
went back in.

Soon after, one of the girls got sick, and I had to take her
place, cross the room, and wait on their table, which is something I'd always known was going to happen one way or the
other, their table.

Five or six of them. Pretty loaded. Goofy. Looking me over. I
avoided looking at him. Looked at the others. They were tattooed. Panthers climbing arms, claws raking bloody trails in the
skin; green-hued snakes entwined with daggers; map of Vietnam a grinning death's head, dice caroming beneath. I'm not too
freakish about tattoos. My father has a fading 82nd Airborne.
And a hula girl. A couple of times Vicki and I even considered
getting tattooed, and once, I remember, we started driving and
looking for a place, but we got too stoned, disco biscuits, could
hardly drive, and besides, I don't think either of us could decide
on anything; we couldn't stop laughing. I avoided looking at
him. Kept my eyes on their tattoos.

But then I became curious. And after all, what could happen?

I decided to try not to be afraid. I glanced at him. But he wasn't looking at me. He was looking down, concentrating on something. Downcast eyelids an ash-violet, as though dusted with a fine metallic powder. The bridge of his nose, thin and delicate. Again I thought, beautiful. He was printing something on a scrap of paper. The pen hooked back toward his chest, so awkward. How could anyone hold a pen like that? Left-handed. But that wasn't it, what surprised me. It was his arms. Not a mark. Not a scar, not a single tattoo, the only one at the table without. Smooth except for a light down of golden hair on his forearms. As he printed, I watched the muscles in his forearms. I'd never seen tight skin like that. He finished, looked up, smiled. The rest of the table looked at him expectantly. They loved him, waited on him. He extended the card between the tips of his second and third fingers. Pointed it at me. I ignored it, but he kept holding the card. I held out my tray and he dropped the card on the tray. I let it lie there, though I could see his name printed in block caps—and his phone number. What a dreamer.

Then he did something funny. He held up his palms as if to show me his hands concealed nothing, the way a magician would show you his hands. Gave a little shrug. I had the feeling he was very strong and very weak at the same time. Almost like there was a hole in him. As I walked away, I heard the whole table suddenly laugh. I turned and threw the card behind me on the floor, and they whistled and cheered and laughed louder.

The shrink asked me, why would you go out with a man who made you so nervous, and I told him, I don't know, but it happened.

The shrink said, if you can remember what you were thinking and feeling, then it might give us something, we might begin to understand.

I've told you before I don't think there can be any explanation.

We're not looking for an explanation as such....

It just happened. I woke up one morning with him and then he was there to the end no matter what I did to get rid of him. And if we're not looking for an explanation, then what are we doing here?

At this point, I think we're talking.

I laughed. Talking. Everyone has their con. Even you. You probably most of all. Have it your way. Talking.

At times there was something familiar about Lewis. As if I knew him from somewhere. When I thought of him, I had an intuitive sense of what he was doing with his buddies at that table. The way they waited on him, deferred to him, the way I sensed he controlled them. It was something about the way he looked which made him right, gave him the last word. It had been like that for me in high school. A confidence, a style. My friends waited on me, wanted to be with me. Something about the way I looked, too. It was familiar. I sensed it in Lewis. Maybe he sensed it in me.

But beyond, I don't know if anything would have happened, except for the simple fact that Lewis was always there and he was always waiting and in a way it got to be enough in itself, his waiting. There used to be a good old boy, Duane, who parked his white Cadillac by the quad to watch all of the sweet young nookie going by year after year. He'd watch and wait and ask if you wanted to take a ride. He asked me once. He asked everyone once. He was a joke. He's there now, waiting. Lewis was always there and waiting, I could feel him waiting, and one night I came to work pissed about something, got more pissed, somehow knew it wasn't going to go away, Lewis waiting, that it had to happen.

I have to say this for Lewis. He was gentle. Even shy. That first night we went for a walk after work. I remember Armenian's face, startled, through the porthole in the kitchen door; he'd caught sight of us leaving together. We walked along and there was nothing to say. We kept walking. I was concentrating on avoiding him, touching, brushing. Knew just what I was going to say when he put his arm around me. But he didn't and we kept walking in silence and finally I understood Lewis really didn't know quite what to say, but that he would walk ten miles just to be with me. I didn't feel like walking any ten miles. I'd already done my ten miles in Armenian's. I stopped. "I don't care how this sounds, but I want to go home, sit down, and have a drink. Original, huh?" With his blond hair and gray eyes, he was luminous. "You can do whatever you want."

I turned away quickly, half-hoping he'd leave. He didn't. It didn't matter. Leave. Not leave. It would have happened somehow, sometime. Perhaps it had already started.

He was sitting on the porch step below me, we'd been drinking bourbon, I kept looking at the blond down on his forearms, and finally I took a swallow of bourbon, reached over and ran one fingertip down his arm. "Nothing personal, you understand." But it was me. I was the one. I touched him. His skin surprised me. Incredibly soft, though hot, almost burning. But it was me. Sooner. Later. I knew. I was a little drunk. He smiled. A nice, gentle smile. Then we drank some more, and I watched myself unbutton several top buttons and part his shirt. I wanted to see his chest. I'd never done that with any man before, and in a way, I don't have a lot of use for most men's bodies, but I had to see Lewis.

I know what it looks like now, the shrink telling me it was there and waiting in him, I know why the shrink's been working that, reprogramming and all, I know what he's up to, but I don't believe anyone or anything and I can't blame it all on Lewis. I wasn't any little Alice in Wonderland. I used to have some pretty hot little sessions with my boyfriend in high school before my parents came home from work—my father was working days then, too, so the house was empty. I always kept it under control. And when I was ready to lose it, I picked the time, the place, when and how, and it happened that way. It wasn't in the back seat of anybody's car. And I was prepared, I wasn't about to get knocked up, either.

And that's the way I kept it. I picked the time and place and kept things under control. I slept with who I wanted when I wanted and when I said it was over, it was over. Once I was on a train and started talking to the guy next to me, he had nice eyes and hands and a soft voice and a way of pausing to think before he spoke. After a few stops, we got off together and went to a motel and spent the day in bed. I don't do that all the time.

But I wasn't any little Alice in Wonderland and when I went with Lewis, I don't think there was any way I or anyone else could have known. Not then. And maybe there wasn't anything in him yet. But maybe there was something in me that put it in him. We. Nam. The shrink said, it was there and waiting. I don't believe anything. After everything is said and done, it was *me* he'd been waiting for, wasn't it?

So we got drunk and went to bed in a tangle of clothes, no better or worse than anyone else, and in the morning I looked at him, that tight skin, smooth, not a mark on him. Whatever it was that had been there and waiting for me, I felt it was gone, and now I could get on with it, see him, not see him. He was different, too, than I'd expected. Had been the whole time. Quiet. Gentle.

I borrowed Mary Beth's car to drive him back to the base, we stopped at McDonald's for coffees and drank them as we drove and when we were almost there, he said, "When am I going to see you again?"

Before I could say anything, I saw this tableful of buddies laughing, I saw Lewis back there at the base spreading it around, his big score, the one in Armenian's, lots of nice details, and suddenly I pulled over, hit the brake, grabbed him by the shirt, and said, "I don't know, but you've just had yourself a pretty good fuck, and if you breathe one word of this, you'll never see me again." He looked astonished, reached for my hand, and started to laugh.

"Don't you dare laugh at me." I pushed his hand aside, shook him so hard his head banged against the window.

He kissed my hand and said, "Okay, okay, I wasn't going to say anything."

"Give me your word."

"My word!"

Later of course I found out he was a black belt and a self-defense instructor, knew all kinds of martial arts, tai chi, karate, knew eighty-seven ways to kill a man with a three-inch pen-knife, and there I was banging his head against the window.

He straightened his shirt, fussed with it a second, inspected a loosened button, "Not a pretty good fuck..."

I jerked away and grabbed the wheel. "Get out. You can walk and go fuck yourself."

"...a great fuck."

I looked at him. He smiled and then we burst out laughing

and maybe that was the first moment I really liked him a little. I stopped laughing. "I'm serious, Lewis."

Then he did it again. What he had done in Armenian's when he'd given me that card. Just turned up his palms, empty.

I don't think he ever did say anything. I would have been able to tell. He wasn't a liar. Not the way most people are liars. Tell lies. That wasn't it. I don't believe he ever said anything. It may even sound funny to say, but I probably could have depended on him.

When we got to the guard's checkpoint, I let him out. He leaned back in the window and said, "I love you."

"Little early for that, isn't it?"

"I've always loved you. See you later?"

"Give me a little time."

"But you'll see me?'

I sort of knew, but I wasn't sure. "Give me a few days." He looked a little vague. "Your word, Lewis."

"My word. I've always loved you."

He leaned in to kiss me goodbye and then I watched him walk past the Marine guards, salute, disappear inside.

He did what I asked and stayed away. He kept his word.

And I saw him again. In a way, I think I liked Lewis at first because he was simple. Not dumb. Simple. He was what he was. Lewis. None of that dreary, college boy soul-searching. The melodramatic little crises. Lewis wasn't complicated. He liked to have a good time. He liked to spend money. He never let me pay for anything and always brought me little things from the PX. We'd go to the movies, drink, get stoned, go down to the beaches at Kitty Hawk, sometimes do things with Mary Beth and Tommy.

He was already in the real world.

He rarely swore or was crude around me. Sometimes he could get pretty goofy and stupid, but he was always gentle, and one time, even though I sensed why, I said, "It doesn't fit, Lewis, you and your grunt buddies, hanging out with them, you're not that way."

He looked startled. Then seemed to recover and said, "They're good guys, really."

He told me he'd finished high school, hadn't done badly either; said he'd been a good athlete, letters in football and baseball, but he'd gotten in a few scrapes, one thing led to another, and finally one night, he and a couple of guys got drunk, stole a car, and when it got sorted out, the judge gave him the idea the service might be a better place for him than jail. After basic, he'd been sent right to Vietnam. He didn't tell me anymore, then, about Vietnam. Just that he had done two tours and that now he was a self-defense instructor. He didn't say much about his family, either, but somehow I got the idea that his parents had been divorced a long time, or perhaps his father was dead, and he had been raised by his mother. He might have had a sister living somewhere. I can't say for sure. He didn't know what he wanted to do after the Corps, but he once said, glancing over at my books on the desk, that the Corps had been his college and he knew what he needed to know. After the Corps, he thought he might be a cop. In fact, Lewis told me, there was a local police-community action program where you could sign up to ride with the police on a shift and see what their problems were, a kind of public relations program, and Lewis had made a date to do that. He was interested in being a cop.

The shopping center is behind me and now I'm walking through the subdivision, each house like the next, some small variations. My father is a good carpenter, can build anything, once built a room addition onto one of our houses. Did everything himself. The wiring. The plumbing. He could build a beautiful house. Why he chooses to live in houses like these, I don't know. My mother, I guess. She likes them, feels safe in them, their being new. Clean. Two-story houses, small rooms, tight spaces. We've always lived in houses like these and in each house my father has planted beautiful vegetable and flower gardens, completely landscaped the yards, planted shrubs, fruit trees, evergreens, shade trees, mimosas. The things he plants rarely die. I used to dig the holes with him. The close smell, the dark earth. The trees from the nurseries, root balls, heavy and tight in burlap and twine, lowering them into the holes, the sweet piney smell of humus. He would graft stems from rose-bushes, make them into something marvelous. And fruit trees. He took these muddy yards with broken surveyor's stakes and turned them into beautiful green landscapes.

He planted one yard up beautifully with pines and mimosas and Chinese elms and then we moved, but occasionally I would walk or drive out of my way to see how everything was growing even though other people lived in the house. I did that for several years, and then once I drove by and couldn't find the house. Confused, I drove round and round the neighborhood, then went back and realized they had cut down the trees. I could see one stump remained, the rest had been dug out, burned out, I started to cry, I went home and was sick for days. Cried. I was filled with hatred. How could those people do that to those beautiful trees? I wanted to kill them. I never told my father, though maybe he already knew that they'd been cut down. If he did, he never said anything and I never asked him. It made me wonder what else my father kept inside. My father has always kept everything inside. I don't understand how anyone could have cut down those trees. It still makes me sick.

I walk along, I am going to make it home easily this time, maybe later Vicki will come over and we'll go out for a drink or something, the sky is no-color white, a car accelerates behind me, sudden screech of brakes. I stop in the middle of the sidewalk. I must keep going. I can't look down at my feet. I look ahead. The streets are empty. There's never anyone out. They're all in their houses. Or the houses are empty. Everyone away. I can almost reach this tricycle, but I stand trembling. I hear a sudden laugh, the car accelerates, tires screech, fade down the street. My eyes are hot and weak, and I can feel them on my cheeks, trembling.

Lewis. The Corps is my mother and father, my college. Did Lewis say that? I'm sure he said that. Maybe not, but I thought so. He'd been standing by my desk. He picked up one of my math books, sniffed it like a dog, wrinkled his nose, made a face. I laughed.

"I don't have them for their smell."

He picked up another. Funny to see Lewis holding a calculus book. He never read anything. He'd look at the paper, maga- zines, flip through them. He didn't know what to make of it, math, chemistry, me, a woman. I could tell he thought it was some woman's whim. Again, he sniffed the book.

One by one. Smelled them, turned, sniffed the air, said, "I don't know what's in books, but I know what I smell." He did it in such a way that it was real to me. He was smiling, but serious. He tipped his chin up. Sniffed again. Rushing softness of air. We laughed.

"I'm relieved. What if they smelled good to eat? I'd be out of luck. And do you know what you smell, Lewis? What do you know?"

He smiled slightly and sniffed, and we laughed, but looking at me with those ash-gray eyes, I really did have the feeling that he knew something, that things came to him in the air.

And as I went to the desk, it stayed with me, and it came to me, he must know something, have known something, two tours in Vietnam and not a mark on him. I glanced over, but he had turned away, was getting out laundry, gazing at the TV.

Though books weren't real to him, he never interfered with me. Never kept me from studying. In his own way, he respected me. I know he did. Maybe respected me too much. Maybe I wasn't real enough to him. Or too real in an unreal way. That doesn't make sense. Attributed things to me. Maybe that was it. Made me things I wasn't. Invented me.

I watched him a moment. The TV had a wire hanger for an antenna, he was fooling with it. TV on a wooden ammunition crate. Stenciled black letters, USMC. Weapons. Serial numbers. Lewis turning the antenna, picture bouncing. TV always on softly, Lewis always moving somewhere between me, my desk, my back bent over books, the kitchen and the TV. He needed the TV on, needed me near. And more and more, I could feel him waiting. He was waiting again. Waiting the way he'd been waiting in Armenian's. I'd picked up on it. But waiting for what? Just for me. Endlessly. It made me feel panicky. There were things I wanted to do, places I needed to go by myself, things I needed to talk about that didn't really matter to Lewis. Weren't real to him.

Not that I didn't like him. But somewhere in the back of my mind, I knew it would have to end. I'd have to do something. I thought vaguely of vacations, excuses, ways of letting it cool off. I wasn't thinking of leaving school. I'd never loved anything more.

My mother and her community college...I'm not even sure what it is my father does in that manufacturing plant. He hardly talks. Sits at the table reading books on gardening, turning the book sideways to read tables and diagrams....

Behind me, the TV soft, Lewis bent over now, polishing his shoes. Whisper of his brushes. Straightening and folding my clothes. Placing my shoes in neat pairs in the closet. Straightening things on the dresser. Adjusting hairbrushes and combs. Baskets with bobby pins, earrings, hair bands. Side by side. Straight rows, perpendicular. Marine training. Lewis attending to everything but the plants. For some reason, he never watered them, groomed them, touched them. Never paid any attention to them at all—except one plant. The prayer plant. And while he never touched its leaves, he would move it, carrying it toward the window, away from the window. He seemed endlessly fascinated by the movement of its leaves, their reach up in darkness—shiny, spotted surface, flat underside—their recoil from the light. He'd stare at the leaves and sometimes I'd laugh. He must have moved that plant five or six times a day. Like a kid.

When I think of Lewis, I see him doing fingertip pull-ups from the moldings over the doorway; or Lewis half-crouched, eyes straight ahead, doing tai chi, each movement giving rise to the next, a flower opening in time-lapse photography, endless dreamlike movement. But mostly, absurdly enough, I see Lewis ironing. He stands by the window, clothes piled in the chair, on the bed, and lips pressed together, he irons a pile of shirts. The steam iron hisses, spatters, releases clouds of steam; he sprays the collars and cuffs with starch. He does his tunics, shirts, pants. Beautiful perfect creases. He presses all of my blouses, skirts, even my jeans; when I put them on in the mornings, I can feel the starch, the shaping pressure of the steam iron. He reminds me of myself when I was modeling. I was always fussing with an iron, starch, makeup, always posing, worrying about how I looked, catching glimpses of myself in store windows, mirrors. It got to be a weight, but something I couldn't quite lay down, either. When I went away, I debated trying for some modeling jobs, but then thought this might be a good time to make a break, so I found the job in Armenian's. Started wearing clothes that weren't perfectly pressed. Several days old, I could smell myself in them. A nice soft smell. When I came home, my mother thought I'd turned into a dirty little hippie. Her screaming. Home fifteen minutes. I put my hands over my ears and went to stay with Vicki.

Lewis at my back. Steam. The creak of the ironing board. TV flickering, voices soft. Pressing clothes. I looked over. Eyes downcast. Eyelids almost closed like he was sleeping, dreaming. Lids that delicate ash-violet. Rose petals. Blush of organs, genitals.

What do Lewis and I talk about? We do not talk about books, we do not talk about the news, we do not talk about people. Lewis irons. I do my calculus and work at Armenian's. Lewis straightens things. He moves the prayer plant. Toward the window. Away from the window. Sometimes he is too beautiful. Sometimes Lewis clowns. By himself. Or with Mary Beth. He is not funny, not really, though his attempts to be funny are funny. He is, however, an astonishing mimic, which I think is how he keeps his grunt buddies laughing. He does not like words, but at times it seems he can change his face and appearance completely, become people: Armenian, good-humored, beleaguered; Mary Beth, pert, bright-eyed—he *did* get that look of mischief. Almost scary: Tommy, laid back, moving easy. He never did do me though I was half-tempted to ask him, but I didn't. I guess I was afraid of what I'd see. Lewis and I do not talk. Not really. We are in the same room, we breathe the same air, we metabolize together. I do not know what we know.

Lewis. Always there, always waiting. Me, knowing I would have to end it. Wanting to end it. Not wanting. Late in the day, a panic to see him, perhaps he was someone I had imagined, no one could look like Lewis. He had something about him. Even his dumb grunt buddies knew that. And then, when I would see him, I would want to touch that skin once more.

Maybe it's weird, but he was like a drug and I couldn't get enough. I loved to fuck him and though we fucked and fucked, the more I fucked him, the more endless it felt, a thing which fed on itself, it was outside of everything else, it had no context, made no context, brought nothing else into it; it felt like this, like craziness, something of itself, the horizon, always in front of you. Sometimes I was determined to fuck him as hard as I could as long as I could until I came out on the other side of something and if I didn't, then I'd know it wasn't possible with anyone if not with Lewis and I'd never see him again. I don't know what other side, though sometimes I could sense it close.

Then Lewis brought me the ring. When he came in that evening, I could tell he was pleased with himself. Something in his walk. His posture. He hung up his coat, reached into the pocket, took out a small box, and handed it to me. I wasn't paying much attention, I didn't stop to think. Or pause. Prepare myself. I opened the box, and when I looked, I couldn't say anything. It was so sweet and so awful. A diamond. Perhaps that's what I mean by attributing things to me. No, that doesn't make sense. A diamond. I turned away, but he had seen my face, I know.

Now I must pay close attention. If it begins anywhere, it begins here. It was not there in him, there and waiting. No. If it begins anywhere, it begins here.

I look at the ring, I turn away, he is very close, he is watching me, he has said, I've always loved you; I have never understood that *always*. He has brought me a ring. He has never said a word about a ring, an engagement, marriage. He simply brings me a diamond, a soft voice and his declaration of love which has never made any sense to me, anyway—*always* loved you—as though it is outside of time. He said that the first morning when I drove him back to the base. As though he were clairvoyant, some medium. How could he have *always* loved me? Whenever he says that, I feel a little lightheaded, like I am outside of time with him, like he is talking to me from some other place. Still, I ignore it. I never ask him what he means, *always*. It's too infinite and drowning. I have been on the verge of asking him, but never could. He would not understand and maybe I am afraid of the answer, that I would never understand, that I would understand. That I already do: a feeling, dizzy, like looking down from a ledge. He gives me the ring, *always,* endless houses, empty, a TV, no books, someone at the sink, I come up behind, or I have vision from behind, the windows are steamy, the house is close and smells of stale air, patches of snow in my father's garden, outside, sky no color, my mother? Myself? I can't see who is at the sink, the windows are beaded with water, a chill to the fingertip, doors, some part-open, some part-closed, doors ajar, doors closed, windows, divided spaces, bedrooms, bathrooms, closets, drawers, some part-open, a wedge of dark-ness, some part-closed, my father never speaks, my mother drags on her cigarette, stares into space, she has bags under her eyes, puffy white skin with a grayness beneath, a shadow, her blond hair gray at the roots. . . .

Ring in hand, I turn away, I see the wooden ammunition crates, USMC, black stenciled letters. I do not know what Lewis is seeing. Me. I hear myself say, Lewis, we are going to have to talk. I do say that.

But then something strange happens. We do not talk at that moment. Perhaps if it had been that moment. If it begins anywhere, it begins here. But then we do not talk. Lewis goes into the kitchen, comes back with a glass of ice water. The moments gather, they divide, subdivide, quickly, like cells, reproduce, grow. As if he has not brought the ring. I cannot remember what I do with the ring. If I touch it. Close the box. If I set it down, give it back to him. What. I never see the ring again. I have no memory of it. I know he brought me a diamond ring, but I do not know what happened to it after I turned away. I know we are going to have to talk, but we do not talk.

All night long we do not talk. It is unbearable. Moment after moment, I am numb, I think we are going to start, but something in me cannot begin. I know it is up to me. Lewis has few words. We act as though nothing has happened. We eat together. I sit down to study, Lewis watches TV. The air does not allow real words to pass into it. It is hungry, but cannot take real words. A hollowness in the mouth. Swallowing. TV soft. Lewis does tai chi, his slow-motion dance. Mary Beth comes to the door, pretty Mary Beth, and we joke for a while. Lewis mimics people, Mary Beth laughs, everything is the same. Mary Beth and Lewis joke and flirt.

I keep hearing myself start the words, but they do not come. It is too big, too much, the voices, the silence, the secrets.

Now I must pay close attention. If it begins anywhere, it begins here. Lewis is the same all night. And perhaps I am the same to Lewis. What does he see? Know? He knows something. He must. I know the stiffness in my neck and shoulders. I can hardly turn my head. Lewis drinks glasses of water. Clinking of ice. How many glasses? I don't know, but every time I look up, he is drinking water. Maybe the same glass. His pupils seem large, dark velvety. I actually get to some strange place where I can concentrate. I do chemistry problems. I sit motionless in a chair hour after hour writing on a yellow pad. The silent flicker of my pocket calculator. Numbers, decimals. The stiffness in my neck. Eyes closed, Lewis does tai chi, drinks ice water. Once when I look over he seems to be glistening, a fine veil of sweat. Perhaps not. Even from over here, his body smells sweet. Once I notice him gazing down at the prayer plant, turning it slowly.

I start wondering what to do about bed. Getting into bed. Taking my clothes off. Lewis and I getting into bed. I pick up Gray's *Anatomy* and study the illustrations. You might do anything you want. Can. Gray's *Anatomy*. The illustrations are beautiful and ordered. Red for arteries, blue for veins. Perhaps that is why my father has always loved to read technical books. They are beautiful and ordered. Calming. Calming against voices.

I close the book and wash up. We get into bed without looking at each other, turn off the bedside light, my eyes closed, I feel him against me, his smooth skin, our bodies ravel in a familiar way, though it is dark, I keep my eyes closed, I see us from the ceiling, from the roof, I am in the dark air above the house, it turns me on to imagine myself small and being fucked, myself small, Lewis big, raveling, I am under a man in a room, I see the diagram, red for arteries, blue for veins, everything is peeled back in layers: muscles, cartilage, tendons, bones, nerves, things go together, ravel tight, something I know for sure, tighter, a sharp tearing, knowingness, begins to slip silently away, I can't stop it, coming apart, as I drift toward sleep, I say, Lewis, we have to talk.

I come awake first. It is still dark. Lewis is sweating, groaning, thrashing. I turn on the light.

"Lewis!" He is glistening with sweat. His eyelids and lips twitch, become still. He seems to be listening with his skin. "Lewis, wake up!"

He listens from faraway, as though he were hiding in a tree high above the ground. His lips move. He groans. A single word, thick slur of sleep, Nam. Then his eyes open. Just the whites showing as though his eyes are tangled beneath his lids. The sheets are dark with sweat, his shadow drained off him and run down into the bed like sand. He opens his eyes, gray, ashwhite, they look at me from faraway. He becomes aware of me.

Now I think he was never not aware of me, that he was always aware of me, even when he was sleeping.

He sits up and holds his head.

"You were having a nightmare. Are you okay?" He nods. "What was it?"

"Nam." He shakes his head. "Nam."

His voice is flat and faraway from sleep. The first time he told me. About Nam. That he was dreaming of them. The bodies. The ponchos blowing back with a loud slap in the wind, bloody faces. Bodies. How fast they would bloat, streak, change colors, swell with gas in the heat. Ponchos blowing back, bloody faces.

Now I must pay close attention. If it begins anywhere, it begins here.

No. It has already begun, hasn't it? I must pay close attention.

Once he'd started, there was something I needed to know. I wanted him to stop, but I listened. It felt like something I had always known.

That night was the first Nam dream.

He asks for water and I bring him ice water, the ice clinking, the heat, he says, Nam. He sweats.

His voice is flat, faraway, like he is telling a dream. Across the room I see his boots, shined, side by side. The wooden ammo crates. Under the TV. The bedside lamp. The rough splintery wood. Black stenciled letters. USMC. Light on the ceiling, circle of fuchsia.

Lewis talks. Charlie took two grunts prisoner. Charlie held the village, and they were outside the village. The grunts could hear the screams, but they couldn't do anything. The grunts—the prisoners—screamed all night. Before dawn, the screams stopped.

In the morning, they were reinforced and counterattacked, the VC disappeared into thin air like smoke, they found the two grunts hanging naked upside down, every inch of them sliced from head to foot, balls cut off and sewn in their mouths.

His words the black stenciled letters on the ammo crates.

"We took one look at those bodies and we went crazy, we dragged every living thing in the village out into the open....

I listen.

Maybe I should have stopped him, but I didn't. I couldn't stop him. I didn't want to.

Men. Women. Children. Babies. Buffalo. Dogs.

He is drinking ice water.

Blood. Men. Women. Children. Babies. Buffalo...

Blood. His voice is hoarse.

Dogs, he says. Dogs.

I want him to stop, but I listen. I think it is a relief to finally hear though I don't know why. I needed Lewis to say it. I'd always known. Something in me. Close. I couldn't stop him. He said it for me. Maybe it's my fault. Maybe I should have stopped him. But it was too late. It had already started somewhere.

Dogs, he says, once more hoarsely, lies back, stares up at the ceiling. Fuchsia. Stares a long time. I turn off the light and we lie still and I see Woo in his goofy plaid sport shirt, he is walking with his wife and children, I hear the reasoned delicacy of his voice; in the dark, Lewis says, I thought about you all the time I was there, I have always loved you. Then he is quiet. His breathing deepens. I see Woo and his wife and children covered with blood. I feel the heat from Lewis' body. I hold my breath.

His body is hot, feverish, like something jewelled and camouflaged that lives in a rain forest, something that could remain
motionless for hours on end; the bedroom darkness is a broad
shiny leaf, we lie beneath it, together in shadows, Lewis and I,
Lewis jewelled and glittering, camouflaged, motionless. I lie
beside him, holding my breath.

I bend, pick up the evening paper, put the key in the lock,
open the front door. Close the door and lock it. I stand in the
front hall, hold my breath and listen, look into the living room,
the dining room, open the paper: *New evidence points toward JFK
conspiracy.... Soviet agent in Oswald's grave?...Unable to get
permission to open grave...two-figure inflation...*

I walk into the kitchen, drop the paper on the table. Breakfast
dishes still in the sink. I wander from room to room. Stop.
Listen. Back to the front hall. I glance up the stairs. Start up.
Decide not to. In the kitchen, I fill a pitcher, start watering the
plants, plucking off dead leaves.

When I first came home, I slept in my old bedroom across the
hall from my parents. It made me feel safer, my father wasn't far
away, he kept a loaded shotgun by the bed. A loaded thirty-
thirty in the downstairs closet. I've hunted with him, watched
him handle guns all my life, and there is something about the
way he handles guns which I've always admired. A deftness. A
certainty. But when I came home and watched him load the
guns, it was different than hunting. Something in his jaw. A
finality in his hands. He's always been a realist and I don't think
he had any doubts about what he might be dealing with. It
made me feel better to sleep in my old room; he wasn't far.

They have a little thing on their bedroom door—a love
barometer. One of those joke things. It has a dial: in the mood;
not right now; definitely not now; maybe, try me; a little later.
It's been *not right now* for as long as I can remember. I don't
know what my father does to get off, though if I were a man, I
couldn't imagine wanting her so...

Anyway, I felt safer across the hall from my father. But then I
couldn't sleep at night. I'd get sleepy, doze, but come wide
awake. I'd get up. Read. Write things. I felt like I was in there

holding my breath. Finally, I decided to move into the basement. Half is a workshop—my father's decoys, old fish tanks,
tools—and the other half is paneled, has a bed, shelves. My
father checked the locks on all the doors and windows and gave
me a loaded gun to keep by the bed. He taught me to shoot
when I was a kid and he has always trusted me with guns. I felt
a little better in the basement, though a couple of times I almost
panicked. Did panic. But mostly I felt better. I could keep the
portable TV on and move around without holding my breath,
my mother is such a light sleeper, up in my old bedroom I felt
like any little movement I made was going to wake her, disturb
her. Even with me in the basement, a lot of times I'd hear her
come down to the kitchen at four or five in the morning, pour
herself a drink, pace. Chain-smoke. The doctor told her, keep
smoking, you'll be on a machine in five years. She keeps
smoking. She wants to die. She knows her life is a big nothing.
Too late now. She's done nothing. My sister, a carbon copy.
Except Donna's divorced. When my mother told me it was
going to happen, I was in the eighth grade. I went out, it was the
middle of winter, snow piled in the street, I walked around the
neighborhood, cried.

Though I know that's not the way I really am, nothing, that I
came out of that big nothing, have that big nothing in me,
sometimes I still feel that way.

My mother up there drinking. Chain-smoking. Pacing.

She'd pace from one end of the kitchen to the basement door,
stop as though she were going to reach for the knob, then I
could hear her turn, her steps creak back across the floor. What
was she doing when she'd stop? Trying to make up her mind?
She'd keep this up for hours. I felt like shouting, "Oh, come on,
open it! You know I'm awake. You're awake, I'm awake. Open
it, come on down, say it: I should have stayed home and gone to
the community college, say it. And then, bad enough I went
away like any other normal person would have done, but I
should have stayed in the fucking dorm, right? Go, say it all, get
it over with, you've been dying to tell me since I came home,
come on, I know it's killing you, you'll feel like a million dollars,
I should have gotten married at seventeen, you did, three kids,

miserable, a little ball-breaker, stuck it out, or how about like Donna?...

But I wouldn't say anything. I'd lie there and she'd pace back and forth driving me crazy. Maybe she was trying to show me how many miles she could put in each night over me. Was that it? If so, it's the only exercise she's ever gotten. She must have walked farther than Lewis and Clark.

I water the plants. The phone rings, I put down the pitcher, go to answer it; I stare at the phone. Raise my hand. Maybe it's Vicki. We'd talked about going for a drink, but didn't decide anything definite. The receiver vibrates in my hand, but I cannot lift it. I have a sick feeling in my stomach. Finally the phone stops. I sit down for a few minutes, then refill the pitcher, go on watering the plants.

When I was little, maybe seven, my brother and I used to play a game. If I was seven, he was already fifteen. It was his game. He made it up. We lived in another house then, but the same kind of house as this, except our bedrooms had a connecting closet. He taught me the game. To crawl through the closet at night after everyone was sleeping. Crawl under the clothes. I liked to feel them hanging above me. A cedar smell. Into his room. The smell of hair on his pillow. I don't know what we did. But I know, knew even then, that my father would have killed him, my brother, for whatever he was doing. I never said anything.

The shrink would misunderstand something like that. I would tell him, that is not it, nothing is it, *I know*, but he would look at me as though only he knew what I really knew and didn't know. He would take away what I know. Vicki would understand.

Sometimes when I talk to the shrink, I wish there were words to differentiate *know*. I took an anthro course freshman year; the Eskimos have dozens of words for ice and snow, the Africans for grass. They see things in the ice and grass we do not see. They need those different words. Sometimes I wish I had at least a dozen words for *know*: know with the head, which part of the head, all parts of the head, know with part of the head, all of the heart; know with both head and heart, and completely; and know beyond knowing, evidence or not, beyond words or anything, just know; and know and can't take away, no matter what good reasons people give. Eskimo ice, African grass, everything, plants, stones, air, know.

The shrink would be tolerant and amused and take this as further evidence that I do not know. But Vicki would understand.

The phone rings again. I ignore it and go on watering the plants. Neither my brother or sister went to college. My brother went into the Air Force and was trained in computers, came back, found a job as a computer programmer, married his high school sweetheart who he had shit on and who he stills shits on. He used to be nice-looking in a bland sort of way, but now he's got a kid, he's mister respectable, and so he's gotten down to the serious business of sitting around, drinking beer, watching the Superbowl, getting fat; he and his wife, both a couple of pudge balls. I can tell my father doesn't think much of him. My brother lives maybe a ten-minutes' drive from here, a house like this, the old beige and off-white sleepwalk, when he comes over, I don't know what it is, even though he's got a wife and kid of his own, he sulks at my mother. He feels she slighted him with her love, that he didn't get enough, and get loved right, this big, fat pudge-ball, my balding brother. So he's still sulking. He has even begun to look like a soft, round baby—pale and sunless.

The phone finally stops ringing, I put the pitcher on the counter, think of turning on the tube, think of calling Vicki, but just sit. In a while, they'll be home. In grade school, I used to come home from school about now, let myself in, and play. House quiet. I'd make up games until my mother came home. It was the best part of the day. When I'd hear her key in the lock, I'd feel this big letdown, she'd shout up the stairs for me, her voice hoarse and shrill, and I'd feel sick.

Now Dad's working days again so he can be back here nights. He doesn't want to leave us alone. I wish my friends could see the sweet side of my father. They always used to be afraid of him, even in high school. He'd never say anything and they'd think he was gruff; they didn't understand he was shy. They would see his decoys in the basement and think the worst. They didn't know he used to raise pigeons, take care of them when they were sick. When I was little he used to hold a pigeon in his hand and they would talk back and forth, cooing, and I always knew what they were saying.

And fish. We used to have fish tanks all over the house. Huge tanks. He'd make these beautiful underwater gardens with plants, crystalline rocks, shells. At night, room lights off, I'd stand, fish floating above, colors flashing, waterlight shimmering and stretching over me. I'd watch for hours. I remember I turned once, he had come silently, he was standing in the doorway. I could see him smiling, the underwater light shimmering over him, flashing off his glasses like fire. Next time I turned around, he was gone.

I look at the clock. In a while, they'll be home. I get up and turn on the tube. Merv Griffin. I turn it off, pluck a dead leaf from a plant. The thing is no one can really see how good my father's been on this. How hard it must be on him. He's straight. Doesn't drink. Doesn't smoke. Doesn't approve of girls fooling around. Ordinarily I think he would have killed me if he'd found out I'd been living with a man. But he hasn't said one word to me through all of this. Not one word. He's kept my mother under control, too. Maybe for the first time in his life. I'm not sure how, but I sense it. He's been very good.

In some ways, it's my mother who's surprised me. I think part of it is she's more scared than I am. The other day she opened the hall closet, something fell from the shelf and she screamed. My father and I came running. Here she's lived this deadly dull life and always felt safe in her new houses and now there is this thing loose, her worst fears have come to pass, new houses or not, locks or not; she stood there, two shattered light bulbs at her feet, face in her hands, sobbing, and I felt sorry for her; sometimes from the way she acts, you'd think she'd been the one, not me.

In the morning, my mouth and eyelids were thick with silence, I drank several cups of coffee, but I was still faraway and couldn't get back—myself opaque, a hangover or virus. And my tongue, slow and thick, like a nerve had been severed. No words. Lewis never said that much anyway, but I knew he was far away, too. Looking at his face I couldn't tell if he was thinking about Nam or the nightmare, the ring, what. We were buried under strata of silence. I wanted to shout, "Do something, Lewis. Anything! The ring, Lewis, the fucking diamond. Show it to me, show me the diamond. There was a diamond. Do something."

But I knew he had seen my face and somehow I didn't dare say anything about the ring. Either last night was unreal or this morning was unreal. Or, as it was turning out, both were unreal.

And now there was a sense of something close, that thing I had always known. I kept looking at Lewis and hearing the clink of ice in the glass. And once, catching sight of the stenciling on the ammo crates, USMC, I saw letters, words, hundreds of words compressed together, everything Lewis had told me last night, Nam. And one word repeated over and over again: blood.

I turned away. Lewis was so incredibly pretty that morning. His eyes. Skin. I borrowed Mary Beth's car and all the way to the base I kept looking at Lewis and wanting to pull over, pull him into the woods, tell him, fuck me, Lewis, fuck me, make everything real again, but I couldn't take my foot off the gas pedal.

When we got to the base, I pulled over and told him I'd like a couple of days to myself. Door open, legs out, Lewis glanced back. "Because of what I told you last night?"

I shook my head, "No, just a lot of work. I need some time to myself." He looked scared, the way he had last night when he'd come awake. Alone. "Just a couple of days, Lewis," I said softly.

He glanced past me, drew into himself, then farther, into a military bearing. I watched him walk past the Marine sentry, exchange salutes. As I drove back toward town, I began to feel something I couldn't identify; it started as keenly missing Lewis, finding his absence unbearable. Then it gave way to a gentleness I'd never felt toward him, a tenderness. Finally, as I reached school and parked, I realized perhaps I was in love with Lewis.

And all through my lectures, I could hardly concentrate. I was thinking about Lewis when he'd been in Armenian's, before I'd known him. Suddenly it all made sense, his mimicking and clowning to amuse, his closeness to his buddies. It was simple. So many of them had been killed. What did I know? Work. School. Modeling. Summer jobs. I was just normal, where did I get off, judging someone like Lewis.

That afternoon I tried for ten minutes during a lab to weigh out something on a scale, but I couldn't get it to balance, powder spilling everywhere, and finally, I knocked the tray over, stood there shaking and walked out.

Outside, Duane in his white caddy watching the girls, the girls sleepwalking by, asleep and dreaming. Duane watching. The rolling hills, the Jeffersonian architecture, beautiful as ever, but now unreal, like a stage set, a mask. I walked in one direction, then another. I couldn't make up my mind. I was stumbling over my feet. The pool. Suddenly I wanted to be immersed; I remembered how it had been after work, evenings, before Lewis. The silence of the pool, floating, the velvety rainbows around the lights high overhead. Through eyes half-closed, they were like suns or stars slowly revolving. I started for the pool, but when I got close enough, I looked through the glass and could see there was a swim class going on; the sight of so many naked arms and legs and necks made me uneasy. Some students were lying on their stomachs on the pool deck imitating the crawl, kicking and lifting their arms and turning their heads. Others were already in the pool which was too filled with swimmers and splashing white water.

Then I thought of Woo. We would talk, go for coffee, I wanted to hear his voice. He was such a sweet gentle man, his voice was so calming. I started for his office, but on the way there were too many people coming out of stores, crossing the campus, getting in and out of cars—men, women, children. A sign in a window, *blood*, in some oriental language. Looked again, *book*. Husbands, wives, brothers, sisters, which ones would kill, were killed, I must have been staring because a lot looked back at me, startled, then turned away.

The math building, janitor running a buffer, polishing linoleum, he looked up without expression. On the second floor, his office. Woo's. Dark. I knocked. Walked up and down the empty halls. Waited by the men's room for several moments. Back at his office, I pressed my nose to the opaque glass, peered in. I could see the silvery glow of a window. His desk. I wanted to hear his voice. I started to write him a note, thought of calling him at home, left.

That night in Armenian's, I mixed up orders, gave out the wrong change, spilled things. Noisy and smoky. Star Wars, Raiders, Defenders, video games, disintegrating blips, mechanical explosions.

Armenian waving from the kitchen. "Eaten yet?"

He indicated a stool and got a plate out. I shook my head, no. He offered me a cigarette, patted the stool, we smoked.

"What's the matter, Kim? Even your first night you weren't like this."

We sort of laughed. Without mentioning his name, Armenian said the only thing he would ever say about it.

"Before it started, you said you didn't like him, do you remember?"

"No, did I?"

He nodded. He took out his wallet. Placed the twenty on the table. "Go on, take the night off, you're a good girl, Kim. I know you."

I pushed the money into his chest pocket and kissed him on the cheek. "I'll be alright."

At home I put all of Lewis' things on one side of the closet. We weren't really—officially and by agreement, sign on the dotted line—living together, but a lot of his things were here. Too many. I pushed them all onto one side of the closet. Put some of the loose things in a cardboard box. Then I took a long shower and studied. Before I got into bed, I picked up Gray's *Anatomy*, opened it, anatomy diagrams, slammed it shut. As I got into bed, I looked at the sheets. A shadow, where Lewis had been sweating. I pulled back, yanked at the sheets, stripped the bed, and made it up with fresh sheets.

But the bed seemed empty, and I felt disconnected and strange without Lewis. I could sense the darkness and night around the house, as though I could float off the bed, float through the window, keep going, float up above the house, drift away into nothing. I kept tossing and turning, getting up for water. Recalling a magazine article. Rescue missions. Vietnam. Helicopters, clean-cut boys, smiles. Writing letters to Mom and Sis, the wife or girl back home. Rescuing downed pilots. Floating above the house. Monsoon clouds, black underbellies. Skimming over the treetops. Gaps in the clouds. Jungle. Red clay. Muddy river gorges boiling, red torrents. Jungle treetops a solid green floor, someone down there, I was being lowered through the clouds, treetops coming up beneath my feet....

In the morning, exhausted, I got some coffee, stared at my books. There was something I wanted to ask Lewis, something more I needed to know. I didn't know what.

And I knew that I was going to have to say something to Lewis. I didn't know how. Or what. It had gone too far. Maybe I loved him. I would have to say something.

When I got home, the phone was ringing, Armenian, could I work tonight, someone out sick, I was suddenly relieved, grateful for the distraction, sure I would, I hung up, jumped in the shower. In a robe, still dripping, I ran into the bedroom, opened the closet door, jumped back. Someone. Something. A uniform. Full-dress uniform. White hat, white gloves, spats...

While I was out. My heart pounding. Suddenly I knew it had to go, he has to go, that's it.

We hadn't talked about the ring; it had disappeared. Now this. Suddenly, I understood, though I doubted he did, that this was it, his reply.

"Kim."

I jumped. Gasped. Covered my mouth. He appeared from out of nowhere. Startled me, scared me.

"How long have you been here?"

"I got here while you were in the shower."

"Well, Jesus, Lewis, why didn't you say something? Let me know? You scared me."

My heart was pounding. I was avoiding his eyes, but Lewis always knew everything, anyway. I'm sure of that now.

Suddenly I said a little too loud and hot, "I thought you were going to give me a few days."

He didn't answer.

"And what is this?" I pointed at the uniform. "And just coming in like this when I'd asked for a few days. You don't ever ask me, talk to me. You wait and never talk. What are you waiting for, Lewis?" He didn't say anything. "This has to go." I waved at the dress uniform. "Now. Tonight. Everything."

Lewis was always graceful and surefooted, but he looked off-balance and might have stumbled backwards. He looked helpless. I thought suddenly of Marines hanging upside down, screaming.

"Lewis," I said softly, "we can talk about it. But please get your stuff out of here. I can't talk right now. I'm working tonight."

He walked across the room. Stopped. Glanced at the bed. Drifted back. Looking at me. His eyes clear, gray-white, unreadable. I was sure he was going to hit me.

"Lewis," I said softly, "please."

"I have always loved you."

It was as if he were talking to me again from somewhere out of time. Before I could say anything more, he drew himself into that Marine bearing and said, "I'll have to borrow a car."

"I'd drive you if I could, but I don't have time. Anyway, Mary Beth isn't here."

"I'll hitch to the base, I can get one there."

"Thank you for being so reasonable about this, Lewis." I suddenly felt tender toward him, "We have to talk about some things. Make them clear. But please have everything out tonight by the time I get back."

He had resumed that Marine bearing and his eyes were clear and unreadable.

I went back into the bathroom to put on some makeup and by the time I came out, Lewis was gone. I felt bad. I had known something would come, but... I started brushing my hair, caught sight of the uniform in the mirror. I turned. The white gloves, the blue. The red escutcheons. I put down my hairbrush. Walked slowly to the closet. Something weak in my stomach. I touched the sleeve. Watched myself unbutton the jacket, slip it off the hanger, drape it over my shoulders. I glanced at myself a long moment in the mirror, then carefully lifted the jacket off, hung it back on its hanger, and closed the door.

After work, I went straight to the closet. Still there. I was trying to decide if I was surprised or not when the phone rang. Probably Lewis. Excuses. I let it ring. Finally snatched the receiver. Lewis. Not Lewis. Someone else. About Lewis. The emergency room. Yes, alright, I'd come. Mary Beth and Tommy stretched out on the bed, tickling each other, laughing. The car keys. Stumbling. The front walk.

Glare of the emergency room. Nurse at admitting. See what she could find out. She disappeared behind a door. A doctor came out, followed by another man, younger, maybe thirty, short hair, Lewis' CO? No, not a grunt, something different about him, a look of fatigue and worry, circles under his eyes.

They looked me over, the doctor introduced himself, said Lewis would be alright, started giving me a report: ...a neat wound, the major one. The other, a classic self-defense wound, the doctor put up his hand to show me how the hand goes up to block an impending blow, traced a line across the hand, the edge, to show me where Lewis had been hacked. Neither were too deep, and the one on his trunk had missed vital organs. Both wounds on his right side. Lewis still wasn't reacting much, shock, but he was tough, and he would be fine. The doctor explained the antibiotics and pain-killers, said there should be no problems, but if there were, to call this number. He was about to say something more, but the PA called him. He handed me the prescription, two envelopes with capsules, nodded, and strode off quickly. Just as he reached the door, he turned once, held up his hand in some acknowledgement to the other man, who was approaching me. He introduced himself as an Allan someone, police, a few questions.

Was I his girlfriend? Lewis'?

No, just a friend.

"Are you taking him home with you now?"

I hesitated. "I guess so. For tonight, anyway."

He looked me over and thought about that. He asked me a few more questions, what did I do, who did I live with, how long had I known Lewis?

"Do I have to answer these questions?"

"No."

"Then if you don't mind, I'd rather not."

I had nothing to hide, but I didn't feel like answering personal questions. Why should I?

He gave me a tired look, started to say something, thought better of it.

"May I ask you a question?" He nodded. "I've been here twenty minutes and no one's told me what's going on. What has happened?"

He told me Lewis had been hitching back to the base to borrow a car. A couple of guys stopped. As he got in, one pulled out a razor.

When he said slash, I caught my breath.

The cop traced a line across his stomach. Eighty-seven stitches. It made my cheek flush hot and cold. That tight skin. Lewis got no real description of the guys. Nothing on the car, either. No license number, no make. To be expected, since it was dark and happened fast. No witnesses. Of course. The cop said that last with a kind of ironic fatigue. I looked at him. Short brown hair, a tired-looking shirt, gray slacks. He had two deep smile-lines in the middle of each cheek and I knew talking to him any more would be a waste of time.

"Are you alright?"

I shrugged. "I guess." I suddenly felt tired.

His eyes slid across my body, away. "I'll be off. He's in there." He nodded at the doors, turned, and walked toward the ambulance ramp.

I don't know what I'd been expecting, but it wasn't Lewis on the other side of the waiting room watching TV. *Kojak* reruns. His right hand was bandaged. A white hospital top. Pants ripped and muddy. As I approached, I saw his eyes were glassy and faraway. When I noticed the dried blood stains on his pants, I felt that hot-and-cold blush on my cheek, close now, *Kojak* was pink and green, sickening. Said softly, "Are you alright, Lewis?"

He pulled his eyes away from the TV. "Kim." I could hardly hear him.

I extended my hand, but couldn't really get myself to touch him. I waved my fingertips. "Come on, Lewis."

He got up stiffly and followed me.

Across the drive, I could see the cop with his inside light on. His head was down and he was writing up a report. Lewis glanced at him as we drove by. Said, he told you? I nodded, yes. Neither of us said anything more. I suddenly felt numb, exhausted, as though I could put my head down on the steering wheel and sleep. I hardly followed when Lewis started talking. His voice was soft. He wanted me to know that he had lied to the cop on one small detail. He knew the guys. A couple of gamblers from D.C. He owed them money. They had threatened to come down, but he never thought they would. He glanced over at me.

"I didn't want to lie, but I couldn't tell the cop that. It's gambling, Kim."

I nodded. "How much was it?"

"A few thousand."

"A few thousand! How few?"

He hesitated, embarrassed. "Just under five."

"Jesus, Lewis. I didn't know you gambled. Five thousand."

"It was stupid. Some football games. It snowballed."

"And what about those guys? They still didn't get their money."

"I know," he said quietly.

"Will they be back?"

He didn't answer. I was about to say, they will, won't they, but I was too tired. "Lewis," I said softly. "For Christ's sake. Five thousand. Look what they did to you."

He didn't answer.

We must have slept in the same bed that night. I guess. We did. The white bandage around his waist. Hip to rib cage. Tight, clean. His staring up at the ceiling. Then his light regular breathing. Already asleep before I turned off the light. In the dark, I listened to cars coming and going in the street. Doors slamming. Stomach flutter. Razor. White bandage. The dark stains on his pants. I touched my breasts. Stomach. Razor. Drift sleep skid, sixteen, mother's car, winter, too fast, silently skidding on ice, fast, soundless, staring ahead and not knowing I was skidding, falling asleep, snow's silent speed, sideslip, afterward, couldn't ride in a car for a long time, skin silently parting.

After that, Lewis stayed. He was always there, silently drifting in and out of my room while I studied, trying to stay out of my way, always waiting, trying to be sweet and please me. Maybe I'd be lying to say we didn't have some fun. We did, I guess. We'd go here and there, occasionally do things with Mary Beth and Tommy. I know Lewis had a long thin scar across his stomach, a deep hack below his little finger. I saw them, felt them, but I honestly can't remember a mark on him. He is smooth.

I kept on working at Armenian's. I did my school work, but now it was murky. Part of me seemed to be preoccupied or missing. Something darkened the solutions; I could feel my mind working. Something in the way things had gone with Lewis in the days before he'd been slashed by those two guys from D.C. The expression on his face, his voice, Nam ... poncho slapping back from bloody faces, those two grunts hanging upside down, screams. Something. I grew still and watchful, I was holding my breath and listening, and I could hear him, holding his breath, too; maybe he didn't know it and maybe it wasn't even so. Maybe it was the sound of my holding my breath, just me, though I think not. I was listening for something. It was like listening to stone. Everything has its sound, even stone. I was listening to stone.

One night as I was leaving work I noticed I hadn't been to the pool for a while. I thought of the pool, its silence, the colors, the lights drifting and revolving overhead. I started walking that way. Even if there wasn't time for a swim, I loved the way it looked at night. The blue water through the glass, the lights soft and gold on the lawn and trees outside. In the winter I loved to look at the snow and think how just on the other side of a thin sheet of glass, not even half an inch thick, you could be in another world. I walked toward the pool and when I saw it, I stopped. Beautiful in the dark. A few swimmers. I started down the path. When I looked up again, the swimmers were closer so that I could see their wet skin glistening. I stopped. Skin. Backs.

Necks. Thighs. Stomachs. Someone rose from the diving board, floated. So much skin. I felt odd. Lightheaded. I turned and started for home.

Lewis stayed. At work, Armenian looked at me and I knew Armenian was thinking, but not saying something. I wanted to visit Woo, and several times I thought I would, but somehow I couldn't bring myself to stop at his office. I wanted to see him. I still loved to listen to his voice, that delicate accent, but as soon as the lectures were over, I would leave quickly from the back of the hall. There was silence around me and everyone seemed to be listening to the silence of everyone else. I studied math. I studied chemistry.

I'd come awake in the middle of the night to his heat and stillness and it would be far away, who he was, and long minutes before I could remember his name, all the time he would be like a cellular furnace silently regulating itself, carbon, hydrogen, oxygen, heat, infrared. I would almost know something, the words, the right words, and finally would remember his name, Lewis, but that wouldn't stop it, it would go on and on in the dark, carbon, hydrogen, oxygen.... I'd wake exhausted by chemistry.

But I was working on it and knew something was coming soon.

The nightmare woke me suddenly. Voice hoarse, thick, slurred. Nam. The bedside light. Lewis glistening with sweat, the flat voice. Nam. Shattered palms. Bodies turning colors in the heat, bloating, the slap of ponchos, the bloody faces, Lewis drinking ice water, his eyes clear, faraway, unreadable. Lewis talking in a flat hoarse voice, Nam, close, myself in a bathrobe hugging my sides and staring at the creases in the sheets, Nam here.

In the morning, I knew something. I couldn't say what it was, but I knew. And Lewis knew I knew. Lewis always knew when I knew. We had breakfast and all the way to the base neither of us said a word. I could feel him listening. I could feel Nam in him. I drove away fast without a word and all day long I could feel Nam and couldn't look at people and knew I had to get away from Lewis, leave him.

By the time the call came, I was so exhausted from lack of sleep, I didn't think anything. I went and got him. The doctor. The cop. One across his right shoulder and down his arm, a second one higher, across the back of his neck and curving up far enough to reach his cheek. I brought him back and helped him undress. Bandaged. He stared at the ceiling. After a few minutes, he was asleep. I sat for hours with the desk light on and watched him sleep in my bed.

I don't know if I was surprised or not when the cop came a couple of days later. I was probably beyond surprise. I'd never thought anything much about going crazy, but if I had, I probably would have imagined it was dramatic, like a revelation. It's not. It's dull and flat and not knowing anymore. Things go from color to black-and-white. You don't notice. You don't know it's begun. When it began. Anything can be anything else. Everything hurts, but you don't really know that, or know how much. Later, the unceasing conversations. The cop came a couple of days later and met me outside my last class. I was just going about my business. Sitting in the lectures not understanding a word. Not even knowing that.

He approached me quietly, fell in step with me, Allan somebody, he reminded me, he asked me if we could talk. I don't know what I said, but I went with him. . . .

We got in an unmarked car and drove slowly out of town, he was quiet, he was looking at my tits, going to make a pass, I'd scream, I had my hand on the door handle, he asked me to tell him about Lewis, I didn't know, did I have any idea who had slashed him—he glanced over at me—nothing goes any farther than this car, he said, you can say anything, hard to talk, like the nerves in my tongue had been severed, I told him about the five thousand, the two guys from D.C.

He listened. And the second time?

The second time I didn't know. I didn't know anything, but they'd never gotten their five thousand the first time, the guys from D.C. so it must have been them again. . . . I'd say a few words and my mind would blank, he was driving so slowly, I could feel cars coming up behind, hanging back there, hesitating, waiting, then pulling out, passing, I asked if he could drive faster, he speeded up, I watched the road, some more questions, I must have answered, he kept looking over, he asked me about Lewis, what? Anything, I told him Lewis was neat, quiet, considerate, that he didn't talk much, anything else? I said he has nightmares, yes, what were they? about Nam, Vietnam, Lewis had done two tours, the cop glanced over, I turned away from him slightly, did I know more about the nightmares, I crossed my arms over my tits, faces, I said, bloody faces, dead Marines. . . . I went blank, he waited, two hanging upside down, mutilated, screams . . . we were out in rolling grassland, horses grazing, screams, I said, screams, the cop was slowing up, cars were passing, he turned off onto a country road, I turned away from him more, started shaking, my arms were crossed so tight over my tits my shoulders ached, we pulled off, stopped, I'd scream if he touched me, the cop turned in his seat, said quietly, he never was in Vietnam. I said, you don't understand, he did two tours, he has nightmares, the cop said, he may have nightmares, but he never was in Vietnam, I said, how do you know that? he said, we've checked his service record. I said he has nightmares, I know he's been there.

Nam, I've seen the faces, bloody faces, he was there, the cop didn't say anymore, I said, he's a Marine, isn't he? I take him to the base every morning, I see him go in, past the sentries, the cop said, he's a Marine, but he has never been in Vietnam. Even as I started laughing I felt I was opening myself up for a weakness in myself that I would not be able to close later, but now I couldn't help myself, I laughed. The cop watched me. I laughed and laughed, a funny laugh, it sounded hollow and metallic, echoey and faraway, like a nitrous-oxide laugh. I said, would you think badly of me if I got out and peed. I have to pee. I laughed. I do. The cop, Allan somebody, looked up and down the road. Go ahead, there's no one out here. I opened the door. Promise you won't look. He said, I'm married and have two little girls, and I promise I won't look. He lit a cigarette and turned the other way and I squatted beside the car, laughing and pissing and watching the horses graze on the other side of

the fence, the knock of their hooves, rip of grass, I got back in
and sat down and neither of us said anything, my mind was
blank, no words, he offered me a cigarette, we smoked, then I
said, I should have told you about the two guys from D.C. right
after Lewis told me, but I knew you wouldn't catch them and it
would have been disloyal to Lewis and . . . He was too quiet and
I looked over. He was shaking his head. There were no two guys
from D.C. I said, then whoever they were. He shook his head,
threw his cigarette out the window, took out his pen. He held it
in his left hand. Lewis left-handed, all of them were on his right
side, none exceeded his left-hand reach, they were too neat, too
even, the ER doctor alerted him the first time; they couldn't
know for sure, but they were suspicious. But then the second
incident, they were certain. He held the pen, drew it across his
stomach, across his right shoulder and down his arm, across the
back of his neck, up across his cheek. Face, he said. The knock of
their hooves, several psychiatrists agreed, once it reached his
face, they said, it would be her face next. . . .

He put the pen back in his pocket. I touched my face. Said
something.

He said, we don't know why. But we do know he is the real
thing and anyone could have been fooled. Anyone. The real
ones can be very, very clever.

But why? I said, he said, I don't know. Each time he sensed
he was going to lose you. Asked me if I'd get out and walk a
little with him, that he had something to ask me. I said I didn't
think I could walk just now and he said he thought I could, that
he knew a lot about me and thought I was very special and very
tough and that he thought I could walk now and that I could
help them, that he had a request to make, but let's walk a little
first, get a breath of air.

So we got out and he was right, I could walk, we walked
slowly along beside the fence watching the horses and he
started explaining something about psychiatrists, the law, a
judge's order, formal charges, I couldn't really follow, it kept
coming over me in waves, never was in Vietnam, no two guys
from D.C. . . . When he turned, he said, he is the real thing, and
we want him, but we're afraid that if there's any change in his
routine with you now, he'll take off, we need just a little more

time at this point. He hesitated, I wouldn't ask you this unless it was absolutely necessary, but it is necessary. There is little danger now....

So he asked. Could I go back and stay with Lewis. One more night.

He loves you, he'll stay with you and we're sure you're safe with him at this point in time. The psychiatrists we've been consulting feel he's a long way from another episode.

Before I could say no, he said, you know, if we'd wanted, we could have told you nothing, just left you with Lewis until we were ready to move. He had debated doing that, but he had considered me.

I said, he already had left me with Lewis after the first time— if that's what he meant by considered me.

He said, that wasn't true, he told me as soon as he'd been absolutely certain which was only several hours ago. And, he reminded me, I'd withheld specific information which might have helped him and insured my own safety early on.

So maybe the cop set me up for it; I know I am a coward, after being with Lewis, I knew I was nobody, a big nothing, it was a chance the cop was giving me, a chance to show him something, I had always felt special, but now I wasn't, now I was nothing, I don't think it was revenge I wanted. I don't know what it was, but I said, yes, I'd do it, stay with him one more night, one of the horses farted and I turned away embarrassed and started walking back toward the car, the cop a half step behind me, we got in and he looked across the seat, reached over and squeezed my hand and I said, I hope you know what you're doing.

He started the car and on the way back he said, just stay with him, take him to the base in the morning as usual and that will be it, the last time you see him, we'll have what we need by then, he'll be in custody by noon, I wouldn't ever see him again.

As we reached town I was thinking, he will know; he dropped me off near school and as I walked home I was thinking, Lewis will know, Lewis always knows.

Inside no one was home, I didn't know what to do, so I started washing dishes, thinking this is ridiculous, but I didn't know what else to do; then the door opened and Mary Beth came out, looked at me and said, what's the matter?

I said, what do you mean?

She said, you look upset.

I said, can you see something?

She shrugged.

I turned off the water and said, what time is it?

She told me and I said, I'm okay, I just did badly on an exam, that's all.

She said, don't take it so hard, I said, I won't. She went back to her room.

Then I walked into the bedroom and sat down on the bed, I couldn't think, I walked over and looked at myself in the mirror and I couldn't tell anything, but Lewis would know, Lewis always knew, I went to the closet, got out a bag, and dropped a few things in, the cop was wrong, I wasn't special, I wasn't tough, I was nothing, I was getting out, I couldn't stand to see Lewis again, I didn't have any idea what I'd do, but Lewis would know, and though the cop had figured some things out, he really didn't understand about Lewis, I heard the front door slam, someone on the stairs, I pushed the bag into the closet, closed the door, Lewis came into the room, he looked the same, so pretty, his sleeves were rolled down, the one on his arm didn't show, some of the bandage above his collar and cheek, he stopped in the doorway, I said, hello, surprised myself, hello, so calm and cool, he was quiet, I turned on the TV, he came toward me, kissed me, pulled away and looked at me, he took off his coat and started for the closet, Lewis, I took his coat, he glanced over, I opened the closet door, standing between him and the bag, sliding it with my foot when he turned, I hung up his jacket, I thought, he knows, Lewis always knows, he watched me, his eyes were clear and unreadable; I said, I've got to get some work done, are you okay? He nodded. I sat down at my desk, he sat down to watch TV.

I opened my chem book, sat there, I was perfectly still but my neck trembled and stopped, trembled, spotted Gray's *Anatomy*, I stood suddenly, knocked over the chair, Lewis glanced over, started to get up, I said, that's okay, picked up the chair, Lewis changed the channel, fooled with the antenna, I said I'll see about some dinner, maybe we'll eat with Mary Beth and Tommy, he said okay, my heart pounding, the cop saying, you're special, I walked around the kitchen opening and closing cupboards, I wouldn't be able to cook, put food on plates, the smells, chew, swallow, he'd know; in the bedroom, I went back to my desk, he said, what's for dinner, I couldn't answer, he said what? I started to shake, he got up, I thought, oh, no, I'm going to cry, it's over, I could hear . . .

Lewis gets up behind her, Kim standing quickly to face him, the lamp fell over on the desk, glare of light on the walls, fuchsia, the walls blazing, Lewis picking up the lamp, Kim noticed the prayer plant, never screwed when she had her period, starched, pressed, he seemed too aware, sometimes Kim wanted it period ache desire, the prayer plant by the window, Lewis never touched the leaves, Kim suddenly knew, blood, he couldn't stand blood, the prayer plant, Kim picked up the plant, Lewis watched her move it away from the window, Kim smoothing the leaves between her fingers, Lewis watching, Kim knew now, Kim acting embarrassed, Kim knew now, would he, it had started, please would he, Kim calm now, I watched Kim give Lewis the money, even making a joke, he wouldn't be embarrassed to go to the drug store and ask for something like that, would he, Lewis confused, uncertain, Kim knew, only a few minutes, always heavy when it starts, go herself but it caught her, Lewis taking the money, going to the door, going out, coming back, arms around her, holding her, holding her tight, pressing against her, telling her he loved her, Kim holding still, a plant, Lewis listening, Kim still, a stone, Lewis listening, Lewis letting go, backing away, confused, sound of him going down the stairs. Rattle of the front door . . .

Stood in the middle of her room. Lewis always knew. I walked slowly to the head of the stairs. Looked down. I couldn't see him. I leaned over the bannister and looked into the shadows. I couldn't see him. He'd been confused, hadn't he? Now gone. A few minutes. Maybe. In the bedroom. The prayer plant. I opened the closet door, pulled out my suitcase. Moving so slowly. Filled it with books, hadn't even gotten to my clothes, realized I wouldn't be able to lift it anyway, too heavy, books, he'd conned me like Lewis, I wasn't special, tough, I was nothing, the weakness in the laugh, I wouldn't be able to close it later, now, ever, there wasn't much time, Mary Beth, I looked into her room, empty, looked for the car keys, heard a door slam downstairs, heart pounding, I ran to the front window, Mary Beth backing out of the driveway. Mary Beth! She didn't hear, I called again, Mary Beth! She looked around, I waved, shouted, up here! She glanced up. I screamed, WAIT! she shouted, I'll be right back, she held up ten fingers, ten minutes, NO! I screamed, WAIT! She was rolling, she hit the brakes, money, I'd need money, I looked around, I heard her revving the VW, I ran out to the landing, looked down the stairs, what if he came in, I started down, hanging onto the bannister with both hands, taking them two at a time, stumbling, twisting my wrists, I yanked open the front door, looked around, down the walk, cutting across the grass, I could hear Mary Beth laughing, I sprawled flat on the grass, lay there, got up, ran into the street, yanked the car door, Mary Beth laughing, revving the VW, I got in, drive, drive! she laughed, I said, it's Lewis, she kept laughing, threw back her head, held her sides, the VW revving, look at you, where are you going? she couldn't stop laughing, I grabbed her, Mary Beth, it's Lewis, he's going to kill me, she laughed and looked at me and then stopped laughing, he's going to kill me, they don't know, but Lewis knows, Lewis can't help it, Lewis is like a plant, like a stone, he can't help it, hurry, he's coming back. She just stared at me and her eyes got wild, the VW idling, I thought no, she's not going to be able to drive, but she popped the clutch and we took off....

As we drove, I was looking for him at every corner; wherever I went, he'd find me, I said, the airport, Mary Beth, the airport, the closest airport was a drive, she never hesitated, she took off, I was getting worse by the second, the weakness in that laugh was opening wider and wider, I was shaking all over, Mary Beth took me up to the ticket counter, people were turning around, I looked down, my dress was torn, knees skinned and grass-stained, hair in my eyes, I couldn't understand, read the video monitors, Mary Beth pulled out a charge card, held my hand, Mary Beth and the ticket agent talked and talked, he kept punching keys and reading the video, shaking his head and punching more keys. Something finally settled, we started walking toward the gate, Mary Beth talking, telling me she'd call my parents, have them meet me. I kept looking for him, Lewis always knew, the bloody faces, a row of men, backs to us, their eyes narrow and faraway, their lips pressed together, they were playing Star Wars games, Raiders, Defenders, Mary Beth put her arm around me and walked me past, I heard someone whispering, people turning around, Nam, the bloody faces coming toward us, screams, like plants, I said, like stones, Mary Beth said, yes, she knew, she understood, like plants, like stones, her arms around me and talking to the stewardess, the stewardess and Mary Beth each with an arm around me, Mary Beth kissing me goodbye, she was crying, I said, I'm sorry, she nodded, she couldn't speak, I said, don't go back there, he'll be there, she nodded, the stewardess' arm around me, she led me through a door, into an open space, night, lights flashing, generators whirring, aviation fuel, up the stairs, the captain, his hat, epaulets, he said something to the stewardess, she took me through the empty cabin, in the back, sat me down, put her arm around me and put a drink to my lips, I said I'm alright, I'm alright, she said, I know you are, honey, the cabin filled with people, passengers, the plane took off, she was smoothing my hair back from my eyes, she sat with me, held my hand, took me off the plane after the other passengers, walked me through the airport, my father, my mother, she had her arm around me, the weakness in that laugh opening wider and wider, knees giving way, my father kneeling down, looking up at him, he picked me up in his arms, my mother's face over his shoulder, Nam, I said, like plants, like stones, I know.

Now I'm better, I think. Last week I took another MMPI and tomorrow I'm supposed to get the results. The first ones were very low. I had never scored that low on any test in school. There used to be a place in me where things hit—like dropping a stone in a well and waiting for the splash. Now there is silence; things fall through an opening in me.

Even my body stopped. I didn't have a regular period for two months. I knew I couldn't be pregnant. More like my body wanted to run and hide itself from me. I guess for being with Lewis. I don't know. But it came back again a few weeks ago. So I must be a little better. I doubt anything like that can show on the MMPI. Periods. Gone. Back. Maybe.

And I've been going out again during the day. Vicki's. Today I made it home without too much trouble.

I think I'm better, though there was one night I came awake down here, light on, I didn't know where, the closet, I had the gun, I made myself pick it up, go to the closet, I could feel him, the red escutcheons, the white gloves, I yanked at the door, dark, screaming, I heard something behind me, I turned, aimed, he grabbed, slapped me, called my name, I fell, the startled Egyptian eyes, my father kneeled down, the decoys, empty fish tanks all shining...

They're both home now. I hear them walking back and forth above the kitchen floor. Talking. Muffled voices. Floor joists creaking. Scrape of a chair leg. In a while, my father's head will appear at the top of the stairs. Dinner. Dad's paper folded beside his plate. Eating. Reading. Glances at me.

Maybe I'll go out with Vicki in a while, though now that it's dark, I don't really feel like it. People out there in dark cars moving fast. Maybe Vicki will come over and we'll have a few drinks, watch the tube, get high. Sometimes I get kind of horny, but when I think about it, think about men, it just goes blank. I'm not sure which scares me more. Men, or never wanting one again.

Sometimes I think about Armenian and Woo—even the cop. I left without saying goodbye to anyone. I wouldn't want them to think I was that kind of person.

I think about things I haven't thought about in a long time. The other day, an old boyfriend. He was a painter. He took a lot of nude pictures of me for figure studies. After we broke up, I wanted them back. I'd think about asking him from time to time, but somehow it never happened. Once in a while it still bothers me.

I wonder about a lot of things—like if Lewis had those

dreams before he met me. Or if they started only once he was with me. That part bothers me. Though he never was in Nam, I know he was dreaming of Nam. Some place called Nam. I don't think he was lying. Not in the ordinary sense, a lie. He was having real nightmares. The way he woke sweating. Groaning. The screams. The bloated bodies. The bloody faces. I saw them, too. I know. He knows I know. Wherever he is, he still knows I know. Beyond him, beyond me, a third place, Nam. His waiting for me in Armenian's. He must have seen something in me, known something. I really do not think I am a bad person. I really don't. If he'd been different, or I'd been different, maybe I could have loved him, and then maybe . . . sometimes it is just too hard and confusing to think about.

The last time I saw Lewis, when he came back into the bedroom and put his arms around me, I was sure he did know, but maybe he didn't want to know, either, maybe he didn't want to kill me. Not really. I'd like to think that. Of course I'll never know and, in a way, can it matter, because even if he wanted to kill me, it wasn't hate, he loved me, he just didn't know what he was doing any more than the prayer plant knows, my periods know. . . .

When I said that the other day, didn't know what he was doing, the shrink just smiled. It was near the end of the session, and after the smile, I wouldn't say anymore. We sat there for ten minutes. I wouldn't say a word. He asked me once what I was thinking about and I wouldn't answer. I was listening. I could feel him listening.

I lie here listening to the creaking of the floor joists, muffled voices above. In a while I'll go up for dinner. My father. My mother. I continue my unceasing conversations with everyone. I talk with my mother, I talk with Vicki, I talk with Mary Beth. . . .

Mary Beth wrote to tell me he's disappeared; that he is AWOL and the Feds and the Corps want him. It must kill him about the Corps. It was everything to him, mother and father— did he say that? or did I only think it?—and like a little boy, he wanted to be a war hero. I'm sure that's what he wanted. To be a war hero and love me, though I think he invented me.

Anyway, he's disappeared and I doubt they'll ever find him. I go on having unceasing conversations with my father, with my mother, with the cop, with the shrink, sometimes with Woo....

I do not talk with Lewis. I listen. He listens. We look at each other. He is smooth. There is not a mark on him.

Lewis has disappeared and no one knows where he's gone.

I do not talk with Lewis. I listen. He listens. We do not say anything, but he is out there somewhere, and wherever he is, I know he is dreaming of Nam. I try not to think about it too much.

We All Share the Sun and Moon

G RACE DROVE NOW. L.A. had fallen behind them, and they were climbing the Grapevine. Jed opened the windows, flicked off the air-conditioner to ease the engine against the steep grade, then glanced over at Gracie. She seemed to be gathering herself, going deeper into silence. Nina slept in her car seat in back; Teddy, too, was quiet, running toy cars along the seams of the upholstery and talking to himself.

Grace said, "The thing I don't want is to get there and just fall into something indefinite with them . . . I want to hear what they have to say. Let them know what we think. Do whatever we can and leave. Three or four days, Jed. That's it."

He nodded, "It can't be the way it was a year ago."

"Watch me, Jed, and if you think I'm starting to sink, tell me. If I don't hear, pull me back. I trust you to see it. I'm counting on you." Though she was tall, she stretched up to the rearview mirror to check on the children; didn't say anything more.

Last time, they'd been the ones to take Jan to the hospital. Jan had lost her job, she'd let go of her apartment, was retreating from a boyfriend, and several weeks before had moved home. This was an old pattern. Moving home was always the end of the cycle. She was sleeping in the back room off the kitchen, her things piled in there with her. She'd been marginal during

Thanksgiving dinner—poked at her food, left and come back in her car—but not too bad, really; if you hadn't watched her closely, you might not have known. Grace's older sister, Sally, had been there with all of her kids. Jan had gotten through the day without incident, though the flood of her unquiet had been pervasive: a sudden frightened glance; the disheveled hair, an oddly sensual cascade of wisps and tendrils.

When everyone had gone and they'd finally settled the children, Jed and Grace lay in bed holding each other and talking quietly. The door of the bedroom pushed open and Jan took a step into the room.

"Can I come in?"

Jan looked at Teddy sleeping on the cot. She gazed at the baby. She walked to the dresser, got down on her hands and knees, and stretched underneath. Her long flannel nightgown slid up the backs of her thighs, uncovered a curve of hip. She unplugged something. The clock radio went dark. She slid out. "It's not safe. This house is not safe. We can't stay here."

Grace pulled on a robe, put her arm around Jan, and led her into the darkened hall. When Grace returned, she said, "Jan's unplugged all of the appliances throughout the house. Says they're all too hot, the house isn't safe. People are listening on the TV. She wants to go out. We'll have to take her in. I'll make a bottle for the baby and tell my mother."

Jed dressed. He said half-seriously, "Jan's been home three weeks, everything's in a holding pattern; you show up for Thanksgiving, she goes over the edge. It's a silent collaboration."

In the car, Jan asked, "Where are we going?" and Grace said, "To a safe place." Jan held onto the door handle, and Jed quietly reached behind her and pushed down the lock.

Then it had been the white lights of the hospital corridors, the red tape of admissions forms and a long wait. Finally, the psychiatric nurse led them to an examination room where a doctor joined them; after a consultation, they drifted into the corridor, the door left open so Jan could see them. The doctor said in a low voice, "She'll have to stay. Do you want to tell her? Or do you just want to go? It might be easier on you to go."

Grace said, "We'll tell her."

Jan stood in the middle of the room, arms crossed, looking this way and that. Behind her, a diagram of the heart and lungs. She looked small, emptied of everything but fright. Grace put her arm around Jan's shoulders and told her that they were leaving, the doctors would help her, that they'd be back in the morning. Jan stared ahead, the corners of her mouth turned down, a distracted look in her eyes. As they'd turned to go, Jan's eyes went flat with panic, she grabbed Jed and Grace—handfuls of their shirts, "No! Don't leave me!" They talked more, settled her down, but when they turned to go, again she grabbed their clothes and wailed. The doctor appeared followed by an orderly who carried heavy leather restraints.

The doctor said, "Nothing will change. She'll keep you here all night. You'll just have to go."

Grace stood immobilized. Jed and the doctor pried Jan's fingers off Grace's shirt, Jed pushed Grace toward the door, Jan wailed, "No! Don't leave me! Grace!" The orderly encircled her arms and upper body from behind, and she began to struggle.

Grace's face went wet with tears; she looked at the closed door. Jed put his arms around her and, talking softly, walked her down the corridor, there was nothing more you could do, Gracie, she'll be alright, they'll sedate her, she'll feel better in a few minutes, she'll sleep, and Grace had let him walk her, nodding, crying, saying, I know, you're right, it's just that Jan was the one I could talk to once, no, I know....

At the end of that Thanksgiving weekend, Grace had been exhausted. After several nights back home, she came moaning awake with a nightmare: she had no body; she was just a pale form, a ghost, and no one could see her—an old dream which went back to her being a teenager. Grace didn't exactly know what the dream meant, but she told Jed she used to waken from it feeling weepy, cut off, alone. She didn't like the dream returning after all of these years. Here she was married with two kids.... It made her feel that things didn't really change.

And in a few more days, Grace came to realize that hospitalizing Jan had revived an incident. She reminded Jed of the episode—how when she'd been twenty, she'd gone to live with her boyfriend, Paul. Her mother had cried, said, "I didn't raise you to do this," and then had not spoken to her for a year. Grace said, "Even in high school, I knew I had to leave or I'd just become whatever they were becoming...I mean, Sally's more than duplicated my mother, had five children, and along the way thrown in some serious fundamentalism to boot. Look at the doors they've closed on themselves. Look at Jan."

At twenty, Grace stayed in college, but lived with Paul. They were together for several years and then it had been on-again, off-again for several more painful years until they'd drifted apart for good. When the breakup appeared to be final, Grace went sleepless for five days, started hallucinating, and a friend had taken her to the hospital. "For seven days, I saw things. I saw blood going down the drain instead of water when I showered. I saw Paul on TV." She shook her head, "The psychiatrist kept trying to get me to go out with him the whole time I was there. He was also teaching himself to play the sax—he turned out to be crazy—you could hear these broken riffs coming out of his office." Grace said, "When you're in craziness, you just have this feeling you know everything; I could look out the windows and see the clouds moving, the mountains, the sky, and I just understood how everything went together. Maybe the worst part is that you know, but you can't tell anyone else. I see that in Jan, in her isolation. It's terrible. Then, suddenly, it was gone, I was okay."

Jed said, "It's very hard for me to imagine you in the least bit crazy. What do you think it was?"

She started to say something, laced her fingers together, worked them this way, that, pulled them apart. She kissed him and he laughed softly. But when he looked back at her, she was gazing through the sliding glass door and had a look of doubt on her face. That had been over a year ago.

Teddy kicked the back of the seat, asked fretfully, when are we going to be there? Jed said, soon, not much longer, and Teddy said, that's what you told me before and kicked the back of the seat harder. Jed said, want to come in front? and Teddy said, yea-ah, barely consoled, and climbed over and sat on Jed's lap. Jed said, "I have something for you. A surprise." He reached under the seat, pulled out a box—a stegosaurus: three dozen plastic bones, vertebrae, and assorted pieces to be fitted together around a spinal column, and a thimble-sized, wind-up motor.

Grace reached over and smoothed Teddy's neck. "When'd you get that, Jed?"

"When you weren't looking."

"Sweet man." She touched his cheek. In another moment, he felt her receding. He'd seen that look the other night. A late phone call, a long conversation. When she'd come back into the bedroom, she'd said, "Ready for this? Jan is pregnant."

Jed looked up from his magazine. "How pregnant?"

"No one knows, but Sally says Mom's known for six weeks."

"Six weeks? How could your mother not have said anything to you?"

"That's my family. If it's not talked about, it's not there. Why should I be surprised at anything?"

"Is she having the baby? Can't be."

"No one knows that, either."

"How can Jan raise a baby? And where's the man?"

"Oh, he's some lowlife and he's not having any part of it." Grace folded a towel, started another, said, "I only know what I know from Sally. She's known for a while, but hasn't said anything. The family silence. Deny. Keep up appearances." She put Teddy's underwear and T-shirts in a pile. "Sally's final comment before she hung up was, 'It's all so unnecessary.' Perhaps one of the more monumental understatements. Of course she's against abortion, but when I ask her who will take the baby, Sally has nothing to say."

Grace put off calling her mother. Jed said, "You better get in touch with her, Grace. Say something. It doesn't matter what. Just break the silence." Another couple of days went by before she picked up the phone. And it was only after she'd turned off the reading light later that she said anything. "When I asked Mom why she didn't tell me about Jan, she said she didn't want to worry me. When I asked her if she was going to tell me at all, she didn't answer." The windows glowed across the room as Jed's eyes got used to the dark. "Mom must feel that they've tried everything, nothing's worked, and this is what Jan needs. I think Mom wants Jan to have the baby and Jan's picked up on it. Maybe she even picked up on it before she got pregnant." Grace fell silent. She turned on her side, placed her hand on Jed's chest. "I'm amazed."

As they approached the summit of the Grapevine, over-heated cars were pulled off the road, and then they reached the top and started down. They descended into the June heat and glare of the valley, the oncoming ugliness of Bakersfield, and Grace put up the windows. The baby woke precipitously with a scream, and Grace eased the car onto the shoulder. At the baby's cries, milk had surged dark into her shirt. She pulled it up from the waist, placed Nina at her breast. The cries stopped. Jed looked at Teddy, made fists, wha wha, Teddy. Teddy smiled. The car had the closeness of milk and baby wipes, the sweet acidity of flesh, a long drive. As Jed opened his door, Grace said, "Watch the cars as you come around, Jed."

Sweating in the heat, Jed stretched, peered into an orchard, which grew up to the highway. He could smell water flooding soil, the scent mingling with hot tar and gas fumes. He looked down the rows of trees, each receding in pleasing patterns of shadow and white sunlight. Jed peered in the window at Grace; the baby nursed quietly at her breast. He was often surprised by Grace, his children, that he belonged to them, they to him. He stretched and watching the oncoming cars walked around to the driver's side.

They were past Bakersfield when Grace said, "I've been fighting this, but I can't help feeling that Jan has this uncanny ability to set things in motion and make us do what she wants. Even when you try to ignore her, she's still in your mind. Somehow she reaches hidden places, draws everyone in. I keep wondering if this is some kind of revenge or just my paranoia."

"Revenge for what?"

"I don't know." Grace shook her head. "Jan takes away my words. Let's not talk about it anymore."

They stayed with a good friend of Grace's. After a swim, lunch, and a lull of uncertain procrastination, they left the baby sleeping and drove silently toward Grace's parents. In the kitchen, Anna, back to them, worked batter in a stainless steel bowl. Grace had almost reached her when Anna gave a start, put her hand to her chest, laughed slightly. She had short gray hair, a child's perfect nose, dark eyes that gave out warmth, but little as to what she might be thinking.

Her face softened as she took Grace's face between her hands, kissed her. Grace was almost a head taller than her mother. "Oh, and Teddy...." Teddy was already headed through the kitchen. She kissed Jed, wiped a streak of flower from Grace's cheek. Were they hungry, did they want to eat? She started for the refrigerator. No, we're fine.... And where was Nina? Sleeping at Karen's.

"We're staying there. Just thought it would be easier for you, Mom. Jan home?"

"She just went to the store," Anna said in a small voice.

"What's happening with her?"

"Well, she was better for several months, now she's up all night. The other day a stranger brought her home. She was wandering in traffic..." Anna trailed off

Before she could say anymore, the front door pushed open and Jan walked in. "Oh, hi, guys, when'd you get here?"

Grace kissed her. Jan came to Grace's shoulder. Seeing them side by side always seemed incongruous to Jed. More like mother and daughter. Grace said, "We got here a while ago. We're staying with Karen."

"Here, Mom." Jan placed a bag on the table. "Just passing through or is there a purpose to your visit?" Her voice had a tangled nervous edge.

"We're on our way north for a vacation. Puget Sound."

"Out of the heat. My, aren't we lucky, Grace." Jan glanced beyond them into the backyard. "Is that Teddy on the swing?"

"That's Teddy."

"He's gotten so big. How old is he now?"

"Five."

"Is that really Teddy?"

Anna looked into the grocery bag. "Was there change, Jannie?"

Jan reached into her pocket and slapped a crush of bills and change on the table. She walked through the back room, crossed the yard. She came to a stop beside the giant cork oak. Her father stood by the tree. She shaded her eyes and looked up at Teddy, who rose and fell in long high arcs. Her head went back and forth as she followed his swinging. They heard her laugh, "Is that really you, Teddy? You're so high...."

Jan turned abruptly, crossed the yard, slammed the back door. She stopped, stared at Jed and Grace. As if working up to jumping a crevice, she appeared as though she was going to say something; whisper or shout, Jed couldn't tell. "Making cookies for the Vietnamese refugees, Mom?"

"You know I am."

"Save me one." She went on staring at Anna.

"What are you looking at?" Anna said. Jan walked out of the kitchen.

They tried to make small talk, realized they were speaking in hushed voices, and Jed went out to shake hands with Grace's father. Teddy had a chair pushed against an enormous fig tree, was trying to climb its trunk. Overhead, the leaves made a canopy, green figs in the shadows. The darkness of the tree always made Jed want to climb up into the heavy branches until he had disappeared from view, just stay there. He left Teddy struggling for handholds and slipped into the back room to read the paper. Jan's things from her apartment were crammed everywhere—a dresser, mattress and bed, books.

He had dozed off when Grace touched his shoulder. "Jed, let's go in a minute." She seemed rushed.

Jed caught her hand. "What's the matter?"

"I know it's probably off the wall, but I'm afraid to leave Teddy alone with Jan. She keeps staring at him and I don't have a clue what she's thinking." She turned and walked away quickly, glanced back.

He spotted a scrapbook, opened it. Snapshots. A man with his arm around Jan. Her remote smile. In some, she looked beautiful, a little like Grace. Jed searched the pictures of Jan looking for Grace. Features. An expression.

As they were pulling away, Jan ran across the front lawn, rapped hard on the window. Her face seemed to be broken into fragments. "You know, Grace, you've got to do something. I've asked them to have the TV checked, but they don't take me seriously. People are really listening." Grace walked Jan into the house.

"What's wrong with Jan? Who's listening to her?" Teddy held the half-assembled stegosaurus.

"She's just upset, Teddy. She's going to be alright."

"Why's she upset?"

"She's confused. She doesn't understand some things."

"What things?"

"Who she can trust. What's real."

Teddy didn't say anymore. He wound the tiny spring to the stegosaurus and watched the legs move slowly.

They drove back toward Karen's, the sun slanting through the thick oleanders and eucalypti. Jed said, "Is there a baby?" Teddy looked up at Jed, then Grace. "Or does she just think so?"

"There's a kind of weight on her. Though the same thought did occur to me."

Jed looked into her face, searched for the pieces of Jan Grace always feared she'd find in herself. He saw the strain of being home. He said softly, "You're all right, Gracie."

"Her social worker would like to see us tomorrow. Will you do that with me?" Jed nodded. "And we're having a family meeting, late afternoon. Mike and Sally's idea. You know, no matter what we—or anyone else—thinks or says, there's no way to get Jan to do anything."

Jed turned onto a main street, flipped down the sun visors, and raised a hand to shield his eyes. Grace pulled Teddy onto her lap, pressed her cheek to his hair. She held him to her chest. Sometimes he struggled out of her arms, sometimes he sat back and gave himself over to being loved. Now carefully holding the stegosaurus, he sat back in her arms and silently watched the road, his eyes deep and clear blue in the slanting sunlight, pupils tiny and secret.

The social worker came to Karen's in the morning, and while Karen watched the baby and kept the kids busy swimming, Jed and Grace talked with him at the dining room table. When Grace spoke, she sounded tired. She recalled Jan's history, which went back fifteen years. The cycles, the nowhere jobs, the succession of boyfriends, the disintegrations, then going home. Finally, a hospital. She said, "No one knows what to do with her or what's really wrong. They've hung the word schizophrenic on her, a convenient label, but it doesn't feel right. What do you think?"

The social worker spoke quietly, often pausing. No, schizophrenic didn't seem right to him, either. The other day when he'd been visiting their family house, he'd noticed how Jan kept staring at her mother. She'd actually moved her chair to keep Anna's face directly in front of her. To him, it was the gaze of a very young child—maybe between one and two, who doesn't yet have enough ego to let her mother's face out of sight. That, and the way Jan kept coming back home—suggested she didn't get something she needed from her mother at that vital time.

The social worker said, "Your mother has that little voice. Often I can barely hear her. She keeps a lot inside…feelings, emotions. Perhaps has always done so. Jan goes out, tries to start a life, meets the same impasse in herself, goes home, perhaps looking for whatever she didn't get. Maybe it's easier or safer for her to go crazy than do the next thing. Your mother says she was a perfect student, went to UCLA for two years, and then came apart. But until then, she was never any trouble at all. That fits the pattern of a child starved for love who is doing everything she can to be perfect—to win love."

When the social worker said starved for love, Grace looked so stricken, he said, "I'm not saying your parents aren't loving—clearly they are. I'm projecting that something important didn't happen between Jan and Anna when it was supposed to have. And Jan hasn't been able to go on since." He fell silent. Said softly, "Did you know that Jan has had two abortions?"

Grace shook her head no. The social worker said, "Your mother's just learned that. It's come as a terrible shock. Perhaps with each pregnancy, Jan was trying to move on—but couldn't.

Maybe this pregnancy is another attempt at her trying to break the impasse."

After he'd gone, Grace opened the sliding glass door, and the sound of splashing came into the room. Grace looked up at the ripples of water and sunlight on the living room ceiling. "I remembered my mother being exhausted when the third child came—that was Jan." She watched the ripples overhead. "I think Sally got the message it was okay to have kids. She has five. I got the message watch it if you don't want to be stifled. I don't know what message Jan got." She pushed open the pool gate. "I think my mother wants Jan to have this baby." She latched it carefully, and walked across the deck toward Karen, who put an arm around her. Then Grace turned, and raising her skirt to her hips, she waded slowly down the steps into the water, a troubled look on her face.

In the afternoon, she phoned from her parents to tell Jed she was taking Jan back to the psych ward. Jed watched the cleaner following the contour of the pool. "Why don't you wait for Sally—didn't you say she was supposed to show up later?"

"She's here now."

"Well, let Sally take her. Has Sally ever taken Jan to be committed?"

"No, but she can't."

"Why not?"

"She just can't. The kids are with her, it's just something Sally can't do, anyway."

"But why always you? Remember last time?"

"I don't know why me. My mother and father are exhausted. My mother says it would tear Sally apart to do it."

"Oh, but it's okay for you! Grace, you asked me to pull you back if I thought you needed it." Grace didn't answer. "Grace?"

"Jan keeps leaving lists around the house."

"What do you mean, lists?"

"Lists. Lead. Dioxin. You know, they're her way of asking, what can be making me this way?"

"Let Sally take her."

"Are you okay watching Teddy?"

"I'm fine, but..."

"I'm leaving the baby with Sally. That's one thing she does very well. Karen will help you with lunch when she gets back from shopping or you can just take them all to McDonald's. Jed, I've got to go. I'll be by to pick you up later. We're having the family meeting before dinner."

Sally handed Grace the baby, whose eyes were starting to close. "She's such a little sweetie. I hope you don't mind, but I nursed her while you were gone. It seemed the only thing to do. But..." Sally looked seriously, "You'll understand if she shows a mysterious preference for me when she's older." They laughed. Sally reached around Grace for Jed, kissed him.

In another moment, Mike arrived in a sweat, shook Jed's hand as he squeezed by. He'd been a promising illustrator who now worked as a landscaper. He greeted Grace's parents, settled himself, then looked at his boots, stroked his reddish beard, and started. "We can't decide anything for Jan, but I thought we could get together and see if there was anything we could do to help her." Grace rocked Nina gently. Outside, Jed could see the kids running in the yard.

Grace's father said, "Well, we wouldn't want to impose anything."

"I've been trying to find out for two weeks how pregnant she is." Grace looked around. "Does anyone know?" No one knew.

Mike said, "I spoke to her social worker." Jed nodded. "He said that Jan had let him make an appointment to get an amnio next week. Even if she's confined to the hospital, he'll see that she keeps the appointment."

Sally's face closed at the mention of an amnio.

Anna seemed faraway, but now said, "I took her to the doctor when she thought she might be pregnant. Jan wouldn't tell me the results...the doctor wouldn't, either," she said in her small voice. "All of the young women were there with their babies..." She drifted. "You know, Jannie was no trouble as a girl. She was such a good student. She spoke perfect French. Her teacher said she had a gift for languages." She looked out the window and said with resigned irony to Sally and Grace,

"Well...after talking to the social worker, all I can say is be careful if it looks like your kids are being too perfect, maybe something's wrong." Anna sniffed, her eyes moistened, and she said, "I just don't see why Jan can't have this baby and that's all."

"Mom, she can't have this baby because she can't raise it. I'm just coming back from taking her to the psych ward. Where would the baby be now?"

Anna said, "Well, maybe she can have it. Sometimes things don't go as planned, but turn out fine. I got pregnant once using birth control and never regretted having Jan."

"You weren't in and out of psych wards for fifteen years."

Jed peered out the window. Teddy had pushed the lawn chair up to the fig tree again and was struggling to climb the trunk. The chair was trembling. Jed wanted to go out there before he fell, but restrained himself. Grace said, "Well, I'm not going to leave this meeting without saying what I know some of us don't want to hear. If it's not too late, I think Jan should have an abortion." She hesitated, and Jed didn't think she could go on. She shifted the baby. "I've never had an abortion and don't know if I could. Jan's had two abortions already and that's a tragedy. But..." Grace's voice faltered, came back strong, "...the fact remains she can't raise a child."

Sally started to say something, but Grace said in a hoarse voice, "Please let me finish. Sally. Let me. If she had the baby and gave it away for adoption, would that be good for Jan? Remember Marilyn Anderson, Sally? She was in my class? She got pregnant, had the baby, three days later gave it up...always looked like a piece of her was missing. Remember that look on her face...Sally?" But Sally wouldn't look at her. Grace said, "I don't see any other way but an abortion—if it's not too late."

"What about the baby's life, Grace? You're standing there holding your baby. What about that life?" Sally's face was tight and hot, her blue eyes brilliant.

Grace said, "I'm sorry to offend you, Sally, I really am, but we can listen to each other. And I still haven't heard anyone say who would take the baby. Would you? Sally?" Sally didn't answer.

* * *

After dinner, Jed left Grace and Karen in Karen's kitchen. Outside, dusk was seeping into the trees and gardens. Jed walked until he reached the banks of the irrigation canals and then, as the sun set and the stars came out, he followed the canals for miles trying to put to rest a growing anxiousness he felt waking in him. It was always there, but now he could feel it stirring.

When he returned, the house was dark. Teddy was sleeping in his swim suit and T-shirt on a mattress at the foot of the bed, the baby slept on several folded quilts by the wall. Jed looked down at Teddy, his arms and legs thrown out as though he'd been stopped by sleep in mid-stride. Again, Jed felt that sense of surprise and amazement at seeing his children, as though they were someone else's, that it was someone else's life, that his realest self must always be alone.

Jed smoothed Teddy's hair. He listened into each draw of Teddy's breath. After the accident, each of his brother's inhalations had stretched, elongated, and then, just when it seemed the bridge to the next breath must break, there'd been the beginning of the hoarse gasp, months and months, the tubes and fluids silently working, over a year before there'd been some level of consciousness; his mother had stayed by the bed, sung and talked to Ben, held his hand, massaged his arms and legs bowed in paralysis, grown old at his side; then years of rehabilitation, his wife left him, children, years more, a month ago his brother had pecked out a four-line letter on a typewriter with a faded ribbon: *I have a new walker. It's quieter. The neighborhood kids aren't so afraid of me clanking down the sidewalk. They let me get close enough to touch their heads.*

Kneeling quietly on the mattress, Jed let himself down beside Gracie—the rise of her hip beneath the sheet. She turned over, reached for him. "Walking all this time?" she said through sleep.

She kissed him. Jed felt the fatigue thicken in a languid way toward desire. The curtain rose in a cooling stir of breeze, settled. As Grace fit herself to him and they began to make love, the baby came awake with a cry. Grace took a deep breath, reached down. She nursed and settled her, turned back to Jed. They made love. Afterward, Grace said, "I'm glad I love you. Tell me you love me."

"I love you."

Grace was silent. "Sometimes I think you're all that stands between me and my family."

Jed watched the curtain rise overhead. "It's just the way it looks when you're back here. You were good at the family meeting. I know how hard it was for you to speak like that."

They drifted into the rise and fall of their children's breathing, fragile, rhythmic, which filled the dark room, and which, breath by breath, lifted and carried them into sleep.

Nothing more had been settled when they left. Jan was still in the hospital. On Puget Sound, they settled into exploring the woods and beaches, reading, the pleasure of having fires some nights. Jed played whiffle ball with Teddy in the meadow by the cabin, followed the trails over the grassy hill and down the bluff to the beach. There was a long fishing pier which had a Marine Life Center on the end, and this quickly became one of Teddy's favorite places. Teddy would run into the barn-like building and stand silent before the octopus which hung suspended in the shadows of a tank. He fell in love with Kirk, a gap-toothed hippie who ran the place. He was sweet and patient with kids and would invite Teddy to help him clean a net, feed the crabs; he'd place a dead fish in the tidal-pool tank, and several mornings later, there would only be the gluey bones under the starfish. Kirk would explain everything to Teddy. Fish. Tides. Late one morning, Kirk and Teddy stood in the open door, and Jed heard Kirk saying, "...and we all share the sun and moon, Teddy." They were looking up at the waning moon still shining in the morning sky. Jed couldn't imagine what question Teddy could have put to Kirk.

The first week passed and Jed became aware that he and Grace hadn't spoken of Jan or gotten any news on her. He could feel Grace again wrapped up in her wordlessness, but decided to let her be. One evening, Grace returned walking through the long grass of the meadow, the distant snow-covered peaks fading into twilight. Far behind her, the white lights of the ferry cleared the point. She sat beside him on the front steps.

She said she'd just been to the pay phone and spoken with Mike. Jan had responded to her medication and come out of the hospital. Mike said it was just eerie how normal she seemed. The social worker thought it best she not return home, but break that pattern and get herself a new place. In the meantime, Jan had been living up in the Sierras with them—Mike, Sally, and the five kids. They watched the white lights of the ferry getting smaller. Grace said, "Jan had the amnio. There *is* a baby. It's normal. She's decided to have it."

"You thought that's what your mother wanted."

Grace nodded in the dark. "I still do."

"That it might make her well."

"My mother believes what she has to believe." Grace paused. "Mike says that Jan's going to give the baby up for adoption." She shifted several coins slowly from one cupped palm to the other. "She's not telling my mother. She'll find out, but no one's telling her. Jan got some kind of message from my mother, alright. Have a baby. Only it's just upside down and backward. My mother will go crazy when she finds out she's giving it away." Grace shook a quarter in her palm. "Crazy."

A few nights later Grace called and got Sally, who was exasperated. First, Mike had spent his time after work visiting Jan in the hospital. And that was good, it really was. And it had to be done. And then Mike had taken Jan to look for an apartment. That was important, too. Now it was adoption counseling. Mike hadn't spent any time with Sally in six weeks. "And she says that now Mike has started to talk about wanting to adopt the baby."

Jed laughed once. "They've got five. What's going on?"

"Sally says it horrifies Mike—letting a baby go out of the family."

"What does Sally say?"

"Sally says Jan has to go as soon as her apartment's ready."

"Has anyone told your mother about the adoption?"

"Sally says she knows."

"And?"

"And what? It's as bad for her as you can imagine."

After that, Grace didn't call. They walked on the beaches, took expeditions. The baby started to crawl and then pull herself up on chair rungs and give crowing laughs.

One afternoon, after they'd been on the beach several hours, Grace began loading up to go back to the cabin. She put the baby in the backpack; Teddy played in and out of the pilings under the pier. Grace said, "We're heading back to the house for lunch; we'll see you there."

"Right, see you all up there." He'd put together his surf-casting rod and was on his way to bait shop. When he returned to the beach, Gracie, the baby, and Teddy were gone. Jed walked out to the point and cast for half an hour. Moments after he'd returned to the cabin, Grace said, "Where's Teddy?"

Jed balanced his rod against a stump. "What do you mean, where's Teddy? Isn't he with you?"

"No."

"Where is he?"

"I thought he was with you."

"You said, 'We're going back to the cabin.' We."

" 'We.' I meant Nina and I. I left him down there. I thought you knew he wanted to fish and was staying with you."

"No one said anything about Teddy fishing. You told me earlier he was hungry."

Afterward she said, it was the first time in their marriage she'd ever felt afraid of him—she'd never seen such a look of hatred and fear on his face. Jed ran out the door, back across the meadow and down to the beach where he stopped, looking this way and that. He realized, the Marine Center, that's where he'd be, with Kirk. He ran down the pier, but the doors were locked. He looked on the floats, the launch ramps, and with a constricting terror he couldn't hold back, he glanced over at the parking lot, the cars, the RV area. Now each car glinted hard and terrible in the sun. He looked up the beach road at the cars leaving, each with dark shapes in the windows. He ran down the dock, into the parking lot, checking into cars. When he was winded, he walked, then broke back into a jog. He ran up to children, peering suddenly into their faces, and leaving parents looking after him.

When he had reached the point, panting and gasping for breath, he stared out at the ocean and at what was left of the waning moon shining pale, a great dead stone falling in the sky. He groaned and stumbled toward the ocean, then turned and started back down the road. He would call the police. He walked up the hill and followed the road to the park ranger's office. Ahead, he saw a police car next to a ranger and he broke into a run. He had almost reached them when a man got out of a car holding a boy's hand. It was Teddy. Enraged at the sight of a stranger touching his son, Jed ran faster. Then it made sense to him. The man and police and ranger started talking to each other. Jed shouted, "Teddy!" Teddy turned, his face flushed from crying, and ran toward Jed, and as Jed picked him up Teddy began to cry, "Where'd you go, Dad?"

It was another day before the glint of terror dimmed. Teddy seemed alright, yet subdued. But Jed felt withdrawn and couldn't control his moods. Once as Grace hunted for the checkbook, he snapped, "You have the same blankness that makes things just seem to happen in your family." He went out by himself and he walked for miles in the woods, and when he thought of Grace, he could see Jan's face beneath. He returned and said, "I'm sorry, I didn't mean what I said, I don't know how I could have said such a thing to you... anyway, it was my fault...." He could see her watching him looking into her face. Not trusting himself, he lapsed into a nervous silence.

He began to have nightmares: he was looking for Teddy, he was back in a hospital.... One night he woke with a gasp, Teddy was lost, had been gone for days, he hadn't noticed, how could that be? now he was looking through the classified ads for him, he knew he wouldn't find him, he put his head down on the paper, in the Marine Center, the octopus hung motionless in the shadows, beneath the starfish, there were the gluey remains of something....

In his room, Teddy slept as he often did, arms and legs

thrown into a twist of motion. A foot hung suspended off the mattress. On the night table, crab shells, special beach stones, drawings, chunks of legos. Gently, Jed placed his leg back in bed, covered Teddy, and then lay down beside him in the dark. After a while, the space between the windows and shades separated, and the smell of Teddy's hair close in his nostrils, Jed slid into white jagged predawn sleep.

Days went by, but Jed couldn't rise from some choked place in himself. Walking on the beach or through a field, he'd suddenly feel a lurch of dread as his feet stirred the long grass; the sky and ocean would go vast and empty; and the movement of cars away from him, the dark shapes of heads inside, the glint of sunlight off their hard enameled bodies would jolt him with terror. Then one afternoon, as Grace hung clothes, Jed said, "I think we should take Jan's baby."

"I see . . . first Mike and now you . . . what's happening to you guys? I love babies, too . . . it's just raising them . . . " She snapped open a wet towel, hung it, playfully sang, "Oh, where does the time go?"

"Grace, I'm serious."

She turned. The baby reached for a handful of her skirt, pulled herself up. Grace studied him. "You are, aren't you?" She lifted up the baby. "Is this what you've been so quiet thinking about?"

"No."

She started to say something, changed her mind. Then she said carefully, "I am not going to say anything now. If you feel this way in a few days, we can talk about it."

"I'll feel this way in a few days."

"Then we'll talk about it."

"Why not now?"

"Because I'm not ready to talk about it now." Jed looked over to see Teddy watching them from the doorway. There was no telling how long he'd been standing there listening. Grace started for the door. "Teddy, do you want a sandwich?" He looked past Grace at Jed, then back into his room, and slammed the door.

* * *

Now that the children were sleeping and most of the packing was done, Jed sat at the table and read the paper. Grace was cleaning out the last of the kitchen cupboards. "Two tea bags left. Tea?"

Jed shook his head, "No thanks." Just before the water boiled, he said, "Yes."

Grace made two cups, sat down. "Jed..." He looked up. "I want to talk to you. Can you hear me out and not say anything tonight? Just think about what I'm telling you." Jed nodded. "You said a few days ago you wanted to take Jan's baby. I've decided not to ask for an accounting. On a lot of levels I understand why. I'll never forget that look on your face the other day when you realized Teddy wasn't with me. And I know you haven't had a real night's sleep since." Jed started to say something. Grace held up her hand. "You said you'd hear me out."

"I'm not going to talk about your brother. But I will say something about my family. I've watched my mother and father struggle with Jan for the last fifteen years. I don't think they've suffered any less over her because there are three of us." Grace twisted a paper clip. The tea steamed untouched between them. "The last time my father took Jan to be committed, he walked out of the hospital crying. And you've seen what they're still going through."

Jed stirred in his chair. "I don't know if Jan really intends to give up the baby. Who knows what she'll do, or what she really wants? If she knew herself, would she have ever gotten pregnant? And that carries forward. Who knows what she'll do or want after the baby's born? Grace touched her cup. "When she's well, she'll want the baby. Whoever takes the baby will be tied to Jan and her sickness forever." She went silent. "Still, if it's important to you, I'll consider it. Do you still feel the same way?"

"I still feel the same way."

Grace walked to the sink. He knew that she was right about everything—of course she was right, but he couldn't speak.

Unable to cross to her, he felt her great beauty as pain. Stepping outside into the long grass which grew around the house, he looked off at the dark sound.

The car was packed. Grace had taken Teddy down to the Marine Center to say goodbye to Kirk. After a while, they came back up, Teddy trying to whack Grace's legs with a stick as they walked. Grace said, "The Center's closed today, Kirk's not there, and he's mad." She bent to pick up the baby and Teddy took the opportunity to hit her hard on the calf.

Jed rose quickly. "Give me the stick, Teddy!"

Teddy ran out of reach, yelled, "I hate you!" and flung the stick at Jed.

He dashed into his now-empty room.

Jed tossed the stick into the meadow. "He's been so angry at me."

"He's upset about leaving."

"It's more than that. Maybe he blames me for the other day. Thinks I meant to leave him." Shaking his head, Jed went inside for a last look in the closets and under the beds. Things would be better once they got started. But as they drove, a hangover of wordless dread stayed with Jed.

When they arrived at Grace's parents' several days later, things were much the same except that Jan's belongings were gone from the back room, one of the cars was missing, and Anna was walking stiffly. In her small voice, Anna told them that she'd been in an accident a few weeks ago. A few weeks ago? Why hadn't anyone said anything? Anna didn't reply. She'd spent several days in the hospital with bruised ribs; the car was totaled. How had it happened? Grace's father said that she was just preoccupied, drove right into oncoming traffic as though it wasn't there. Everything considered, she'd been lucky.

They'd been there only a few hours when Jan walked in. She was in a stable phase, and it was hard to believe she'd ever been anything else. She wore a maternity blouse bordered with a flower pattern and looked very pregnant. She went into the kitchen, took something from the refrigerator, and returned to the living room. She was more beautiful than Jed had ever seen her. Her surface agitation was gone and Jed had the uneasy feeling that her craziness was an act or illusion. Only her eyes, large and dark, lingered too long on things, hands, faces; it was almost as though she hadn't seen them before or was trying to remember the words for them in a foreign language.

No one said anything about the pregnancy. They talked about the summer. They talked about people they knew. They sat in the living room with the curtains drawn against the afternoon sun, a single thin beam cutting across the carpet, a soap opera on, the color in the TV too blue.

Though Jan had her own apartment, she came over all the time. She'd appear suddenly. Early morning. Mid-afternoon. Evenings. She was in the living room one evening when Teddy handed Jed a set of keys. "Can I have these?"

Jed said, "I don't know whose they are. They look like they belong to a car."

Jan turned from the TV. "*Did* belong to someone's car. L'auto n'existe plus, right, ma mère?" Jan laughed quickly. "C'était l'auto that mom decided to juxtapose with blueberry pie à la mode, n'est-ce pas, ma mère? Ma mère, elle avait fait tort. Est-ce que le juste phrase, Mom? I can't remember. Peut-être c'est un faux pas. Oh, my mind must be gone." She clutched her forehead in mock confusion. Jed looked from Anna to Jan, each balanced at opposite ends of the sofa; he heard the sting of Jan's perfect pronunciation. Anna didn't look up from her book. Jan handed Teddy the keys. "Keep them, Teddy. L'auto n'existe plus."

Before he opened his eyes, Jed sensed Grace gone from the bed. The house was still, the window pale. He pulled on shorts. Grace nursed the baby quietly in the back room. Gray dawn light. Jed made coffee and got the paper. Later, rubbing his eyes and squinting against the morning sunlight, Teddy came in. Jed extended his arms, but Teddy wouldn't look at him, pressed his head into Grace's lap; she smoothed his hair, talked to him softly. Still rubbing his eyes, he went into the backyard and peered up at the fig tree.

As Jed and Grace were readying to leave, Jan came in. She poured coffee and sat down by herself in the back room. Her hand rested on the roundness of her stomach. Once or twice he saw her lips moving.

The beginnings of goodbyes started, but the moment hadn't really come to leave. There were phone calls to make, a few last things to be done. Jed went through the house. "Where's Teddy?"

Grace diapered the baby. "He was in the backyard."

Jed looked around. The crepe myrtle in pink bloom, the orange trees, the enormous cork oak.

"Teddy?" Jed walked into the yard. Already it was hot. "Teddy!" He opened the side gate, called, searched the house, the front yard, looked up and down the street. In the backyard, he called again.

A voice answered, faraway. "Yes."

"Where are you?"

"Here."

"Where?"

"Up here."

Jed looked up into the thick green leaves and branches. Teddy hung deep in the heart of the fig tree. "Did you get up by yourself?"

"Yes, just today."

"Teddy, did you hear me call before?" He didn't answer. His hands and face and shirt were smeared with ripe figs. "If you heard me, why didn't you answer?"

"Are we going?"

"We're going."

"By ourselves?"

"Yes, by ourselves." Jed could see Teddy's blond hair and light eyes in the shadows.

Teddy looked past Jed. "I can't get down."

"We're going by ourselves. Who else would be coming with us?"

Teddy shifted position on his branch, a cluster of figs splattered thickly on the walk. "The baby."

"What baby?"

"Jan's baby."

Teddy's face was hidden in the shadows and leaves. "No, Jan's baby is not ready to go anywhere yet."

"But is it coming when it's ready?"

Jed glanced back at the house and saw Jan standing alone in the kitchen window, the sky and trees reflected silvery-white in the glass. Her hand rested on her stomach and she looked up at something distant, the waning moon. Teddy shifted and leaves floated down. "No, Teddy, Jan's baby is not coming even when it's ready. What do you think of that?"

"Good."

"Did you want it to come with us?"

"No, Dad. Get me down."

Jed held up his arms. Teddy crouched in the lower branches, checking his footing. He hesitated. Jed said firmly. "It's okay, I've got you." Now Teddy looked for Jed's eyes. Jed nodded again. "It's okay, come on." With one last hesitation, he gathered himself, let go of the branch, and fell in a shower of leaves. Jed took his weight. "I've got you." Teddy wrapped his legs around Jed's waist and squeezed. "Let's find your mother and get going."